Frederic Jessup Stimson

Guerndale

An old story

Frederic Jessup Stimson

Guerndale
An old story

ISBN/EAN: 9783744747288

Printed in Europe, USA, Canada, Australia, Japan

Cover: Foto ©Andreas Hilbeck / pixelio.de

More available books at **www.hansebooks.com**

GUERNDALE

An Old Story

BY

J. S. OF DALE

" En los nidos de antaño no hay pájaros de hogano."—*Don Quijote.*

NEW YORK
CHARLES SCRIBNER'S SONS
1882

Trow's

Printing and Bookbinding Company

201-213 *East Twelfth Street*

NEW YORK

PREFACE.

I N these latter commercial days of ours, when a rise of one-eighth of one per centum in the rate of discount causes more stir than was anciently felt at the downfall of a religion, and even our passions are regulated by the laws of supply and demand ; in these days, when the strength of popular emotion is accurately tested in the stock market and not often felt in any other way ; in these days, when honor is replaced by adroitness, justice by good nature, and the occasional highwayman by the common swindler— in all these days it is natural that the character of our fiction should follow the nature of our thought. These are the piping times of peace : we lazily adapt ourselves to the laws of expediency, and are possessed of too much good taste to be either very good or very bad. So we all preserve a specious mediocrity ; and society is somewhat insipid in consequence. Sometimes, still, we long for the heavy villain of our forefathers ; for a little shadow, to lend a more strik-

ing contrast to the unquestionable valor of our sons
and the indisputable virtue of our daughters.   The
modern novel has replaced the mediæval romance,
snubs are dealt instead of stabs ; the *chanson d'amour*
has become *vers de société*, and every young lady is
quite competent to be her own duenna ; maidens
are mistresses of etiquette, and our bloods and blades,
our lions, roar you an 't were any sucking-dove.

Is it then that passions fade in the garish light of
civilization ?   Was romance the outgrowth of barbarism, and earnestness of intolerance ?   Is the exaggeration of an emotion, of a virtue, in equally bad
taste with the exaggeration of a manner or voice ?
Has poetry fled, and left us in a desert of common
sense ?   In answer to some of these questions, I have
committed this history to writing.   Should it seem
to the reader exaggerated, improbable, let him remember that we are all now too polite to bring our
real lives upon the stage of society ; and let him not
forget that real lives may yet exist.   Every nature is
stretched upon the Procrustean bed of convention.
Romeo no longer prates of his love at the street corners, nor does Othello use the fatal frankness of a
pillow ; Tarquin studies propriety, and Achilles dis-
sembles his wrath.   So in our tragedies : we no
longer kill half the company openly and above board
in the fourth act.   *Nec Medea trucidet liberos coram
populo :* the evident deed has given place to the complex emotion ; the objective to the subjective.   We

must seek the romantic in thought, not event; in character, not action; in our real selves, not the selves men take with them to the club. And I sometimes fancy that when we do this, we find as much romance in the world as ever.

Now, when I had finished this story, I threw it over to a friend of mine, a literary and artistic fellow, who is mentioned frequently in these pages. I am nothing but a plain civil engineer; and am wont to rely upon his judgment in these matters, as he himself is on the *dilettante* lay. This, I am told, is an Italian word, meaning "one who likes;" and my friend is a dilettante; which I take to be a fellow who does nothing himself and dislikes everything anybody else does.

Well, he brought the MS. back next day, and said, in his laziest and most critical manner, that what particularly struck him in the way I had told the story (with the details of which he also was familiar), was the caption I had chosen for the first chapter. "For," he said (being also a little on the musical lay), "you have carried out that idea in your workmanship; and the metaphor of the melody or symphony (which I observe you cribbed from Schopenhauer), is not ill-chosen. Thus, applying it to Guy's history, in the first book you strike the keynote and give us an *adagio*. Then a *scherzo*, and an *allegro affetuoso;* in the fourth book an *andante;* and finally a *presto*, with recurrence to the theme and key-note. Insensibly, your style has conformed to this idea, which I am not sure is a bad one. For a life is made up of a few movements, all bearing a certain relation to the 'key-note of character : the peaceful *adagio* of childhood, the *allegro* of youth, the *presto* of the Sturm und Drang period." At this point I shut him up ; but he insisted on my putting his idea in a preface.

Having apologized for the story, I suppose I ought now to apologize for this preface. I am aware that the custom of writing prefaces is old, and, like that of heading chapters with apposite quotations, a grave offence against modern taste. I am in the quandary of the Hindoo philosopher, who supported his world by an elephant, and the elephant by a tortoise ; and I see nothing for it but to follow the good old precedent, and leave the tortoise unsupported.

                              J. S., OF DALE.

DENVER, MARCH 31, 1881.

GUERNDALE.

Book First.

CHAPTER I.

"Now, just as the very essence of Man consists in this : that his Will strives, is satisfied, strives anew, and so on for ever ; so the essence of melody consists in a continual departure from the key-note ; it wanders in a thousand ways, but always comes back to it at last."

ON one of those dreamy afternoons in August, when all audible life in the country drowses away to a faint murmur, and we float through the day as the shifting clouds drift across the sky, you could scarce do better than saunter into the old churchyard at Dale. There is an indefinable charm about our New England graveyards which is often lacking in more pretentious cemeteries. There is little gleaming marble and heavy stonework ; and the greater part of the rude slate slabs is just sufficiently moss-grown to deaden the sound of the dropping nuts. The signs of recent bereavement are few ; most of the stones are softened and stained into harmony with the sap-stained pines about them. The quiet tenants of the place seem rather spell-bound than dead; and the sunset air breathes softly about the old carven letters, as if wooing the dead to forget that they had ever lived. Life seems so old a story, and so long, so very long, ago. And even in the first rich bloom of autumn, just when the fruit of the labored year is most perfect, nature seems to have an occasional day of hush and pause, as if debating whether it were worth while to go through the old story of winter, spring and summer once more. None are more sad than these days, when the earth, in all the flush of accomplished labor, sighs. It is like the sadness of a man at the crown of his ambition; of a bride in her honey-moon.

Dale is an old Massachusetts village, lying nearly lost, far up among the Berkshire hills; and such a day as this was wearing away the letters on the churchyard stones, many years ago; and some such fancies as these were drifting through the mind of a boy, lying by the bole of a tall hemlock, and look-ing dreamily from under his long lashes at an old, slate gravestone. Had you come upon him sud-denly, you would have started at seeing him, so intensely still he lay; as one starts at a squirrel, motionless, just before it flashes along the wall and vanishes. Even his eyes, deep and dark as they were, seemed rather to absorb light than to give it out. Otherwise, an ordinary-looking boy enough, except for a vague expression of sadness, which, after a moment's study, seemed not so much an expression as an hereditary cast of feature. He had been reading, with some difficulty, part of the old inscription on the slate before him :

" . . . departed there
" To singe ye Mercies of Goddes hande
" And see ye Paines wb vexe ye damned."

and, in a curious, half-boyish, half-mature way, was thinking about it. From the part of the epitaph that was yet legible, it seemed a matter of some doubt to which of two possible places the departed spirit had gone. And yet the nature of the stone was clearly intended to be laudatory : carven thereon was the rude semblance of a weeping willow, shading an urn of classic shape, while a bat-like cherub surmounted the name :

Mistresse Anne Dyar
obit ye 7th of July 1709, aet. 81.

He wondered whether Mistresse Anne Dyar knew she was dead, and if she were aware of the ambiguity of her epitaph. Or perhaps the unknown rhymer really thought that the windows of heaven commanded, as an advertisement would say, a fine view of hell.

All this rather carelessly ; for hell had long since ceased to be a very tangible fact, even in the year of grace 1858, and in the mind of an impressionable boy. To be sure he had heard old Dr. Grimstone lay down the precise location of hell, and then enter, with appalling realism, into a detailed description of the ground-plan thereof. He had even taken, as intended for personal application, the reverend Doctor's denunciation of children of sin and creatures of Satan, and had slunk home considerably abashed in consequence. But when the Doctor, between churches, came to his mother's house for dinner—which occasionally happened, for his father had been a clergyman—and laughed very heartily at his own jokes, besides calling him "Sonny" and giving him a quarter, he began to fancy that the good old Doctor's eloquence depended very much upon scenic effect, and that the Devil was not such a very terrible personage in private life after all. He knew that most of the people in Dale, if asked directly as to their belief in the localities aforementioned, would have answered unhesitatingly in the affirmative ; but was not this from motives of propitiation and a prudent regard for possibilities ? Did people really care as much, hope as much, fear as much as they pretended ? It was very pleasant lying half buried in the long churchyard grass that afternoon. Life was rather an easy, simple thing, and all about him seemed to suggest a sort of grave amusement at people's making such a to-do about it.

Suddenly the boy started up upon his elbow. His whole appearance and attitude changed ; he no longer seemed part of the hour and the place, but a truant school-boy who had strayed thither by mistake. His eyes sparkled with fun as he ran rapidly across to the high stone wall which skirted the dusty country road. Soon after, the prattle of a girlish voice was heard. The boy crouched for a spring

over the wall and a merry surprise, but drew back
suddenly into the shade, as he heard a strange voice
pronounce his name.

"Guyon Guerndale—who is he?"

"Oh!" said the girl, "don't you know?" And as
the two little figures pattered away, Guyon heard the
beginning of a long explanation. But he still remained in the shadow of the wall, as if surprised or
shy ; and, as the two children disappeared among the
willows at the bend of the road, he turned and wandered slowly home, keeping by the meadows at the
base of the churchyard.

CHAPTER II.

"Alles ist nicht todt, was begraben ist."—HEINE.

IN the days when the hilt of a sword better fitted
a gentleman's hand than the quill of a pen, and
when the owner of the sword was probably simple
enough to take more pride in his well-shaped leg
than in his clerkship—in short, in the year sixteen
hundred and eighty-eight, there lived in the county
palatine of Durham an old cavalier and baronet, Sir
Godfrey Guerndale. A right stout arm and a right
true heart had Sir Godfrey, and made bold to believe in God and the king. Devoted to the house of
Stuart, he followed its fortunes to the bitter end,
though its fortunes were but misfortunes, and the
end his ruin. While he saw and deplored the
cowardice, irresolution, and misgovernment which
worked the downfall of that dynasty, he could not
see why, if James Stuart was a coward, Godfrey
Guerndale should be a traitor. So he was ever ready
with his counsel and his sword ; and the one was
despised and disregarded, while the other was used
and thrown away. Finally, the battle of the Boyne
was followed by ignominious flight and abandonment
of the cause he thought righteous, and Sir Godfrey
was in disfavor for the same loyalty and devotion

his rightful lord had so little prized. His lands encumbered, his fortune wasted, his very plate melted down, he found himself, in the prime of life, without a cause and without a king. Disgusted, once for all, with the unworthy Stuarts, he refused to take part in the numerous Jacobite intrigues which even then were forming; unwilling to accept as final the results of a half-fought contest, he disdained to seek favor at the hands of one whom he considered an usurper. Like many another loyal gentleman, taking with him what remained to him of fortune and of faith, he sought refuge and retirement in the new world. His wife, a French lady of the Court of Louis XIV.—one of the noble family of La Roche Guyon—refused to accompany him, and saved him the trouble of compulsion by leaving him for an old friend, an ancient companion of the Merry Monarch. Remaining about the Court of St. Germain only so long as was necessary to run his sword through this gentleman, Sir Godfrey departed for America. His only son, then a youth of fourteen, accompanied him—more by his father's will than his own inclination; for Guy was a precocious boy, and even at that early age considered his father a fool. There also went with him an old and valued servant, John Simmons by name, who passed the rigors of the long voyage in drinking strong liquor and cursing Dutch William and his master's French wife.

All this did not tend to give Sir Godfrey a taste for New England society, which consisted chiefly of Puritans, who would, in the words of Sir John Denham, "quarrel with mince-pies and disparage their

best and dearest friend, plum-porridge ; fat pig and
goose itself oppose, and blaspheme custard through
the nose." Sir Godfrey was fairly disposed toward
these people, and presumed, as he intended not to
trouble them, they would do, or rather leave undone,
as much for him. Having acquired by purchase
from the Indians a large tract of land in what was
then a wilderness, Sir Godfrey lived the retired life
of a studious country gentleman, and waited and
watched for the birth of a Stuart worthy to be restored.

But that event never came. The old baronet lived
long enough to give the name of Guerndale to the
settlement springing up about him, and died, as he
had lived, a disappointed man,.soured by the treason of his friend, the falseness of his wife, and the
unworthiness of his king. He was not much known,
and perhaps as much feared as respected among the
simple and bigoted Puritans of the neighborhood.
His quiet memory soon faded away, and what little
is now known of him is due chiefly to the researches
of genealogists and antiquarians. In the early col-
lections of the Massachusetts Historical Society there
is some mention of him, and I think Jones mentions
the Guerndales as among the Tories of the American
Revolution. All the early traditions of the family,
however, cluster about his son, "Bad Sir Guy," a sobriquet first awarded him after his death. His reputation, being positively evil, soon obscured that of
his father, which was negatively good. He failed
utterly to understand Sir Godfrey's Quixotic devotion to an idea, and his sole desire was to return to

that country from which he regarded himself as un-
justly exiled ; and not to the Court of St. Germain,
out of power, but to the Court of St. James. But
he no more wished to return as a needy supplicant
of royal favor than as the blind adherent of a lost
cause. He meant to regain that position which his
father had cast away so foolishly; to shine again
among the gallants of the Court ; to be once more
lord of those broad demesne lands in Durham, held
by the little onerous service of guarding the bones of
St. Cuthbert from the devil. For Guyon did not
fear the devil, and did not think this would be difficult.

Still, to accomplish all these things, money was
necessary ; and money he would have. He must
return in a manner befitting his rank and station.
He was not a miser ; he did not desire gold for its
own sake, but as a means to an end. But that means
was indispensable ; and he must get it all costs. His
father's attachment to the king was loyalty ; his own
was measured by self-interest. He became a tool of
young John Churchill, and afterward a soldier under
Queen Anne, thereby mortally offending his father.
It were an endless task to mention the numerous
blots on his reputation. Thirty years ago his memory was yet alive in Dale. If we are to believe the
old gossips, pillage, piracy, and treason were among
the least of his crimes.

He soon disappeared from the army, leaving an
evil odor behind him ; and it was hoped he was
dead, until, after his father's death, he turned up at
Guerndale with a young and beautiful wife.

Old Solomon Bung, the village story-teller, always accompanied this part of the story with a knowing shake of the head and the fragmentary phrase, " But they *do* say . . . ." Whatever they do or did say, the memory of this poor girl is the one bright edge to the story, for she loved her evil lord devotedly ; and with her sad, but winning smile, she soon became a universal favorite, particularly among the poor, or that class which most nearly approached the poor in those days of rustic plenty. Even wicked Sir Guyon seemed the better for her ; and all might in the end have been well, had it not been for the catastrophe which brought the name of Guerndale into lasting notoriety.

Old John Simmons had faithfully aided his master, Sir Godfrey, in the labor and troubles which attended his settlement in New England. When the mansion-house was built, he settled contentedly down in one corner of it with his pretty little Puritan wife, who acted as housekeeper for them all. If we may trust old stories, one of their sons, Philip, was by no means a comfort to his father and mother in their declining years. Living some distance from the nearest settlements, he was not imbued with the spirit of the honest people of the neighborhood, but became a protégé and a pupil of the many roving Indians who yet lingered about the place. To succeed his father in the servile position he seemed to Philip to occupy, soon became distasteful to him ; and when old John died, an event which happened about the time of Sir Godfrey's death, Philip took his father's hard-earned savings, and his own pickings and stealings, and bought a parcel of freehold land adjoining the Guerndale estate. Here Sir Guyon found him on his return, married, and living the life more of a hunter or scout than a farmer. In him he recognized a kindred spirit, and soon revealed to him his schemes for obtaining that wealth which Guyon so eagerly desired.

The real resources of New England were then but little known. Projects which now would be attributed to the visions of a madman, were then soberly undertaken, and regarded as prompted by a laudable spirit of exploration. The old myth of El Dorado had not quite disappeared from the minds of the settlers; nor had they yet realized that the true wealth of New England lay rather on the surface of her soil and in the depths of her seas, than in the veins of her barren rocks. Misled, like many a better man, by the glitter of a valueless mineral, Guyon passed his time in delving at the base of the rugged hills which lay behind his house. At his directions, a rude smelting-furnace was erected; and respect for his elder's experience and determination soon brought Philip Simmons, insensibly, to the same position of dependence and servitude which, in his father, he had despised. Again, though in a less laudable pursuit, a Simmons was the faithful servant of a Guerndale. No one else was admitted to their labors; secretly, so far as they could, the two mined and smelted; but in vain. Yet people were curious; and doubtless many an eye had watched the half-swaggering, half-servile demeanor of Philip, and the grim, eager face of Sir Guyon, when the features of both were stamped with the same greed, as they turned over rock and sand, or cowered silently at night over the red furnace-fire.

One night, from farm to farm ran the report that Simmons had been murdered. A boy had been out hunting that afternoon, and had lost himself at dusk among the hills. Tradition says that it was a misty, rainy day in November, and little was to be seen in the hills save the sombre outlines of the nearest pine-forest, and the varying shades of blackness in the mist that marked the height of the trees. So the boy had easily become confused as to the way, and it was with unusual gladness that he saw bleared in the mist the red glow of the furnace-fire. Made bolder than usual by the inclemency of the weather —for even then the forge was regarded among the common folk as a place at most times to be avoided —he hurried on toward the door, but stopped on hearing the sounds of an angry altercation within. Catching, amid the curses, the words "diamond," "halves," "my fair share," he rushed to the little square window. Over it was stretched a sheet of isinglass ; and through this he got a distorted view of the interior. At one corner stood Guyon Guerndale, his face pale with rage, his left hand clutching a diamond which the boy said afterward was as large as a pigeon's-egg. Opposite stood Philip Simmons, his back against the door.

"Bah, fool ! let me pass ?" hissed Guerndale. And Guerndale made as if he would pass through the door, which Simmons still held. "Pshaw, Simmons ! be a faithful servant, as your father was before, and trust to me for your reward! I may make you a gentleman yet—who knows?" Simmons, with a curse, threw himself upon his master, striking him with a clenched fist upon the lip. At this a great flood of scarlet swept over Sir Guyon's pale cheek ; he drew his sword from the scabbard he had buckled over his working-dress, and struck Simmons to the ground. Striking him twice again, he dashed the lantern to the floor and strode out of the cabin.

All this time the diamond was flashing in his left hand, and the boy believed him to have taken it with him. Rooted to the spot with fear, he could do nothing, but heard Guerndale's heavy tread down the bed of the brook which formed the only path out of the valley. Presently the cabin took fire from the lantern, and by its first flames the boy saw Philip Simmons still lying on his back, with a wide gash beneath his upturned chin. He turned, and fled to the village.

A party was at once made up to proceed to the smelting-furnace ; the cabin was found in ashes, among which was the body of a man. A hue and cry was raised for the murderer. Guerndale, not expecting so speedy a pursuit, was found in his own house, calmly making preparations for flight. At first he seemed not to suppose that the villagers would dare to apprehend him. Brought to bay, he showed fight ; and, anxious as they were to take him alive, he was killed by his own shot, after he had cut and slashed a dozen of his pursuers.

That night his lady died, leaving behind her a boy, destined to be sole heir to the Guerndale estate. Not a very large principality, you will say, for all that the king's escheator cared to trouble himself about was forfeit to the crown. Hard indeed would have been the boy's lot, had not some yeomen, well-to-do, who owed their all to early kindnesses of his mother, taken and cared for the poor little creature, who already seemed unfortunate in being born alive.

Meanwhile, Sir Guyon Guerndale had been buried, after the good old fashion, at the meeting of four roads, with a stake through his heart.

CHAPTER III.

"All men are born free and equal."—Old Song.

TIME went on, change succeeded change, fortunes were made and lost, families were founded and dispersed, the little settlement of Guerndale grew slowly into a country town, and yet no change came in the fortunes of the family that gave the place its name. It ever seemed that they lived only in the past, and had their hopes buried with their fortunes, at that fatal date in the early part of the eighteenth century. To be sure, the square old country-house was left them; but land, wealth, and position were gone. The disgrace of the family remained, and stamped itself upon the nature of the descendants of Guyon the murderer. From father to son they lived a life of dreams; absorbed in books and contemplation, that strain of ambition and action, which had been so evilly used, seemed to be ended and buried with its last possessor. His son, who came into the world at that dark moment, struck the key-note of the lonely, introspective nature which remained dominant in the lives of his descendants. Each in turn wrung from the soil the scanty subsistence he required, married in due time, without love, and died in course, leaving, at most, two sons to perpetuate the misfortunes of their race. Family pride they had, but this served rather as a motive for holding aloof and brooding on the past, than for taking part in the stirring events of their day. In the Revolution they were Tories, but took no active part, and were easily overlooked in the confiscation which followed. In brief, they all seemed born under a cloud; each felt it his duty to marry, and usually married beneath his station. Unknown among the later aristocracy growing up in New England, they refused to face the trials and rebuffs which they would unavoidably meet if they emerged from their traditional retirement.

Curiously enough, no one had ever seen the diamond since that dark November evening, but it was believed the fatal jewel was yet retained in the family of Guerndale. This added not a little to the distrust with which the possessors of the stone were regarded. Keeping the object of the crime seemed, as it were, a ratification of the crime itself. Yet the family never would part with the jewel; and years ago, I remember, it was believed by the older people of the town that fortune would never come back to the Guerndales until they lost or threw away the ill-won heirloom—a common tradition enough in cases of this sort.

So time passed, and brought neither happiness to the family of Guerndale, nor kindlier feelings toward them on the part of the neighbors.

Meanwhile, the nature of the place changed with the nature of the country. The Revolution came and went, leaving a slight accession to the ill-repute in which the family were held. The town of Guerndale became the centre of an important farming district. Then a few manufacturing establishments sprang up along the brown little river. Social distinctions were levelled ; aristocratic ideas gave place to democratic dogmas ; the township, from an oligarchy, became what my friend Randolph used to call a demagogue-archy. Even the old Guerndale murder became a thing of the past—as obsolete as an old English tragedy by the side of Camille or Frou-frou. Only the impalpable feeling of the towns-people toward the Guerndales remained. A slight odor of disfavor still hung about them, as the scent of oil still lingers about the rotten Nantucket wharves. Any old-country feeling of respect for the founders of the town must have disappeared early in the present century. Many people were now there, more wealthy and influential, who could claim to be what is in New England considered of " good family." Several names had appeared, with due iteration, every thirty years or so in the Harvard triennial catalogue, where you might in vain have looked among the fellows and graduates for a Guerndale. Several families had acquired wealth and position in New York or Boston, and left a glory behind them in the little town of their nativity, or returned to grace their ancestral acres with pretentious modern mansions. The Simmonses, for instance—they had lived many years on their farm, quite as long as the Guerndales ; and a scion of that stock had made an enormous fortune by introducing salt fish into South America. He had come back to Guerndale, and had been well known as the richest man of the place ; and the prominent Boston family of Symonds are his descendants. This Simmons or Symonds (who built the Symonds Memorial Hall, at Harvard) was very active in changing that town-name which had ever been felt by the more progressive citizens as servile and un-American. Who were these Guerndales, that they should inflict their name, and their disgrace with it, upon an American township, as if it were their property ? They owned less land than half the farmers about, and every one knew they had not a cent to bless themselves with. So argued Squire Simmons, and, thought his fellow-citizens, argued well. But then came the question of change. Here opinions were more conflicting. Some favored Ephesus, some Arcadia, some New Moscow, others Anemonevale. Squire Simmons argued secretly, but long and earnestly, in favor of Simmonsville ; indeed, it was said that he offered to build a town-clock and a wooden steeple in the latest style, upon the old stone town-hall, if they would adopt that name. But to this proposal there was much quiet opposition, in spite of a flaming leader in the *Guerndale Weekly Palimpsest*, calling attention to the "unprecedented munificence latent in the generous proposition of one of our townsmen, that true gentleman, whom we feel it an honor to call our fellow-citizen, Joseph Simmons, Esq." Strange to say, among the old farmers there was found some reluctance to having the name changed at all ; conduct which was characterized by those citizens who, having before lived in other places where things were done much better, might naturally be supposed to know, as "narrow-minded, mean-spirited, and, worse than all, un-American; for the name ought to be changed, in the interest of progress and reform." However, the resultant of all these conflicting forces was a compromise. An objectionable syllable was dropped, and the town was called Dale. Dale it is at present, and Dale it will probably be to the end of the chapter. Squire Simmons was in high dudgeon, and shortly afterward he departed to settle permanently in Boston, having previously cut up all his outlying land into small lots, which he sold at ten cents a foot to the employés of a large factory he was then building in Dale.

Meantime, old Mr. Godfrey Guerndale, the grandson of the wicked baronet, was at work—as, indeed, he had been for years—on the second volume of his "History of the Usurpations of the British Crown," noticing little what was going on about him, and caring not very much. This valuable work was never finished, but was left as a sacred legacy to his son, the third Godfrey, who was sent to college that he might acquire a taste for literature, which should enable him to complete it. At college he was shy, reserved, and apparently morose; known, or rather unknown, by the appellation of "Owly." Mr. Bonnymort once told me that he was his only friend, but Guerndale found it impossible, with his nature, inborn or acquired, to be completely unreserved, even with him. To the surprise of every one it turned out, after graduating, that he had privately married an orphan girl whom he had met at the house of one of the professors. He studied for the ministry, but was never able to get a parish, although he had set his heart upon being settled in his native town. His dearest ambition was to gain the respect and love of his neighbors, and break the strange blight that seemed to hang over his family. In this he was disappointed, and he died young, leaving one son, Guyon, who was about ten years old at the date of my first chapter, and the world, and more than the world, to his widowed mother. Unwilling to bear his daily absence at school, Mrs. Guerndale taught the child herself; moreover, Guyon himself was loath to leave her, shunning the companionship of other children. He seemed conscious that he had little chance of success in this world. For he might be sure that whenever his action or his inaction was equivocal, the worst interpretation would be put upon it. The presumption was against him. Not even the neighboring farmers looked upon the boy with favor. He was a pale, uncanny child, with eyes of a mature expression ; and they, who remembered the past better than the villagers, shook their heads and said that the name was unlucky, for there had not been a Guyon in the family since the wicked old baronet, who, it was even then remembered, slept his troubled sleep at the cross-roads.

CHAPTER IV.

" Plus doulces luy sont que civettes ;
  Mais toutes foys fol s'y fia :
  Soient blanches, soient brunettes,
  Bien heureux est qui rien n'y a ! "—*Villon.*

" A child . . . who sends, like a star, the first rays of her love and thought
through the white cloud of infancy."—*Maurice de Guérin.*

THE old Guerndale mansion is large and square,
and its color has, from time immemorial, been
brown. It is built, like all old Massachusetts houses,
of wood, and the great beams of hewn oak, hard
enough to turn the edge of any axe, bend and bulge
through the ceilings and floors. It stands on a knoll,
a little set back from the country road, and guarded
by four gaunt, Lombardy poplars. In the shade of
the house lies hushed a clear little brook, still foamy
and breathless with its hurried tumble from the hills ;
but, after a moment's pause, it glides under the road
and sparkles down through the meadow, happily un-
suspicious of the coming mills and dye-houses. Guyon's earliest memories were associated with this
stream. There is something companionable about a
brook ; it lightens up a wood as a wood-fire does a
winter room. Its moods vary, its caprices change,
so that it is hard indeed if a sympathetic nook may
not be found somewhere along its course. This

brook, in particular, was the only playmate of his
early childhood. His home stood remote from other
houses; he had no school acquaintances, and such
few children of his own age as he had occasionally
seen in the neighborhood rather shunned than en-
couraged his advances. Thus he learned to seek diversion by himself, and the brook became a great
favorite. It was not long before he had followed its
course up to its boggy source amid the hills, beyond
the site of the old forge about which he used to play.
The brook floated his little navy and turned his wa-
ter-wheels with that cheerful evenness of humor so
pleasing in our inanimate friends.

There are times when one finds even one's best
friend rather dull; and one September afternoon, in
the year eighteen hundred and fifty-seven, Guyon
found himself rather poor company. Some boys had
just passed by with their fishing-poles, and their
happy Saturday-afternoon talk had aroused an after-
tone of loneliness in his own thoughts. Sensitive to
moods, as all children are, though incapable of analyzing them, it never occurred to Guyon to join the
fishing-party; but, as usual, he started up the brook,
taking with him a lately completed craft whose geometrical mould bespoke the inland origin of the
draughtsman. He walked up the hill-side toward
his favorite pool, where the water circled round in
momentary irresolution before plunging out from the
edge of the forest. A shady, dewy little place it was,
covered by a luxuriant grape-vine, which was the
reason that his ears were first to warn him of an invasion of his haunt. Feeling instinctively the strat-

egy of surprise, he crept up cautiously and peered
through the vine, the sweetness of the song he heard
tempering his wrath as he approached, and inducing
a mood fatal to salutary sternness, for he had omitted
to adopt the ancient Odyssean precaution of stopping
his ears. And a pretty picture he saw. Seated in
the shadow of the grape-vine was a little girl, pluck-
ing the crimson leaves and throwing them into the
pool, where they eddied around in a circle, as if dancing to the song softly crooned by the little siren
above them.

Guyon stood as if spell-bound, as I believe his
predecessors in that adventure have usually been.
How long this tableau might have lasted, it is impossible to say ; but, his eagerness getting the better of his equilibrium, there was a sudden plunge,
a scream, and consequent confusion. The little girl
started back in affright ; but, as Guyon emerged ruefully from the water, the sublime gave way to the
ridiculous, and he was greeted by a frank burst of
laughter. Rather surprised by the novelty of the
emotion, yet relieved now of embarrassment, his own
features broke gradually into a somewhat depreca-
tory smile, as he waited for her to begin the conversation. This she finally did, on the offensive.

"Why did you come tumbling into my brook for ?"

Evidently, evasion as to motive and riposte as to
ownership were necessary.

"'Tisn't your brook ; it's mine."

"And what is your name ?" (A boy would have
said, Who are you ? but, with natural feminine diplo-
macy, she produced the same effect less rudely.)

"Guyon Guerndale."

And then he hesitated, as if conscious that this was no recommendation.

"Oh, what a queer name!" And then, seeing he was wounded, "Where does your papa live?"

"He doesn't live anywheres. He's dead."

"Oh, I'm so sorry!" And she timidly put a soft little hand out to his. I grieve to say that my hero (but, quite as much to his own surprise as hers) dropped his head upon his knees and began to cry. Then, suddenly, he started up as if ashamed.

"What is your name?" he said, rather rudely, by way of asserting his manhood.

"I am Annie Bonnymort, and I live down in the big, white house by the river. Come and sit down, Guyon Guerndale, and see how pretty the leaves go round. And, please, don't cry. But I'm afraid you're all wet?"

"Oh, no. I'm not wet," stoutly asseverated the new-comer. "Besides, I like it."

Whatever inconsistency there might have been in this last remark, it was overlooked; and the children were soon at ease in each other's company. The boat was brought out, and pleased Annie so much that he eagerly promised to make her a still better one, if he could find another shingle. And then confidence led to confidence; and he told her, with true masculine egotism, that he was very lonely, and there were very few boys around whom he liked, and Ned Dench and Johnnie Strang had gone off fishing; but *he* didn't care one bit. And then Annie said that she didn't like boys very much—at least, *most* boys ; and Guyon at once mentally classed himself in the smaller division, and Ned Dench and other objectionable creatures among boys in general ; so that the evening mist came floating up from the meadow before Annie suddenly remembered that she must hasten home, or Papa would be angry. So she went to find her nurse, who was snoring under an oak-tree, and all three walked back together.

"Papa says I may go to church with him to-morrow, like a lady. Do you go to church ?"

"Not always," said Guyon, feeling suddenly that church was a somewhat desirable place.

"Do go. You are big enough to go always." Which would not, perhaps, have been a satisfactory reason for a mature mind. But Guyon looked forward that night with unusual pleasure to church the next day, where he would see Ned Dench and ask him how many fish he had caught. He did not think of Annie.

But it is not the first time in the history of the world that two people have met at church.

2

CHAPTER V.

"There's a great text in Galatians,
Once you trip on it, entails
Twenty-nine distinct damnations—
One sure, if another fails."—R. BROWNING.

"Yet the meeting-house is a kind of windmill, which runs one day in
seven, turned either by the winds of doctrine or public opinion, or, more rarely,
by the winds of heaven, where another sort of grist is ground, of which, if
it be not all bran or musty, if it be not *plaster*, we trust to make the bread of
life."—THOREAU.

THE next morning, when the pine-boughs near
his window were first blurred upon the redden-
ing horizon, Guyon awoke and hastened out of doors.
Involuntarily he turned his steps toward the scene
of the meeting of yesterday. Except that the frost
of the night had turned the vine-leaves a deeper red,
nothing had changed about the little pool, and yet
it seemed to him there was a difference. This nook
in the forest was now a place to him, differentiated
in his mind from any other little woody glade; and
the day had become a date, a milestone in the vista
of the past. He felt this confusedly as he looked
about him; there was the mossy rock which had
been the cause of their involuntary meeting, and
relieved him from his natural shyness; there was
the little bank where she had sat and scattered the

leaves on the black surface of the pool; and the little shingle-boat was probably caught on the ledge of
rock just below.   He almost thought that he would
tumble in again for such another afternoon, for he
was not a child to whom a damp pair of shoes meant
a cold, and an involuntary bath a serious illness.
But to-day he felt the unwelcome stiffness of his
Sunday clothes—an irksome change from the week-
day suit, which had grown as wonted to his little
person as the feathers to a water-fowl.

This reminded him—without the usual pang accompanying the thought—of church, and he went
home to be brushed, after which necessary ceremony the boy and his mother set off in the family
"carryall," driven by the "hired man;" for it was
still the time when, in country towns, the dignity of
independent labor was felt, and any faithful retainer
of the families of Dale would have objected to the
word *servant*.

The church was like many another New England
meeting-house—white, wooden and perched on the
top of the hill, as if to attract, by its conspicuous
presence, the attention of the Almighty to the piety
of the town.   Behind it was a long shed, where the
sedate steeds of the neighborhood were tied with
their noses to the wall, as if, with the aid of wall and
blinders, to produce a state of introspective abstrac-
tion favorable to religious thought.   Occasionally
even this means would fail, and the most eloquent
pause of the preacher be broken by a musical phrase
known and employed as such only by Raff, and far
from an ornamental *fioretura* to the conventional

melodies of the choir, whose "Duke Street" and "Amsterdam" rang far down the village street.

When the widow entered, they had ended their voluntary; appropriately called a voluntary, for they chose their time and harmony *ad libitum*. This overture had the double advantage of bringing the minds of the congregation to a proper state of anxiety, and affording them an excuse for turning around and watching the incomers. As each beribboned girl flaunted up the aisle, the interest became more intense, especially among those girls who felt their own efforts for Sunday review less successful. The boys attracted less attention, and while their faces blushed with conscious cleanliness, their looks betokened disgust with all this Persian apparatus and mutual condolence for not being elsewhere. This uneasiness increased during the service, as their hands sought their trouser-pockets and felt the sad absence of the accustomed jack-knife and fishing-line.

Guyon Guerndale paid little attention to his companions in misery. He was watching a gray-haired gentleman who had just walked in, hand in hand with a little girl whose light brown hair and dark brown eyes made a pretty contrast to the grave white and black of her father's head. Guyon had thrilled with pleasure when this gentleman recognized his mother with a stately bow; and it must be confessed that the fact that the Lord was in his holy temple was not so vividly realized by him as the more material presence there of Annie Bonnymort.

However, the long sermon was endured by him

with exemplary patience. Old Dr. Grimstone took for his text: *And Zebedee went down into Bashan ;* which he developed, as usual, in many logical divisions, somewhat as follows:

I. *a.* Character and previous history of Zebedee.

β. Elucidation and explication of mistakes which had previously been made with regard to the character and previous history of Zebedee.

II. *a.* Enumeration of the motives which might have induced Zebedee to undertake the journey to Bashan, but were not, in fact, those which did induce him to travel thither.

β. Probable reasons why Zebedee did not go to some other place than Bashan.

γ. Why Zebedee did go to Bashan.

III. A few remarks on the history—natural, sacred, and profane—of Bashan ; with an apologetic digression on the bull.

Here the doctor made a pause and took a glass of water ; which moment was improved—by the boys openly, and their elders covertly, in glancing around at the clock. Deacon Shed gave a start, and looked about defiantly. Solomon Bung passed down a parcel of " lovage " to his protégés below him in the gallery, for Solomon Bung blew the organ. This delectable delicacy was received with some excitement, in the course of which a palm-leaf fan slipped from the railings and fluttered passively down on the head of Squire Strang, the lawyer, who bore it for the moment with Christian fortitude. Dr. Grimstone mopped his face, and continued—while Squire Strang looked up to the gallery with a savage frown—" A few words more, my dear friends." The boys knew this to mean twenty minutes, and murmured slightly among themselves.

IV. What would have been the possible consequences, had Zebedee gone elsewhere.

V. Triumphal return to the key-note, and reiterated assertion that *Zebedee went down into Bashan.* This *fait accompli* satisfactorily disposed of,

"AND NOW"—said the doctor.

The boys sprang to their feet; there was a general rustle, and all rose for the benediction. The doxology was sung with vim and rejoicing. The boys waited with tense muscles for the last *amen*, and then, unanimously, were no longer there. Most of the old ladies stayed behind to compliment the minister on his sermon, or gossip lightly on men, women, and things—chiefly women, and the appurtenances thereunto belonging. Mr. Bonnymort came up and began conversation with Mrs. Guerndale, and the children were once more together.

The next half-hour was spent in walking home under the elms; and Guyon returned to the quiet old house, happy in having been so lately happy, with an invitation to tea at Mr. Bonnymort's. And much care did his patient mother bestow upon his attire (which necessary offices seemed to him less irksome than formerly), for were not the Bonnymorts among the nicest people that had ever gone city-ward from Dale? And though Mrs. Guerndale lived a retired life, she was not without that knowledge which gives the word *gentleman* its connotations; and liked to think that, shy and old-fashioned as he might be, there was not a better-mannered boy than her son in all Dale.

So Guyon went over to tea, sleek with that unusual sleekness which careful mothers consider perfection in a boy's dress ; paler than ever in the plain black suit and tie which he still wore on Sundays, in memory of his father. Mourning in New England had a faint smack of ceremony about it, which made it linger longer about one's Sunday dress than the less pretentious week-day garb. Somewhat embarrassed of his person was the boy, as he entered the house ; but the kindly old gentleman soon put him at his ease, and he thought afterward, with some surprise, that he had found it less difficult to talk to him than to most of the village people ; even less so than with the smart boys of the neighborhood, who usually made him painfully conscious of his own demerits. He had, indeed, been somewhat awed when the three marched solemnly in to tea, and were waited on by an old man ! But this was soon lost in observing how prettily little Annie—though only nine years old, she had told him—poured out the tea, which was then solemnly borne around upon a silver salver. For poor Annie, as Mr. Bonnymort said, with a quiver in his voice, had lost her mother, and seemed older than her years.

After tea the children laid many plans for future amusement. The boy promised to take her up in the woods—up in the great gorge where the ruins were ; and Annie said papa had promised to send her to Miss Laighton's school : was not he going too? And Guyon, who had learned to read and write at home, and always rebelled bitterly at the constraint and enforced society of school, felt suddenly a lively desire for further instruction. Meanwhile, Mr. Bonnymort read a strange language in a splendid large book, which Annie catching sight of, begged to see, for it was full of wonderful pictures. Nor were the children satisfied until they had seen them all; the earlier ones, which were dark and terrible, as well as the later ones, which were brighter and brighter, until the last was almost a blank page for the light. But in every picture was a dark, sad-eyed man, holding an angel by the hand. And Annie said she liked the bright ones best; but Guyon did not know, for, he said, perhaps they would not have thought them so lovely if they had not seen the sad ones first. At last, when the book was ended, it seemed to him time to go. Mr. Bonnymort asked him to come often and see him and Annie, for his father had been an old friend of his at college.

And Guyon walked home through the autumn evening, wondering if Mr. Bonnymort ever liked his father as much as he liked Annie, and decided that he would go to school and study, and learn things, and in the winter go "coasting" with the other boys, and play with them, and make friends with them; and so on, more than he ever thought of the future before: for somehow it seemed to him there was much more in the world he wished to do than he had supposed.

CHAPTER VI.

" Loved, if you will: she never named it so :
*Love comes unseen, we only see it go."—*AUSTIN DOBSON.

ONLY after many struggles with his shyness did
Guyon finally set off for school, one frosty
morning in November ; the first of a numberless succession of mornings in which he was to hurry across
the meadow, along the river, and up the avenue to call
for Annie ; then down the long street to the little
schoolhouse. And yet this first plunge into the realities of life was less terrible than he had feared. He
had learned to read and write at home, and never had
that bodily fear of books which seems to possess many
a healthier boy, as of a drawer of dentist's tools, or a
pill-box. But his great difficulty was to get along with
the other boys. He was with them, but not of them.
So you might take a bottle, webbed, and mildewed
with the damps of some ancestral cellar, the wine
ripened and mellowed, and saddened by long time
past, and decant it into a quart-jug of the sharp,
hard, New England cider. No such far-fetched
simile ever occurred to Guyon ; but he was even
then vaguely conscious that the mixture was not
happy. In the real, objective, wilful life of other
boys, his own had no part. When they thought of

2*

him at all—which was much less often than Guyon fancied—they thought of him with that careless contempt which one boy has for another who is not up in his games ; who cannot throw a stone so far ; who does not excel at top or trap, ball or marbles ; who is not blessed with the desired and influential friendship of Jim, the brakeman, much less Jo, the engineer ; or Solomon Bung, supreme over all in luring the muskrat to the steel-trap, the rabbit to the seductive "twitch-up," or in setting night-lines for those fresh-water ghouls, horn-pout. Moreover, a crime above all others, Guerndale liked girls—for his company with Annie did not escape notice.

This ignoring of girls is a curious phase in the development of the masculine mind. There would almost seem to be a polaric relation between the sexes ; a magnetic attraction or repulsion, which varies with different ages as a magnet itself varies with the spots on the sun. Thus, from infancy to youth, boys run away from girls. From youth to marriage, girls run away from boys. After marriage, they run away from each other.

Much healthy contempt was therefore felt for Guyon as a girl's boy. Such weakness and frivolity could not be pardoned, and his position was not a pleasant one in the social microcosm of school. And even the girls, though more lenient to his great fault, found it hard to overlook the bad taste of his preference ; for Annie had taken that doubtful place which results either in sovereignty or complete disapproval, as the breath of popular prejudice turns the balance. Unfortunately, or fortunately, her

father forbade her presence at a Sunday-school pic-
nic ; and when Amanda Shed expressed her opinion
that Annie was "stuck-up," it was universally felt
.that this judgment was final ; and Annie was a *pou-
voir fini* from that time forth.

And Guyon himself soon fell under the iron rod
of the great Amanda. This young lady possessed
in a high degree a fondness for the unknown in mas·
culine character. A similar trait is observed in all
children ; but in girls, it is the more noticeable, as
exercised upon a higher object. For, whereas boys
experiment upon *corpora vilia*, girls wish beings possessed of a soul. Boys impale beetles, decapitate
turtles, starve reptiles, interfere with the domestic
arrangements of birds, and tie tin-kettles upon dogs'
tails ; it is true. But girls scarify, excoriate, and
otherwise exacerbate the boys themselves ; and while
these latter either lose their cruel curiosity on arriving at manhood, or apply it to the legitimate vivisec-
tions of science, girls do not so, but continue their
evil practices, apparently with a mere view to sport.

However, in both cases the object is the same :
boys desire to study the effect of physical emotion,
girls that of psychical emotion, on other organisms
possessed of will. Both boys and girls desire to see
which way the worm will squirm, and whether the
nature of the squirming will vary with the nature of
the stimulus ; and in neither case is there any sympathy with the suffering of the *corpus vile*. The boy
regards the movements of the tortured turtle with
the delight of gratified curiosity ; girls and women have perhaps the additional pleasure of a

gratified sense of power; but that is all. Indeed, the boy is perhaps the more humane operator; for boys do occasionally end the process in a feeling of disgust, remorse, or affection, according as the tortured animal shows fight, dies, or pleads for compassion. If it be visibly proved that a turtle cannot live with a brick on its back, the boy may suffer a transient regret at the animal's death. If the cur he has sought with views of kettles, or caudal applications of fire-crackers, show gratitude for his notice and lick the hand of the operator, perhaps the latter feels a responding affection; instances have even been known where he has adopted the dog. But no such weakness has yet been observed in female operators: the woman never allows the subject of the experiment to enter into subjective relations with her; still less does she adopt the poor devil of a dog. Throughout the operation she considers the animal in a light purely artistic. If the animal die, her blue eyes open wider in a stare of mild surprise. If he become aggressive and a bore, she utters a petulant expression of disgust and throws him out the window. If the animal limp away with a broken heart, she looks up with a pleased smile from her successful experiment, and turns her attention to the next subject. Look at Miss Dubloon and poor Harry Maravedi, down at Surfside last summer. Had Miss D. any idea of marrying him? did he ever cause her any emotion whatever at any moment of the flirtation? Not the slightest. My word, she simply wished to try whether he really would fall in love with her; and if so, which way he would squirm.

Her curiosity satisfied, the *corpus vile* has gone out on a cattle-ranche. All of which is a good deal of explanation and analysis for the simple motives of a country girl like Mandy Shed? My dear fellow, the nature of the animal is the same all the world over. In the simplest *débutante* or "bud" you will find all the curious convolutions of the full-grown flower.

When Guyon first dawned upon the horizon of Mandy Shed, he was an unknown and curious fact; quite different from the well-tested male creatures by whom she had been so long surrounded, and among whom the *mot-d'ordre* was contempt for everything feminine. Her curiosity was aroused, and thus the strongest and most essential condition of the reaction was provided. So she began by treating Guyon with soft-soap and smiles. He was impervious. Then, a provoking indifference failed of effect. Alternate malice and caprice won him not, caused no squirming in this oddly mailed animal. Finally, she asked him to the pic-nic.

Guyon was not page-in-waiting at a French court, and his answer was fatal.

He said, " Is Annie Bonnymort going ?"

It will readily be imagined that he joined her in the pleasant country about Coventry. And often, in later life, he wished that a considerate world of grown people had acted as kindly as his childish enemies.

For they left him with Annie ; and the winter wore on, and Guyon and Annie and the woods grew up together. In the morning he dragged her, on his sled, to school, and back at night, coasting down all the hills on the way. And Saturday afternoons were devoted to all out-doors; than which, Guyon grew up to think, nothing, not even Annie, could be more pleasant.

For there were afternoons when the sky was gray, and the country like a drawing on a slate; and yet in the woods the usual places of shade were all white, and the boles of trees were white, and the feathery labyrinth of twigs above was all white tracery against a white sky; and perhaps far over the gray landscape, on the horizon, was the great gleam of a sunlit mountain, Graylock or Monadnock. Then there were afternoons when it was spring, despite the stillness and the snow; the white shroud shrank visibly, and around every tree-trunk was a little crack between it and the snow melting, as if to give it room to grow; and a little tinkle came faintly through from the hidden brook like the music of another Orpheus to move the world and vivify the very moss on the rocks. And there were days with a sky of May, when the liquid air could be seen, and yet through it the country beyond, like a landscape pictured in a crystal; when each varying shadow came out in unexpected richness of color, like a painting newly oiled. And the boy's eyes would glow, and his face flush, and his limbs grow nimble—even his shyness vanishing, in the loveliness of the living world. And Annie, only partly sharing his excitement, would wonder at the change. And even then, if Ned Dench or Ury Sprowl came by, he would suddenly shrink back into his usual quiet self, like a chameleon.

Guyon must have felt instinctively that the boys did not like him, and he would offer no foothold for their ridicule. So the boys would go by, laughing, probably really not thinking much about him, while Guyon would brood for hours on the unpleasant things he thought they thought of him. And he grew fonder yet of Annie.

CHAPTER VII.

"Défaites vous de votre optimisme, et figurez vous bien que nous sommes dans ce monde pour nous battre envers et contre tous."—PROSPER MÉRIMÉE.

IT was a year after all this, the day of Guyon's autumn afternoon reverie in the churchyard. Annie had expected a cousin that afternoon, who was coming to live in Dale, for a time, and so Guy had gone off under the pine trees to watch the squirrels. Then he went home and found what would most have pleased him at any other time—a message from Mr. Bonnymort for him to come and take tea with Annie. He felt that he should probably meet there the owner of the strange voice, and shrank with all his old timidity from the meeting. Still, he also felt anxious to see him; he wanted him to understand thoroughly that he, Guyon Guerndale, was Annie's chosen companion and friend, and that a third would be admitted to their pleasures only as of courtesy, not of right. For he never doubted that Annie would feel as he did; he judged her by himself. Moreover, he had found a new brook up in the hills, and had been reserving for Saturday the great delight of exploring it; thus he had a certain advantage of position as to the newcomer.

When he had walked across the wide piazza, less

eagerly than usual, and was about to enter the hall, he stopped on seeing within a lady, dressed in a confused elaboration of silks. She turned about, with a portentous rustling, advanced a step or two, and said,

"What do you want, little boy?"

Guyon was frightened and perplexed. There was something about the attendant sweep of silk with which the lady moved—their crisp rustle seeming to exact your attention, and preceding slightly each movement with an ominous noise of preparation—which made the whole effect of her approach rather overawing. Then, what was he to say to a question "what he wanted?" Should he reply *tea?* Or, that he came by invitation? He was just beginning, "I think Mr. Bonnymort expects me—" when a clear, boyish voice broke in,

"Hallo, Mamma, that's Guerndale. *I* know him. Saw him this afternoon sleepin' down at the cemetery."

At this, the lady smiled graciously to Guyon, who was looking with pleased surprise at the speaker, and said that he might come in. "Oh, and you are young Guerndale? That is my boy—Phillie Symonds, and I am Mrs. Symonds."

Guyon did not seem so much impressed with this announcement as she perhaps expected, but "Phillie" was already hurrying him off to the garden. "I say," said he, "don't call me Phillie—Mamma always calls me that 'cause she thinks I'm a baby. My name is Philip Schuyler Symonds. But you can call me Phil. And your name, what's—oh, I know, Guyon. What a queer name! I can't call you that,

you know—it's too long. I might call you Guy.
Where's Annie ? she's a brick, isn't she ? that is, for
a girl. I told her so. Have you got a gun ? I have.
It's got two barrels, too. It's Jim's, but I took it
when we left Boston. Don't tell Mamma, though.
She don't know. I'm goin' off shootin' to-morrow."

He was a handsome boy, with a rosy, bright face,
and yellow curls, which grew well down over his
forehead and fell, now and then, over his quick gray
eyes. Guy felt companionship with him a novelty.
There was something aggressive about his movements ; everything he did impressed you with that
nervous wilfulness, rather than will, which springs
from animal spirits and careless self-confidence. It
was all quite new to Guy, this active, intrusive, objective person, who entered so directly into relations
with his own self ; not as other boys had been, whom
he suffered passively, so little did their orbits cross
his, but as a force of character, necessarily deter-
minable for friendship or the reverse. Guy thought
all this with that deep consciousness of a thoughtful
childhood, which feels, though it be but vaguely,
more than the philosophy of manhood can express.

Meanwhile Philip trotted along, chattering questions and paying but little attention to the answers,
to the little old pond in the garden. This pond was
a hot, sleepy place in summer ; stone-rimmed, with
water none too clear, giving a safe asylum to the fat,
yellow bull-frogs that gravely thrust their green
heads through the scummed surface of the water, or
basked contentedly on the old logs that floated here
and there, motionless, stuck fast in the green slime.

The pond was shut in by a fringe of dingy ever-greens, that kept off the light and seemed to inten-sify the heat. Philip at once seized a stick, and be-gan threshing the water, usually hitting with a huge splash the place where the lazy green head had just been, but was no longer. With a natural delight in destruction, the two boys had soon a dozen or more of the frogs ranged on the stone curb, and the pond so well beaten that even its most imperturbable denizen had sought refuge in the muddy depths. Their game exhausted, conversation became again in order.

"What fellers are there here?" said Philip.

"I don't know; I don't like them. At least, not very much."

"I saw one boy as I came up from the depot. I think I can lick *him*," he added meditatively. Guy looked at him with some admiration.

"Do you collect eggs?" continued Philip. "Mam-ma says I mustn't take but one at a time, because I don't need but one of each kind. But then, I do; 'cause I can swap the others off. This would be a bully place for teetlybenders." And the boy looked around, as if at a loss for action.

"Oh, I know what I'll do. I'll stump you to jump over here!"

And running back, he cleared the narrow part of the pond at a bound, and landed, with a crashing of bushes, on the other side. Guy had a dim feeling that he was being curiously involved in uncongenial pur-suits. However, not wishing to lower himself in the eyes of his new companion, he made a rush, tripped on a bush, and alighted in the water, two-thirds of the way across. Philip threw himself upon his back and kicked up his heels in an agony of delight. As Guy struggled up and rubbed the mud from his eyes, he became aware that he was an object of ridicule. Making a rush at Philip, the two boys closed, and this time both rolled into the water, Guy undermost ; while a patriarchal bull-frog sat gravely on an old tomato-can, and enjoyed the dissensions of his whilom oppressors.

How long this duel would have lasted it is impossible to say, had not Annie Bonnymort been a horrified spectator of the scene ; but, by her mediations, peace was restored, and the sorry train returned to the house, Philip defiant, Guy abashed, and Annie crying bitterly at the end of the procession. Mrs. Symonds received them with horror and opprobrium ; and reproaching audibly " that rude country boy," began coddling Philip, to the latter's intense disgust. Nevertheless, he was consigned to the upper regions in charge of a stout serving-maid ; and Guy, receiving an intimation that that other boy had better go home and change his clothes, found himself upon the dusty road with a burning sensation of misbehavior and disgrace.

And so ended our hero's first appearance in society.

CHAPTER VIII.

" L'amour propre, c'est la plus grande de nos folies."—LA ROCHEFOUCAULD.

IT was the first time in his life that Guyon had a decided feeling of hate ; for his self-respect would not suffer him to hate the other boys of his acquaintance for disliking him without cause. It was not that Symonds had led him to jump and tumble in the water, had rolled him in the mud ; but that through him he had been snubbed and disparaged before Annie. And the next morning when he hurried across the fields to her house, rather late, and found that she had left for school with Philip, he hated him more than before. Hastening his steps, he stalked silently by them on the way and took his seat in the school-room without speaking to either. At "recess," he met Annie's invitation to come and play with the remark that "she might go and play with Philip—*he* had sums to do." And wilfully bending over his desk, as she turned away, he did not see the look of sorrow and wonder which came into her soft eyes.

"Ho, ho, Guy ! I wouldn't get mad about nothin'," cried Philip, as he went by.

"I am not mad," replied Guy, with more dignity than truth. But Philip had vanished, leap-frogging the row of desks as he went, to the admiration of the crowd of boys about him. And so for several days he stood upon his dignity, satisfied that his conduct was very right and noble, though he could not have told himself what cause he had to be offended.

Now Mandy Shed had never quite got over her pique at Guy's injury to her spurned beauty. Not that she particularly cared about him, but she did care about the evident preference of any one for Annie Bonnymort. And thus it happened that Uriel Sprowl came up one morning and found Mandy and our hero in close conversation. The interview was evidently of her seeking; but all the more fired with jealousy was the noble soul of Uriel Sprowl.

"Hallo, Mandy! what are you talking to *him* for?"

"I'll talk just to who I like—just! You haven't any say about it, anyhow."

"Perhaps I ain't; but if I was you, I wouldn't talk to a thief like him."

"He isn't a thief!" cried Mandy, indignant.

"Yes, he is—or his father was! Oh, I know all about it! Sol Bung told me."

"Yes, and he murdered a man, too, and got a big diamond for doing it. Sol Bung told me, too. And that's the reason he lives off all alone by himself, and don't talk to nobody—*I* know!" This from Ned Dench, who had come up after Sprowl, eager to express his own disapproval of the boy whom no one knew.

"It's not true," said Guy, pale, but quietly.

"Well, if 't warn't your pa, it was your grandpa, anyhow, and it's all the same thing."

"You lie."

"Pretty poor lot, all of yer, I guess," retorted Sprowl; "and, if it comes to lyin', yer lie back."

How the matter would otherwise have been decided it is impossible to say; for Guy resorted promptly to primitive, but honest Saxon, methods of procedure by waging his battle then and there. Sprowl found himself lying upon the ground, looking up at the blue sky, with a feeling as if most of his teeth had been driven in.

Upon this, Ned Dench also rushed for Guy; several other boys joined him; and Sprowl picked his own self up and hurled it at our hero with all the fury of revenge. Nevertheless, Guy backed calmly up against a stone wall, and was preparing to take it out in fighting, when there was a wild rush of tossing fair hair and arms and limbs in the midst of his assailants, and he suddenly found himself surrounded by the prostrate forms of his enemies. In the middle stood Philip Symonds, his gray eyes fixed and blazing with excitement.

"That's like you, darned mean sneaks! Three or four of you to pitch into one man at once! Come away Guy, we'll give them some more when they want it!" And, linking his arm in Guy's, he led him away, too much surprised and overcome to make remonstrance. The allies sat upon the ground and stared ruefully at one another. Mandy Shed emerged from behind a tree, and looked at them silently, her black eyes flashing with delight. But no one spoke, save Ned Dench, who drawled out with gravity, as he rubbed his bruised elbows alternately with the palm of each hand,

"Wa'al, fur fireworks!"

Thereby evincing the philosophy and good nature of the New England countryman.

As the three other children were walking home, Guy turned and said, with a low voice, and in a manner quaint and constrained : "Mr. Symonds, I was wrong in being angry with you this morning. And I am very much obliged for your help. I shall not forget it. And, Annie, I wish you to hear me say so."

Philip opened his eyes somewhat, but said : "Why, Guy, that's all right—of course I wouldn't let those fellows go for you all at once. Only I wouldn't git riled just 'cause I tumbled in the mud—"

"I was wrong" interrupted Guy, hastily, with a slight flush. "I have said so."

Annie pressed his hand, and the children walked along in silence.

CHAPTER IX.

"In quella parte del libro della mia memoria, dinanzi alla quale poco si potrebbe leggere, si trova una rubrica, la quale dice :—*Incipit Vita Nova*."—DANTE.

FROM the famous day of the fight, the three children became fast friends, and Philip, in particular, grew to be a very idol for Guy. No one could do anything so well as Philip, no one was so true, so plucky, and so strong. Annie, for the future, held but a second place in his mind, though they saw almost as much of one another as ever, for Philip soon made friends and admirers of all the boys of the neighborhood. While he was off with them as leader in some boyish diversion, Guy, who still shrank from any one but Philip, would be rambling about alone or with Annie. But he took more pride in the prominence and prowess of his friend than if it were his own.

Perhaps, the boy brooded more than ever. Whenever he was alone the memory would recur, morbid and persistent, of what Sprowl had said. What had he meant by it? He had always felt that other children shunned and avoided him. It was, then, because there was some disgrace connected with him and his family? No, that *could* not be true, it must be only because they did not like him. At all events,

3

Solomon Bung was the man who had told the story, and of Solomon Bung he would have an explanation.

But old Sol was not an easy man to find, unless you lay in the grass under a meadow-willow, some fine summer's day, looked up at the sky and waited for him.

One night when the crickets and tree-toads were still, and the gray meadow-mist rose thicker than ever beneath the first breath of autumn, as Guyon was passing through the marsh-land near Weedy Pond, he saw the well-known motionless figure of Solomon Bung. He was seated on a decayed stump by the margin of the water; the cork of his fishing line bobbed merrily among the lily-pads, and the smoke of his briar-wood pipe curled gently up about his weather-beaten face. Old Sol had knocked about the world in his youth enough to enjoy the dear delight of doing nothing, now he was sixty. Much as Guy wished to speak to him, he was too diffident, and he probably would have passed by in silence, had not Sol, with an encouraging "wa'al, sonny?" invited conversation.

"Do you get many fish?" began Guy, with some trepidation, for he felt the honor of a talk with so famous a personage.

"Wal, no, can't say as the fish be as plenty as they used. 'T ain't so much for the pout 'n' suckers I come. It's sorter quiet out here by the pond o' nights, 'n' a man gets away from the everlastin' cackle o' the wimmin-folks."

"It *is* nice!" assented Guy, eagerly. "I like to be alone, too."

"Wal, there's loneliness an' loneliness. 'T ain't good for a little shaver like you to see too much of hisself."

"I don't like the boys at school."

"No, an' 'taint nateral you should. Their ways ain't like your folks' ways, ever since—ever since the country was settled. But what's this folks say about a rumpus you an' that 'ere Sprowl boy had the other day? Folks do say as how you 'n' he had a qua'l."

"He said my grandfather was a murderer and—and a thief; and I told him he lied. He said you told him so; and oh, do tell me—you know it can't be true——" And poor Guy burst into a passionate fit of crying. Old Sol lay down his fishing-rod and his pipe and his bait-box upon the long meadow-grass, and took the boy tenderly in his arms, while his leathery old face lengthened into such an expression of pity as a large quid of tobacco stuck in one cheek would allow.

"Why, sonny—why, Guyon boy, don't cry so, now don't! Why, my good little boy, what do you care what that 'ere darned Sprowl or any other cuss said? 'n' what difference does it all make, so long as you did n't do it? 'T warn't you as killed old Simmons, anyhow."

"I don't care what Ury Sprowl said," struggled out Guy between his sobs. "But he said you told him so, and, if it wasn't true, you had no right to."

"Wal, my boy, I'll tell you all about it. Only don't cry—there's a good boy! You see, the fact is, it's all true, an' it ain't. An' it happened so long

ago that it don't make no difference to you, anyhow
—now, does it? Why, I know fellers whose fathers
made their money in real downright cheatin'—*I* call
it so—an' they hold their heads now jest as high as
the next man, an' a heap higher than you nor me.
Why, there's old Simmons—Symonds he calls himself—they do say as how, when he fust went into old
Nat Langdon's counting-room, he stole hand and
fist from the uneddycated heathens and Catholics,
and such like poor devils!"

"Is that Philip's father? For he is my best
friend, and his father is a gentleman in Boston, and
I know he would not do anything wrong." Guy
looked up and spoke earnestly through his tears.

"Wal, sonny, that's neither here nor there. However, as I was goin' to say, the fact of the matter
was, you see, that your grandfather's grandfather—
Sir Guyon, as old folks used to call him in them 'ere
effete times—was a mighty queer sort o' man. He
was a graspin' old cuss, and his great idee was to
scrape up enough of the shiners to take him back to
England, where he could live with the kings and
princes of them old monarchies. Now, you 'n' I
ain't such darned fools as to go and suppose as how
there's gold, or anything else but gravel an' pyrites,
in these old hills. New England hills is pretty poor
plowin'. But in them ancient times folks didn't
know no better. So when old Godfrey Guerndale
died—the old gentleman that bought all the country
round here—his son, bad Sir Guyon, he came back
an' struck up a great friendship with a chap named
Phil Simmons, that was one o' the forefathers of

your friend we was just speakin' of, or akin to him,
anyhow. He was a good-for-nothin' sort o' cuss that
used to be a-gipseyin' round mostly, summat like
me, only he was an ugly devil an' graspin'. Anyhow, the long and short of it was, they had an old
furnace up here in the hills an' used to roar away at
it o' nights like mad, an' on Saturday nights, too.
Folks tell as how they really did find a diamond, or
a carbuncle, or suthin' of the kind ; anyhow, they
got into a muss, an' your gret-gran'father, he knocked
young Simmons on the head, dead as Chelsea, sure
enough. An' he would not let himself be taken
alive ; so he was shot down like a woodchuck, and
the rights of the story never got rightly known.
Some say as how he shot himself. I don't guess
but what your gran'father warn't so much to blame
as some other folks ; quite likely Simmons had the
first lick in the row an' got lammed, and sarved him
right ; but it never came out. And your folks
hain't, perhaps, been in much favor since ; an' that's
nateral. People will talk, and then they've had a
way o' keepin' off to themselves a good deal, and that
ain't helped 'em. Folks thought as how they might
be a little stuck-up. But some say that old John
Simmons, he that wuz the father of the one that was
killed, he stuck by your gret-gran'father, 'n' was
with him before he was killed 'n' tried to get him off
out o' the country ; an' old Guerndale he gave Simmons the stun' to keep for his boy, your gret-gran'-
father. Ah, well," added Sol, relapsing into silence
and seeking for his pipe, "'t ain't no use !"

Sol used to tell afterward how Guy's face had become "sorter white an' set-like" during his narrative. However that was, the boy had stopped crying and remained silent for some minutes afterward, a pause which enabled Solomon Bung to eliminate from their muddy element several horn-pout, and deposit them gasping in his basket.

"And what became of the diamond?" asked the boy, finally.

"Wal, folks used to say as how your family kep' it. People don't think much o' them sort o' things now. But Guyon, boy"—and Sol lowered his voice —"they do say it was foretold that your people never would be happy or get like other folks until they gave away, or lost, or somehow got shet o' that 'ere precious stun! There was suthin' kind o' queer about the way it came to ye, an' it can't bring no luck!"

The old fisherman began gathering up his basket and preparing to go. Guy still sat on the grass, looking into the black water.

"Ain't you comin'?" said Sol. "Most time for you to be a-bed."

"Not yet," said the boy. "Besides, I go home the other way."

Solomon Bung, after urging him some time in vain, slowly plodded across the spongy meadow to the edge of the low wood. When he reached there he turned and looked for Guy. The boy was still sitting beside the dead tree-trunk, quite still, his hands clasped upon his knees. The white mists from the pond rose up so dense about him as almost to veil his form, dimly outlined against the sombre mere. To the west the sunset faded in pale yellow streaks, running in long bars across the sky, behind the high black pines. There was no noise but the hoarse croak of the frogs and the cry of a hidden water-fowl.

"Can't exactly make that boy out," said old Sol, as, after several unanswered calls, he turned and took his way through the wood-path. "Seems to care a lot about what folks think of him ; an' yet he does pretty much as he likes, an' is powerful sot in his ways."

CHAPTER X.

. . . "You hold our 'scutcheon up,
Austin, no blot on it! You see how blood
Must wash one blot away; the first blot came
And the first blood came. To the vain world's eye
All's gules again—no care to the vain world
From whence the red was drawn!"—ROBERT BROWNING.

" A ciascun alma presa e gentil core. . . .
Salute in lor signor cioè Amore!"—DANTE.

GUY never knew how long he stayed there, sitting with his head upon his breast, his dry eyes peering into the still water. He was almost too unhappy to move; he sat there blindly and let his sorrows pass over him like a flood. What matter if he never moved? Why not resign himself? What difference did it make? So absorbed was he, that the first he knew of any one's approach was the touch of a little, soft, warm hand. There was poor little Annie, breathless and trembling, looking at him with anxious eyes.

"Why, Guidie, where have you been? Why do you stay away so late? I went over to get you to come to tea at Cousin Philip's, and they did not know where you were. But your mamma said she thought you had gone down to the pond. So I ran down here; and oh! Guy, I was so frightened! It was so late, and the woods were so dark, and—but, what is the matter, Guy dear?"

For suddenly great drops of tears rolled down the boy's face; and she had never known him to cry. But he made no sound, until, as she took his cold hand in her warm ones, out came the whole confused story of his trials and troubles; distorted and exaggerated, as children's griefs are, but withal a keener sense of injustice than is left to callous minds of men. But, somehow, when Guy, broken-voiced, reached the end, with Annie's tender brown eyes fixed in sympathy, it seemed to him that he cared less than before. After all, while he and Annie were walking homeward through the wood, he did not care so much what Ury Sprowl and Ned Dench might be saying. And so they came back through the shadows, hand in hand; and Annie, now sobbing herself, begged Guy not to mind it. It was only the foolishness of those people; and they were not nice, any of them. Besides, why should he mind if what they said was untrue? Her father would not think so, she knew.

But Guy suddenly felt a longing for a world where people were all like her father, and did not act or think in a way he felt was not—not nice. He not only felt discontented with Mandy Shed and Dench and Sprowl and the other children about Dale, but with the place itself and home and narrowness. Guy was not old enough to even imagine malice; he could not understand that people should do ill merely for the pleasure of ill-doing. He wished to go back with the Bonnymorts, when they returned to the city, that October. He wished to go anywhere.

Tea at Mrs. Symonds' was a somewhat formidable affair; but he heeded it little, to-night; still less, Philip's many inquiries as to why he had been so long fishing and how many pout he had caught. He became more interested when he heard Philip talking about going off next week to St. Mark's, in Rockshire, for his first term at school. He was going to room with Leffy Lane, he said; but he did not want to. Leffy was a muff, and—hallo! why would not Guy go with him?

Guy looked at Annie, across the table.

"I should like to, ever so much," he said; then, seeing Mrs. Symonds' look, "if Mrs. Symonds is willing, I will."

"Oh, that would be perfectly splendid—as girls say," cried Philip, adding the latter clause as an apology for his unmanly enthusiasm. "And we can come to Dale here, for our vacation, instead of Boston; and we'll take our double-runner, and Snap, and a lot of fishing-poles, and——"

"Be silent, Philly, don't scream so, child," interposed the dominant of Mrs. Symonds' metallic voice. But, after tea, Mr. Bonnymort and she had a long conversation, one side of which was very much to his credit, so far as Guy overheard, and the other not at all. Finally, Mr. Bonnymort called Guy to him, and asked if he had spoken to his mother about this.

Guy said no; but that he knew she would let him. And, truly enough, the sad-eyed widow would as soon have thought of opposing his father in the

flesh as of offering let or hindrance to anything
Guy willed.

"Ah," said Mr. Bonnymort. "Well, Mrs. Symonds has no objection to your going with her son;
only, of course, you must get your mother's permission."

This she gave, with many tears and much inward
repining. She did not say that she could not bear
to have him leave her; she seemed afraid to let him
go. She too had caught her husband's curious,
shrinking dread of the world. She pleaded for delay,
that he was too young, that he was not twelve.

"My grandfather was only thirteen when he went
to the war," said Guy.

"Yes, and he took the wrong side," sighed his
mother.

"No, Mamma," said Guy, "he was loyal. I know
the Tories were wrong; at least, Miss Laighton says
so. But they *had* to be loyal." At which Mrs.
Guerndale smiled and kissed him, and said that only
women reasoned so, now-a-days.

So Guy was to go to school and learn to meet the
world and conquer it. Philip was much busied
about his pets and traps and implements of sport;
but Guy and Annie passed the last week in making
the tour of the neighborhood. It was then late autumn; the last of the cardinal flowers found by Guy
flamed in Annie's hair; but the wood was ablaze
with golden rod, and the beautiful clematis vine and
the pale purple aster. The children spent one day
about the mushy and somewhat ineffective shores of
Weedy Pond; where Solomon Bung watched them

silently, with his kind old face, lest they should get
into danger. Then they followed up the brook
to the little pool where Guy had first tumbled into
Annie's acquaintance. Then over the brow of the
hills beyond, where great lazy Monadnock loomed
in the crisp autumn air like a dream, and brought a
like look into the boy's eyes. They often visited the
old forge or furnace on the shady side of the valley.
One day they were sitting there looking over at the
brown sunlight, as it fell on the opposite slope of
wood and fern. There was a haze and a hush in
the day, falling like a shadow of thought on happiness; but above the sky was purple, and shimmer-
ing down came the long silver skeins that the mother
Mary weaves in heaven, as the old Provençal peasants say: "Weaving the birth-robes for them that
are just born, being dead."

Guy had been entertaining Annie with a long vision
of his future. How, if a war broke out, as men said
might be, he would go and win such honors that he
might come back and wear the fatal old diamond on
the hilt of his sword if he liked, and no man should
say him nay. And, if he died, he would leave fair
fame behind him and a kind memory for his sons.
Annie, somewhat grieved at her own absence from
all these brilliant dreams, hinted that she feared he
would forget her, when all these fine things came to
pass. And Guy said that he never would.

The next day, the morning train took the boys off
for Discord. But not before Guy had taken Edward
Dench and Uriel Sprowl, Jr., successively behind
Uriel Sprowl's barn, and then and there given each

in turn, in a fair field, what Sol Bung called "an all-fired good lickin'. He hez the old Guern'l spunk—no doubt on 't—an' he'll try an' make a start."

"So he be gone up to Discut, be he?" said old Sol to me. "Wal, wal. They do give youngsters a powerful deal of schoolin', now-a-days."

Sol turned his quid meditatively for several minutes. "Mebbe, it's a good thing" he added. "Mebbe, now, ef I—"

But it was never known what things Sol thought he might have accomplished with educational advantages. The high, shallow accents of Sol's helpmeet were heard at this moment, in the direction of the back-yard, but approaching the speaker, the volume of their acerbity increasing inversely as the square of the distance. Sol hitched his trowsers.

"Wal, wal—'t ain't no use."

And, as he spoke, he gathered up his rod and lines and moved off rapidly and smoothly in the direction of Weedy Pond.

Book Second.

CHAPTER XI.

"In that I live, I love ; because I love,
I live : whate'er is fountain to the one
Is fountain to the other ; and whene'er
Our God unknits the riddle of the one
There is no shade or fold of mystery
Swathing the other."—TENNYSON.

GUERNDALE never liked me at Discord, and
we saw very little of one another. Doubtless,
I should then have put it that I did not like him,
for I thought he was a muff and a fool, and prided
myself on never changing my opinions. I do not
know what he thought of me, but he never liked
me. He was not a boy of much promise at games ;
being, indeed, very young, besides weak and slender.
Symonds, who was one of the jolliest and pluckiest
little cubs we had in the school, was a great friend
of his, but even Phil, as I saw, felt sometimes ashamed
of Guerndale's moodiness and want of spirit. We
used to wonder what made them such close friends ;
but, perhaps, it was natural, for Guerndale almost
worshipped Philip. There was little enough the
poor little devil could do for a man like Symonds,
one of the most popular fellows in the school ; but

he stuck to him like a leech. I do not think Guerndale really was such a fool as he looked; indeed, once in a while he would seem to try and be more like other fellows. I remember one day we were sitting around the south door, talking over a fourteen-mile run of hare and hounds the day before. Guerndale really had done remarkably well as a hare, for he had a surprising knack of finding his way in the woods. Lane spoke of it, and Tom Brattle said Guerndale could do well enough when it came to running away. This was, perhaps, rather a mean thing to say, and Philip flushed up a little.

"I do wish Guy, you wouldn't be such a flat," said he. "Why, there's scarcely a fellow now that can't beat you at anything."

"Let the little muff alone and come out for football," I cried. "You can't make a silk purse out of a sow's ear." This sally of mine made quite a success, which pleased me hugely, for I was not usually very ready with my tongue. Guerndale turned quite white, but said nothing, and afterward joined us in the field—rather to my surprise, for he usually wandered off alone in play-hours. Now I was one of the biggest and strongest fellows in the school, and Phil Symonds, though younger, was a beautiful rusher. I remember well how he and I chose up— for it was a scrub-game—and he, rather reluctantly, took Guerndale as his last man.

"What am I to do?" asked he.

"Oh, I don't know," Phil answered. "You might as well help tend goal, I suppose. You can't do anything else."

Guy silently took his place, and I led off. The game was pretty close that day, and after an hour we only had two touch-downs. Then I got the ball out bounds, and made a far throw to Lane, who caught it and by a quick side run got well behind their rushers; I, of course, ran in from out bounds a little ahead of the line, keeping well along with Lane, and when Phil caught him, as I expected, he threw the ball to me. I took it neat, and tucking the leather under my arm started, all Phil's side after me. But I was well ahead, with only Guerndale between me and their goal. "You're off side," he sang out; but I was mad at his cheek, and told him to "shut up" and that he was a "darned little fool," or something of the sort. Just then I stumbled over a hillock and dropped the ball forward. Madder than ever, I rushed on after it, now near enough to the goal to try a running kick. Guy must have seen my intention; but none the less he threw his little corpus upon the ball head-foremost, just as my heavy boot struck square, luckily, on his shoulder only, and I went over like a ninepin amid a confused noise of cheering and laughter; while Guerndale sang out "have it down!" Down he had it, sure enough, and himself on top of it, and fainted away at that. And then I was too blown to do much, and a straight winder of Phil's ended in a goal for them.

I speak of this incident, because it is about the only thing I remember of Guy at St. Mark's. Curiously enough, I find I have described it quite in my old self as a boy. I can see, as I write, what I then thought and believed, what I was, what sort of a world I centred, as if I were back there again. But my language of those times will not carry what I have to say now. So the reader will please forget me, as I shall forget myself.

All this was some years before we went to college, and by that time Guy was quite changed by his long life in a large school. He was now a wiry, active fellow, somewhat serious and reserved, but far from morose. Indeed, he was most enthusiastic when roused by anything he liked or believed in. The summer we were sub-freshmen, Philip, Lane, Guerndale, and I walked through the White Mountains, and I saw more of him. He had deep brown eyes, which seemed to drink in light without returning it, except now and then a reflection of the sky, and a deep, bass voice, and when alone he was nearly always singing. He had two great beliefs, ideas, objects which quite surprised me when I first discovered them. One was his intense belief in the earnestness of life; it was so earnest that it almost seemed forced or artificial, or as if it depended on some other feeling. He took things and thoughts so deeply into his consciousness that I believe anything wrong or unhappy in them caused him acute pain, like a bruise or a broken bone. Another was his ideal way of thinking, and he seemed to think the world really corresponded to it. He idealized everything—his friends, his favorite public men of the time, his favorite authors, and particularly men's motives. He really seemed to think that all men acted like the knights in the Faery Queen, his favorite poem. I used to envy him his enthusiasm, his passion of admiration, while it lasted, and would pity him somewhat contemptuously in his poignant unhappiness when his ideal was shattered, as would sometimes happen in those days. All women are hero-worshippers, and he was very much like a woman, or rather a young girl. We often laughed at him for this, and for his dreams.

Still he had great energy and plenty of ambition for active life—for coming out of the cloud, as he used to say, and living in the open. His belief in things was intense—I mean, in men and thoughts, not works and facts; rather in the future than the present. And added to this was his belief in himself. Guy was not exactly conceited, but I believe he thought that he could remove most external things that vexed him, as a surgeon excides a tumor. In the middle of the civil war he had sought his mother's permission to enlist, which was refused, as he was only fifteen; but I think he would have gone all the same had not the war ended. He used to glory in the North and its victories, and declaim eagerly to such of us as would listen to him about the effect of a war undertaken from noble motives in purifying and perfecting our country.

All this rather bored us, I think. He was too high-strung altogether for a lot of jolly fellows on a walking trip. In conversation he shot too many arrows in the air to be amusing. I never could make out what the devil he was driving at. Still, he came as a friend of Phil's, whom we all liked.

I remember, one afternoon, we four were trudging along the bad road between Jackson and the Glen, when a little phaeton rattled by, carrying a pretty girl with a pink parasol. A young man, faultlessly dressed, was leaning toward her to whisper something in her ear, with an air of matter-of-course about him that we all felt was quite beyond us. Then they looked at us and laughed, and Lane spoke up : "Why, that's Norton Randolph ; he's going in with our class." We all of us raved about the pretty girl except Guerndale, who persisted in comparing her to a tulip ; but when we went to Cambridge in the autumn, and Randolph appeared for the first time in our midst, it was with a certain glamour of pink parasol. He had that delicious manner of a man of the world fascinating to youth, and we were all prepared to be influenced by him. He was dimly reported to be very rich and to have travelled much abroad ; moreover, he had a general sort of air of having been all through college twenty years before, and only being there again to see how we managed it.

But I am dropping into myself and my impressions again ; so here goes for impersonality and a new chapter.

CHAPTER XII.

Oh, if I had course like a full stream,
If life were as the field of chase ! No, no ;
The life of instinct has, it seems, gone by,
And will not be forced back. And to live now
I must sluice myself into canals,
And lose all force in ducts."—CLOUGH.

IN the old halls of Cambridge there was nothing sufficiently luxurious to suit the cultivated tastes of Mr. Norton Randolph. Moreover, he said, the college halls were infested with proctors, and proctors were a race of very impudent fellows who would come into your room without being announced. We paid great attention to what Randolph used to say, in those days. It was not only his great age that impressed us—he was twenty-two—but the superior way in which he spoke of things in general and the world in particular.

By reason of his aversion to proctors, he eschewed the quadrangle, and occupied the floor of a house in the town. Thither he was wont to call a few chosen spirits every night ; but first let me describe his surroundings, as I remember them.

He occupied a study and a bed-room. On the floor of the latter was a large metal bath-tub, perfectly flat and surrounded by an ornamental rim of wrought iron. This he had imported from England, a Christian tub, as he said, being not procurable in America. Besides a bath-tub, it was a trap for burglars, as any one entering the room carelessly was sure to trip over it. And its width was carefully measured, so that a falling proctor would just reach the opposite iron rim with the bridge of his nose. For this purpose, it was frequently borrowed and placed in dark entries by men who gave wine-parties.

This machine of cleanliness and defence was familiarly spoken of among Randolph's friends as the Frog-pond. Besides it, there was a wardrobe, a clothes-press, a dressing-table, and a large table at the head of the bed. On this you might usually find a reading-lamp, a box of cigarettes, a hookah, the latest number of the *Revue des Deux Mondes*, *Punch*, *Figaro*, the *Petit Journal pour Rire*, and the *Saturday Review*; a volume of Montaigne and of French memoirs; a prayer-book of the Protestant Episcopal Church, a siphon of seltzer, and a bell. On the walls was a miscellaneous collection of armor, from a Japanese spear and a mediæval broadsword down to a pair of Guérin's best fleurets, and a triangular, beautifully engraved rapier. The floor had no carpet, but was covered with furs and fox-skins. The window was always opened, even on the coldest days.

The study was a room some twenty feet square, the floor of which Mr. Randolph had caused to be painted of a bronze green. There were many Persian rugs. The walls were lined with dwarf book-cases, and covered with old engravings and modern etchings of the rarest sort, except over the door, where was hung, in a meretricious gilded frame, a chromo of Washington, Abraham Lincoln, and General Ulysses S. Grant, with the legend *Pater—Salvator—Custos.* Randolph always said that he preserved this work of art as epitomizing the gradual deterioration of his country. The book-cases were filled with small duodecimo volumes (for he used to say that nothing could be carried in the head which was too big to be carried in the pocket), a lot of Elzivir classics, Greek and Latin ; all the older Italian and Spanish poets, and a smaller number of modern works, represented by Cervantes, Calderon, Rabelais, Montaigne, Voltaire, Swift, Byron, Goethe, Heine, Schopenhauer, Diderot, and de Musset. For he used to say, laughingly, since the time of Cervantes and Rabelais it has been impossible to take the world *au sérieux,* and his library was chosen accordingly.

But the centre-table was Mr. Randolph's especial pride. He maintained that a gentleman's centre-table should resemble the room in Dürer's *Melancolia,* and his own, accordingly, was an *omnium gatherum* of books, works of art, sporting utensils, cards, smokables, notes, letters, beverages, sketches, photographs, maps—everything *except* a daily paper ; for Randolph preferred, as he used to say, to view his times from an historico-critical distance, and not through the shilling spy-glass of an illiterate reporter. When he wished to let his friends know "what things propped his mind these dark times," he used to have his centre-table photographed, and send them proofs. For he never wrote letters, on the principle that he never had any thoughts worth writing down.

"I sometimes wonder, Guerndale, why you came to College."

The speaker, Randolph, was lying lazily on a divan, smoking a cigarette.

"I ?" cried Guy, surprised, and getting up to walk nervously about the room. "Why—of course I came here. My father came, and it was his last wish that I should come."

"Really ? Do you know, you surprise me." And Randolph rolled another cigarette. "Fellows whose people have come before them usually take it in a different way. Now, you really seem to believe in it all."

"Believe in it ? Of course I do. Why did you come yourself ? "

"Oh, I don't mean the mere coming. But there is only one attitude possible for a gentleman now-a-days : to sit and think. Life doesn't amount to anything ; and most of us have only come to Cambridge to learn to be gentlemen."

"You mean, to be mere dreamers ? "

" Dreaming isn't so bad. Most fine things left us are dreams. Besides, the real may be the false and not the true. There are visions truer than truth, as some poet says."

" You don't mean all that !" laughed Guy.

" I do, by Jove !" said Randolph, more earnestly. "Why, if it seems absurd, take one of the stock aphorisms that they cram down our eclectic throats

now-a-days—a man is a man, not for what he pos-
sesses, but for what he is. Now, what a man pos-
sesses is material ; what he is, is ideal. According
to this standard, you are only superior to a hod-
carrier in the ideas which you have that he has not.
But ideas are thoughts—visions—dreams ! Q. E.
D."

"Oh, well," said Guy, "in that half-metaphorical
sense—in that light, it may be true."

"I can't help it if you grasp the wrong light, can
I ? The white light of truth, in passing through the
turbid and many-sided prisms of this world, gets
broken into many lights and various colors. A
humble chap like myself can only grab an occasional
refracted beam and sling it at you. You must put it
in the right light yourself."

"'The idea is the act in a weaker form,' and it is
only worth anything because of the act. I wish to
do something with my life," said Guy.

"Bah ! you can't even think anything new, much
less do anything new. Besides, college men are out
of date ; they're not in sympathy with the masses.
Life, my boy, is nothing but a grim pleasantry—a
silly little toy, given to man to amuse himself with
as he likes ! He usually breaks it, sooner or later,
over something or other, and it doesn't make much
difference whether he breaks it in pursuing a muse
or a mistress."

"What immoral French idiot said that?" sang out
John Strang. "I know you cribbed it from somebody, you second-hand satirist."

"Strang, my son, you may go now, and shut the

door behind you. Your mind is too mechanical to appreciate the finer play of fancy. Moreover, your base insinuation of plagiarism falls flat. As an epitome of modern thought, a cultivated man must plagiarize. There is nothing new under the sun, as that jolly old boy said in the Hebrew bible."

Strang said he had to go, anyhow, to run with the crew, and closed the door with a grunt of disgust. Randolph turned to Guerndale, with a sweet smile.

"No," said Guy slowly. "I mean to live my life for what it is worth. And if you mean that, because a fellow is highly educated, he is to take no interest in things, it is absurd."

"Schopenhauer said that the peculiar character of the Americans of the Northern States, was vulgarity; vulgarity in all its forms, moral, intellectual, æsthetic, and social. And Renan—let me show you what Renan says." And Randolph lazily reached for a book on the centre-table, and opening it showed to Guy a scored passage :

"Les pays qui comme les Etats-Unis ont créé un enseignement populaire considérable sans instruction supérieure sérieuse, expieront encore longtemps leur faute par leur médiocrité intellectuelle, leur grossièreté de mœurs, leur esprit superficiel, leur manque d'intelligence générale."

"Now, my boy," continued Randolph, "you must either do like the people, be of the people, or dream —if you like—dream what the people of this country ought to be and arn't. If you mean to dream, Harvard College is the best place for you ; otherwise not. A college-bred man in America, must

4

wince in all his business, even in his social relations
—in short, he must go through life holding his nose."

"Pardon me, Randolph," said Guy, excitedly.
"I know you don't think what you say."

"Since the French Revolution, who ever could?"
muttered Randolph, *en parenthèse.*

"But," Guy went on, "if you mean that a high
education unfits one for American life, I deny it.
There *is* a lot that is vulgar and corrupt in American life I know; and there is just a want of gentlemen—men who have been born to ease and
enlightenment, who have got education without
narrowness, and have not been taught petty shifts
and mean motives by the *res angusta domi;* men
who have been bred in the higher views of life.
There is such a thing as having too many 'self-
made' men. Take politics for instance. What we
need there is men whose honor is above suspicion,
who have love of country without bigotry, and education without false pride in it; men who are willing—as I mean to be—to plunge fairly into the
stream, neck and neck with the self-taught mechanic
and the untrained immigrant; men who dare meet
and confront a demagogue on his own ground. Such
men are rare with us; but we can each try to be one."

The boy's words came tumbling, one over another,
almost too rapidly for utterance; he rose and walked
nervously about the room; Randolph eyed him curiously.

"My dear fellow, you talk like the back part of a
spelling-book. Now don't say bosh! and look disgusted. I admire you."

Guy threw himself into a chair, lit a pipe, and puffed impatiently. "I wish you would talk seriously."

"Ah, don't require impossibilities. The world went on seriously enough for an indefinite number of thousands of years. Now its mood is humorous. Still, I am delighted to hear you mean to pull American civilization up a peg or two. I was reading an amiable old Chinese prophet, the other day, who wrote seventeen hundred years before Christ. His name was Lao-Tse ; he was blue about the state of China, which he predicted would result in the arrest of culture and partial progress backward. The sagacious old heathen, as A. Ward would say, was right, and the signs of the times he saw remind me hugely of America to-day—indolence, indifference to metaphysical and ideal good, practical materialism with corrupt conditions of Government. See what this Chinese critic complained of—" and again Randolph took a book and read.

"'The common people of the realm are, alas ! too rough, too uneducated, too comfortable—if their meat and drink tastes good, and the girls have a trinket, and they have a snug little household, that's enough. The people take pleasure only in material things, they delight in the commonplace, they only know what is daily, ordinary, common.' I'm not a snob ; it may be that all old families are descended from robbers or ladies of doubtful reputation. But there is at least some advantage in having the successful thief a few generations back. The refining influence of money is all very well ; but I confess I like friends with whom the process began with their grandfathers.

> " ' Priez pour paix, douce vierge Marie,
> Reine des cieux et du monde maîtresse ;
> Priez, princes qui avez seigneurie,
> Gentils hommes avec chivalerie
> Car méchants gens surmontent gentillesse.'

"However," concluded Randolph, "pitch in, by all means, if you like."

"You know what I told you a year ago, when we were Freshmen," said Guy, confronting him and then turning away. "I had a quiet, sad sort of life when I was a boy, and never thought I should care much for action. Direct conflict with other peoples' wills was distasteful to me. They jarred upon me. But suddenly I changed. I felt ambitious—I don't know why."

"You don't know why?"

"No, but I went to school with Phil, and then came here. And I can't tell you, Randolph, how pleasant it has been for me, knowing you. You are the only fellow I do know well, except Phil. You are a great deal too blasé, but then I think you understand things better than most men. Only, I really can't see why you took a fancy to me?"

"Because you read like the pages of an old book, my boy, before the leaves have turned, or been turned, as the case may be," said Randolph, smiling. Just then the door opened with a hearty kick upon the panel, and Guy took his leave, as a troop of young men came in, singing. As he crossed the yard, he wondered whether many men did not, after all, think like Randolph. His moods were not so very new to Guy. As a child, he might, in his childish way, have thought very much like Randolph, except for the latter's humor. For humor is a light of the mind which only comes at maturity, and has a brighter glow in the decay of everything else. How did it happen that he himself was so changed?

Outwardly, perhaps, he was not. He was shy and sensitive ; as a rule, men did not see much in him. But that was natural ; for he was not much, he felt, especially by comparison with the men about him, his friends. For Guy had chosen them as friends for the great qualities he saw, or fancied that he saw, in each.

Guerndale was a tremendous idealizer as well of his friends as of the world in general. He believed that every one of them was the expression and embodiment of some high type of character or some great excellence, which too often existed only in his own mind. In his imagination he carried a collection of heroic ideals, and each man he met and liked was at once properly ranked, and erected in his appropriate niche. Thus his mind became a sort of Walhalla of worthies, the realities of whom he believed he saw in the world about him. So he undervalued himself ; and, perhaps, we were too ready to take him at his own valuation. And he, in turn, was terribly afraid of being a bore, and inflicting his own unworthiness upon our valuable society. He was a little like the rich and diffident fifth member in deal old Murger's *Scènes de la Vie de Bohême*, the only worthy and useful fellow among a set of scape-graces. I did not think so at the time, however.

So, when Guy entered the old, smoke-stained, low-studded, deep window-seated room which he shared with Phil Symonds, he felt bashful at disturbing the gayety of the scene when he knew he could not add to it. For Guy was not good at songs and stories and young men's conversations.

A dozen or more students were lounging about in great boyish *abandon*. One, sitting at an old beer-ringed piano that filled one side of the room, was struggling with a college song, while a group of others waited with eager breath to encourage the performer by a chorus in which confidence was more noticeable than precision. Symonds and John Strang alone were not drinking and smoking, being both provisionally in the University six, and were telling an interested group of a brush they had had in their barge with the Freshmen shell. Little Billy Bixby was throwing poker hands with Van Sittart, of New York, stopping now and then to tell a story of the unmentionable order—what John Strang used to call profane histories—and sipping from a tumbler of brandy and absinthe at his side. This was a beverage he had lately introduced into Cambridge, and his friends watched him drink it with interest not unmingled with admiration, for it was said that old Dr. Wayland had warned Bixby that six months of it would kill him. In a distant corner was standing Mr. Lefauconeur Lyndhurst Lane, buttonholed earnestly by Seth Hackett, who was partially revealing some scheme of society log-rolling. Lane's attitude was, perhaps, expressive of boredom, but his face was as faultless as a society expression and an eye-glass could make it.

"What show for the crew, Phil?" sang out Van Sittart over four aces, by way of keeping his countenance.

"Pretty fair, I guess. We haven't much beef in the boat, but they say half the Yale crew can't pull their own weight."

"Pluck and science against muscle, as usual," said Bixby, after making an unsuccessful "raise" of ten dollars on a "full."

" Billy, you can't play to-night. Better keep that little appointment of yours—it's past eleven," and Symonds sauntered up, his golden hair tossed back, a twinkle in his merry gray eyes, the tight blue jersey open at the neck, showing a superb throat, still flushed with the evening run of the crew.

"I've got a *detur*, Phil," said Guy, timidly, by way of announcing his presence, which no one had yet noticed. This bit of news was received with derisive laughter. Hackett, who was secretly grinding for honors, but feared such ambitions, if known, might injure his political influence in the class, laughed louder than the rest.

"A *detur*, by gad!" laughed ˙Phil, "what is it, young 'un? A 'college bible' or Edgeworth's Moral Tales?"

"Throw you poker hands for it!" said Van Sittart.

"What the blank *is* a detur?" cried Bixby.

" *Cui habet, detur*," growled Strang, amid cries of Shop! Shop! "Shut up, you fellows on the piano there—*bien chié, chanté*, as says the gentle humorist. There is something, in the sanctity of the hour, that suggests, to the wearied spirit, beer!"

"Beer on Guerndale! Magna—prosit!" cried Van Sittart, who had spent a semester at Heidelberg.

Symonds went to a little refrigerator, and produced another dozen bottles of the required beverage.

"Sit down, and have a game, old man!" said Bixby.

"You ought not to, Phil—you're on the crew, you know," remonstrated Guy, who was anxious for his chum's success.

"Dry up, Guy," said Symonds angrily. "Time enough to train before the race." And the three drew up to the table, Guy, who had a morbid fear of being thought ungracious, joining them. Bixby went off on some mysterious errand in a coupé. Lane took his leave politely ; Hackett offering him his company across the yard, which Lane refused, on the ground that he meant to stop and see Tom Brattle. But he did not do so, for Hackett saw him walk across the quadrangle to his own hall.

"The damned snob!" muttered Hackett, as he looked after him, grinding his heel into the gravel.

When the bell rang for prayers, the four were still at the card-table. Guy went out for a morning walk, feeling ashamed of himself for having done what he did not like for fear of incurring odium.

Van Sittart and Bixby, who humorously complained that the Faculty could not expect a fellow to sit up until such an unearthly hour for prayers, went home ; while Phil, having lost largely, dismissed his guests with a parting joke at the door and then went sulkily to bed and slept till noon.

4*

CHAPTER XIII.

"Ne dites jamais de mal de vous-même. Vos amis en diront toujours assez."
—Prosper Mérimée.

"Eat, drink, and play, and think that this is bliss :
There is no heaven but this ;
There is no hell,
Save earth, which serves the purpose doubly well . . . .

"Eat, drink, and die, for we are souls bereaved :
Of all the creatures under heaven's wide cope
We are most hopeless, who had once most hope,
And most beliefless, that had most believed."—Clough.

"MY dear Guy! what is the use of your grind-ing away so over mathematics? Mere form without content. Two-and-two-make-four-and-can't-make-five narrow, pestilent bigotry!"

"Exact science," interposed Strang, with a grunt.

"All cant—and cant I hoped Kant put an end to! Exact sciences! When you talk like that, I think, like poor dear Heine, of his old doctor, Saul Ascher; —Saul Ascher, with his abstract legs, his tight, tran-scendental-gray body coat, and his stiff, cold face, that might have served as a copper-plate to print a geometrical diagram;—Saul Ascher, who was a right-line personified, and had philosophized every sun-beam, faith, and flower, clean out of life, and left nothing for himself but a positive cold grave;—Saul

Ascher (pass me a cigarette, please, Guy—thanks, much), who had an especial malice for the Apollo Belvidere and the Christian religion; he lived on co-ordinate paper, and when he died you felt as much emotion as when you said, 'Let the line A B be extended to infinity!'——"

"Hold on!" said John, "till I write that down! Put in my examination-paper in conic sections, it might soften old Calculus."

"No," added the speaker, "but what do you mean by talking of exact sciences? How do you know the whole thing is anything more than phenomenal and provisional, anyway? Time and space, thank the Lord, are mere temporary curses, and won't afflict us always!"

These energetic speeches came softly out with the quiet, rich accent of Norton Randolph. Randolph, even when he used to swear, which was seldom, swore you an 't were any sucking dove. He now spoke in precisely the tone he would use if remonstrating with a girl for not dancing with him.

"Training for the mind!" replied Guyon, with a cloud of smoke.

"Gymnastics for blind puppies!" sighed Randolph, weariedly. "In the first place, the people don't want trained minds, and you want to suit the people. In the next place, mathematics are not half the brace that a little judicious metaphysical fog is. Leave Cartesian co-ordinates for Cartesian contradictories. You will wake up some day, as Hamilton did, like another Faust, and find that quaternions are as empty as the multiplication table."

"Oh, dear!" sighed Guerndale. "I wish the war were still going on! There, at least, Randolph, is one thing you can't deprecate."

"I, my dear fellow? I never deprecate. All things are very good, no doubt. And one thing is as good as another. Besides, I admire the war. It is the only instance within my knowledge, in modern times, of a purely ideal motive swaying mankind. It was superb to see a whole nation make a fool of itself even as one man! It was sublime! They could not have been greater asses if they had been poets. Moreover, they abolished slavery."

Guerndale looked at him, not knowing if he were in jest or serious.

"O, come, Norton, you can't say that there is no such thing as patriotism?

> " Breathes there a man with sense so great
> That this or any other State
> Is all the same to him?"

laughed Randolph. "When I was young, apple-tarts were my passion. Now it is fame, freedom, truth, and *potage bisque*. Why, my dear fellow, fame is being known to people one despises. Power is the consciousness that an aggregation of forty millions of fools can probably pummel one of twenty, unless the latter are very much bigger fools than the former. Love of country is selfishness, and as such a perfectly dignified and proper thing. It rests on the desire to preserve self and property from enemies. But now there are no external enemies against whom it is necessary to combine. The best civil government is the direct and local. What have you to show, then, that this country could not be better governed if split up into sections?"

"Like Greece, you mean? A lot of little states warring among themselves?"

"Well, even if they did," answered Randolph, "war and conflict develop the purest emotions and the highest nobility of character. And, at all events, under small local governments, the drains and roads and prisons might all be better, which, as modern science shows us, is the one great thing. What you feel is simply the barbaric and vulgar pride of being a forty-millionth of a big and bad thing rather than a millionth of something better. I can remember when I used to feel just your way: whenever I went to New York I used to choose the biggest steam-boats by preference. I have got over my worship of size and quantity. Now I would rather go to Europe in a yacht than in a Cunarder. If you want spread-eagle, go to Hackett. He is practising it for cau-cuses; it is his cue, and he will give you a dose if he gets the idea you like it. By Jove! why don't you form a sort of political partnership with him?" And Randolph laughed from the depths of his easy-chair.

"I don't like him!"

"*Raison de plus!* He will secretly respect you. He will pose as the self-made man, the spontaneous pillar of his country; and it will be his duty to hate you as a conservative and an aristocrat. But he will only call you foul names in public, and all you have to do is to take them in a Pickwickian sense. Besides, if you don't make him a friend, he will certainly over-match you. He is mediocre, and the people want mediocrity. As my old friend Lao-Tse said, the people like shine, not light; they don't want the lamp of truth, but fireworks. Now, you are a bloated aristocrat, and will be so impudent as to think you can teach the people something. Moreover, Hackett is smart, and will hob-nob with them; and, you can say what you like, your style of education and breeding will put you out of tune with them. The elegant simplicity, the reserve, the polite manners of the great world, cause not only a deep aversion for coarse men, common men of all parties, but a true hate, which even goes as far as a thirst for their blood!"

"Pooh!" said Strang. "I happen to know that you cribbed that from Guérin's memoirs, for I read it on your table the other day. And just below that place he says: 'Il n'y a pas un homme qui ait le droit de mépriser les hommes.'"

"Well, it is true," said Randolph. "I remember how the men at the Union Club thronged to the windows as the Irish societies passed by down Fifth Avenue, at the time of the draft riots; and we all said the time was coming when we should have to shoot those fellows down. Now, Hackett is enough akin to the proletariat to know how to manage it."

The door opened and Hackett entered.

"We have been talking politics, Mr. Hackett," said Randolph—"a conversation rather in your line, I fancy?"

Hackett looked suspiciously at the speaker, and accepted the proffered chair with an assumption of ease.

"Really, don't you think it is rather warm for such an appalling subject?" and he rolled a cigarette with a languid exaggeration of Randolph's manner.

"Mr. Guerndale has been treating me to quite an extreme dose of abolitionism," said Randolph.

"Ah!" said Hackett, after a moment's delay; "I think it is a great pity that the two sides should have been so exaggerated in the war. I think, at best, it was an unfortunate business. The effect is very noticeable here. A charming element of college society is lost to us in the Southerners. I don't know as we shall ever recover it. By the way, you are from Virginia, are you not?"

Guy walked to the window.

"I don't know *that* I am," said Randolph, slightly emphasizing the word in correction of Hackett's grammatical error. "My father was; but, as we have just been saying, the feeling of birth is an obsolete and narrowing sentiment."

"I came to speak to you, Randolph, about a little club we are organizing: both for dining, and to enable us by organization to give a more definite influence to our opinions among the class. By getting two or three of the more prominent men of each section, we may privately exert a very considerable influence, perhaps, even to a majority. And at the dinners we hope to have elegant—a—charming times. I hope, Randolph——"

"Really, Mr. Hackett," began the latter, but he was saved the. labor of replying by the entry of Lane, Bixby, Brattle, and Symonds in a burst of laughter, caused apparently by some story of Symonds as they were coming up the stairs. Soon after Hackett rose and took his leave, somewhat awkwardly, and with an uncomfortable sensation of probable comments behind his back, which he could neither avoid nor conceal. Nor was he disappointed.

"There," said Strang, "goes a pure skunk."

All assented with more or less enthusiasm; even Phil Symonds admitting, with a sort of jovial disapproval, that he was a damned fool. Lane alone was silent, but, upon being playfully urged to express himself, blushed deeply and confessed that he thought him "a cad."

"I don't see what that sort of fellow comes here for," said Bixby.

"Comes here for? I fancy that it pays him better than any of us. The faculty like that sort of thing. They regard him as a successful graduate. He will be near the head of his class; orator if he can; leaves here with the endorsement of all the professors, two or three scholarships in his pocket, and is a university man." So said Randolph, and Strang nodded his head.

"Yet," said the latter, "one does admire success."

"Do you?" said Randolph, coldly; "I don't."

Strang shrugged his shoulders. "What are you going to do this summer, Billy?" said he to Bixby, who was already late in his second glass of "Bixby's mixture."

"Go to Paris, I think. Run down to Monte Carlo to have a time. Want to come?"

"Can't," said Strang, "After the race I am going on an engineering party out to Colorado. Better
come, Phil," said he, turning to Symonds.

"Much obliged. I'm going yachting with some
fellows, and then down to Newport to stay with
Randolph. I like to loaf in summer myself."

"Why don't you go down to a sea-side hotel then,
and loaf on the piazza, and drink cocktails, and sit on
the rocks with the girls?" grunted Strang. "They
are even sillier in summer than in winter."

"O, they're well enough if they're pretty. What
more do you want?"

"No more can we expect, certainly. What went
ye out for to see?" grunted Strang. "A silk dress
shaken in the wind? Well, good-night; training
time, you know."

"Queer stick, that Strang," said Brattle, as the
door closed behind him.

"Damned cranky cuss," snarled Bixby, over his
third glass, "cocky enough for his own statue."

"Well, it takes all sorts of men to make a world,"
said Van Sittart.

"He means well," threw in Randolph, with a tinge
of amusement in his voice.

"Any of you fellows want to come in behind the
scenes? Some devilish pretty girls in the ballet. I
knew the prompter in Paris—a little Italian fellow—
and he'll get me in."

"Thank you, Billy, not to-night, I guess," said
Brattle; then, as Bixby took his leave, "how any of
you men can stand *that* fellow, I *don't* see."

"Oh, Billy isn't so bad," said Randolph. "A cup

of sack, please, Guy. Thanks. Billy isn't half such
a fool as he looks."

"Little Parisian snob," said Lane.

"Why, Faucy, I never knew you to be so worked
up," laughed Randolph. "What's the matter?"

"Well," said Lane, smiling and blushing, "just
because he's got a lot of money, and impudence, and
bad style, all you fellows let him go on. His father
was an oil man or something like, and they live
over there because people won't receive them here.
Well, good-night; I've got a party in town."

"Jove, Randolph," said Van Sittart, who had
hitherto been absorbed in poker with Bixby, "your
Boston men are the weakest little snobs of the lot.
What difference does it make who a fellow's people
are, if he shoots and drives a good drag, and plays a
square game of poker? Time enough to cut him
when you get married."

"Lane's a curious chap," said Brattle. "He's my
cousin, and we've always been together, and he's a
good-natured fellow and all that. But he never had
an idea that hadn't been previously strained through
the minds of all the old dowagers in Boston. Yes, I
suppose he *is* a good deal of an ass. Hullo, Phil—
you going, too?"

"Yes," said Symonds, "Guy and I have put on a
brace for early hours. Good-night, boys!"

"Good-night, Phil! good-night!"

"Good-night, Guy," said Randolph, going with
him to the door. "Don't forget that walk to-morrow!"

"Why the deuce does Symonds chum with that

poor little devil of a Guerndale? said Van Sittart.

"I'm not sure that I shouldn't put it the other way," said Randolph. "What do you think of it, Brattle?"

"O, Phil likes to be admired, and he can't find anybody else to do it, I suppose," said Brattle. "You might as well room alone, old three-of-a-kind. Ta-ta!" and Brattle, decorated with a velveteen smoking-jacket and a huge pipe, took his way across the yard.

"Disagreeable, sarcastic devil, that Brattle," growled Van Sittart. "Excuse me a moment, old man, but as soon as he gets well along I'll follow."

"Stay as long as you like, Van. By the way, I hear the play was pretty high the other night?"

"Yes, devilish rough it was, too. You know that little fellow, Pruyn, of Princeton, is engaged to Miss de Ruyter, of New York—a regular love-match, they say—and they are to be married in a month. Well, they haven't either of them enough money to pay the parson; and Phil and I got Pruyn up to his room and got a five dollar Van John on him, and he was out $2,000 before he knew where he was. He gave us his I.O.Us. for $1,600 to me, and $400 to Phil; and I know he's sure pay; for he's just that sort of a little conscientious fool that would; but, gad! I shouldn't be surprised if he hadn't money enough to buy a wedding-present!"

"Capital joke, by Jove!" said Randolph. "Why didn't you let me in?"

"Well, we didn't think of it in time. But, good-night, Randolph, much obliged for your hospitality."

Left alone, Mr. Norton Randolph betook himself with a sigh of relief to Thackeray. A deep smile on his face remained as a sort of after-glow of the gayety of the evening. After a chapter or two of " Vanity Fair," he turned to La Rochefoucauld ; after half an hour of which he wrote and sealed the following notes :

> " CAMBRIDGE, FRIDAY.
>
> " MY DEAR PRUYN.—I won several I.O.Us. of yours the other night and have bought the rest at twenty per cent. on their face indebtedness, thinking you might not like to have them floating about just now, and would prefer having them held all by me. So I am now your creditor ; but for four hundred only. You may pay when you like ; but let me give you your revenge first. Yours,
>
> " N. RANDOLPH."

> " CAMBRIDGE, SATURDAY.
>
> " DEAR MR. VAN SITTART.—Pruyn has commissioned me to square all his I.O.Us. If you will bring me yours, I can draw you a check for the full amount, $1,600, I believe ? Yours very sincerely,
>
> " NORTON RANDOLPH."

" By Jove," said Randolph, rising wearily, " they all say every other fellow is a damned fool ; and I suppose I am the greatest fool of the lot, after all."

And going to bed, this inconsistent cynic smoked for an hour, reading over his hookah a comedy of Calderon.

CHAPTER XIV.

"Autrefois," dit le Diable, "pour te punir de ton impolitesse, j'aurai pris et emporté ton âme ; mais qu'en faire aujourd'hui ? J'ai des âmes à revendre."— J. JANIN.

"The works of Dr. Channing—the last words of religious philosophy in a land where every one has some culture and superiorities are discountenanced—the flower of moral and intelligent mediocrity."—MATTHEW ARNOLD.

RANDOLPH used to say that he liked to get up into the afternoon. It was the best way of realizing the land where it was always afternoon. Perhaps, it was this habit which gained for him Strang's jesting sobriquet of "the mild-eyed melancholy lotos-eater." His morning lectures suffered somewhat in consequence ; but he chose his "electives," as the optional courses of study are termed at Cambridge, with a special view to the times of day the lectures would require his presence. It was, accordingly, about one of the following day when Randolph was interrupted over his coffee by Guerndale's arrival, fit, as he expressed it, for a walk.

"What sort of weather are they giving us ?"

"Glorious ! do come on, and don't dawdle ! "

"My dear fellow, a gentleman is never in a hurry. Are you sure the day is well out of curl-papers ? Besides, let me see if I haven't a lecture this afternoon ——"

"You promised last night to come ——"

"Do wait a moment, Guy. I only want to make sure that I am cutting a lecture to heighten my enjoyment of the walk. Yes, I've got a recitation in Ethics—just the thing !"

"What a delightful old poser you are !" laughed Guerndale. "And how absurd your studying Ethics !"

"Not at all," said Randolph, seriously. "It's the best fun in the world to see them analyzing and ornamenting the roof after cutting away the rez-de-chaussée and the entresol. It's one of the best jokes of the lot."

"You seem to regard everything as a farce gotten up for the amusement of Mr. Norton Randolph," said Guerndale, as they walked out into the street.

"Certainly, my sprouting Telemachus. Did you ever read Carlyle? Well, Carlyle in my opinion is one of the grandest and most consummate humbugs that the world ever produced—but he said one good thing. He said that humor is the mood of a god. Fancy how bored the holy first cause and sustainer would be with the inanities and antics of his creations below here if he couldn't view it all in the light of humor? Do you know what is the best definition of a Bourgeois, a Philistine? He is a man who takes things in general *au grand sérieux*. Fancy God taking men au sérieux ! The Aristophanes of heaven, as Goethe says !" And Randolph switched off some daisies savagely with his cane. "God help us, if he does."

"It seems to me you are suddenly taking things rather seriously yourself."

"Oh, no, my dear Guy. I beg your pardon. The broadest farce and the deepest tragedy are so exactly alike that it is almost impossible to distinguish them. However, modern times have almost done away with both, by inventing burlesque. The seriousness of people to-day is mere stage-seriousness—buckram and humbug. That is, I mean any seriousness except such as attends their chase after money, and the gratification of their passions ; since Quixote men have grown ashamed of honor and love, and think only of pursuing their fortune and gratifying their lust. It is the seriousness of the chief augur at the auspices ; of the charlatan with his tongue stuck in his cheek."

"I don't think the world is all humbug," said Guy.

"Neither do I. But humbug is the tribute men of sense pay to fools. And if a man wants worldly success—the fools being in the majority——It is a great merit in Carlyle to attempt to show people their own stupidity. But the trouble is, Carlyle is a fool himself. He complained that people are all talk and no do, and there is no other fool who talks so much as he, and so little to the purpose."

"Still," said Guy, "I do not think that life is a farce. And in the same volume of Carlyle from which you quote, he has taken as a motto, Schiller's *ernst ist das Leben*. Because you laugh, the world is not laughable. Besides, I think you are more or less of a humbug yourself. There may be some people who learn the sad learning of laughter, but not at your age."

Randolph winced a little. "By Jove, Guy, usually you seem like a bear with all his troubles before him, but sometimes you have a gleam of perspective. As to being a humbug, of course I am. Most men, who don't like the rôle of Manfred have to make believe a good deal. But, I stick to it: the part of amused spectator is the proper one for a gentleman in this world."

Guy shook himself impatiently and walked faster.

"No," said Randolph, "hear me. I think there are four ways of taking this world: the Comical, the Serious, the Serio-Comical, and the Tragico-Burlesque. There are people who take life comically, who go in for fun and folly. They are the fools; they are also the happiest. Then there are those who take this terrestrial life of grub and grind and petty successes *au grand sérieux*—they put everything on a level and look at it seriously. These are the Philistines, and are second to the fools in good fortune. The remaining two classes are both intelligent, both unphilistine; men who look at things serio-comically—they are the men of talent and of high success, besides being the most agreeable. And lastly, the poor fellows who alternate between tragedy and burlesque. They are the geniuses; they usually die miserably or are driven mad; and are called morbid by the average sensual man. They hate convention, and scorn meanness both of thought or aims; they are snubbed by the Philistines and stoned by the rabble. Only once in a while a Dante or a Rabelais survives to shame his fellow-cits. There you have mankind, their nature

and their works ; the first seek amusement, the second
are busy with affairs ; the third achieve, the fourth
suffer. Comic, Serious, Serio-Comic, Tragico-Burlesque—Fools, Philistines, Great men, Geniuses—
Amusements, Affairs, Achievements, Agonies. You
pays your money and you takes your choice," Randolph closed, with a grin.

"And which do you prefer ?"

"Well, the world in general laughs with the fools,
praises the Philistines, worships the great men, and
damns the geniuses. I laugh at the fools, despise
the Philistines, have a reasonable respect for the
great men, and pity and love the geniuses. Tell
me, Guy," said Randolph, after a pause, "I hope I
haven't shocked you ? *I* don't believe that God is
human at all ; but if people will insist on giving him
finite passions, I think with Heine that humor is
the only suitable mood."

"Oh, no, I am not shocked."

"I thought not. Van Sittart and Bixby and
Hackett would have been shocked. So would every
one over forty of decent character. But I thought
you and I had breathed the same air—the air of a
dead faith. It hangs over this New England country like the sad gray sky of Hawthorne's novels.
Religion here was once a passion ; and we are living
in the ashes of it. Isn't it strange, this New England history of *mœurs?* I think there is a worn-out
enthusiasm, a sort of nervous prostration in the very
atmosphere. We seem to be born in it. You and I
are not the only ones."

"No," sighed Guy ; and he thought of his father.

5

"Do you know," added he then, dreamily, "I have always had a sort of favorite vision in my mind of what you mean. Think of those grim, narrow, hard old Puritans—you hate them, no doubt."

"I hate them?" interrupted Norton. "Why, my dear fellow, I deplore their absence. Didn't my amiable old great-grandfather write a famous sermon on 'the Heart of New England Torn by the Blasphemies of the Present Generation'?"

"Well, we admire them," continued Guy; "for they at least had ideality and a purpose—think of the first scenes, the rude board chapel in the midst of a clearing; on all sides the unbroken forest of a continent; and the solemn congregation worshipping a cruel God without book or liturgy, holding a rifle instead of a prayer-book. Ah! there was something fine in that."

"That will do for one picture," said Randolph. "And then the present reaction, the failure, the corruption of it, the change from the cold, grim poetry of their ideal to the easy fat content of material success."

"They came to worship God—they realized a balance of trade in their favor ——"

"Yes; and then the perfect failure of that highest attempt to realize religion; pure religion, abstracted of all earthly attractions, non-emotional, non-sensuous. For they did fail completely. Think of that same old barn-like church now, standing gaunt and lonely in a cluster of modern French roofs and gingerbread moulding. Religion has degenerated into a curious social custom. I look at a New England meeting-house in much the same outside way that I should look at a Chinese joss-house—it serves as a sort of social nucleus to a parish where they period-ically run into debt, and cut down the preacher's salary. If old Dr. Norton were to appear to me in an indigestion—I think that would be the proper modern explanation—and talk about my heart being 'rent by the blasphemies of the present generation,' I should tell him that 'Fear God,' perhaps, made many men pious, but the proofs of the existence of God have made most men atheists. No ; Puritan-ism—neither faith nor metaphysics, the mathemati-cal religion—is a failure. The Roman Church has, at least, the talent of making herself loved and her children happy. At all events, Puritanism will do no longer—look at the church named Plymouth, and think of the satire of the name. The people want bread and circuses ; candles on the altar and theatrical performances in the vestry, or that worse modern vulgar abomination which is known as sen-sational preaching. Oh, it is very funny — very funny—damned funny."

"Oh, come, Randolph, you make everything out too bad. If one form of religion has run its course, it is not a reason for thinking the world worse. You say yourself you don't want it—why do you expect other people to need it ?"

"Perhaps," laughed Randolph, "I am like Billy Bixby, who admitted to me one day that he never went inside of a church himself, but that it would make him seriously unhappy if his mother and sis-ters ceased doing so. . . . The truth is, Guyon, we live in an intellectual air of failure. The best we can say is, that our forefathers came for one thing and found another—a balance of trade, as you suggest. It may be, what we found was more valuable than what we sought—I do not know. Still it is failure ; if it is failing only in the way that fellow failed in getting what he wanted, who was always unlucky, and while boring for water, struck gold. You know Morris' 'Earthly Paradise ?' We seem to me like the men in that book. We sought a high ideality—what we have found is a vulgar reality."

"But, Randolph, I hate to hear you talk so. When I said we had realized a balance of trade in our favor, I did not mean it as a reproach. It is surely a good thing—at least, no bad thing. We have not kept up the old ideas of the Puritans simply because they were narrow and bad. We have realized at least one ideal—we are free—we are educated ! "

"O my *dear* boy," said Norton, "don't drop back into spelling-books. If you think the tyranny of the coarse rabble better than that of the finer few, I don't. As for free education, consider the fitness of things. There must always be in this world a certain number of hewers of wood and drawers of water. If among that class arise one who is capable of better things, and really wants education, let him have it at as little difficulty to himself as possible ; but what is not worth desiring and acquiring is not worth having. Do not cram education and discontent down the throats of those who do not ask for it. Leave them to their toil, that their sleep may be sound, and their digestion unimpaired. In the social organization, we cannot all be conscious nerve ganglia; there must be the healthy unconscious bone and sinew and muscle as well. Free education means free and accessible; not compulsory. Let the clown remain a clown till he wishes to be something else."

" But they vote," said Guyon.

" Ah, yes, they do. I forgot that. Well, as long as we gauge our civilization by the broadest base, perhaps, it is as well to raise that base as high above the mire as it can be put. Since, by our systems, we level down, not up, perhaps we had better make the lowest level as high as we can."

" But, Randolph, I have cornered you there. And besides, I don't see why you deny the refinement and happiness and purity of our general civilization. Why not raise the mass as well as the few ? "

" Then, I say, give them a practical industrial education, make them cooks, mechanics, engineers. With all our cant about democracy, there is more absurd cant about 'genteel' professions than ever. Our education is founded on old ornamental models, designed to finish that useless article called 'gentleman.' Now that the masses feel their power, they not only want to destroy present swells, but they want to be nobs themselves, just as the old swells were. Which is impossible and absurd. Granted, one man is as good as another, then we must all turn to and work. If you can be as good a judge as I can, why I must be a house-painter just as soon as you; instead of which every country boy wants to be a counter-jumper, because he thinks it more genteel than learning a trade. Why, really, Guy, all the old foolish ideas of the land-owning class are being picked up and refurbished for the modern emancipated peasantry. Every country girl wants to be fashionable, and every carpenter's son wants to be a merchant."

" I think, myself, the 'Latin and Greek and Art antique' business is a little overdone."

"Guyon, let me tell you a story. My father told it me, and I know it is true. Some years ago there was a respectable Protestant mechanic in Boston who had one daughter. She showed great promise, and some ladies took an interest in her. They sent her to a good school and gave her what is called a fine education for a woman. That is, she acquired refined tastes ; knew a few facts ; enough about the history of the world to make contrasts and draw conclusions ; learned French and music, and fondness for that cleanliness and elegance of person and surroundings which is an expensive luxury of the favored few. For even to be clean in this world requires money. Well, they did this, not with the view of making her a teacher, which is but a limited field, but, with great ideas, looking to give her a higher life and influence for good in her own class. She was pretty. Well! At twenty she came back to her home—a small suite of rooms in a dirty tenement. They gave her a piano and left her, each saying *that* was true charity. Still she seemed unhappy, so that it was a relief to such as kept track of her when she married a railway employee—a steady, industrious fellow, I believe. She did not make him a good wife : so, far from admiring her, he found her a bur-then. He never understood her, then he despised her, finally he took to drink and beating her. She met a man whom she liked—a gentleman. Her husband was not. A year after, you met her on the street corners. She went to the devil—if there is one. Her husband died of drink, her father of shame. What do you think ?"

"I think it a case of ill-judged charity, and that it proves nothing," said Guyon. "Spite of all you say, I think our civilization pure and noble. American girls are the most refined and the most virtuous the worl' has known. Take the type of girl described in Mrs. Stowe's novels ——"

"That is a type that is passing away, it is a relic of the singular ideal life which *did* prevail here— owing to universal plenty and intelligence—up to a few years ago. Go along our seaport towns now and you will find universal discontent, vulgarity, a cheap imitation of bad city fashions and vice. New England will shortly be the most immoral country we know. And the sinister fact about it is that this un-happiness and immorality will be found not in the highest classes or the lowest, but in the great middle class on which the social life and future of a nation depends. We are accustomed to shrink with horror from French novels and French morals. To-day the bourgeoisie of France is purer and happier than our own."

As Randolph ended they saw a fine apple-tree in

a field by the roadside, and he suggested that stealing apples was one of the most delightful of diver-
sions. When they had filled their pockets and descended from the tree, they were disturbed by the
sudden appearance of a large dog, increasing hugely
in apparent size as he descended the hill toward
them. Randolph, laughing, suggested flight, and it
was with some exertion that they got over the gate
a short distance ahead of the dog.

"No," said Randolph, attacking one of the apples, "Compare Spenser and Spencer. Spenser
based the world on love, loyalty, courage, faith, and
courtesy. Spencer bases his on life, on competition,
and that adaptation which, were there any true faith,
would be cowardice. The latter may be necessary ;
but which is best ?"

"A third is possible," said Guerndale. "Co-
operation—based on sympathy."

"Co-operation for what ?" said Randolph.

Guerndale could not answer. Finally he said,
"life."

"Is life an end or a means ?"

"O, a means, of course ! "

"Means to what ?"

"Happiness," said Guerndale, hesitating.

"Yes, so we come back to that happiness, the old
summum bonum ; with the difficult modern addition
that it must be reached here and now, for Spencer
and Co. have suppressed a future or ideal existence,
ex hypothesi. Ah, the philosopher's stone was a less
wild dream than this. And, as for your sympathy, go
into your highest, best, most perfect circles of soci-

ety, and you find as yet no approach to the sympathy which makes such co-operation possible. It may come with the millenium. Why, now one cannot even fall in love!"

"Love?" said Guerndale, musingly.

"It is a vulgar expression, I know. Look at the crew."

They were standing on one of the bridges over Charles River. The sun was just setting behind the brown country hills, and through the oily surface of the water came a boat shaped like a dragon-fly. The six oars rose and dipped like one, and as the barge dashed beneath them they could see the mighty play of the muscles on the bared backs, the flush of exercise on the faces, and even the clear healthy eyes of the oarsmen. All the vigor of animal life and contest seemed personified in the firm flesh and deep breath and strain of the stroke, and there he was, Phil — Phil Symonds — and Guy uttered a cry of recognition as he swept beneath the bridge, his yellow curls tossing in the sunlight, his oar dipping clean in the water with clear even sweep to the recover.

"Don't you think they can beat Yale?" cried Guy. "I know Phil will, and if they are only all like him."

"Ah," said Randolph, "perhaps, the old Greek life was the best after all."

Just then a carriage drove by with the windows filled with the heads and arms and legs of a half-dozen of students driving to the city for a supper and theatre. A wild song came from the party, led

5*

by Billy Bixby, waving out of the carriage window an empty bottle by way of baton.

"Greek again," said Randolph, with a smile. "Corinth *versus* Sparta. After all, perhaps, either is better than Manchester."

When Guerndale told me this conversation, I said that Randolph was a damned fool.

We had a way in those days of applying that epithet to our friends.

CHAPTER XV

"An occasional booze has a favorable tendency to excite the faculties, to warm the affections, to improve the manners, and to form the character of youth."
—LORD CAMPBELL, *Chief-Justice of England.*

" Quae fecisse juvat, facta referre pudet."—*Ovid.*

I DID not mean to drop myself in at the end of the last chapter, but those old days when we all lived and loafed and thought and drank together in old Cambridge seem so vivid in my memory even now, that it is hard to talk of them impersonally. I did think Randolph a fool, with the usual qualification we then employed, but he was a curious and an interesting one. Besides, although he had the crudity of statement peculiar to youth, I don't think he was quite such a fool as he seemed to be. I can easily understand the influence he had over Guerndale. He could laugh at everything you said, and yet with such an exquisite sympathy and appreciation of your meaning, that you thought he must be right in laughing. He laughed softly and sweetly, and gently led you to see the absurdity of your own enthusiasm. And he was always on his guard against expansion, excitement, enthusiasm. He never gave himself to you unreservedly, but always kept a part to himself. His idea was neither to deceive himself nor to be deceived by others, to act as if always in the presence of an indifferent and cynical spectator. And finally he became himself that spectator. Had Norton Randolph been a friend of Menelaus, never would the swift straight ships have been launched over the wine-color'd sea, nor the ten years' pulse of battle flowed and ebbed about Troy. So I used to think, at least. But suppose he had been Menelaus himself?

I am not fond of poetry usually, but Homer always had a fascination for me, and the reader must pardon a little occasional shop from him. And, if there is something strained and halting about my metaphors, and something a bit jerky in my style, I am writing this part of my story down in Arizona among mountains, and heat, and torrents, and "ye dam salvages," in a climate where a good honest English rail telescopes out at noon like an angle-worm, and life is too rough for art to be over easy.

So, many a walk and talk did Guy and Randolph have together, and though I think Guy thought Randolph in one way not up to Phil Symond's elbow, Phil stood, perhaps, at a disadvantage on a long talky walky, as Strang used to call these peripatetics. Then Guy got into a way of taking curious courses of study, I think at Randolph's instigation; namely, metaphysics. For if there be an entire impossibility of knowing anything about the Lord in a practical way, as these same metaphysicians tell us, what the deuce is the use of befogging one's brains and making one's self unhappy over their quiddities and systems? I consider Locke a sensible

philosopher, and I mean to have my boys read him—
when they are old enough to know better. But Randolph, and afterward Guerndale, used to turn up their
noses at Locke, and say he was no metaphysician at
all. If they meant by this that he said there was no
such thing as metaphysics, I think he was quite
"right. But I have always noticed that those fellows
who believed least in religion, and hated the church
as the devil hates holy-water, particularly if there
were no music and flummery about it, and they came
of sensible Unitarian people, were just the ones who
spent most of their time in hunting after some abstract, or Noumenon, or God knows what modern
substitute for Himself, and seemed to be most unhappy because they could not find it.

As for Randolph, Guy used to say that his light
laugh would set you to thinking more than one of
old Dr. Grimstone's sermons. Personally, I don't
see the value of such thinking, and, as for laughing—
why, the man would laugh at the Mont Cenis tunnel.

Well, Guy began with a course in Descartes
(whose writings I don't so much object to, as his
"I think, therefore I am," seems to afford some
sort of a solid basis to start on; though, indeed, I
think Herbert Spencer is much more likely to be
right when he inverts it and comes out somewheres
about *I am, therefore I think,* after no end of evolution and rigmarole from protoplasm)—then he ran
through the gamut until he finally smashed up on
Schopenhauer. After this Guy got a liking for
Montaigne with his "que sçais-je?" and Charron
with his "Je ne sais," and some other duffer with

his " Qui sçait ? " and so on.   Then he brought up
on Rabelais, whom he hated ; and, the worse for
Guerndale, I thought ; for he wandered from him
into romanticism, and then into ecclesiasticism and
agnosticism ; and read the " Confessions of St. Augustine," and of Jean Jacques Rousseau, and of de
Musset, and Janin, and every other so-called con-
fession that St. Augustine, or any other drivelling
idiot, ever wrote.   He cut all his mathematics and
science ; and then he left the classics because, he
said, they lacked " breadth of horizon," which expression I have since found in " Daniel Deronda,"
a book somewhat popular, as they tell me, in the
States.   About the only sensible things he did keep
were some hours in American History ; at which
lectures he used to have continual rows with Tutor
Otis about Franklin, and Adams, and Hancock ;
though I never could quite make out which side
either of them took.   Then he stuck pretty hard to
his Political Economy, which he seemed to have a
fairly good head for ; and I think he always had a
notion in those days of going into politics, much
as he has changed since.   Curiously enough, this
brings me back to the next scene that I especially
remember in college ; and I find I have allowed myself to run away with myself again.   I have been
telling not what Guy saw, but what I saw, when I
expressly proposed to myself the opposite !   I must
keep myself and my way of telling the story out of
this, if I can.

The evening began with a stupid discussion on a
dry enough subject—political economy.   Guy and

Randolph were talking in the latter's room. Guy, who was conservative still, from force of habit, had been attacking communism, internationalism, and the general tohu-bohu which sometimes looms up before us in these years. Randolph listened, smoking as usual. It was one of his fits of depression ; but outsiders never knew when Randolph was "blue," except that he drank more and talked less than usual.

"But, my dear fellow, you have got to come to it," said Randolph, cutting the leaves of a periodical called the *Popular Radical*, a new production which some friend had sent, claiming to present the latest discovered nuggets of truth. It had also a diabolical cover of black and red ink, and letter-press printed in all the colors of the rainbow, which latter was said to be a new device to prevent weakness in the eyes caused by reading its pages. I believe the benefit of this discovery did not extend to the brain.

"Come to what ?"

"Communism, in some form or other."

"Why ? "

"You yourself have been studying economy lately. Haven't they taught you that the profits of all labor must be divided in three parts : first, for the plant, which is raw material and machinery ; second, profits, which you give to the capitalist ; and third, and only third, wages fund, which is to remunerate the laborer ? "

"Well ? "

"Well ! It is a perfectly established fact that the

proportion of profits which goes for plant has grown, and is growing larger and larger. More and more machinery is being needed; and, of course, the reward of capital can vary within but small limits; so, less and less remains for the merely human force, the laborer. It is demonstrable that, under present conditions, the state of the agricultural or manufacturing laborer must become more and more miserable as compared with that of the community at large."

"A cheerful outlook you take!" said Guy.

"Well," continued Randolph, "there is just one way of escape. Teach the laborer to be a capitalist. Give him an interest in the profits. There you have co-operation—which is over the bridge to communism—and there we are."

Guy was silent a moment. "And do you think co-operation will succeed?"

"No. At least, not under present conditions. It is being tried in England—at Rochdale, and at some of the collieries. But while the education of discontent and the charity of pauperization go on, it cannot succeed. Then, when it fails, and the masses starve, you and I will have to shoot them in the streets, my boy."

"You talk like a young Carlyle," laughed Guy.

"My dear fellow, don't insult me. Carlyle's writings are one huge, chaotic mass of rant and grumble. He is always telling people to *do*, and never by any chance telling them what to do. Now, I say that it is perfectly obvious what to do. We have taken away from the people God, and, what is more important practically, the idea of future compensation. They have not found it out yet ; but when they do they will naturally proceed to smash things. As in this country they can do this by the ballot, I do not mean that there will necessarily be any fighting here, though it is possible. Still, things will, in a general way, be smashed."

"So far you suggest as few remedies as Carlyle himself," said Guy.

"My child, I have the floor." ("So has your argument," muttered Strang; but after a moment of speechless contempt, Randolph continued.) "Now we know that life, up to the highest human society from the lowest single spore, is the object of all effort ; and all successful effort requires strength. I propose, as the only way of impressing the necessity of social, moral, and physical strength on the people, that all criminal, infirm, and insane persons be etherized. Their remains will, of course, be utilized in some practical commercial way—leather, bone fertilizers, and the advancement of science. This may strike you as harsh, perhaps, cruel ; but it is not so. I can show you that the misery consequent on crime, lack of adjustment to environing circumstances, and, above all, weakness, is far greater than would be caused by my process. Besides, it is obvious that these weak creatures and their descendants, being ill-adjusted to their environments, must, in the long run, die all the same, after having caused an incalculable amount of woe and suffering to others."

"No society has the right to kill, except for self-preservation," said Guy.

"This is self-preservation. Moreover, we should try to inculcate a public sentiment that to be etherized under such circumstances, for the good of the State, is a high and noble duty. This we can do, for similar things have often been done. Look at the Hindoo widows, who burn on their husbands' funeral pyre; or, take a modern example, and see how many men are ready now to die for an imperfect State in a contemptible foreign war. In my ideal State every man or woman will see that it is far more for the general good for them to be etherized than as now, in England, for soldiers to die in a skirmish in Abyssinia or Ashanti. Besides, think of suicide. In the millenial country I speak of, when a man becomes so weak as to wish to die, it will become for the highest good of the State that he should do so. Self-murder will be quite a noble act, and every suicide a martyr."

Strang snarled with disgust.

"Cork up, old man; all taken from your favorite, Herbert Spencer, or logically deduced," retorted Randolph.

"But, Norton, you forget one thing," said Guy. "You speak of the State as a thing by itself worthy of love. But the State is a mere assemblage of human beings, and if man does not care for his fellow man—which seems to be a necessity of your plan, for it shuts out sympathy, pity, and mercy—he will not care for that aggregation of his fellow men which you call the State."

"Yet patriotism has existed. If the State is to be preserved——"

"Save the State?" cried Bixby, who had entered, and overheard the last remark. "Oh, dammit. Let it spoil, and get a fresh one. You can't preserve a nation like pickles or canned asparagus."

"Patriotism has existed," Guy replied, "when men loved their fellows and their descendants; when the State was needed as a protection against outside barbarians; when men believed in immortal life; when they believed in helping the weak, in charity, and the use of social virtues. But in your plan all these are wanting, for they are rooted in religious belief."

"It is true," said Randolph, meditatively. "We suppressed God *ex hypothesi*. Nevertheless," he added, "I believe I am right. Something of the sort exists now among the Chinese, and has for thousands of years, and they, poor creatures, are still in the darkness, and have not the broad certainty of vision of our disbelief. Don't demur," Randolph went on; "I say disbelief. All thinking men are so calmly certain of their materialism that they do not care for longer argument. They treat the writings of clergymen who dabble in science with supercilious indulgence. We have got so far on that we even speak of Christianity and other superstitions with polite regret, as one is courteous to a beaten adversary. Curious how the world has grown in a few years! You remember, even so late as Thackeray, it was said about a skeptical old major, that whenever he went to church, he did it with a sort of martial bearing, as if going into battle; and that when he received the benediction he took it erect, with frock coat tightly buttoned, so that there was about him a certain suggestion of receiving his adversary's fire at ten paces!" Randolph stopped to ring the bell. "No one is even afraid to go to church any longer, except for being bored. I think some of the most indifferent men I know would go, if they would only allow smoking."

Just then Randolph's servant entered and received some cards on which Randolph hastily scribbled a line. "I am going to have some fellows up here for a little wine, Guy," said he. "You see, they are not only much better fellows, but much better philosophers than you and I, and can enjoy it."

"But, Norton," said Guy, "you have been drinking steadily all the evening."

"Bien, après? I must get into training. Man, being reasonable, must get drunk, you know."

"Randolph, you know perfectly well, you never were drunk in your life," said Guy angrily.

"Not for want of trying, however!" laughed Randolph. "No, to tell the truth, and talk seriously, a relic of Puritan prejudice sticks to me in that respect. I cannot throw it off; somehow or other, as a matter of taste, intoxication is disagreeable to me. Ah, we are weaker than our forefathers, and, if we are not, our stomachs are. Rum and true religion—both gone! What *are* we to do!"

"Oh, dammit!"

"With pleasure, but you can't," said Randolph calmly. "There is no longer any such thing as damnation."

Bixby was so charged with profanity that, upon

being suddenly touched or spoken to, he emitted a
"dammit" very much as an electric machine does a
spark.

"Sit down, Bixby, take a chair; I have just asked
Symonds and Lane and a few fellows round to a little
wine, which I should be happy to have you join, if
you have no more tender engagement?"

"Randolph, let up on that sort of taffy. What
have you got to drink?"

"Champagne and chambertin."

"Not bad, but a leetle washy, unless you mix 'em;"
was the opening speech of Brattle.

"O come, old man, put fizz into good chambertin, you know; why, dammit,"—and Bixby took
a bumper of the burgundy by way of steadying
his nerves—"that's like your Boston young ones,
though——"

"If your object is to get drunk, why don't you
stick to Medford rum, which is cheap and expedi-
tious?" grunted Strang.

"No," said Randolph, "by all means let us get
drunk with good taste. This is an æsthetic sym-
posium, as becomes a cultured Harvard man, and
not, as is coarsely expressed in the police reports
of the daily papers, a simple drunk. Mr. Bixby, I
am sorry I have no absinthe, but if green chartreuse
is strong enough——"

"Ho, boys, already ahead?" sang out Phil, as
he surged in like a spring tide. "Sorry I can't
join you, but I'll put you to bed, you know. I
would, if it weren't so thundering near the race
though."

"I'll see that you don't, if I'm to pull seven," said Strang. "Sh! there is that infernal Hackett—I know his step."

"Hush," said Randolph, "the oak is sported all right; he can't get in; and, if he knocks, we're not at home."

All were silent, and sure enough there was a knock at the door. No one answered. Another knock followed. Amid breathless silence, the door, to their intense astonishment, slowly opened, and Hackett appeared on the threshold, where he stood in some confusion. A roar of laughter burst from the room, only Lane, Guerndale, and their host retaining their gravity.

"Good evening, Mr. Hackett, we thought you were the proctor. Will you not join us?" said Randolph, suavely.

The effect of this excuse was somewhat spoiled by an explosion from Bixby; but Hackett appeared not to notice it, and took a seat rather more diffidently than usual. A silence followed.

"Really, fellows, this is dull as an examination;" said Brattle. "A Rubicon to take away the chill!"

Randolph took an immense glass tankard, containing, perhaps, a gallon, which he filled with burgundy and champagne, and passed around. Each made it a point of honor to drink as long as he could at a breath. Lane started, drinking delicately, and keeping his eyes in the glass. Brattle followed, with a tremendous pull; Bixby did equally well. Guy did not like the mixture, but drank it calmly; Strang and Symonds both sipped it and passed it on to Hackett, who drank noisily, but, as Strang noticed, very little. Randolph received it back, and drank long and deeply, which had little effect on him, except that his face grew paler and his manner even more courteous than before. The party, however, was more animated. Story succeeded story; Phil Symonds having a great reputation as a *raconteur*, while Strang's deep, jovial humor floated the lighter ventures of Brattle and Van Sittart. Hackett called for a song, and the suggestion "came home to him to roost," as Bixby said. So Hackett rose and sang, in a loud and somewhat uncertain voice, a ditty which, though a good example of the lyrical art of the day, would possibly not edify us if transcribed in full. Relating how the hero was the drummer of a wide-awake firm, "and ran from city to city," the fascinations of the commercial element in our society were expressed in the statement that

> " Lou lives in rooms, with a little brass bell,
> And her mother is gone to the workus,
> And I waltz around quite the Sunday swell,
> On a Saturday night for the circus."

Touching slightly on the catholic tastes of the drummer aforesaid, as shown by his fondness for various young ladies, it ended by giving at once the philosophy of the hero and the moral of the tale :

> "And when women are false and biz is bad,
> I wait, like a saint, until Sunday,
> And the devil take the girls, I say, by gad,
> As I get blind drunk before Monday.'

"Hooray, Seth, old man! Good enough!" cried Bixby. "By gad, fellers, that's the best song I've heard since I had the measles."

Randolph had evidently listened with some disgust. "Will you have some more wine, gentlemen?" said he. "Pass the glass to Mr. Hackett, Baker." Then, turning to Guy, "The sooner we get that fellow drunk the better."

Baker was an English groom, who made one of the most perfect in-door servants I ever met. I once saw Van Sittart drink a bottle-full of Worcestershire sauce, and then throw the castor at Baker's head for giving him bad wine, and that invaluable man bore it all with gravity imperturbable.

"Send around the Rubicon again!" shouted Brattle, who had a weak head, and was growing rather uproarious in consequence. "We drink like Freshmen to-night."

A second time the bowl was passed around. Hackett drank less than before. Guy was growing very gloomy, and drank more. Passed back to Randolph, he drank long and deeply, until the word "Rubicon" was plainly visible, blown in the bottom of the glass.

"Hooray!" shouted Brattle. "Let me finish it, old boy!" And snatching the tankard, he drank the half-pint remaining. This, however, finished him, and he rose, and, staggering to the door, sought the cooler air of the street. No one seemed to notice his departure except Randolph, who politely escorted him down the stairs, and returned to call upon Strang for a song.

"One dead man already!" cried Phil Symonds. "Well, he died in a good cause, so to close up the ranks! Courage, my children! and I will pipe to you what John would call a Tyrtæan ditty!"

"Shop!" cried Hackett, "fine him a bumper."

Symonds took no notice of this remark, but began in a full, rich baritone. Phil was fond of careless, reckless glees, and cared more for the spirit than the melody. So he chose that song of the British soldiers in India, when the pestilence was upon them, and there was no escape, and they sat carousing over their card-tables, drinking the health of the next one that died. It was a favorite song in my time in college:

> " For God's sake, let no bells be ringing,
> Let tinkling glasses be my prayer ——"

With the refrain, strengthened by much pounding of the table and clinking of glasses:

> " Here's to the dead already,
> And hurrah for the next that dies!"

I looked musingly about our table as he sang, and speculated on the future of the men: at Randolph, grave, with his habitual half-smile, impredicable, inexplicable; at Hackett, Randolph's antithesis, long, sallow, with unkempt hair, and keen, furtive eyes, pretentious and insinuating of manner, though loud of speech; at simple, jolly Bixby; Lane, conventional and polite; handsome Phil, with his flushed face and superb figure, towering above us as he sang; and Guy, thoughtful, earnest, reserved, imaginative; fated for noble things, it sometimes would seem to

me. Which would stay longest in the race of life ?
—Symonds, Bixby, Hackett ?

When Phil finished, every one was more or less off,
except, always, Guy and Randolph, and Hackett,
who was not nearly so drunk as he pretended to be.
Even Lane, the quietest of men, became animated,
and we suddenly heard his voice : "Szthe diff'rence,
fellers——"

"Hooray ! Shut up, boys, Faucy's got a story !"
cried Bixby. "Fire away, old Blood-and-thunder !"

Lane was usually called Blood-and-thunder on account of the amenity of his manners and the calm of
his deportment.

"I say !" began Lane, in a very loud voice, which
weakened as he proceeded, "the difference between
a gentleman and a cad is, that when a cad gets drunk
he is drunk, and when a gentleman gets drunk no
one knows anything about it."

"Yer don't say !" said Bixby. "Who told yer
that neaow ?"

Lane turned with dignity and eyed him for a moment, but suddenly altered his course and walked
straight and erect to the door. "Good-night, gentlemen," said he.

Randolph bowed politely. Van Sittart threw an
olive at him, which hit the door as it closed rapidly,
and, immediately after, a rumble and a crash in the
front hall assured us that Lane had safely fallen
down-stairs.

"Did you ever hear the new Toper's Chorus,
boys ?" said Randolph.

"No, No," was the cry in answer, for Norton rarely consented to sing, and, when he did, sang well. He poured out a glass of brandy in a slender crystal tumbler, which bore the old Randolph crest and motto "fortiter!" and stood up perfectly self-possessed, though he must have drunk more than any two men in the room. His face was very pale, and his eyes somewhat larger than usual ; but his hand was as firm as a woman's.

"It was written," said he, "by a friend of mine, who had a very liberal education and a large fortune. I believe it was the only thing he ever wrote, and he died the next month. It is a very jolly song, and he wrote it just before he shot himself."

Ye men that have a sense of things,
    Now senseless evermore ;
Or have, as poor old Dante sings—
    Intelletto d'amor'—
Come, drink with me—the toast I vow
    Will take you well, I ween.
I drink to things that are not now,
    If they have ever been.

I drink to right, I drink to wrong,
    I drink to good we seek ;
I drink to mercy in the strong,
    To courage in the weak ;
I drink to life, I drink to death,
    I drink to things forbann'd ;
I drink to hope, I drink to faith,
    I drink unto the damned.

I leave the hell we know so well,
    To toast the heaven o'er us ;
I toast the life that bibles tell—
    And happiness before us.

The fair true maiden whom we love
  Or shall love, when we see one—
I toast the love that reigns above,
  And God, if so there be one.

I drink to worlds that are to be,
  I drink to truth and beauty—
I toast all things we cannot see—
  I drink to life and duty—
All things that we have never found,
  Both human and divine,
We jolly topers ! Drink around !
  We'll find them—in the wine !

Little attention was paid to the song.   Such men
as had their senses left did not like it.   " O, dammit,
I say," began Bixby.

"Why do you object—because of the sentiment?"
laughed Randolph.   "My boy, this song, at least, is
not vulgar, like Hackett's.   Moreover, ' les chants
désespérés sont les chants les plus beaux.' "

Guy was leaning his head in his hand, saying nothing.   It was three in the morning ; Strang and Randolph helped Van Sittart and Bixby home ; Phil went
back with Guy.

Randolph did not return to his room ; but spent
the remainder of the night in a distant walk over the
country hills, alone, smoking many cigars.   As he
returned, the college bell was ringing for morning
prayers.   Randolph had an excuse from prayers on
account of an unhealthy influence the family doctor
had discovered for him in the morning air ; so he did
not stop, but went to his room, which was foul with
ashes and tobacco smoke, and littered with over-
turned empty bottles and broken glasses.

He took the first horse-car for the city, and passed
the morning walking through the hospitals, and talking with such of the poorest patients as interested
him. Rather a curious occupation for Norton Randolph—we would have thought, had we known it in
those days.

CHAPTER XVI.

"L'honneur—c'est la poésie du devoir."—A. DE VIGNY.

IT was in the middle of the annual examinations. At Cambridge, these trials, coming with the canker-worms, occupy the better part of June. The day was warm; and about three in the afternoon of that twelfth or fourteenth of the month (I remember the date, for a staple of conversation that day consisted in cursing the Faculty for not "letting up" on examinations for the seventeenth), a somewhat picturesque group might have been seen assembled at the upper end of the "yard," the part which the grave and reverend seniors most affected. We had struck all work some days before (out of respect for the examinations); and our chief occupation, when not undergoing that torture, was to lie on our backs in the grass, with our heels in the air, and smoke cigarettes. University air, in midsummer, is conducive to scholastic repose.

This circle of promising youths was then disposed in a variety of attitudes under the elm trees. Most of us were lying on cushions brought from neighboring window-seats; the costumes ranged from the recherche velveteen shooting-coat, through knicker-

bockers, and Norfolk jackets, and white flannels, to
the normal costume of the American citizen. The
circle was surrounded by a somewhat turbulent company of bull-pups, in assorted sizes, of the most ugly
varieties. The peace of the hour was only disturbed
by the occasional passage of a carriage more stylish
than usual through the quadrangle, or the descent of
a canker-worm, depending from his swaying skein,
upon the face of one of the smokers.

"Yes," said Phil, "I think they might at least
shut up their old mill on the seventeenth of June."

"What is the seventeenth of June, anyhow?" demanded Bixby.

"Some event in biblical history, I believe," said
Randolph drily. "Ask Van Sittart; he is under the
impression that the Mayflower was the first Cunarder
that came into Boston harbor."

"What's in you, old Ineffable?" cried Phil. "I
think you are even lazier than usual."

"I am reflecting," said Randolph, gravely, "whether the pleasure of cutting my examination and
lying here to smoke cigarettes in your charming
company will make up for the pain of being 'conditioned' in Athenian Art."

"Conditioned" means, or used to mean when we
were in Cambridge, being "plucked," "ploughed,"
"pulled," "slung," or any other euphemism for being rejected at an examination. It was possible to
remove a "condition" by a second trial; otherwise
it hung over one's head indefinitely to prevent taking a degree. Men were known in this way to ac-
cumulate as many as twenty by their senior year.

Randolph had quite a rolling snowball of them; in
fact, I believe a "condition" in Greek composition
had prevented his ever getting any "matriculation"
or entrance papers. He had a certain, calm faith that,
some time or other, they would give him a degree, if
he wanted it. Besides, he had once passed an examination (on a bet); and at another time had astonished a professor into giving him ninety per cent. by
out-arguing him on an economical question. This
latter marvel he celebrated by a grand dinner at
Taft's—an inn by the side of the sea we much frequented—by reason of which dinner, two of our party
were suspended; so that it may be doubted whether
the final fruits of Randolph's scholastic exploit were
good or evil. I wonder whether old Taft's is still
running! Your dinners were good, old man, although your turbot was chicken-halibut, and your
wines dear and sweet. But it is far I would go for
one of them, out here in Arizona.

"Hello! Hackett, my accidental—I mean occiden-
tal—Demosthenes, what's the news?" sang Strang.
"Are you well up in making the worse appear the
better reason?" Hackett was our class-orator.

"How much of an ear-ache are you going to give
us, Class-day?" queried Van Sittart.

"Hope there's nothing in your jokes to call a
blush to the cheek of the most fastidious et cetera
and so forth?" laughed Phil. "Remember the dear
little girls."

"Better take a tub and file your finger-nails,"
sneered Van Sittart again, rudely.

"Talk lower, or he'll hear," whispered Guy.

"What the deuce is the matter with you? Whose blank business——"

"Oh dry up, you two, it's too hot to fight," cried Phil. Guy's face had flushed up, and Phil's bluff, good-natured tones came just in time. Hackett seemed not to hear all this, but took a seat next Randolph, who liked him least of all, and yet, with the exception of Guy, treated him most politely.

"Heard the news, boys? Strang and Guerndale have got honors—Science and Philosophy."

A prolonged yell of approbation greeted this announcement, with much clapping of hands. This caused several windows to be opened in various parts of the quadrangle, whence the occupants protruded their heads, with shouts of "more!" "mo-a-ah!" pronounced in the most grotesque and elaborate falsetto. After looking up and down, and across, and observing that the excitement was caused by neither a pretty girl nor a dog-fight, the windows were closed, and the occupants thereof returned in some disappointment to their studies. A peripatetic proctor said,

"Less noise, gentlemen!"

"Oh, go to blazes!" cried Bixby.

"You're dished, poor boy," said Phil. "I saw a wicked look in his eye."

"Well," said Bixby, "I guess another one won't hurt me. Chance it, I'm all up, anyhow."

"Young men: In the face of this most wondrous and passing strange occurrence which has happened to two of our company, it behoveth us to accept the gifts of the gods with a fitting reverence, and that

6*

those upon whom this rain of honors comes should show themselves truly grateful. Wherefore, let us dine at my expense—and credit." So spoke Strang, the eupeptic, if impecunious. "But, Hackett, where are you, this day of glory?"

"Oh," replied the orator, with elaborate carelessness, "I got double honors."

"Congratulate you. Well, Brattle? Lane? Phil? Randolph? Guy? We start at six. All agreed? You'll come, Bixby?"

Whether Hackett was purposely omitted in this invitation, I do not know. But he seemed provoked, and added, with malicious pleasure: "And Mr. Bixby is quite right. His degree is thought very doubtful."

"What? Billy Bixby lose his degree? By Jove! Too devilish bad, old fellow!" Quite a chorus of sympathy. Then we all looked to see how he would take it. A moment of breathless silence followed. Bixby's command of terse Saxon execration was known to be boundless. Several windows in the quadrangle were again opened. The inmates of Holworthy leaned out as one man. He began feebly, with a "d." Then he changed his formula. "The Faculty may—may go to—may—oh, lord——"

"Wait till dinner, Billy," put in Randolph, soothingly.

Ah! how well I remember that dinner. What a parcel of precious young fools we were! The ceremonies were opened by Bixby, who rose gravely and read from a paper, in all dignity, and, in solemn emphasis, the following toast:

" By the Sentence of the Angels, by the Decree of the Saints, we anathematize, cut off, curse, and execrate the Faculty of Harvard College, with the President, Proctors, and Parietal Committee thereof. In the presence of these sacred books, with the six hundred and thirteen precepts which are written therein ; with the anathema wherewith Joshua anathematized Jericho ; with the cursing wherewith Elisha cursed the children, and with all the curses which are written in the Book of the Law : Cursed be they by day, and cursed by night ; cursed when they lie down, and cursed when they rise up ; cursed when they go out, and cursed when they come in. The Lord pardon them never. The wrath and fury of the Lord burn upon these men and bring upon them all the curses which are written in the Book of the Law. The Lord blot out their names under Heaven. The Lord set them apart for destruction from all the tribes of Israel, with all the curses of the firmament which are written in the book of the Law. There shall no man speak to them ; no man write to them ; no man show them any kindness ; no man stay under the same roof with them ; no man go nigh them. Thank you, old man," said Bixby, when he had finished, to Randolph, " you are very kind." And he drank a glass of wine with much satisfaction.

"Yes," said Randolph, " I think it is a neat example of a quiet family curse—illustrative of the amenity of sectarian manners. The Jews applied it to Spinoza."

But I do not remember the dinner so much as a

talk we had afterward ; though I believe the grub
was good.   I had gone in for grind that year, and
had given up the crew ; but Phil was still stroke, and
had to cut the dinner on that account.   Bixby and
Brattle were a bit sprung coming home, so we put
them with Lane, as the quietest man to drive them,
while we came back in the other carriage.

   "Strång," said Guy, "why did you ask us all to
dinner before Hackett and Van Sittart, and leave
them out ?   They must have been quite hurt."

   "Why, hang it, young 'un," shouted John, "you
had'just had a row with the man yourself, and he
treated you like a pickpocket !   I can't stand either
of those men ; I've stood 'em for four years, and now
we're graduates, and I've had enough of them."

   "There's something fine about Hackett, after all,"
said Guy musingly.   "Energy, purpose—I wonder
what he'll do in the world."

   "Become President of the United States, probably," said Randolph.   "What are you going to do
yourself ?"

   Then, I remember, bit by bit, and phrase by phrase ;
as we grew more confidential, Guy told us of his
thoughts and aims, much as I have tried to sketch
them in this book.   How he had been lonely and shy,
and then ambitious and desirous of the world ; how
he had come to college with all sorts of fervent theories and immature plans.   "But now, I don't know.
Somehow or other, at this time, something seems uncertain and most things trivial.   I doubt, after all,
whether all progress—in any direction—is necessarily
a good thing.   And shouldering the wheel backward

is an ungrateful sort of task. Conservatives are always at a disadvantage. As Billy Bixby says, ' let it spoil and get a fresh one.' "

" Ah ! that's it," smiled Randolph, " the sooner things burst, the sooner we can set them up again."

" But I am not such a poco-curante as the mild-eyed here," laughed Guy, " and it grinds me."

Guy had one peculiarity which I long ago discovered. He rarely talked slangily or flippantly, but when he did, he was always deeply in earnest. He had a horror of a scene, and a great fear of "posing."

" No," he continued, " I believe in doing, still in doing, if you know not why, or what you do. This Weltschmerz nonsense is nothing more than a sort of world-dyspepsia. We are weak, and life is too strong a food for some of us. I should be just as ashamed of giving in to it as I should of being melancholy and misanthropic because my dinner was too much for my stomach. Exercise is the remedy for dyspepsia ; so occupation for Weltschmerz. There are plenty of worthy things now-a-days. And neither are these necessarily in what you call the Philistinism of science, or in what Strang calls the affected in-doors twaddle of culture and art. Look at the last six or seven years of history—our war, for instance."

" Guy, my boy, you are beginning to talk seriously, and I do not believe you more than half believe what you say." Randolph, too, had evidently found out Guy's ways.

" I do," said Guy. " It was great as the Iliad."

" My dear fellow, the Trojans at least had a woman in the case to lend it human interest. No, but seri-

ously," he went on hurriedly, "if you had been actually in the ranks, *passe encore*. But we are coming
to a time of reaction, corruption, low ideals, vulgar
competition, general disillusion. You are too late,
my boy, ' *Tout est pensé, tout est dit, tout est fait.*'"
And Randolph relapsed into a grin.

"Stuff," replied Guy. "Excuse me, Norton, but
the same man who said that gave the anti-phrase:
'Everything is old, and everything is new.' What is
noble and good can bear repetition. '*C'est imiter
quelqu'un que de planter des choux.*'"

"My dear fellow, you have chosen an unfair example. Planting cabbages is one of the few thoroughly worthy occupations that remain to mankind."

"Look here, you fellows, I am going to talk a little
romantic nonsense. Norton, you, at least, believe
in honor, do you not? And honor is but a finer,
more imaginative, form of duty. If this life is all unworthy, we can at least live it worthily. I started
with a definite purpose. I meant to lead an ambitious, active life. And I, too, have been discour-
aged. Definite faith, to me as well, is an impossibility. But life, the progress of a life, is like
ascending a mountain. In the early morning, when
we start, we see the glorious peak, the first ideal of
youth, full in front, fair in the sun. Then comes the
haze of mid-day ; foot-hills, forests, dark valleys come
between ; clouds veil the summit. Never, perhaps,
in this life do we see the final height again. We
only now can see the poor little ridge before us,
scarce worth our climbing. But if we bravely follow
the first ideal, keeping it in mind, always ascending

ridge after ridge—that is duty. For what is a great
life but the dreams of youth realized in riper age?
And so, only assuring ourselves that we are still
ascending, we shall some time reach the final height,
as sure as God lives."

"As sure as God lives,—perhaps."

"'*Ein Gott lebt—lasst euch nicht irren des Pöbels
Geschrei!*' And it is right to have ideals; and
youth is the time for them. Thought is given men
to remind them that there is truth immortal; and
beauty, music, poetry, love, ray through this life's
clouds like a bow, to make men mindful of things
that in this life we never find; dreams they are now,
but dreams that are truer than the truth that here
we know. And so I hold that our ideal may be more
real than this world's reality. And when we reach
it, be it with this life or the millionth life after this,
though each little stage seems final death, as each
mountain spur looks to us the last—though each
little stage is taken with no memory of the last—
when we reach the final height, the mists will drop
away, and the weary wanderings of all our lives will
lie far down below us, like a distant view. And we
shall reach it, though it be beyond the realms of time
and space, above the so-called laws of mortal science,
cause, and will, and soulless matter. '*Hoch über all*,'
as Schiller says."

"Very pretty," said Randolph.

Guy gave a shrug of displeasure.

"Guy," said Randolph seriously, " do you suppose
any one around you lives with an ideal like that?
You might as well seek to steer by the stars of

heaven through the Erie Canal. Those commod-
ities are worthy which have exchangeable value—
not intrinsic, mind, but exchangeable value. This
alone is real ; and, when we leave our main business,
we moderns do not want ideals, but amusements.
We live from day to day, not from day to eternity ;
we work a day's work for bread, dress-coats, brown-
stone fronts, and cigars ; our day's work done, we
want circuses. Bread and circuses ; get them ! Why
lay up treasures in heaven ? We'll never see them
again. Be smart, wide-awake, go ahead, pushing, a
live man, as they say in the business advertisements.
And pushing does not mean climbing—but elbow-
ing one another down."

"But even this life lets in desire for fame, renown ;
what is a desire for immortality but a wish to live
beyond this world ?"

"Men no longer want that. They want the adula-
tion of their contemporaries. Why should we do
anything for posterity ? Posterity never did anything for us. Men want flattery—after the comforts
of life are obtained, we all like to be envied by our
fellow-cits. Social success is more prized than immortality. Immortality ! What is it after all ? Who
wants it ? Who first thought of it ? Heine says,
'some fat, comfortable burgher sitting, some soft
spring evening, before the door of his comfortable
little house, with his long clay pipe in his mouth,
who thought how nice it would be so to go on veg-
etating into eternity without letting his pipe go out'
—or perhaps some young lover—bah ! Love, immortality—what nonsense we are talking !"

"Norton," said Guy earnestly, "do you know our old family motto? It is, 'Seule la mort peut nous vaincre.' It is a fine old phrase and I mean to be true to it. And death itself does not kill one's character, one's children, one's works, one's fame."

"If character is merely doing, you might emulate the piston-rod of a steam-engine. But, of course, if you wish to perpetuate your family—make several fools live where only one lived before—or are so content with yourself that you wish to project your little individuality beyond your natural life—— As for works, the world is quite content with itself, and won't let you tinker it up. Men are extremely comfortable. Look at that row of 'genteel suburban residences!' The very slope of their French roofs suggests a tawdrily dressed girl over the piano in the front parlor, her 'young man' expected in the evening, mother in the kitchen making bad pies and doing all the other work her daughter is too fine to do; a vulgar and overworked father with a deficiency in his accounts, mural decoration of shells and autumn leaves, and 'God Bless our Home!' in red and blue chromo over the mantel-piece."

"Well," said I, "why is not this a very fine state of things? If Henry IV. was right in wishing every peasant in France to have a fowl in his pot of a Sunday, why are we not glad that each citizen has a house, though it be ugly, and a piano, and a ribbon for his daughter—even if they do prefer chromos to etchings and burlesques to Shakespeare?"

"It *is* a very fine state of things. That is just it. They are perfectly comfortable and don't wish to be altered ; and here Guy comes and makes a pother about ideals, and ultra-mundane aims, and beauty, and honor and all that. Their preference for bur-lesques shows how they would treat him. We bur-lesque everything now ; in politics, social life, taste, literature, even religion. What are Beaconsfield, Spurgeon, Beecher, but bouffe ? I myself am a part of it. I, too, burlesque everything ; I even burlesque the cynic ; and am only half earnest in my cynicism."

"You certainly do—I will not," said Guy. "You know I told you the story of that old murder about the diamond. I do not believe it. I believe that my great-great-grandfather was first attacked, and that Simmons, his old servants say, was false and tried to rob it from him."

"Was not Symonds one of Phil's people ?"

"I believe so. A great-great uncle, I think."

"Why, I thought the Symonds were great swells," said Strang.

"There are no swells any more," said Randolph. "Only snobs. There are not a dozen pre-revolution-ary families in American society. Everybody's grand-father was a peasant, or an innkeeper, or a grocer, or a fisherman, or a soap-boiler, or a barber, or a cobbler. So much the better for their descendants. But go on, Guy."

"Well," said Guy, "you may laugh ; but in all seriousness I resolved that I would keep that dia-mond always. There was an old superstition that our family would never be happy until we parted with it. One of my childish ambitions was to prove that it was rightfully acquired, and all the old scandal a lie. I would meet the world, and conquer it ; and show the diamond when I had got back all we lost. This was my first childish dream. Not a very noble one, and rather silly, I suppose. Still, 'seule la mort peut nous vaincre.'"

I was amused at this queer little streak of romance 'in Guy's character. But the reader must remember that all this talk was after dinner ; and we were driving in the evening along the sea, and we were very young in those days, after all.

There was a long silence after this remark of Guy's. The black outline of the city lay across the water ; the blue hills to the south had an ashen sheen beneath the summer moon. Behind the domes and spires was a great glare of yellow sunset, with bars of ruby clouds.

"Is it not beautiful ?" said Guy.

After another silence, Randolph spoke. "It looks like an omelette aux confitures," said he. "Guy, my boy, when you reach the seventh heaven you speak of, I hope you will call the attention of the authorities up there to the bad taste of our American sunsets."

.   .   .   .

On that same thirteenth of June two people were sitting at a late dinner in the coffee-room of the Royal Hotel, at Oban. They, too, were looking at the sunset ; and the myriad faint hues of the heather and the northern sea were deepening slowly into night. "Yes, Annie," Mr. Bonnymort was saying, "I think it is time for us to go home. I have taken passage in the *Scotia* for the last of the month. You see, we have been away seven years, and it is time you should go into company. We can go up to Dale, this summer; and you must rest and gain strength for the autumn. But do you not wish to go, little girl?"

"Yes, if you wish, Papa," said the girl. "But I do not wish to lose you."

"My child, you will see more of me than ever. I shall have to act as your duenna. Heigho! I wonder whether little Boston has changed much since my time? I fear I am of the old school now."

"What has become of Guy, I wonder?"

"He has gone to College, and is doing well, I believe. He used to be a nice boy—but something like his father."

So it was decided that the Bonnymorts were to return home.

CHAPTER XVII.

"Instruction supérieure sérieuse."—RENAN.

"Qui est-ce qu' on trompe ici ?"—FIGARO.

COMMENĊEMENT day at Cambridge. It no
longer caused the stir and excitement of yore
in the country round about, when the Muddy River
roads were filled with a procession of carriages rolling out by the wide estuary of the Charles ; when the
Cambridge Commons were crowded with booths of
hucksters, merry-go-rounds, and cheap jacks ; when
the provincial clergy and gentry drove solemnly out,
behind their powdered negro coachmen, in chariots
or "carrying-chairs," belozenged or emblazoned with
the arms known to Salem, to Portsmouth, and the
old coast towns now decayed. Then, even the sailors
on the ships at the foot of Queen Street had a holi-
day, and rolled out to see the young senior sophis-
tors receive their degrees, and fuddled themselves
over black strap and other allurements in the process. Now, the extra-collegiate world troubles itself
little over the great event ; and the two or three hundred young bachelors flung upon the world scarce
cause a ripple as they sink in the sea of commerce
and craft, where few—alas !—are to reappear on the
surface. The little leaven of our so-called great uni-

versities is hardly felt in the national yeast, which patent baking-powder froths and scums the mess up into half baked results much the same.

Not so, however, think the fair sisters and cousins of these young fellows, as they flock in ribbons and furbelows to the dusky red halls, and listen in unappreciative admiration to the dissertations and disquisitions, hearing with much the same feelings a declamation on Italian Poetry and an exposition of the Nebular Hypothesis. But it happens, by some strange chance, that the most charming of these visitors usually find their brothers *dolce faciendi niente* on the lazy sward of Holworthy. For eleemosynary are the systems that govern the old college; and scholarships and collegiate honors and fellowships are like the needle's eye to the rich. " Let him work who must " is the principle ; which the lazier fellows are only too ready to take advantage of.

In the great College Hall the triple-headed cerberi, the men of marks and honors, the future clergy and magistry, have been holding forth to an audience sleepy in the heat. Behind them are the gowned professors ; below the three books on a field gules of Harvard, bearing the motto "veritas!" But, up in the college yard, prone upon the grass, lay such of our friends as had, in college, sought "veritas in vino " only. For Guy had fallen among a precious lot of scapegraces, I fear. Most of his friends were only sent to college to learn to be gentlemen ; and they began by learning how to do nothing gracefully, and perhaps some never got beyond these rudiments.

However, if in those days we were only artistic

loafers, we have not all done so badly since; and even then there was plenty of honest work. Some were there, men of marks and men of mark; for there is a class between Philistia and the Lotus-land, after all. Hackett — that angel of intercourse between the powers that be and Cockaigne — appeared, with a budget of news, as usual. "Strang, old man, I am sorry to say ——"

"Ah, I know," said John. "Don't bother."

"You have lost your degree," ended Hackett.

"*The* devil," cried Phil. "What, Strang, the blameless, the hard-headed, the sprouting Telemachus—Why, in the name of the powers behind the Dean! I thought you were in the first ten, or some such atrocity!"

"I was," said Strang; "and they assigned me a Disquisition! But I refused to inflict my crude and jejune lucubration upon a fastidious if patient public. Wherefore the Government snailed my sheepskin."

"As for you, Randolph, they say that you have finally acquired a grand total of seventeen unexpunged 'conditions.' They think in three years you may get them off, if you care to try."

"Thanks, so very kind," said Randolph. "I expected as much or rather more. My burden has increased like the national debt—quite like the Pilgrim's Progress, without a sepulchre handy."

"My deah fellah," said Hackett, with his favorite adapted manner; "wheah did you pick up such a curious literatchah? I shall expect to hear you quote scripture next."

"The Bible, it seems to me, is the grandest book ever written, and the first every man should read," said Norton simply.

"One for him," Strang chuckled audibly. Hackett, having no reply ready, turned to Bixby. "Billy," said he, "you're dished—finally. No hope this time."

Bixby jumped a foot. "Oh, come, not really?"

"I regret to say it," said Hackett.

"There goes my three years' vacation all in a heap; I should really like to know what for," he added musingly.

"O, really, my boy, when you drive up Beacon Street, Sunday afternoon, in a Tally-ho coach," said Brattle.

"And scour the country with another Hellfire club like that of Medmenham," added Strang.

"And threaten Tutor Lynx to put him through in Paris," laughed Guy.

"And treat old Professor Blowglass the way you did!"

Bixby's long features gradually extended into a grin.

"I did take it out of old Blowglass, didn't I?" said he with a chuckle. "Gad! how he did run!"

"What was that?" cried Brattle. "That must have been the year I was suspended."

"Why," said Van Sittart, "old Blowglass had his back turned, freezing water in a red-hot stew pan, or going through some such shenanigen, and when he turned round there was a cannon-cracker smoking under his desk, about the size of four Bologna sausages. All the fellows saw it at the same time, and,

by gad, you ought to have seen him skip. Most of
us went out the window; the darn thing was a-fizzin'
and a-sputterin' and old Blowglass, he lit out first of
all."

"Jove!" laughed Brattle, "it must have blown all
the windows out of the old place."

"That's what we all thought," said Van Sittart.
"It was the kind of Chinese cracker they use in
Fourth of July processions when they ain't got any
artillery. All we fellows stood round the door waiting to hear the thing bang. Old Blowglass was in
an awful state of funk, and went out and stood in
the middle of the yard, but the lecture-room was as
quiet as the inside of a gospel shop. Finally old
Blowglass got a lot of proctors and they sneaked in
with their handkerchiefs before their eyes, and there
was the cannon-cracker, and it wasn't loaded at all,
it was only a fuse. Of course they had Billy up before the Dean, but they couldn't do much."

"No," said Billy with a chuckle. "I had taken
the gunpowder out, and I put my kaleidoscope inside, and I told the Dean I was very sorry my new
case had frightened the gentlemen."

"Really, Billy," said Randolph, "such little ex-
periments in fine arts are all very well, but the
French Opera were not quite the sort of people to
bring out, Class day. It shocks our prejudices, you
know."

"O! go it," sighed Bixby. "What else? Any
body else?"

"Van Sittart, I hear. And Brattle is very shaky.
He is dropped, at least."

7

"Ay," said Tom, "methought I heard something fall. I am no squire of low degree. I've no degree at all. That, I believe, has the true Strang ring!"

"My children," said John, "a certain solemnity in the hour betokens dinner. I feel it—deeply." And Strang placed his brown hand above his capacious belt. "Let us shake the dust of Cambridge from off our feet and fly to pastures new."

"I wish old Phil were here," said Guy. "It is probably *jour maigre* with him. Monday is the race."

"Gad, fellows, an idea!" cried Bixby. "Let's coach to Worcester!"

The humor of the group changed at once from the gay tone of easy banter to the gravity with which one considers a serious matter.

"I know a stable at West Cambridge where they have an old Concord coach, we might rig up as best we can, like the real thing," continued Bixby, "and horses from Pike's. Who can drive a four-in-hand? I can't drive all the time."

"Oh, anybody; what's the difference if we do upset?"

"My servant is an old English groom, and will wind the horn for you," said Randolph.

"We can carry the drinks and things inside the coach," suggested Van Sittart.

It was surprising, the sudden influx of energy. The *plastik* of the party had changed at once from ancient Egyptian to a style quite Greek in its motion and activity.

"Let's cut the rest of Commencement," said Bixby. " They don't want us. Let such of us as have degrees depute some of the virtuous to grab 'em out of their darned old basket. We must get off by six; I, thank the Lord, never to return."

" Except," said Strang, "when the asperities of academic life are again mitigated by Commencement punch."

" Speaking of punch," said Bixby, "Van and I will look after the cellar department. Brattle, you arrange about the coach, will you ? Strang can see to the horses. And, Guerndale, go in town and get some rockets and cannon crackers, there's a good fellow. As for Randolph, he is too lazy to do anything, I suppose."

" Not at all," said he ; "I will store my energies against a sudden emergency. Meanwhile, I will stay to prod the plodders."

" But how about feed ?" said some one.

" Oh, any one can see to that ; get Lane," cried Brattle.

" If his aunts will let him come," growled Bixby.

" We're very sorry we can't hope to have you join us, Hackett," said Norton ; "but I suppose your Commencement part will interfere. Come, fellows, bustle—bustle—the most beastly word in the language I know—but we must be away by six."

And Randolph, stopping only to roll a cigarette, walked indolently away toward his rooms. The rest had already scattered, no more to press the sacred herbage in front of Holworthy.

It was admitted on all sides to be a great ride— that of ours from Cambridge to Worcester. A nine-

teenth century edition of Paul Revere. The com-
missariat department, consisting of Randolph's servant and the stores, rode inside, which part of the
coach was accordingly yclept the cellar, and it also
served as a hospital for such of the party as were
overcome by the heat or "otherwise," as Bixby
euphemistically put it. Flags of many and various
shades of Harvard red waved from every corner.
Bixby and Van Sittart sat at the back of the coach,
dispensing ignited squibs and serpents among the
admiring multitude, and occasionally defending our
rear from the onslaught of the barefooted villagers.
The proceedings were otherwise diversified by the
persistent attempts of the same youths to render
"Fair Harvard," on the coaching horn. In this way,
if our entrée into each village was triumphant, our
departure bore more the semblance of an escape.

Thus we rode through the elm-shaded Middlesex
roads, calling at country farm-houses for milk or
other refreshments—our supply of solids being limited—where we were taken for an organized body of
tramps, and where Bixby was invariably found flirting with the daughters of the house in the milk room ;
stopping at country inns by night to pass away the
quiet hours at the card-table, to the wonder of the
natives and the commercial travellers, who were the
usual guests ; driving off in the early morning, with
the nine Harvard cheers and a boom of cannon-
crackers ; sleeping away the hot noons ; smoking,
drinking, and singing on the top of the coach ; up-
setting once, under the guidance of Randolph, who
never could be induced to hold the horses going down

hill, and, to our great grief, breaking a flagon of
excellent champagne cup ; on, like a very rout of
Comus, with the two sheepskin degrees of the party
tied in pride around the whip by their own pink ribbons, generally making of ourselves a fearful example to the bucolic districts ; so that the country
newspapers teemed with the enormities of Harvard
for weeks after, and dozens of country clergymen
sent their hopeful sprouts to Amherst, or Williams, or
Princeton instead ; on, while Bixby drank and Strang
grinned, and Van and Brattle played games, and
Lane preserved his politeness, and Randolph poured
cynicism into Guerndale's ear ; on to Worcester, in a
blaze of flags and fireworks, where tall, thin youths in
linen dusters and high hats, or straw hats and frock
coats, ribboned like an Austrian field marshal in
blue, betokened the presence of the men of Yale.
And these same men of Yale concealed the admiration which our entrée must have inspired, under a
running fire of chaff, which it took the united wit
and tongue of the party on top of the coach to respond to and return in due form. The Yale student,
like most American undergraduates, is *fort en gueule ;*
and it finally became advisable to call up Randolph's
groom, who, versed in the slang of Newmarket and
the amenities of British jockeys, succeeded in "getting off several grinds," as Bixby put it, upon the entire party. From the usual polite personalities, the
talk turned upon the prospects of the race, and argument from probabilities ended in quite a natural
way in *argumentum ad crumenam.* A rapid series of bets
were made and salted ; and Bixby and Brattle were

kept busy with their betting-books, while Strang, an old oar, and known to both colleges, was literally loaded down with greenbacks as stake-holder.

"Gad!" said Van Sittart, "the Yale fellows are actually backing their own crew even. Fifty more? No, thanks—got all I can carry. I say, Lane, take a bet for the honor of the college. We can't have these fellows offering against Harvard, and no takers!"

Lane blushed, and timidly pulled out a fifty-dollar note, which, with a similar contribution from Yale, were stuffed in John Strang's capacious pocket. But still the offers flowed in from the crowd from New Haven. "I say," said Bixby, with the usual formula, as he wiped the perspiration from his face, "I wish some of our men would come. These fellows are as rocky as a country road. Hello, Randolph, in there! Wake up!"

Randolph had retired to the interior of the coach, and was apparently wrapped in slumber.

"O, darn the fifties," cried at this moment a lanky fellow from the sidewalk, wearing a white "plug" hat surrounded by a broad blue band. "I go a hundred or nothin'. Damn you Harvard men, you can't back your own crew. Here's a hundred on Yale! Yale! Ya-a-le 'n no takers."

"Yale, Yale, h—l," grunted Brattle.

Bixby began to sputter viciously from the back of the coach. Then Randolph's quiet accents came softly from the cellar:

"Guy up there? Tell the gentleman from Yale I see his hundred with pleasure, and raise him a thousand."

"I only said I'd bet a hundred," answered he of the ulster, when Randolph's message was delivered by Guerndale, "and really I haven't——"

"Then dry up," put in Bixby tersely. "Put up or shut up!" and the coach stopped before the Harvard headquarters in triumph, while Van Sittart exploded a timely bomb, which soon brought the Harvard contingent about us. An astonished policeman on the outskirts of the crowd struggled vainly to reach the offender, and, giving it up in disgust, contented himself with the arrest of two small boys at a distance.

Guy, however, was a little weary of this. He soon got away from the others, and, hiring a buggy, drove out to the crew's quarters on the lake. He had not seen Phil for nearly a month, and found him browner than ever; his face well filled out, his great blue eyes clear, his body trained down, in fine condition for a pull. A superb six they were, too; but the true Harvard cut—small-waisted, though broad-shouldered, long-limbed, with a general look about them of more blood than bone.

"Well, old boy, our four years are over, hey?" cried Symonds. "I'm afraid we shan't see so much fun again in a hurry."

"I don't know," said Guy. "I don't know what I shall do these next years. To-morrow I am going up to Dale to loaf for a while. Then, I don't know —perhaps, I shall go abroad with Randolph. I wish there were something one could study there besides medicine and art."

"What's the use of going abroad to grind?"

growled Symonds. "Gad! if I could go, I shouldn't take much of that in mine, thank you. But the governor's mad over my debts, and swears I've got to go into his counting-room on the first of August, just when I hoped to get to Paris. O, Lord!" and Phil sighed like a furnace. "By the way, I almost forgot—there's a devilish important thing I want you to do for me, old man—you will, won't you?"

"Why, of course, Phil. What a question to ask of me—as if there were anything I wouldn't do for you; and you know it, old fellow."

"You see I wanted like the deuce and all to pot a little money this trip. If I could raise a few hundreds, I'd go to Europe in spite of the old man. If I could only get out there, he'd send me cash to get back fast enough. Now I went and bet a cool thousand on our crew. And the fact is, Guy," and Phil's voice sank to a whisper, "we aren't going to win this race. Eliot has gone queer in the insides and is all bunged up. I only found it out just now. Now, if I lose this thousand, I can't pay it—anyhow. I bet with men I knew; so I didn't have to put it up, and I thought we were dead sure to win. Don't say anything about Eliot to any of the fellows—at least not until you have got it all fixed up; and I advise you to put in a little on Yale on your own account."

Guy was silent a moment. "I'd rather not, Phil," he said.

"Rather not? why not, Guy? Hang it all, I've never asked a favor of you before; and now you'd rather not? It's all right—I wouldn't bet against my own crew, of course, but to hedge is another matter."

"But I can only get bets on Harvard from Harvard men—our friends."

"You needn't go to our fellows—take it from the older men, the graduates. They've got to lose the money to somebody, don't you see? and better to you and me than those Yale fellows."

Guy's face brightened up suddenly. "Tell you what I will do, Phil; I'll lend you the money to pay, with pleasure."

"Damn your money!" said Phil. And so forth. It certainly looked like serious trouble between those two—the first they had ever had since they tumbled into the pond as children. Fortunately, Guy's obstinacy was overcome by Phil's good nature. Symond's never could be angry long— even with a friend, as Randolph would say. And after a while his hearty laugh rolled out again, and the two sat chatting until it came time for the evening spin of the crew. And Guy sat and watched them go out— prouder than ever of his chum as he saw the start, the style, and fire of Phil's quick stroke seeming to make the boat quiver and throb through the water.

"Forty-two," said a voice close by Guy. "Hm— too much, Symonds."

"Hallo, John," said Guy, "when did you come out?"

"Just now. Five doesn't finish. Who's rowing five?"

"Eliot."

"The man you were talking of an hour ago?"

7*

"You heard it?"

"Just as I came in—besides, didn't know the con-versation was private."

"Well, I'm glad you did, but Phil doesn't want it known. Eliot is out of condition; and Phil wanted me to hedge his bets for him, but I didn't like to, and I am afraid I have offended the dear old boy, though he wouldn't show it, and forgave me directly, like a brick as he is. I hope you don't think I was wrong?"

"I think you were right," said Strang.

"I'm glad you do," said Guy; "though still, you see, I think Phil only meant——he was only hedg-ing——"

Strang began to laugh.

"What's the joke?" said Guy, seriously.

"To hear you arguing for Phil against yourself."

Guy hated ridicule and turned away. Strang looked after him curiously, and then out over the lake. The sun was setting, and the still surface of Quinsigamond like molten gold. Afar down the lake Harvard's returning crew moved slowly, a little dark line upon the water. From the opposite shore was borne a faint noise of the cheering which greeted the coming of the 'Varsity six ; Phil Symonds, stroke.

Guy drove back to the town with Strang. They found the streets crowded with excited students. The ordinary business of the citizens of the place seemed suspended. The highway dignified with the name of Main Street was really animated. On the corners groups of blue and red ribboned young men were eagerly discussing the latest news from the lake. The Boston and New York morning papers of the day contained long articles on the probable result of the race, which were anxiously read by the students, notwithstanding they knew them to be written by Brown of '72, a "scrub," who knew less about the crews than they did themselves. The apartment in the hotels which was graced by the presence of the clerk, usually a rambling hall, with walls covered with gaudy advertisements, and a dirty marble floor, was thronged with that youth which, in journalistic phrase, constituted the hope of the country. The neighboring bar was fringed with a continuous bibulous queue, who poured down many and various "mixed" drinks, and made bets for more. Occasionally a scrap of college song was heard above the hum of conversation, soon to be drowned by the groans of those of the rival college.

Guy and his friends, finding it impossible to get a room, dispensed with the luxury of a bed; but Billy Bixby discovering an apartment held by a weak contingent of Yale men, an assault was ordered, which promptly dislodged the latter; and our friends, barricading the door, held their position against all invaders over a bowl of champagne punch. About dawn the dregs of this were generously bestowed upon the heads of a party who attempted an escalade from the street. A quarter of the garrison kept watch and ward at the window and door while the others played unlimited loo at the centre table. Thus, heedless of complaints from the agonized proprietor, our hopeful graduates passed the night away.

The race was announced for early in the morning,

and by eleven the crews were off. Harvard took a slight lead at the start, rowing in beautiful form. But, with a vicious splash and jerk—rowing, as all critics said, like bargemen—Yale passed them at the mile, and ended an easy winner.

The demoralization of the Harvard forces was complete. Not waiting for the regatta ball, which was to conclude the day, our friends scattered far and wide.

Strang got into difficulty after the race by crushing an Irishman's *os frontis* for speaking in uncomplimentary terms of the esteemed university which had just refused him a degree. Bixby stayed to bail him out, having won largely at loo, the night before. Lane and Brattle betook themselves to their blameless firesides ; Randolph and Van Sittart, to Newport, the former with a promise to and from Guy for an early visit. And Guy took the afternoon train west for Dale, lying in midsummer sleepiness amid the Berkshire Hills.

His head was still racking and his thought confused with the last night's punch and profanity, and the green afternoon had a soothing influence. He smoked and thought dreamily of things in general. He had a curious feeling as if things in general had come to an end. His college life was ended. *Bien —après ?* He did not know.

What, why, wherefore, whither, and every other accursed "*w*" that the devil ever invented, rolled lazily through his mind. Even his enthusiasm seemed asleep. He thought of Randolph, and then, with some uneasiness, of Phil.

Phil had told him after the race that he was going to Europe anyhow ; and he had given a half promise to join him in Paris.

And then he thought fondly of his own mother, living the quiet life of an unobtrusive Lady Bountiful in the old town up in the hills ; living as much in the past as the present ; regretting much, but hoping much also. He knew she was very fond of him ; but he always fancied her to be comparing him with his own father, and he knew enough of him to know that he was very different, and that his father had not had a successful life. A born recluse ; a man whose highest ambition was to be clergyman in Dale ; and, failing in that . . . . At all events, he, Guyon, must not fail. He was for the world, the world still, if in a high sense . . . . Yet was he so sure of that ? After all, what did he see in the world that he really desired ? He could not help understanding Randolph when he said "there was much to envy, little to admire" . . . . Then there was society. *Etre aimable et plaire aux femmes* —after all, was that the highest duty of a gentleman ? . . . . Money—he had enough. Would he take more ? Yes, he would take it, but as for laboring to acquire it . . . . After all, what was he vexing himself with abstractions for ? And he walked out upon the platform of the rear car, where he sat and smoked a concrete cigar.

There is something intensely sad about the New. England country. With an unkempt, half-reclaimed raggedness it joins the wild, sad beauty of a relapse into nature. It is an Italy without architecture, but the moss clings as kindly to the wood, and the vines hang as lazily to the stone walls, as if all the decay of Pæstum fed their growth. Not so in the ugly, successful, manufacturing towns, but in the lazy orchard-bounded country roads, in the mossy vine-grown walls, behind which the square elm-shaded mansions stare gloomily forward over a waste of forgotten agriculture or modern industry. Beauty of art it never had ; beauty in life it never had ; but it has beauty in decay. The square old farm-houses blink through their blindless windows, lonely and forlorn. The young men have sought the " genteel " in cities, and are dapper salesmen or smug commercial travellers ; the daughters—what does become of the daughters?—and around the old fireside, now plastered up and fitted with an iron stove, the old ' squire ' sits with his wife, and finds even his weary hands strong enough to manage the abandoned farm. Meanwhile, higher grow the elms and more gaunt and spectral the few Lombardy poplars before the house; and closer twines the wild grape about the rocks in the pastures, and the barren apple-trees, forgotten in the swamps and woodland clearings. And Guy pondered dreamily of a long talk he had had with Randolph, the night before. " Does it pay?" he had said, " that is the great question. It is a frequent phrase, and, by that very frequency, a good text, too. That question must be asked of every end, thought, action, or mode of life. You regret many things, I regret more, and yet they disappeared in due course before that mighty logic of that modern catechism. They did not pay. . . . .

Look at religion, the idea of God. Dr. Newlite shows us in his book the incalculable number of lives ; the amount of suffering ; the loss of art and knowledge and civilization ; that has been caused by religion, its hate and bigotry. And what has it brought in recompense ? Has it squared the accounts ? No, decidedly ; a God does not pay. Love does not ; purity does not ; nobility does not. Worldly ambition may—if you consider the game worth the candle. I don't." And Randolph had taken a glass of champagne punch and relapsed into his more accustomed badinage. "*Vogue la galère !* I had almost said something I had a distant idea of believing in." Ah, if Randolph had only a dash of Phil Symonds—or rather if Phil Symonds had only a dash of Randolph, thought Guy. And he thought of Phil's honest, hearty smile ; and the plucky way he had pulled a losing race.

So Guy mused, as his train trundled up the gradual slope from the green meadow country about the Connecticut with its clumps of elms, to the woods and hills of Western Massachusetts. Finally the train stopped at Dale, and he sent his luggage forward, choosing, for himself, the two mile walk by the sunset. He knew that the Bonnymorts had come home ; and looked toward their house as he approached it. It was seven years since he had seen Annie. He wondered what she had grown to be like. Two young ladies he saw were playing croquet upon the lawn. Croquet is at no time a very amusing game ; still less so, except to the bystander, when played by two young ladies. So the younger and prettier of the two was knocking around the balls in an aimless way, while the taller girl stood shading her eyes, looking toward the road.

Guy was taller by a head and shoulders than the low hedge which separated the lawn from the road ; and, as he brushed along by the leafage, he looked over into the croquet-ground and their eyes met. Annie came running forward directly.

"Oh, Guy !" she said, "I knew I should know you again. I heard you were coming to-day." Her face broke into the sweetest of smiles, and she pressed close into the thick of the hedge and gave him her hand over the blossoms. Guy felt himself turning quite red. He had expected no such warm greeting, thinking, indeed, that Annie had probably forgotten him. He held her hand rather awkwardly, not wishing to drop it into the prickles, and was conscious of a strong temptation to address her as Miss Bonnymort.

"Why, you have hardly changed !" she went on. "Come around by the gate." But Guy placed his hand on the outer rail, and vaulted over it, hedge and all. Annie's eyes were quite as he had remembered them ; but, now that he was beside her, he saw, of course, that she was much taller, and was dressed in some kind of white, fleecy material The other young lady had gone into the house.

It was already quite dark when Guy went home, walking with the quick, uncertain step of one who is unconscious of his surroundings. But the last few weeks were already an older past than the days when he had been a child in this same sweet coun-

try ; the stars of the sky were full of a strange new
meaning for him, and the sounds of the summer
night woke memories of that old evening when he
walked back from the pages of Dante, years before.
Now as then

> " Lo giorno se n' andava, e l' aer bruno
> Toglieva ; li animai che sono in terra
> Dalle fatiche loro ——"

and the time of day and the sweet season seemed
once more to be calling him to newer hoping and to
higher aims.

CHAPTER XVIII.

"Ecce Deus fortior me, qui veniens dominabitur mihi."—DANTE.

ANNIE BONNYMORT was the daughter of a gentleman, and a gentleman who meant his daughter to grow up a lady, and did not expect her suddenly to become one when first she appeared in company. She had never been at boarding-school. She had never had a dozen or more dearest friends with whom she spent the better part of the year. She had never romped promiscuously in the hall-ways of American sea-side hotels. She had lived much in the country and all out-doors; she had not been afraid of the woods or lonely in them. As a child, she had had unlimited use of the *clef des champs*, without the fear of freckles before her eyes. Much of her life had necessarily been passed abroad, where she had lived very quietly, respecting European conventions, and avoiding table d'hôtes. Her manners were a rare combination of frankness and courtesy, so that a knave feared her, a fool was deceived by her, and a gentleman adored her. Yet, I think she was too simple in thought to see all this; and her nature was such that the characters of those about her were purified and ennobled by passing

through her mind, and all people seemed to her better than they were. Guy once said of her to me,
her thoughts were not thoughts, but sweet feelings.
Above all, she had two great marks of a lady—
sweetness and dignity.

So the next morning Guy woke up, earlier than
usual, and found the world an easier world to get up
into. All his ambitions, beliefs, hopes, seemed to take
new color that July day. He seemed to hold a key
to the meaning of things ; he was not quite sure
how, but knew all would come right in time. He
wondered at this frame of mind while he was dress-
ing, and finally ascribed it, wholly to his satisfac- ·
tion, to the fresh Berkshire air. " What a pity there
i· no country life in America," thought he. " If
one could only do something here—something at
once national and local, as a fellow can in England.
If people could only believe in one's honesty and
singleness of purpose one might go into politics."

It was an odd breakfast table, that of Guy and his
mother. She, a woman of the past ; he, never more
decidedly than now a man of the future. Hester,
the old servant, who had heard his father preach his
first sermon, whom he had married, whose husband
had abused her, then deserted her, and left her to
come back to Dale and live in peace, while she kept
canny hold upon her earnings in the books of the
Dale Savings Bank—put in her name, well out of his
clutches—Hester hovered about them grimly, like
an arbiter between fate and hope.

Guy's mother seemed to him more and more to be
going back, forgetting him out of her life. Every-

thing he did was either like his father or unlike his father; more frequently now the latter than the former.

But Guy was a grown man now; the square, rough-hewn oaken beams in the floor creaked beneath his weight as they had not done under a male Guerndale for two generations, and his mother seemed to feel this dimly, and in some way to relinquish her active part in life to him. She did not oppose him, but her will had none the less a certain inertia of its own which it was not so easy to disturb.

Yes, Guy might live in the city now, if he liked; yes, she supposed he could not stay in Dale. He had always hoped that she would take a house in the city when he grew up? Oh, no, she could not do that! She was too old now. She had hoped Guy would be a clergyman, like his father; but he knew best. Of course he would have to go to the city to practise his profession or business. She did not see why he should have business if he was not going to be a clergyman. No, she could never be happy in the city. Every one had forgotten her now. Besides, it was too far from his—father, she was going to say, but stopped. Why did he wish to go so much? She had always thought he would like to travel after graduating. His father had been abroad before studying divinity, with letters from Dr. Channing and from Mr. Emerson, before he went wrong. His father had enjoyed European society very much. Guy, too, ought to go and see something of the world before settling down. Why did he want to settle down in Boston so soon?

Guy became suddenly conscious of remembering that Annie—Miss Bonnymort—had told him they were to open their town house for the winter, and this first memory prevented for a moment his remembering, in the second place, that he had decided to study mining, and that it was best for him to study a year or two in Boston and Cambridge before going to Europe. "And then," he added gaily, "I can tell whether these old hills really contain anything like precious stones or metals, and make certain that our diamond was never found here, and that Simmons really tried to steal it from old Guy, though bad enough he was, I don't doubt."

This was the first time Guy had ever alluded to the story since his mother had given him the stone itself, in an old locket, and told him to wear it always, as his father had done. If he spoke thus to let in a little modern light and cheerfulness upon the musty old legend, he tried in vain. It was a very serious matter to his father, said his mother, and he should know better than to jest about it. No good had come to the family ever since. Evil fortune was too serious a thing to laugh at. His poor father had always felt that it had prevented his doing much good in his ministry. Mining might be an honest profession; she hoped so ; but desire for easily won riches had been at the bottom of all their troubles.

"My dear mother," interrupted Guy, "you must know that I don't particularly value money, except as a means to an end."

"To what end ? Your poor father was content with the half of what you will have."

Guy had no answer ready, being distinctly conscious of having always maintained that the highest life was one free from all desire, except for self-improvement and the country's good. "At all events I mean to live an open life among men, and come out of the dark corner where we have lived so long, and you must not blame me, mamma dear, for feeling so."

The widow sighed and rose silently from the table. When Guy was away she was devotedly fond of him ; when he was present she enwrapped both Guy and herself in the gloom of the past. "Where do you go to-day?" she said, pausing at the door.

"I—I promised Miss Bonnymort to ride with her to see some poor people in whom she is interested," said Guy. "But if you do not wish me——"

"O, no," said his mother. "I had hoped you would go with me to the cemetery to see whether you do not think your father's monument needs polishing. But of course you prefer your ride," and the widow softly closed the door behind her.

Guy felt all conciliation for the moment impossible. Moreover, he did not wish to break his engagement with Annie. So he threw himself upon the small Canadian horse, and rode across meadow abstractedly, taking the ditches on the way.

In the good old times of the middle ages, when men and women were men and women, we know that that modern sentimentality known as love filled little space of life. Deeds were more common than words, much more common than thoughts ; and love existed purely as a deed, occasionally occurring in the intervals of warfare and wassail. We also know that since the appearance of Werther and Manon Lescaut, its German form has been purely a thought, its French form impurely a deed. But the simple and idiotic sentimentality which has been largely prevalent among the English-speaking races was in earlier times unknown—as all men know.

Consequently, when we read of the sternest and gloomiest face that frowned through the streets in the bloodiest years of Florence ; of him whose life was full of war and hate and envy, and embittered by exile and loneliness, we know that here at least we shall find no trace of it. A man from whom the very children in the streets shrank in awe ; a man whose robes they feared to touch (for he had returned from hell) ; in his book we shall find no morbidness, no smack of Werther or of Gautier. And we look into the second page of his first work and find . . . . "When I first saw her she seemed to me clothed in noblest blushes, gentle and pure, sunny of disposition, girdled and adorned plainly, as best befitted her youth. At that instant, I say truly that the spirit of life which abides in the deepest chamber of the heart, began to tremble so that I felt it in my smallest pulses most fearfully ; and all in trembling, it spake these words : Behold a god stronger than I who, coming, shall rule over me. And at that instant the spirit of the body which dwelleth in that part where our nutriment is administered, began to weep, and weeping spake these words : Unhappy me ! for in future I shall often be hindered——."

Thus we learn that so long ago as Anno Domini 1274, men's stomachs were weak enough to forget

digestion, when men's minds were busied with love.
So Burton speaks of "this heroical or love melancholy, which proceeds from women, and is more
eminent above the rest, and properly called love ;"
and maintains that the "part affected in men is the
liver ; and hence it is more common in men of
generous and noble dispositions."

But, perhaps, the times were as we thought them,
and Dante being but a weak creature, after all, did
not truly represent them.   For see, he says : "and
I say that from that time love had lordship over my
soul, which fell so soon to his disposition, and so
much assurance and dominion did he begin to take
over me, by the virtue which my imagination gave
him, that it behooved me to do obediently all his
pleasures.   And many times he commanded me to
seek to see that young woman ; wherefore I in my
youth, often went about in search of her. . . ."
Silly little children of Florence to be afraid of this
man !   Perhaps, had you run boldly up, he would
have dandled you on his knees and given you lolli-
pops after all !

How strangely beautiful is the mountain air sometimes !   This not particularly brilliant reflection was
Guy's, that morning, as he rode through the meadows in the valley.   Particularly, when coming from
a city or crowd ; and, most of all, in the early morning.   How liquid is the light ; what a golden green
in the meadows ; what a smoky purple in the outer
forest spaces that hedge the intervale !   How white
the water lilies are, studding the still water surface, the edges of the river, and the straight, black-

rimmed ditches; how vivid the purple iris, standing
in long, tall clumps and companies from out the yellow blossomed sedge! How one would like to live
all the year round among all these fair things with
—let me see, what is her name in your case?

Guy's thoughts ended at the dash and went on in
a much more consistent fashion. He had scarcely
thought beyond the dash, yet. Moreover, he was
leaving the meadow and riding up the side of an
orchard slope, not far from the very pond where
Phil and he had had their aqueous rencounter. Guy
sighed a little to think how Phil had improved since
then, how much better a fellow he was than himself.
Still, it was all the better having such a man for a
good friend. Then Phil was going abroad that summer. He had thought of going with him, but, perhaps, it was just as well he should not. It was time
for him to be getting to work. Work was prayer,
some one had said. Not that that was any especial
recommendation. Prayer was the highest act of
man, to be sure; but if that were all he had to do,
he might as well do it in heaven; cut this world,
and be done with it. As John Strang would say,
the highest things were always damned impracticable. Perhaps he, Guy, was a man of low ideals and
worldly ends. Such as they were he would stick to
them. The re-establishment of a name, the respect
and admiration of men were yet good things if won
honorably—perhaps, also, wealth and fashion. He
did not think Miss Bonnymort cared much for Mrs.
Grundy, for people in general—she talked too much
of *things* in general. Was that she on the piazza?

8

some one in white—no, this one was dumpy and different from Annie. It was Miss Brattle. He did not particularly care to see Miss Brattle, yet was dimly conscious of a desire to conciliate her. She looked excessively spotless and cool, with a starchiness that extended somewhat to her manner. Would she shake hands? He extended his own, doubtfully, feeling that it was hot and smelt of the leather reins. He had not worn gloves—he hated them, in the country.

Did he want to see Miss Bonnymort? Yes—Annie was going to ride with him—ah—that is—He felt it was somewhat rude to shut Miss Brattle so entirely out of the excursion.

"Oh, I am to be of the party, too, Mr. Guerndale. I am sorry for your sake—but Miss Bonnymort asked me."

There, he had offended her. So Annie asked her —she said nothing about her, yesterday. Why did Miss Brattle insist on calling her Miss Bonnymort? And why was he so embarrassed? It was only Tom Brattle's sister—and a younger sister, too, he fancied. Still, she was a woman, and that made the difference. His appearance was not irreproachable, and his manners had been careless. A lady should be offended by none of the coarse common-places of life. They were sensitive, shrinking, and pure ; all that entered the sphere of their presence should be sweet and courteous. He felt that her womanly sense had seen through his discourtesy ; he was not even sure that the mental oath had escaped her. Somehow he had not thought so much of it last

night ; but to-day it occurred to him that he really
was not fit to be their companion. He should be
continually wounding their susceptibilities. His
thoughts must be so different from theirs—how
should he refine and mould them to make conversation possible ?

Just then he heard a lighter step in the hall, which
he knew was Annie's. When she came through the
door and gave him her hand, he touched it hastily,
and felt a strange difficulty in looking at her. Since
Miss Brattle's remark, it seemed awkward to call her
by her first name, as he had always done. Even
when Miss Brattle went up for her riding-habit and
left them together, conversation was difficult, and
he could not help avoiding her eyes. He was almost afraid of her ; when he lifted her on her horse,
he was conscious of doing it nervously and clumsily.
With Miss Brattle, strangely enough, he was easier,
though he knew her less well. During the ride this
odd state of affairs continued. Either he had no
conversation, or he became garrulous and inclined
to talk about himself.

Annie looked at him once or twice in surprise;
Miss Brattle evidently thought him a bore ; and finally they engaged in a conversation about people
of whom he knew nothing. When they arrived at
the cottage, he stayed outside and held the horses
absently. He knew vaguely that they were calling
on the Widow Sproul, with whose son he remembered once having a fight. Across the valley was an
old cider mill, in front of which he could see a cart
standing, and a horse with a stumpy red tail. For

many years he remembered the appearance of that
horse's tail.

Coming back, things were a little better; as he
talked of Phil Symonds, and Phil was a subject
about which he could always be enthusiastic. He
felt quite pleased to monopolize Annie's conversation, and to notice that even Miss Brattle seemed to
listen with some interest. Still, when he went home,
it was with a sense of emptiness and disappointment;
his horse's nose a foot from the ground.

He did not notice old Solomon Bung, who sidled
past him, with a rod, as usual. That worthy seemed
to take no offence, but looked at him solemnly, with
that increase of wrinkles about the corners of the
eyes which served the purpose of a smile of greeting. He even turned to look back at him once or
twice after he had passed.

Days soon came, however, which were less disap-
pointing. Miss Brattle went over to Lenox for a
few days, and Guy and Annie had long walks and
rides—days which he put aside in his memory like
sweet sounds, and as indescribable in words. He
grew a more and more constant visitor at the Bonnymorts'; but each time, on first meeting Annie, his
constraint seemed more marked. She was always
frank, and sunny, and kind; but he felt his manners
cold and silent, and his conversation forced. Only
after a few minutes, when they got down in the
woods or fields, did he regain the old simplicity of
companionship. Many times Annie would notice
his reserve, and vex him by asking, with sweet sympathy, about troubles which he knew were imaginary.

Once she took his hand and asked him anxiously if she had offended him. His lips trembled, but he could make no intelligent answer. He drew his hand away hastily and turned away, afraid to meet her eye. He was one-and-twenty and she seventeen.

One afternoon he walked with her to see their old acquaintance, Mandy Shed. Annie, as old Sol Bung expressed it, was a lady as women used to be, and yet nat'ral and not stuck up ; not so Miss Shed, who kept them waiting half an hour while she donned a blue silk and caused a long gold chain to depend from her neck. She was only two years older than Annie, but looked already thirty. Her eyes were still bright, but her neck long, thin, and sallow, and her complexion worn. She spoke with fretful animation of the lack of society in Dale, and said it was much gayer at North Adams. There were some city people there.

Poor Mandy ! the world had not gone well with her. She had been for many years engaged to Ned Dench, who was a salesman in some dry-goods store in the city. He was believed to be doing well ; had occasionally returned to Dale, showy of scarf-pin and lavender trousers ; but his visits were growing less frequent, and it was popularly considered doubtful whether the long-postponed marriage would take place at all. Fifteen hundred a year didn't seem so much in Boston as it did in Dale, and it was reported that Dench had said to one or two of his bosom friends that he guessed he had had all he wanted of that girl. Ned was a rising man, they said, admiringly, as he drove by with her in his buggy, smoking an Havana cigar. Ned secretly felt that Mandy was growing old, and, if he married on $1,500 a year, his cigars would be too domestic for his taste.

It was not a pleasant call, and would have been embarrassing but for Annie's tact and simple manners. Miss Shed's voice was harsh, and her accent voluble, but she seemed at a loss for conversation, and her manners were rude in the attempt to avoid *empressement* or any appearance of seeming flattered at their visit. She thought she might stay with a lady friend in Boston, next winter; who had boarded near Dale, that summer. She was very intimate. Did Miss Bonnymort know her? Her father was John C. Whalen, of Whalen, Young & Skinner. Mr. Dench admired her very much. How was Mr. Dench? Mr. Guerndale must have seen him in Boston. He went a great deal into society. They were very superior people—the Whalens.

CHAPTER XIX.

"Nous disséquons le Christ au pied de l'autel."—DE MUSSET.

DESPITE these occasional new moods of Guy's, and Annie's larger knowledge of the world, it seemed very natural to both of them to fall back into the old relation of eight years agone. Possibly it was an attribute of both characters to remain the same ; to alter little with outer circumstances. Dale itself was much changed, however. A little more of the old life was gone, a little more of the new had crept in. Old Dr. Grimstone was dead, somewhat to the relief of his parishioners. Indeed, his decease had possibly saved him an enforced retirement in favor of the present incumbent, a young man bred on the Western Reserve in Ohio, whom an exaggerated estimate of his own powers had led from the paternal pork-raising to a western college, thence into divinity. But he soon left the fathers of the church for the rising suns of modern thought. Possibly his early cultivation of turnip roots had led him to radical views ; or else, as La Rochefoucauld says, he embraced the wrong opinion because the best places were already taken in the right one. He called himself an eclectic ; he knew the existence and names of

many things; and his mind had hitherto been too
fully occupied to leave him time for turning gentleman by the way. At one time he had dabbled in
metaphysics; but this requiring too much mental exertion—for he was a very lazy man—he now contented himself with the positivists. General denial
is a very comfortable mental attitude. In his sermons he delighted in putting the boldest assertions
of negation in their crudest forms. Nevertheless, he
kept on easy terms with the Deity. He would occasionally mention Christ with good-natured patron-
age, and made friendly allowance for the vagaries of
the Evangelists. When he treated earnestly of
things spiritual it was in quoting from Buddha, Con-
fucius, or the Koran. He read large quantities of
verse in his sermons, which were also full of metaphors derived from business and trade. He was act-
ively interested in politics, affected worldliness in
dress and manners, and hated to be taken for a clergyman. He was very popular in the parish, prominent
in pic-nics and church dancing parties, and a capital
actor in private theatricals. Wine and cards he considered immoral, but, to avoid the charge of phari-
seeism, he frequented smoking cars and familiarized
himself with bar-rooms. He was fond of taking the
maidens of his flock to drive in his buggy on Saturday afternoons, but his attentions were so universal
that scandal never attached.

The Bonnymorts had once invited him *ex officio* to
tea, where he asked "Miss Annie" to go to drive
with him, inquired who her gentlemen friends were
in Dale, sought fiercely to argue with Guy for Tyn-

dall against the Kantian school, and contrasted the enlightenment of his own parish with the dark and superstitious barbarism that still afflicted countries groaning under the Romish Church. He regretted that he never had been across the " pond," and that he had always resided in the country since he commenced his mission. He told Mr. Bonnymort, who was an Episcopalian, that the Anglican Church was effete.

Besides the changes wrought by this servant of the Lord, there were others. Gas had been introduced into the town. Some new manufactories had been built, and there had been a considerable influx of French-Canadian and Chinese working-people. The employers of this cheap human energy had erected for themselves new French-roofed houses, usually prominent of tower or cupola, surrounded by well-shaven little grass-plots, iron statues painted white, and black asphalt walks. These were the prominent parishioners of the Rev. M. Frank Hanna, and had chiefly contributed to the building of the vestry— the new vestry. This institution was in theory a Sunday-school for the children of the parish ; but its more prominent use was for winter dancing-parties, raffles, and private theatricals, when the small pulpit was removed to make place for the stage. Mr. Bonnymort spoke of it irreverently as the " Casino."

Most of the younger people whom Guy and Annie remembered had left the town. Some few of the girls had been married, usually to strangers ; some of the ones so married had returned home ; others

8*

were spoken of vaguely as "living in the city."
Nearly all the young men were also in the city; a
few were said to be "smart fellows" and doing well.
Guy learned these things from Solomon Bung. Old
Solomon Bung took a somewhat cynical view of
matters. He reminded Guy a little of Norton Randolph.

Guy went to church, the first Sunday, and found
a few of the faces he remembered. The church itself was more out of repair than of yore; but the
outside had a new coat of lilac paint. He noticed
the plaster dropping from the ceiling in some places.
The service was quite different from that of old Dr.
Grimstone. It began with a quartet, adapted from
the famous sextet in "Rigoletto;" a fine piece of
music, but not well rendered. Then Rev. M. Frank
Hanna rose, in a tight walking-coat and wispy black
tie, and addressed, in confidential tones, a somewhat
indefinite Deity. This was the prayer.

Mr. Hanna then read a passage from Max Müller's
version of one of the Vedás, and the choir joined in
a hymn. There was a cheerful rhythm to this, which
reminded Guy irresistibly of a college chorus. After it, the congregation settled themselves comfortably, but, strange to say, they seemed alert and
interested—almost as if they were at a theatre.
Nothing of the old sleepy boredom was visible.

Mr. Hanna, burying his face in his hands, prayed for
inspiration "to the same Great Spirit who inspired
Shakespeare—to the same mind that breathed in
the brain of Newton—to the same love that pervaded
the heart of George Eliot, of Joan of Arc, of Christ."

Guy's breath was quite taken away at this, which was rapidly succeeded by the following sermon. Reading no text, the minister began by taking his open watch in his hand.

"If there be a God, I give Him thirty seconds to strike me dead.

"If there be a God, I give Him thirty seconds to strike me dead."

"So spake the French atheist. No doubt it was a mad and foolish challenge. Yet, if there had been a God such as the fancy of olden people pictured—a God to love, to hate, to be angry, to be jealous, a Deity revengeful and fond of praise, vain and vainglorious—such a God would have taken him at his word. The Bible says, *I am a jealous God.* The Bible is wrong." And here Mr. Hanna made a pause, which added to the boldness of the assertion. "At least, the scribe who copied the ancient Hebrew writings made a mistake. We should not be fettered too closely by noun and verb. When I find such crude statements as this, I say the Devil's in it. I mean the printer's devil, or copyist. For the only devil is the devil of our own carelessness, our own weakness. The other was a medieval myth.

"And yet, this remark of the Frenchman's was a notable one. As an indication; it struck the modern balance of mind ; that balance of mind which only bigots call disbelief. It was a noteworthy application of inductive reasoning to the misconceptions of established churches. Let us hesitate before we follow all this book has to say. For the Bible is a book, like another—in most parts, better ; in some parts,

worse.   It is, perhaps, founded on many other books.
If it was a revelation of God, it does not follow that
it was the only one. · It was written by men.   Grant
that they were inspired—so was Plato, Shakespeare,
Mahomet, Swedenborg ; so is George Eliot, Longfel-
low, Herbert Spencer.   And Christ was a good man.
Yes—Christ was a better man than Herbert Spencer.
Christ was the most divine form our glorious hu-
manity has yet assumed.   Are we then to follow him
in all things ?   Shall we not render unto Cæsar the
things that are Cæsar's ?   And I say, my friends,
my brethren, my fellow-seekers for God—for who
am I that I should stand above you on this platform
and tell you where to find Him, when every one of
you may learn as well as I ?   My brethren, put
Christ and Herbert Spencer side by side and tell me
which could *teach* the other most ?   If I follow the
one always with my heart, shall I follow him always
with my brain ? "

Mr. Hanna then went on to relate in brief the process of the evolution of the world ; and how the
masses of self-conscious matter that we call brain
had gradually grown and broadened and become
complex, until each was a microcosm of the universe
outside.   Was it not possible that the Bible, or a
greater part of it, was meant for weaker and more
childish minds ?   It was designed by God, no doubt ;
but was it sure that God intended us always to be
satisfied with this primitive statement ?   Might not
the Scriptures be a sort of primer, until we could
read alone ?   Our minds, too, were made by God.
At all events, they evolved from protoplasms under

his superintendence. The real intention of God—if the Almighty could be supposed to have intention—was to make the human mind a higher sort of Bible, and the truer gospel for us modern ladies and gentlemen the writings and expressions of this mind.

Nay, more, it was possible that even some of the morals of the Bible were provisional—a sort of ethical mother's milk, from which we might be weaned. It was obvious that this was the case in some things. Modern experience had found it necessary to supplement the seventh commandment with divorce laws. The provision regarding graven images had become meaningless. Again, the economical doctrines of the New Testament would not hold water at the present day. It was clear they would result in total pauperization. In fact, many forms of private charity are directly opposed to the great law of the survival of the fittest. Many other texts might be cited which required to be taken with a grain of salt. How would they go with the immortal truth that all progress consists in a change from indefinite, incoherent homogeneity to definite, coherent heterogeneity? Love one another, for instance—as a statement of ethical truth, this is bold and crude. We are required by the discoveries of modern thought to love one another only under certain conditions and limitations.

"No," continued Mr. Hanna, "life is a struggle. What we want is adaptation to our environment—which we call *smartness*—and strength. The *smart* man—the acute, ingenious, intellectual Yankee succeeds, and deserves to succeed. In so-called *charity*, we simply bolster up the weak, at the expense of the strong. We discourage true merit. Let them die. It is right and merciful they should. But, my friends,"—and here Mr. Hanna grew eloquent,—"let us remember there is one thing more. Sympathy, sympathy is the bright star of the future that is to render this world a heaven and reconcile us to the thought that there may be no other. Sympathy. Oh, my friends, my dear friends, it was lately my fortune to come from the metropolis in a railroad car behind a man whom former times would have called a felon. He had committed financial irregularities—he was a forger. The gyves were on his wrist, and at his side there sat a myrmidon of the law. Many and severe were the looks that were cast at him askance by the other occupants of the car— deep and rankling, they entered into the sensitive soul of the man before me. Bright sympathy sprang warm in my breast. I thought that, but for my environment, I might have been as he. He, too, may have sought to be strong. As he pressed his burning hand to his fevered brow, I pictured to myself the sweet home fireside for which he had done this thing—the dear wife, the woodbine-covered cottage, the cherubs clustering around the hearth. The tears sprang unbidden to my eyes. I thought how many in the car might merit shame as much as he. I thought of all he had sought to do in the conflict of this world. Ah, my friends, let us be sure that what we call our laws are right, before we condemn with moral obloquy this man. In the struggle for existence, he had failed—let us take warning by him.

But society was the true sinner—not this man. And it was the fault of us around him that he sat where he did that day. We, to-morrow, may be where this man was to-day. Let us remove the temptation for crime, and let us give the criminal our sympathy! Faith, hope, and love—and the greatest of these three is love! We are all equal. There is a cursed aristocracy of virtue as well as one of rank. What is sin? A faulty adaptation to chance environments. O sinner, disdain not the sinner!"

Mr. Hanna's voice here sank into a hoarse, impressive whisper; then he buried his face in his hands, by way of benediction, and the service closed.

Guy was alone that morning, Mrs. Guerndale having been unusually feeble, and, reflecting on a few inconsistencies he thought he had observed in the sermon, he walked slowly from the church into the churchyard across the way.

Here he threw himself on a bank of brown pine-needles near the old oblong tomb, topped with the argent, bend sable of the Guerndale arms. And so, as he sat there, somewhat gloomy, Mr. Bonnymort and Annie passed by; and she, seeing him there alone, and divining his mood, did not stop, but bowed with such sweet courtesy that it seemed to him he saw all the bounds of happiness. So he left the village and the people, and went into the wood, for a long ramble, thinking of her; and there by Weedy Pond he met old Sol, sitting just above the lily-pads, on the sunny side of a rock, and blinking at a turtle on a log.

"Why, Sol—not at church?" cried Guy, gayly.

"Wa-al, no, Mister Gun'l, I ain't."

"Why, how's that, Sol? I thought you were one of the old stand-bys?"

"Wa'al, Gun'l—ye see, I ain't so powerful sot on religion ; but I do like to hear a preacher thet is ; an' when my wife died, I did take a sorter spell o' goin' to meetin'—didn't somehow like to hev the old pew empty, ye know. But I dunno. I sorter get more comfort out o' God's works than I do out o' that there young man. The fact is, when I experience salvation I take it straight. Damned ef I don't. Bonnymort's folks to hum?"

"Yes," said Guy. "I believe they're here for the summer."

"Wanter know," said Sol.

CHAPTER XX.

"Ni aimer ni haïr : c'est la moitié de la sagesse humaine ; ne rien dire et ne rien croire : c'est l'autre moitié. Mais avec quel plaisir on tourne le dos a un monde qui exige une pareille sagesse ! "—Schopenhauer.

I SUPPOSE it must have happened that night of the walk in the forest. The summer was then nearly over ; two months Guy had been in Dale. All his other plans had been given up. None of our enemies deceive us half so perfectly as we deceive ourselves ; many and ingenious were the theories which Guy developed in his letters to Norton Randolph, to explain his long lingering in Dale. Perhaps Guy himself hardly knew why, though he saw Annie Bonnymort so often. But whoso wished to know what thing love was, might have marked him when he met her, and marvelled at the tremor of his eyes. And it befell, this day of the walk in the forest, of which I speak, as often in such cases comes to pass, that their wanderings were much prolonged ; and they came to a rocky hill, rising out of the forest, whence they saw the setting of the sun.

Now Guy had finally bound himself to go to Newport on the day following, which was a Monday, and Miss Bonnymort was to leave on the same day for some autumn visits. And through this last walk

Guy had been oppressed with a sense of incompleteness, as of something left undone ; yet knew he not what it was, nor how best to set himself to work to remedy it. And having been thinking much of this for many days, the approach of the last evening made him curiously anxious to accomplish what thing it was that lacked. Still, beyond a strange yearning that he might be always in her mind after he had left her, he was conscious of no special thing he wished to do. He did not wish to go ; but there was no help for it, for she was going too, and he thought of it not often. He could easily forego her bodily presence ; but her mind to him was a kingdom in which he wished to rule.

Now it happened that, in helping her up the face of the rock (which was smooth and round and mossy and covered with pine-needles), it became necessary for him to give her his hand. This was a situation which he had hitherto evaded ; but to-day it was imperative, for the place was very slippery. Moreover, it was necessary for him to hold her hand in his some moments, and even to impress a firmer pressure on it when they came to places where the rock was steep. All this he did courteously, as became a cavalier, and yet he found the doing of it most uncomfortable. It seemed as if there were some dumb force within him, struggling for utterance, yet elaborately pent back, and this affair of the hands weakened the barriers. Although her hand was very soft, and white, and warm, and far from an unpleasant thing to touch on a cool autumn day, so much so that when he dropped it hastily, as they reached the top, he did so with some reluctance. And there was a dear little wrinkle where the hand bent forward at the wrist.

They sat down upon the crisp, gray moss, and watched the sunset ; that is, Annie did. Guy looked mostly at the ever-varying expression of her lips. Her eyes, too, were deep, and still and soft, like the haze in a distant mountain valley, and the ends of the brown lashes, just where they curled upward, were gilded by the last rays of sunlight. So he looked silently at the sweet face, no longer child, nor yet woman, and saw the sweet white soul that dwelt behind the eyes, living in a light of love and trust, and little wondered at so beautiful a face, moulded by the soul within. Here the eyes turned upon him, clear and frank, and his own fell in much confusion.

"Guy, why are you so strange ? Sometimes I feel as if I scarcely knew you. You are so different from what you used to be. You are so formal, and far off. Not since you first tumbled into my pond——"

"*My* pond !" laughed he.

"*Our* pond," said she. "Not since then have you been as you are now. Dear Guy," she went on, touching his hands earnestly, "please tell me ! Have I offended you ? Is anything wrong ? Have you any troubles ?"

"'Our pond,'" he was thinking. "Ours—"

"Why are you so silent and indifferent ? Do be what you used to be, when we wandered about these old valleys—don't you remember ?—like the babes in the woods, and I used to think you were so brave and manly, because you did not mind snakes and spiders, and——"

"And tumbling into brooks!" laughed he, nervously. "Seriously, Miss B—— Annie, I have not changed since then in many ways. Less than you can imagine——much less than you believe."

Guy paused a moment, and began scratching off the moss with a pointed stone. It was an old flint arrow-head; some Indian had shot it up into the air a century or so before, and it had fallen here. Guy did not notice its shape, but went on, hurriedly, "Do you remember the last day before I went to school?"

"Do I remember? Why of course I remember, Guy," said Annie warmly, somewhat too warmly, he thought, considering the difficulty he found in reminding her of what he meant, and the way the doing of it made his heart beat. "We spent all the day together, finding the places where we kept house among the rocks, and then in the evening I cried because you had to go."

"You asked me never to forget, and I promised that I never would."

"Did you?" said she. "Did I? Yes, I remember —it was up by the big pond in the woods. Well, we have not forgotten, have we, Guy?" she added, laughing. "Let us part so to-day and always be friends just the same."

"Always," he said, and then, in a lower tone, "Always, always—for me."

"How nice it will be to have you in Boston next winter! You must come to our house very often.

See! the sun is setting—oh, look at that long purple cloud drawn like a scarf about the Greylock mountains! Ah, how lovely—" and the dreamy look came once more into her eyes and wound itself into his heart.

So the bright clouds faded and they watched the colors go ; then they looked in one another's eyes. Guy trembled slightly ; but this time bore the look fully, nor ever flinched. Annie was pleased at this, and smiled ; and a star came up in the east over the lower land, and a whippoorwill down in the valley spoke of the night. It was time for them to go ; so they walked home, talking of old sports and scenes, that were to Guy as if they had been always, and yet to him would never more be old. I think Mr. Bonnymort saw them coming slowly over the lawn ; but they said good-by in the old verandah, and Annie looked up to him and said, " So, Guy—we are just as we used to be, are we not? We have always been like a brother and sister, you know——" She stopped, for here Guy bent down and kissed her, and then felt he could not speak again, but broke hastily from her and went out into the evening.

He could bear no four walls that night. The open sky seemed a lodging scarce vast enough for his heart. That was but one throb in the mighty pulse of nature—dear mother nature, based all upon love, love everywhere! love in the stars that looked down upon him from the soft quiet sky ; love in the winds, in the faint sweet noises of the night ; love in and through the whole world. The beauty of the night,

the beauty of thought, of life ; he was part of all,
and they were part of his soul, and Annie's was the
fairest of it all.   His soul and hers were far apart,
yet they were one, sharing in the beauty of all things
that lived.   And all things did live, nothing was
dead ; the smooth broad meadows were alive, and
the dark hills bending to the lighter sky.   Ah, the
fair world !

So he walked dreaming through his favorite path,
and as he came around the brow of some low hill,
there before him lay a sea—a sea of silver mist, and
all the world was silvern, still and silvern ; silvern in
the white light, rimmed with the purple of the hills
and sky ; a deep black-purple where the silver points
of stars shone through.   All below him and around
him lay the moonlit mist, filling all the valley meadows, sifting softly through the little woody hollows,
where great black shapes of trees loomed up, and
higher hills pent up the fleecy cloud, and through it
came the rifts of evening winds.   He knew not why
the tears were in his eyes, but threw himself upon
the last mossy slope below the forest, and murmured
Che è bella, che è bella, in vague memory of some old
Italian rhyme, and lay there while the hours rolled
over his heart, and thought how it was love   .

> " Che primo mosse quelle cose belle."

Slowly his passion throbbed away into sweet calm ;
his happy heart grew silent, and he thought more
soberly of all he had to do, of all that he should be
to win her.   Of her love he had little doubt : her
soul was very love and tenderness ; he must first de-

serve her love, the winning it would be a later thing. And so, with higher vision than he ever felt before, he planned for himself a straight pathway through the world, that he might not be ashamed to lead her with him there.

Then he steeled himself to sober thought, as he fancied, and to common sense. He felt clearly that romance and sentiment were but slight basis for happiness. Yes, he would succeed ; he would do this, and that. He would not speak to her for a long time yet—a year or more. She was but a child ; if, as he hoped, she was fond of him, he ought not to take advantage of her affections ; he should wait until she had seen something of the world. Yet he had kissed her ! His heart cried " Ah, Annie, Annie——"

Grave Guy ! Sober, thoughtful Guy ! His sober thoughts took no note of time, nor did his mature consideration show him where he was, and the short night went by, and a ray of dawn came through the wood and fell upon his face, lying fast asleep beneath an oak.

Book Third.

CHAPTER XXI.

"So, since the world has thus far whirled
Without change of direction,
Like Buddha I'll sit in the sky
And think on my perfection."

A YEAR passed by. Norton Randolph was abroad, whence he wrote frequently to urge Guy to join him. Vansittart was prominent in New York and Newport. Bixby was believed to be lying *perdu* in Paris. Others said he was travelling about the Continent in chase of some female *feu-follet*. Strang was studying civil engineering in Boston, and, to Guy's surprise, asked the latter to take rooms with him, which he did, and they got along surprisingly well together. Brattle, after a brief tour abroad, had returned with a large consignment of London clothing and Vienna meerschaum, and was leading that group of callow youth which in most American cities constitutes society. Philip Symonds was in Paris, and Guy felt very lonely without his old friend. Phil's great hearty laugh, his healthy view of things in general, had grown to hold a large place in Guy's life ; indeed he had been used to supplying any deficiency in his own animal spirits from Phil's superabundance.

However, if Philip wrote but seldom, great reports of his doings in Paris were brought home by other men ; and it was generally understood that this young descendant of the Puritans was making it uncommonly lively on the Boulevards.

Guy had worked through that year with an intensity of purpose that was too real for him to be very conscious of it. He had occasionally seen Annie Bonnymort, but he had not allowed himself to utter a word of love to her, scarcely even to think of her as the woman he loved, though he thought of her always. It would not be fair to take advantage of her youth and inexperience of men and the world ; besides, he must wait until he had at least shown that he might prove worthy of her. So, if many flowers were sent to her, it was not from Guy ; if any one man danced many cotillions with her, it was not he ; if any one talked sentiment with her (though it was not an easy thing to do, she seeming above and beyond "flirtation"), Guy did not. His manner toward her was indeed marked and different from his manner with others ; for it was frank and simple almost to bluntness. He told her his deepest thoughts with those which were half in earnest, and showed her his weakest with his strongest side ; nor ever sought to flatter her or to impress her with his own merit. But, had she demanded it, he would have shown his soul to her as calmly as his photograph. For, he felt, if there were things in his heart or mind to render him unworthy of her, it would be false to hide

9

them. She should love him as he truly was, or not at all. So he only veiled his love from her. Perhaps in doing this, he veiled the larger part of himself.

With Philip, however, he could freely talk, sure of his hearty sympathy and strong encouragement. The year before, when Philip went away, they sat through many a long evening. And so, speaking of their old school days, and quiet Dale, and Annie, what more easy than to pour his fears and hopes in Philip's friendly ears? Indeed, he told him everything—as he had told him all from childhood up—and Phil had laughed good-humoredly at his earnestness, and advised him to "go in and win, old boy." And Guy looked at his lusty hero, and thought how often Phil had stood by him and what a fine fellow he was, and wished he could be like him, to win Annie's love. Then Phil had gone to England, and Guy had not liked to put his thoughts on paper, even to Philip ; so nothing had been said between them since.

Annie also went away this summer, and Guy did not see her for many months ; but now and then a white letter came, in firm, fine hand-writing, that Guy read oftener, I fear, than even the books on geology he used that summer with his scientific exploring party in Western Virginia.

Randolph returned from Europe in September ; so it happened that Guy made him a visit in Newport when he came back from the South. And one autumn afternoon Randolph, with the clear fair face, drooping moustache, and slight habitual smile, and Guy, with bronzed checks and a big brown beard, were seated in a two-wheeled cart, taking the four o'clock drive on Bellevue Avenue. Guy had just arrived, and Randolph was very glad to see him, though he greeted him with his suave, matter-of-course manner, as if they had parted yesterday. Naturally, they had much to talk about, and where, better than bowling along amid green lanes and flowers with a prospect of the sea (and a cigar) in the distance?

"So, Guy, you never came abroad?"

"Oh! no. I had no time. I—I should have liked to. Perhaps I shall go to Freiberg, next year."

"I saw a great many of the fellows over there— Brattle, Bixby, Phil Symonds. I believe he sailed for home the other day."

"Did he, really! How jolly! Phil hasn't written for months, and I began to worry about him."

"They say he has been shying the paternal ducats pretty freely about Paris. But, Guy, how you've changed – waked up, braced up! I hope you are not going to become *quorum pars magna* as to these things about you?"

"Ah, Norton! Haven't you got over your dawdling with life yet? I think all we fellows were great fools with our callow cynicism. It was merely an excuse for laziness."

"Ah?"

"I tell you what, old fellow, active life is the thing after all. Even ambition isn't half a bad motive."

"Oh!"

"Where should we have been if our fathers had thought and acted as we pretended to do?"

"Why, in that case our fathers wouldn't have left any children, that's certain," said Randolph. "Our noble selves would still have been in the divine nebula of the possible. But what has happened? Have you experienced religion? Grown avaricious? patriotic? Want to go to Congress?"

"No, none of these. But I have grown older——"

"Reconciled yourself to conventional humbug." Here Mr. Randolph stretched himself lazily out, and went on. "The achievement of immortality, my son, is nothing more than 'Arry's idea of the true way to spend a 'appy life. The man of reason does not desire to project his petty individuality into eternity. He who cries loudest for the perpetuation of his valuable self is not the statesman who fills the books of history, but the Philistine. 'Arry, the Philistine, upon whose tomb one reads 'He was born on such a day; married on such another day So-and-so, daughter of some other duffer, esquire; had children certain other bipeds and died.' Such a man naturally wishes a posthumous identity, because he hasn't sufficient confidence that his soul will wash. But men who have really been something and have reason to look back upon their lives with satisfaction— such men yearn for rest after their labors, for eternal sleep. Naked selfishness—nothing else—is the basis of this desire for immortality. The Philistine cannot bear to think that his dear little *ego*—the one thing in the world about which he is most interested, on which he has expended so much pains—should be annihilated. What does the hero in his strong growth care for immortality? It is only to old women, sipping their tea, that it is the air in which they breathe. What has become of Miss Bonnymort? You tell me nothing of her."

"She has been away some months and I haven't seen her," said Guy quietly. "Where are you going to be this year?"

"Oh, I shall do the domestic a while with my numerous sisters—play the pattern son and heir to my pa and ma—and devote what remains of my strength to resisting their combined efforts to make me commit matrimony."

"Are you never going to marry?"

"Certainly, dear boy. But you see, I am very *difficile*. I expect too much. And a girl of the kind that I want would not be likely to want me."

"Why? You have money enough, position enough——"

"Ah, if that were all. But, you see, my requirements are extravagant. I expect the lady to be both gentle and true, and not a fool."

"I have never yet succeeded in understanding you, Norton," Guy complained, with a laugh.

"Perhaps not, my young violet in the parterres of society. My character has all the obscurity of simplicity."

"As simple as an orchid in a flower-pot, my aged and exotic European."

"I say, young 'un, don't steal my thunder. Don't you know that a cynic is the only person who hates to be imitated? Being by the sad sea waves (which I always thought ought to be mad, insane, idiotic sea waves, for their infernal perseverance in tumb-

ling about and accomplishing nothing), I suppose
I may take a cigar. —— Ah, my boy," and resigning
the reins to Guy, he took the lower seat. "I wish
to live, not as a savage or a misanthrope, but as a
solitary man on the frontiers of society, on the outskirts of the world. Consider the birds; they come
and go and make nests around our habitations; they
are fellow-citizens of our farms and hamlets with us;
but they take their flight in a heaven which is boundless. The hand of God alone gives and measures to
them their daily food; they build their nests in the
heart of the thick bushes, or bury them in the height
of trees. So would I, too, live—hovering around
society, and having always at my back a field of
liberty boundless as the sky!"

"I see," said Guy, "that your acquaintance with
the literature of laziness is as varied as ever."

"Call it not laziness—call it still-life. That is the
artistic thing. Yes, Guy—still-life is the thing. The
Dutch school of life. Occupied most with interiors;
so look out only for dyspepsia. Dutch courage,
Dutch repose. I am growing Dutch in everything—
Dutch in restfulness; Dutch in my taste for damning
the sea which first unsettled men's minds; Dutch in
my taste in women and tobacco; Dutch also in build
—an architecture of the human frame so beautifully
adapted for sitting down, that the divine intention is
obvious. . . . For what after all is action? Action implies will, will implies desire, desire implies
imperfection and want and misery. Quietude is the
thing——"

And Randolph took a long pull at his cigar, for

he used to say that no speech was so important as to justify imperilling the light of one's weed.

"Quietude—go through life like a nun, barring the morals. Keep a good digestion and a hard heart."

"Damn," said Guy.

"I say, speaking of hearts, Newport seems to be very much the sort of place that it was in my youth —admirably calculated for working up the raw material of society into the finished product, giving the most natural girl and the most sensible man the *culte* of ostentation and fashion. Here we learn to take the world at its true value ; our emotional weaknesses are safely crushed. Seriously, I think of establishing a sort of moral sanitarium here for the weak in heart. A grand idea—by Israfel the fiddler ! And here, if I mistake not, comes that blameless lordship, John Canaster !"

"Who's that ?"

"Seventh son of the Duke of Maccaboy. I saw him last as a young calf fresh from Sandhurst—now I find him a beef-à-la-mode at Newport ! to adapt an ingenious metaphor from Heine." And Norton pointed to a burly young Briton with a single eye-glass, robed in a lounging-suit of which it took two to complete the pattern.

"Oh ! the little Englishman. But who's that with him ? Phil ! by Jove !" And Guy slung himself out of the dog-cart before Philip Symonds, resplendent of collar and cravat, somewhat hairier, a little airier, but otherwise much the same as ever.

Randolph joined them more quietly, and the reunion was celebrated by a grand dinner at the little club—Lord John lending lustre to the party, and affording a beautiful subject for the mystifications of Norton Randolph, greatly to Phil's amusement and a little to his horror. For Guy's friend was the least bit overcome by the glamour of the peerage, as became a descendant of John Simmons, of Dale. He might have had no anxiety, however; for his lordship's fear of being taken in was only equalled by the ease with which he fell a victim, and the calm with which he remained one.

Philip was in great spirits that evening, and full of talk of the wine, women, and horses he had met on his travels. Little was said about America, except when he asked Randolph about the budding Boston girls, and promised Canaster to "trot them out," when he went there, for his lordship's gratification. How was Annie Bonnymort coming on? he said to Guy. She had promised to be a devilish pretty girl, he told Canaster; very good points; rather thin, though. Yaas, said Canaster, he had seen Miss B. in London. Nice girl, very; neat little filly. Most women in the States were weak on figure, he was told. "Not so with us, egad! Remember when Lady Constance and Lady Alice Evelyn first used to show! We called 'em Big Beef! Haw, haw! And Boiled Beef!" And Canaster became convulsed with laughter over these amusing epithets. "Now in London, Miss Bonnymort was considered——"

"English ladies have good legs," Randolph broke in bluntly, with a curious expression. Guy looked at him with surprise. "I say they have good legs, but big feet."

"Haw, haw—really now, I don't deny it. But how do you know?" And Lord John rolled in his chair with laughter at his own wit. Randolph suddenly changed his manner to his usual lazy calm. At all events, if his lordship had not seen an offence, the conversation was turned from Miss Bonnymort— much to Guy's relief, Randolph made bold to imagine. He poured out another glass of wine, and hummed carelessly :

> "'Madame alléguera qu'elle monte en berline—
> Que, lorsqu'on voit le pied, la jambe se dévine—'

"Come, Guy—I see Phil is about to induct Lord John into the mysteries of poker. You don't care for that?"

So Guy and Randolph talked cynicism for half an hour as they walked home to his cottage, and then Guy secretly stole down to the cliffs and smoked his bedtime cigar over the salt breath of the breakers. Afar to the south stretched the ashen ocean, and he looked dreamily out to the line of the sea and sky, and wondered where beyond the rim a certain ship might be that was bringing the Bonnymorts home from England.

9*

CHAPTER XXII.

We thaet Maethhilde
Monge gefrugnon :
Wurdon grundlease
Geates frige,
The hī seo sorg-lufu
Slaep calle binom.
Thaes ofercode,
Thisses swa maeg.

That of Maethilde we
May have heard
Were unreasonable
Geat's courtships,
So that from him, hapless love,
All sleep took ;
That he surmounted,
So may I this.

—OLD SAXON POEM.

THE ensuing week was passed by Philip in inducting his British lordship into the mysteries of poker and American society. History does not record the amount of British gold which found its way into the pockets of our genial Yankee during this period ; but it must have been large, for Phil was unusually flush for several months afterward. Lord John was possessed with the idea that every American woman desired to marry him ; a pleasant delusion of which Randolph was considerately slow in disabusing him. The latter ineffable personage derived vast amusement from this and other peculiarities, and was fond of mystifying the stranger in elaborate and ingenious ways. "The great thing," he would say, "with American girls, is to understand that they observe absolutely no conventions, and will stand any amount of knock-down flattery. Their

minds being rude and uncultivated, they can enjoy
but the simplest and crudest forms of attention.
European finesse and English delicacy of persiflage
is quite lost upon them. Their characters being
wild and unformed, they have no notion of the ordinary social trammels and polite observances. My
dear Lord John, you must say anything that comes
into your head, and do anything you like. That will
please them."

Whereupon Randolph would retire into a corner
and chuckle in solitude over the social mishaps
which attended the following his advice.

Fortunately his lordship was quite impervious to
snubs; and his heart was quite safe, being well
wadded with conceit. And if John Canaster returned
safe and unmarried to the maternal bosom of her anxious Grace, it was because he was so convinced that
every one wished to wed him that he feared to ask any
one. The Oolongs of New York have to this day
never forgiven Randolph for persuading him to go to
their dinner in a velveteen shooting-jacket, and it is
currently believed that it was as much owing to the
corrupting counsel of Randolph as to the embold-
ening influence of the wine, that the noble Englishman got into that awkward row for kissing Miss
Pussie Van Dam upon the terrace.

A few days after the evening at the club, Guy grew
nervous at Newport. He felt, as he told Randolph,
a strong desire to be at work again ; so his host com-
passionately suffered him one Monday to take the
afternoon train for Boston, where Phil promised to
meet him in a few days. Guy had a restless fear of

ennui, even for that short journey, and bestowed
himself in his seat well provisioned with novels and
newspapers.   But I doubt if they got much more
attention from him than the scrub-oak woods and
rocky meadows through which the train rushed
northward.   Coming at last to the city, he sent his
luggage in a cab, feeling that he would rather walk.
The evening was crisp and cool, and it was only a
detour of a block or so to go through the street
where the Bonnymorts lived.   The house was lighted;
evidently they were come home.   He could not, of
course, go in, but he lingered around the doorstep a
moment or two, and then walked behind the house
and home by the brink of the river.   There was a
light in the second story room which he knew was
hers.

As he entered his own study he was almost overcome by a cloud of dense tobacco smoke, through
which, when his eyes became accustomed to the
smart, he discerned the figure of John Strang, puffing an enormous meerschaum, from which the cloud
proceeded.   This worthy was sitting in the depths
of an arm-chair, at his elbow a huge jug of beer, and
a table which supported the elbow also ; his fist under his chin, a slipper and an open book on the carpet before him.   He did not see Guy for a minute ;
when he did, it was with a start of surprise.

"Guerndy, my boy, were you ever in love?"

"N–o ; why?"

"I am."

"You ?"

"I."

Guy fell upon a chair, and looked at Strang in amazement.

"Ay—in all the plenitude of youth and strength, in the flush of promise—man that I am—I am in love. I thought I would tell you. You would have found it out anyway. Loss of appetite, general debility, emaciation," and John took a pull at the jug and relapsed into silence.

"You in love? My dear fellow, if there is anything I can do for you, you are sure of my sympathy——"

"Damn your sympathy. Guy, this thing must be studied scientifically, and firmly treated. I have been deriving solace from literature, as you see." And Strang indicated with his foot a volume of Spencer on the ground before him. "Burton, in his Anatomy, says the seat of this disease is in the liver. Randolph's friend, Schopenhauer, says it is the affirmation of the will to live. The great Herbert grounds it on the end of all nature processes—the preservation of life. Anyhow, I have got it."

"What is more," continued Strang meditatively, "I take it most unphilosophically, too. For, granted that the reason of this idiocy on my part be well grounded, why should the phenomena appear only in connection with this particular girl? The ends of nature, obviously, would be as well subserved with one woman as another. But to me the operation of the law is narrowed to this one particular object. All the other women in the world are completely indifferent." And John sighed heavily, and shook a bell at his side. "Mary! Mary!"

"Yes, sir!" And the rapidity of her run up-stairs

was evidence that John's nervous condition had been of some duration.

"Another bottle of beer."

The door closed behind the not particularly neat-handed Phillis, and John relapsed into silence. Guy stared at him helplessly.

"Moreover," broke in John, "there is no satisfactory method of explaining the infernal earnestness of this thing. Spencer would not rank the perpetuation of life as a more important end than the maintenance of it. But with me the maintenance of life is of comparatively slight importance. I do not set about getting my bread and butter with the blind, ungovernable passion that prompts me to send flowers to her. I have been told that I am somewhat lazy in earning my daily bread—even with the added inducement of beer and tobacco. Hang it, Guy, I have the feeling of having lost control of myself. I do not like it. I *will* not be made an ass of. I *will* not get away from myself. She asked me to go and see her this evening, and I am not going for that very reason. Volition is liberty." And John recurred to his beer.

"May I ask who —— "

"What's the use? you'll find out soon enough."

"When did you meet her?"

"Last Tuesday."

"Is she clever?"

"Don't know."

"Pretty?"

"Don't know."

"Rich? "

"Don't care."

"When *do* you mean to see her?"

"When I've trained myself so that I don't care whether I see her or not."

Guy smiled, and John continued to puff savagely. "I saw Phil at Newport, John. He looks handsomer than ever, and is coming back to Boston this winter. And you ought to see Randolph again! He is the same gentle old cynic that he always was, only mellowed a little, and I think——"

"What time is it, Guy?"

"Eight, or a little after, I believe," said Guy. "Why?"

"I think I'll go round there after all. It's not too late, is it?"

"Round where?"

"To see that—that girl I spoke of. I think it might be rude if I didn't go."

Guy gave one of his fresh laughs, brought from the mountains of Virginia. "And how about independence and that sort of thing?"

"I have been thinking of that, and it seems to me that if she can control me, there is only one way for me to regain my authority over myself; and that is, to control her."

"And how do you mean to do that?"

"I'll marry her," said John.

CHAPTER XXIII

GUY did not sleep very well that night. He was nervous and excited ; and, in some way, the light that streamed from the two windows beneath which he had been, came stealing over the river to fall into his own dark room. To-morrow evening he should see her ; would to-morrow ever come ? He tried to think of other things—of Newport, of Randolph, of Phil. Dear old Philip ! He would wish him success, Guy knew. And lazy, jolly, placid Randolph—how little he knew the reason of his change, and what lay at the base of all Guy's energy. Ah, well. Perhaps Randolph would not think even this reason enough.

However, work must not suffer ; so Guy rose as usual and went to his school. The lectures were rather prosy that morning ; and when he finally found himself alone, he set to work on some geological report. But his thoughts did not flow so freely as usual ; not even when he wrote the name *Annie Bonnymort* at the top of the blank page. This had been his habit, for some months, when the movements of the heart

deranged the working of his intellect ; but to-day
he could not so drive her from his mind. How
would she seem that night ? How would she greet
him ? When he met her, would she be at all embarrassed ? Her letters had been natural enough, but
it is easy to avoid embarrassment on paper. Could
he still call her by her first name ? He doubted ;
certainly, it would not be easy for him. "Always
the same ;" yes, he would never forget. Always the
same, at the very least. . . . When did he first begin to love her? He could not remember. He had
thought it was that last day of the walk in the
woods in Dale, but he saw now that this was only
the time when he first became conscious of it. Was
it when he first met her, after so many years, the
summer he left college ? No ; it must have been
before that, long before that ; before he went to college, perhaps even before he went to school. Was
it not for some such reason that he first persuaded
his mother to let him go to school ? Yet could he
really have been in love at the tender age of ten ?
He smiled to himself at the thought, but smiled seriously.

He did not mean, that evening, to ask her to marry
him. No, he must try a long time to win her, and yet
a longer time to be worthy of her. But at least he
might now begin trying to make her love him. There
was no longer any need for guarding the secret from
her so sacredly. She might begin to be conscious
of his love, even if years passed before he told her
it was the one thought of his life. How sacred,
sweet, serious, it all seemed—so different from the

'triviality and silliness of courtship as it is drawn in novels; still more so from such love-making as was talked of by Philip and his English friend.

At eight, after an hour of anxious preparation, and not much dinner, he presented himself at the Bonnymorts. Yes; Miss Bonnymort was in, and would see him. As he entered, she rose with her happy smile, and pressed his hand unaffectedly as he sat down beside her. Her father, too, greeted him most cordially, and had a providential engagement for the evening; leaving, as he kindly said, the two young people to themselves. "And be sure you don't go till I come back, sir!" he said. Guy took his seat again with a flutter of expectation. But did two hours ever pass more quickly? And with so little said of what he wished to say. He felt nervously that the moments were flying by, and that, perhaps, he had best tell her that evening; but it seemed to him when he rose to go that they had been like children together: he might have been a boy in Dale, and she a little girl with heart bent on ferns and flowers, instead of a man and woman in evening dress, meeting in a city drawing-room. They talked, as usual, much of Philip, and Annie said, with a little playful petulance, that he had not been to see her. As Guy walked home, he thought with much satisfaction that Mr. Bonnymort was a man of the world, and must have meant the encouragement he had given him. How gracious she had been, and yet how sweet and natural! Was there ever any one who walked so like a *grande dame*, and bore her small head so regally, who had yet such soft eyes as Annie?

All that was bad and weak in him seemed to sink before them, to fade in their light. How right he was in loving her!

So Guy was thinking as he opened the door of his parlor; but, as he turned the knob, he shrank back, abashed to find himself in such a blaze of light. There were Philip and Lord John Canaster and half a dozen other men having high supper. John Strang had relinquished his accustomed easy-chair to his distinguished guest; but he sat in a corner puffing the usual pipe, and was evidently "taking in" his lordship with a lively interest and admiration. Lord John was quite the centre of the circle, and, being in a genial and unbending mood, was telling stories admirably calculated to bring a blush to the cheek of the least fastidious. Phil was in more than usually good voice and laugh, fresh from cricket in the country and still flushed, having ridden in to dinner. Randolph, he said, was coming up to-morrow, and would probably be at Miss Bonnymort's "coming-out" ball the next evening. "You know, Canaster," he said; "the little girl we were talking about at Newport the other day." Yes, Canaster remembered. "What a devilish cranky fellow that Randolph is, though! By Jove, you can't make out whether he is chaffing a fellow or not."

"Randolph is an ass," said Phil, jovially. "But I tell you what, John, old man, now you must see some of our Boston girls. Lord knows, I'm tired enough of 'em myself, but they may amuse a stranger."

"Speaking of girls," said Tom Brattle, "have you heard the story they tell about Mrs. Bill Willing?"

"Mrs. Bill Willing," said Phil, "is my cousin. Still, no matter; go ahead. Fair game."

"Don't let a little matter of family trees stand in the way of a good story!" laughed Lord John.

"Certainly not," said Tom. "Well, you see, Bill returned from Colorado one evening, and found his wife had gone to a party; so what does he do but pop on his dress clothes and follow her. It was in Washington, at a ball given by the Mexican Minister. And there he finds Mrs. Bill alone in the conservatory, her partner gone for an ice or something, and she was waiting for him; so he thinks it would be no end of a joke to steal up behind her, and kiss her and make her scream. So he up and did it."

"Well, is that all?"

"Don't see the point, if he did make her scream."

"Low kind of humor, practical joking."

"But," said Brattle, relapsing into a laugh, "the point is just that he didn't make her scream! Bill kissed her, and Mrs. W. looked around, and saw her husband. *Then* she screamed!"

"Speaking of the Willings," said Phil, after a roar of laughter, "Bill's sister reminds me of that little Bec-de-gaz, as the men used to call her in Paris. Do you remember what eyes she had? And, gad, John, that night when you and Bixby and I had that supper at the Café Américain? By Jove, how——"

"Oh, hang it, Phil, give us a song, and don't let's have post-mortems of past dinners. It makes me melancholy—dyspeptic, in fact. Besides, I hate to talk about girls; it's bad enough to have to talk to them. Why, Mr. Strang, that man's success

among the—er-coryphées and things, in Paris, you
know, was amazing. As to society, I can't judge
over here. But I've no doubt he's equally irresistible."

"Well, the fact is," said Phil modestly, " I've usu.
ally found that what goes down with one kind goes
down with the other—properly veiled, you know,
and all that sort of thing. There ain't so much difference after all. Women are very much alike."

Phil's voice was very rich and fine ; and he sang
his songs with a masculine voice that was irresistible.
Then he drifted off into a lot of French couplets,
with a *Tzing*-la-la ! *Tzing*-la-la ! catch and snap ;
while the other men drank and told stories, and told
stories and drank, and smoked between times.
Strang, I think, did not admire Phil as much as the
rest of us did, and he grew visibly impatient under
the long evening. Finally, when Phil insisted on his
bringing out the card-table, he left Guy to play the
host and went to bed. Guy had been silent and
distrait all the evening ; and now he felt a sudden
anger, a want of sympathy with their moods and
minds. He wondered if Phil thought ever of the
room and presence he had just left. He had warmly
defended his friend to her, that night ; but now he
could not help wishing he would be a little different.

About midnight there was a gentle knock at the
door, and Randolph stood on the threshold, well
dressed, in a loose travelling suit, with a thin umbrella. Randolph had plenty of luggage, but he
never troubled himself with a hand-bag, or carried
anything more than a light stick or umbrella in his
hand.

"You fellows seem to be burning considerable of the candle off at the other end," he said, quietly. "You look like the latter end of a misspent life, already. Guy, my boy, I want a bed. I do not wish to burst too suddenly upon the domestic hearth. Meantime, shall I take a hand? Whist is the best game, though. Philip, do you know why they had just eight people in the Ark? It was to make two tables for whist. Guy, go to bed. You look tired."

After some excuses, Guy was persuaded. Phil and the bluff Englishman showed no signs of fatigue; and while Tom Brattle dozed peacefully on a lounge, the others sat and played. Although Randolph had been in the cars all day, he played a beautiful game; and when they stopped, his pale face shone serene and victorious over the tobacco-mists of the battle-field and a smell of brandy. Guy, in the next room, was asleep and dreaming.

CHAPTER XXIV.

" And I've a Lady—
                —I would put
My cheek beneath that Lady's foot,
Rather than trample under mine
The laurels of the Florentine.
So is my spirit, as flesh with sin,
Filled full, eaten out and in,
With the face of her, the eyes of her,
The lips and little chin, the stir
Of shadow round her mouth ; and she—
I'll tell you—calmly would decree
That I should roast at a slow fire,
If that would compass her desire
And make her one whom they invite
To the famous ball to-morrow night."—R. BROWNING.

"HELLO, John, good morning! Haven't seen you since you got sober!"

"Now look here," said John, as he came striding into the study, rosy with ten hours' sleep and keen for breakfast, "I am not straight-laced, nor unduly prejudiced. But if this retired and modest bachelor's apartment is to be turned into a nocturnal gambling-hell, and blinded and shuttered in the daytime to preserve the noonday slumbers of exhausted debauchees, I——"

"Rise above your predilections, John, and do not get excited before breakfast—or after, either. Take a little seltzer, mitigated with brandy.

'Oft have we seen him, at the break of day,
  Wash with cold seltzer the cobwebs away,
  That cloyed his throat from yester-e'en's carouse.'

Guy, sweet youth, thy eyes do but mislead the morn.
Send for some more coffee and a cigarette, if you
have got one. I made a lot of money for you last
night, and all I crave in return is board and lodging. My family don't know I'm in town. To-day
is Sunday; when I feel able to bear the splendor of
their company, I may venture out. Possibly by
Tuesday or thereabouts. Meantime, I have been to
early service at a little ritualistic chapel I discovered
near by, where they haven't half a bad idea of in-
toning——"

"From cards to church, from church to cynic
sneers," sighed Guy. "You really ought not to mix
things up so, old man. It is so hard to think you
are in earnest in anything," he added, pathetically.

"Is it, really! By Jove!" laughed Randolph.
"Well, there are your ill-gotten gains!" pointing
to a heap of notes on the table.

"Which of course I shall not take," said Guy.

"Well, give them to the poor of the ward, for all
I care—or to Harvard College. Ha! where's John
Strang!"

"John is off his feed," laughed Guy.

"In love?"

"He won't mind my telling you, if he is."

"What, that man of success—that hero for a Sunday-school biography—that walking epitome of the
development of the natural resources of the country?
Well, I shall be delighted to see the comedy. He

must be more fun than Falstaff. How is she—fascinating and false, or true and common-place ? Those are the only two varieties I know. Has he any chance of success ? Strang is not a rich man."

" Come, Norton, you don't think girls nowadays marry for money ?"

" No; I don't think they do. Oh, no. They marry for love. But they are uncommonly apt to fall in love with a rich man. Hallo, Strang!" he cried, as that worthy entered. " Is this true I hear about you and Miss —— ? "

John looked up with a feeble pretence of laughing it off ; but his eyes fell, and he tumbled crestfallen into a chair.

" Oh that men should put things in their hearts to filch their brains away !" sighed Randolph. " Why, John, I have known you a right merry fellow, and as ready with a kiss or a blow as any in all New England ! "

" Norton—you will not talk of it, I know ; and I want your advice. From Guy, here, I have no secrets."

" Well, fire away, John. Alas !" groaned Randolph, comically, " how true it is, that in the stream of life, when the iron pot meets the earthenware feminine jar, it is not the delicate vase, but the hardy pot, that bursts a hole in its side and sinks to the bottom ! Who is she ?"

" It is quite unnecessary," said John, " for you to know that. Suffice it to say that I am, if you will for once excuse profanity, in a hell of a fix."

" My poor Strephon," replied Randolph sympa-

10

thetically, "this world *is* hell—only we do not know it. And the hell of it is that we do *not* know it. Well, first, and most important : of course, you must never let the lady *know* you care for her."

"The devil!" cried John, "I almost told her that the first day I knew it myself!"

"If you had, it would have been all up with you. At least, it is infinitely more difficult. The hardest way to win a woman's love is by loving her. That, when she mentally casts you up, will be the least of your attractions——"

"I don't see why," broke in John and Guy.

"Of course you don't, my children. But it is true. For, on the one hand, it is hard for a woman to respect a man fool enough to love her ; and, on the other hand, she thinks it no merit in him, as it is a thing which every man ought to do. *Le chemin le plus difficile à un cœur de femme, c'est celui de l'amour— crede experto.* See also Sir John Denham :

> 'He that will win his dame must do
> As Love does when he bends his bow :
> With one hand thrust the lady from,
> And with the other pull her home!'"

"I believe," said John, "you don't know half so much as you pretend to, and are nothing but a walking, chattering farrago of quotations."

"*Il y a dans ce monde si peu de voix, et tant d'échos,* said Goethe. I am one of the echoes."

"But what am I to do?"

"I admit it is very difficult," said Randolph. "Usually a woman knows that a man is in love with her before he knows it himself. Still, do not let her

think your attentions are what the little dears call
'serious.' The longer you keep from proposing, the
more she will respect your self-control and admire
you as something difficult to obtain. As the best
way of flirting with a woman is to make her think
you want to marry her, so the best way to marry a
woman is to make her think you only want to flirt
with her."

"Oh, don't, Norton ; I hate to hear you talk that
way," broke in Guy.

Randolph cast a side glance, and went on.

"Another thing, Strang—do not treat her with too
much respect. It is very true what Phil Symonds
said the other night. Much the same sort of thing
pleases women of the whole world and the half.
Deference is out of date. Reverence makes them
laugh at you. Have free-and-easy manners. Give
them plenty of chaff and bonhomie. Don't be afraid
of squeezing a hand or so when you happen to be
given it. Don't try to touch their hearts, but tickle
their vanity. Make yourself the thing ; they prize
the lover's *ton*, not the lover's tone ; and treat your
special Dulcinea more after Sancho's fashion than
the Don's. As Phil says, a firm hand is the thing,
both for women and horses."

"Phil never talked that way!" said Guy, defending his friend.

"Oh, yes," said Randolph, "Phil is a man of
sense. There is no better training for the game
of women of society than the earnest of the women
Phil met abroad. Another thing, Strang ; if you
have any earnestness, solid worth, and that sort of

thing, be sure you keep it out of sight, for it will frighten the modern maiden as much as a dull sermon. The venerable Lao-Tse, who, as I once before remarked, wrote twelve hundred years before St. Paul and three thousand years before La Rochefoucauld, said that men should seek for light, not glitter. And Goethe made a modern application of the ancient Chinese philosophy, by saying that women liked *Glanz, nicht Licht.* They will love you, or at least pretend to, not for what you are, but for what you seem to be."

Guy got up, and walked nervously up and down the room.

"Yes," Randolph went on, "Women like men of distinction ; but it is for the distinction alone. Thus, a title is always irresistible, if only decently backed up. It is His Excellency, not his excellences, that they adore. And be sure of this : she may fall in love with you, but it will not be because you are worth marrying ; but for some whim of fancy, some caprice, because she thinks another girl wants you ; some vanity, if you are generally considered desirable."

"A fellow who has sisters has no business to talk so !" growled Guy.

"Simmer, my fair idealist, simmer. I don't say these girls don't make very fine wives, like Rip Van Winkle's Dutchwomen, when you do get them. The breed is immensely improved on being domesticated. Then they cease to be girls, and become women ; and before they are caught and securely penned up, it is, perhaps, fair that they should have their fling, and do all the harm they can. When they know good from evil they usually have sense enough to choose the good. To conclude, John, never trust them. Pretend, of course, to put all the confidence in them you like ; but never forget that women have no sense of honor. They may be sweet, fascinating, gentle ; but magnanimity is the man's prerogative. And as to sisters, Guy, it is perhaps because I have them that I know so much more of the female girl than you do. Strong, masculine creatures, like John here, idealize women terribly. It is the man that supplies the romance ; women are intensely practical. They are not half the ethereal creatures you think them ; nor so refined, so pure-minded—— "

Bang ! went the door, as Guy left the room. Randolph laughed softly, and going to the mantel lit a pipe.

"Not half of this I meant for you, John," said he.

But Guy was quite angry with Randolph and, gaining the street, walked rapidly away. It was a crisp October afternoon ; the parks and avenues passed by unheeded, and his stride of four miles an hour soon took him out of the town. As he glanced carelessly down the street, he saw a lady's figure far ahead ; suddenly his eyes fell, and he felt sure it was Annie. He wished to avoid her, and, walking by, found embarrassment in the act of raising his hat, usually a simple thing enough.

Gradually the houses fell away ; then he left the main road for a green lane ; that again for the woods ; and soon he was wandering in the hills. His step grew slower as he picked his way among the trees. They were already half bare; so that the sun's rays slanted far within the wood, and fell warm upon the heaped brown leaves.

Randolph's words faded from his memory, and he thought only of Annie. Ah, if poor Norton had only known a woman like her! Coming out of the woods, he threw himself upon the brow of a hill. It was a wonderful afternoon; the dark sweep of forest lay in a glow of the Indian summer; the sky was a golden blue. Long silken skeins were float-ing in the air, those threads of gossamer that come no whence and go no whither.

Yes, Annie must love him; he had so long and so truly loved her. Such love as his must meet with some return, he thought, unconsciously quoting Brown-ing; else there was no right nor reason in the world. He did think of Dante's line—"Love, which suf-fers no one loved to love not in return." When he came back he propounded this to Randolph.

"Ah," said he, "Dante wrote before modern social refinements. Still, he had been through hell, and ought to know." This remark was made by Ran-dolph, leaning against a door-post at the party that evening.

The party, he said, was much as usual. There was the usual number of simple youths, though con-ceited, and girls, commonplace and undeveloped. He pointed out to Guy the young man of society, at the feet of such young ladies as were most the thing, hastily recognizing or cannily avoiding such as were less favored. Happy fellow! He has risen at ten, dawdled at the club, called on his particular female friends of the day ; now he has come from a dinner, and, retiring to rest, will consider the day well spent according to the number of invitations he has received or the favors accorded him in the cotillon. Mild and humanized is this modern Don Juan ; little hurtful to women, more to men, most of all to himself. Here you might see the maiden of the same order ; too frivolous for friendship, scornful of the follies of love, nurtured solely on admiration, she gauges men by the ease with which they talk small-talk and the demand made upon them for dinners and coaching parties. She regards marriage, except under particularly brilliant circumstances, as an eclipse—a sort of drear necessity. But at the same time she likes to have men in love with her, though it is a passion she cannot understand. By a wise provision of nature, she is not of a calibre to break many hearts ; and when she is married she will try to make her married life as much like her single life as she can—in all respects.

Here, again, you might see the gay young man of business, greeting the ladies he knows with jolly familiarity and good fellowship. He is bright ; but his time is too much occupied for more than parties, chaff, and club gossip ; he has plenty of " go " and snap in society, and is known down town as a " pushing young fellow." He reads newspapers, not books ; knows everybody "in society ;" and is liked by " the girls " far more than this other young man, who is critical with culture, and serious with thought, and quite snubbed in a ball-room.

There you might see the young married belle,

more successful than the débutante, happy with six bouquets and the prospect of a late supper, affecting, with rude half-imitation, the immorality of older and more corrupt societies. Not that there is any real crime—oh, no, we are too weak for that. See, she is angry now ; she sees her bosom friend with a new set of diamonds, and will revenge herself by flirting with the husband and giver thereof.

And here, Randolph might have added, is a young lady, with beauty and intelligence and education and purity and gentle breeding as never elsewhere in the world before America gave her birth. And there a young salesman, or physician, mayhap, as wise as Galen, as pure as a woman, as chivalrous as a Bayard ; and withal, this modest young citizen of a Republic, all apothecary that he is, or tradesman, is as true a gentleman as you shall find elsewhere in the world. And here is Guyon Guerndale ; and, if you follow his eye, you will see Annie Bonnymort.

A number of men are about her, all adoring her, Guy fears. He is an imaginative fellow ; but it is quite beyond the power of his imagination to picture a man who knows Annie and is not in love with her. After all, how can he, among so many, be the one to win her ? It gives him no claim that he would and will live and die for her. Any one would do that, he thinks. So he goes up to her timidly, and is rewarded by a pressure of the hand when she leaves with her partner for the cotillon. "See, are not these roses lovely ? " she says, showing him a great scarlet mass ; and then she takes one of them and puts it in his coat—one of his own roses ; for Guy had sent to Virginia for them the day before. "She must know who sent them," Guy thinks, "for there was no card with them, and she would not have worn them if she had not guessed." She had helped to make this intimacy between them ; and now all he had to do was to turn her old friendship into love. So Guy goes up to Randolph, who is still leaning against the wall, pulling his slender, fair moustache ; so radiant that Randolph smiles to see him.

"Well, Don Quixote, have you conquered an enchanted island, or what ?"

Guy can afford to laugh, to-night, at his old friend's cynicism. "You are the Don Quixote, old fellow, leaning on a shivered lance, and looking uselessly on. Can no one here tempt you to break a lance yourself ?"

"Oh dear, oh dear !" muttered Randolph. "My young Don, remember the words of the old Don, grown old and dying—'You'll find no new bird in any last year's nest.'"

Guy looked at Randolph rather vaguely. "Try and fall in love, Norton," said he.

"Odzooks, youngster ! *Quien se casa per amores ha de vivir con dolores*—he who houses himself with love will have trouble for a housemate. But you are young yet—you'll get over it. Aha ! that merry fellow, Strang. Prithee, sweet wag, an it like thee, a cup of sack were no bad thing ! Go to ! Let us to the supper room." And he dragged Guy with him into the anteroom, among a group of men, where Phil Symonds was prominent, drinking champagne and condemning its quality, while Phil himself told

10*

stories. Randolph turned around for Strang, but he had vanished; and they stood at the door of the ball-room, looking on. The floor was crowded with dancers, some solemn of countenance, others laughing; some flushed with excitement, others pale. The less splendid members of society stood at the doors and looked on enviously. There was a harsh chatter of many voices, broken by the blare of a cornet. The air was hot and intensely close, heavy with a smell of supper and wax and lights. Little scraps of lace and tulle littered the floor, and were whirled about in the vortex of the dancers, like autumn leaves.

"Tattersall's!" growled Randolph. "Guy, don't forget the moribund Don's discovery, and seek for the birds of this year in the nests of the last. Ah, who is that bucolic young creature leaning on the arm of Lord John, and looking for all the world as if he interested her?"

"Don't you know her? Miss Kitty Cotton. She's a bud. Isn't she pretty, with her bright rosy face? She always reminds me of Maud Müller."

"Yes," grinned Randolph, looking at Lord John, "Maud Müller, with a rake. I hate to think of that gross fellow rumbling through the maiden med-itations of our fancy free. He judges Miss Cotton, now, as he would a horse. Still, she looks pleased. Perhaps she is willing to have him take her at his own valuation. Tattersall's, again. Ah, there goes your friend Symonds; dancing with Miss Bonny-mort I see."

"Yes," said Guy. "Just like Phil; he hates society; but this is her first party, and he wants it to be pleasant for her. He is her cousin, you know. So he is introducing all the best men to her, and dancing the cotillon with her himself."

"She ought to enjoy herself, I'm sure," Randolph replied, gravely. "You know her very well, don't you?"

"Yes," said Guy, and felt himself blushing, and was angry with himself for it.

"Miss Bonnymort is a very charming young lady."

Guy said nothing.

"Hallo," Randolph went on, in a moment, "look at John Strang! Dancing the german too!"

Sure enough, John was sitting with pretty Miss Kitty Cotton. His elbows were squared upon his hat, and he stared straight forward with an air as if studying a chain of mountains opposite for a practicable opening for a railway. Lord John sat in the row behind, leaning over Miss Cotton's white shoulder, and pouring candied nothings in her ear. On Strang's red face was an expression of blended rage and martyrdom.

"Maud Müller, by Jove!" said Randolph.

Maud Müller it certainly was.

CHAPTER XXV.

"She should never have looked at me
If she meant I should not love her!
There are plenty—men, you call such,
I suppose—she may discover
All her soul to, if she pleases,
And yet leave much as she found them:
But I'm not so, and she knew it,
When she fixed me, glancing round them."—R. BROWNING.

"COME to Europe with me, Guy," said Randolph.

"Oh, no!" said Guy, surprised, "Oh, no. I've got too much to do."

"Bosh!" answered the other, wearily.

This interesting conversation took place one snowy afternoon of that winter. Randolph, ensconced in the sofa in Guy's room, was taking life with the good-natured resignation that was usual with him. He was a most beautiful and artistic loafer, a green oasis in the desert of American social life, as some travelled American, resident in Rome, once said of him. Merely to smoke a cigar with him was almost as good as a day in Naples. He bore about him a mellow atmosphere of intellectual languor that was quite Italian.

"You ought to do something," Guy added, gravely.

"I do. I am a microcosm of the day. I reflect

the manners, customs, and ideas of the time. I can say, like Dobson's sun-dial :

> ' I am a Shade : a Shadow too arte thou ;
> I mark the time ; saye, Gossip, dost thou soe ? '

Bah ! my dear boy, don't blame me. It is the age we live in, as Dante Savage said when blamed with being Agnostic, Ritualist, Comtist, and Pagan, all in one day. Besides, I have a work before me. I think of marching to the relief of Candahar."

Guy looked at Randolph dubiously, uncertain whether he were in earnest or not. For he was quite capable of turning up at Candahar the day after to-morrow, or at any other place.

"America," murmured Randolph, "has had two great missions. Her first, was to liberate the world. Her present one is to vulgarize it. She is now a colossal market. I am not in the market. So, occasionally, I have to fly from America and from other commercial countries, to brush off the dust of business in foreign fields. Now and then, like the raven, I return to look for the first glimpses of civilization above the traffic sea. But I have not yet detected so much as a darned sand-bank. No, it is *not* all affected prejudice. There *is* something narrowing and dark about trade. Anciently, civilization was based on the superiority of one man over another in nobler qualities ; now it is all, who can get the best of the bargain. Now, it is to sell ; formerly it was to excel. Everything nowadays is made to be sold ; just as political economy teaches that all values depend on exchange, not possession. A man has ability, brains—what will it bring? A girl has beauty, purity, refinement—what can she get with them? A man has acquired reputation, honor—what shall be given for them? There was a deeply philosophical youngster down in Maine, to whom his father gave a long lecture on the great value of a good name, acquired by long years of probity and honorable conduct. But when *ought* I to sell it, pa? said he. You know the latest decalogue?

> 'Swear not at all; for of thy curse
> Thine enemy is none the worse:
> Thou shalt not steal; an empty feat,
> When it's so luerative to cheat:
> Thou shalt not covet; but tradition
> Approves all forms of competition!'

Great heavens, my mother wants me to go into business. I don't want to make a fortune any more than I want to go to Congress; and I couldn't do either. Modern trade is simply low competition; vying with Chinese in petty shifts, and Jews in meanness, and Yankees in 'financial irregularities.' If you are sharp and unscrupulous, and popular with vulgar acquaintances, and don't mind lying a good deal, you will get along—perhaps. But you must practise taking advantage of your neighbor; soliciting favors from men you despise; accompanying your Jew correspondents and country customers on low tours of city dissipation. And you must make yourself used to crooked ways of attaining your ends; if you wish your customer to buy one piece of goods, you must make him think you wish to sell him another. Even then, the squarely dishonest man, your competitor, buying on credit, making pretence without capital, who can content himself with a shaving of profit, and does not mean to pay if things go wrong, has an immense advantage over you. Worst of all, you must suit yourself, just as you suit your goods, to the taste of commercial travellers and drummers ; you must tell their stories, and sing their songs— songs like that one Hackett used to sing in college ; and if you wish to retain any part of your gentle self, you must change your manners, tastes, views of life, character, every time you change your coat for dinner, and keep your social life in the evening totally distinct from your business life in the day. That this is impossible, American society is beginning to show."

" You do not mean half of that."

" True, on the other hand, our country (I will not say our civilization) is an immense success. Hog and hominy we can produce in quantities hitherto unknown. And for any one whose wants are limited, metaphorically speaking, by hog and hominy, America is a paradise."

" But the professions are different from the dry goods business——"

" Not a bit. Sharp practice and vulgarity in smaller lumps, that is all. But why, in the name of Lucretius, do you do anything ? The highest aim of life is self-expansion ; assertion of one's essence, as Arnold says. America may be the place for Strang and Symonds, but not for you."

" Because I entirely disagree with you. I believe in America, her civilization, and her future. And I mean to take an active part in it myself."

"Ah, well," said Randolph, relapsing into languor, "pardon my suggestion. When you find yourself ready to adopt it, I will meet you in Florence. Where is John?"

"Calling on Miss Kitty Cotton, I fancy. I wonder if there is any chance of her loving him?"

"Loving? Miss Cotton loving? God bless my soul, Guy, don't use such improper expressions."

Guy laughed. "What new crank have you got now, old fellow?"

"It is very evident, Guy, that you have not felt the refining influence of sisters. Both your mind and your language need chastening. Had you been one of a numerous family, you would have learned that the young ladies of our sort of people may like a man, but never love him. They would shrink from it as improper."

"Correct me as you please!" laughed Guy.

"To put your thought in refined language, such as I hear used by my sisters and their friends, the question is: Will she take him? That will depend upon another question: Can she do better? Now, if you pass John's merits into the personal equation of her mind, you have the exact mathematical probability of her marrying him. The common sense of our fair friends may be trusted implicitly. At least in one respect, we have arrived at the golden age. We might leave our young ladies of society with silken ladders from every window, and not so much as a serenade, far less an elopement, would ensue. Chaperons are now a sort of survival from past conditions. Like the buttons on the tail of a dress-coat, they are merely conventional ornaments or appendages."

"Good Gad!" Randolph went on, sleepily. "Fancy a girl's allowing her heart to fall in love without a warrant duly signed and countersigned from the head! Time enough for her to love after she is married, when she hasn't anything better to do!"

At this juncture a heavy step was heard upon the stairs, stamping louder as it approached; the door was flung open, and John Strang walked in, hurled himself savagely upon a reclining-chair, which crushed under him, and left him prostrate amid the débris, whence he called feebly for beer.

> " ' Why so pale and wan, fond lover?
> Prithee, why so pale?' "

quoted Randolph. "Ah, John—this comes of seeking to perpetuate the universal evil of birth and death. The best gift is a hard heart and a good digestion.

> ' For man may love of possibilité
> A woman so, his hertè may to-brestè
> And she nought love ageyn, but if hire lestè.' "

John gave a grunt of approval.

"How idiotic it is! A man develops his character slowly, acquires his education bit by bit, builds up his strength, and then paf! it is all beside the point; and the sole question is whether the result happens to be pleasing to some chit of a girl. If all that he has made himself does not suit her, let him go hang.

Well, if the assault is to be fatal and final, don't let it come too early."

"Bosh!" said John. "Women are like stinging-nettles. Handle 'em boldly, and they don't hurt."

"Now, with some men I know," Randolph went on, "to be deeply in love is like the state of having committed some disgraceful act. A person who loves sincerely is usually laughed at by the world; and the more earnest he is, the more ridiculous he becomes. He must keep it secret, like shame. His best friends must not know of it; and the stronger and purer it is, the harder it is for him to disguise it, and the more necessary for him to adopt the commonplace and degrading pleasures of those about him. Purity in a man is bad policy; it gives him a reverence for women fatal in love affairs; they like to be treated as a polite man treats a woman of the demi-monde. But tell me, John, since you are bent on continuing the evils of birth, death, sickness, and old age—has your dulcinea the marks of perfection which the divine Buddh tells us they should possess? Are her gait, limbs, and figure perfect? Is she fond of pleasant recreations? Heart virtuously submissive? Handy in female pursuits? No levity? Hating sensuality, anger, and doubt? Ah, me; I fear few of our modern belles would pass the old Hindoo tests."

But John was silent. Either he was provoked at Randolph's raillery, or he regretted his early confidence, and did not wish to talk about his troubles. Instead of replying, he filled his pipe; and his visage grew once more serene under a softening halo of smoke.

"Ah," said Randolph, "that theory that this world

is hell, and we are all the bad people of another world, being punished here for the crimes we committed there, would be a very consoling one if it were true. But conscious existence vibrates like a pendulum between pain and ennui. Why do you lovers seek to perpetuate it? We look in the tumult of this world; we see all men occupied with its torments, uniting all their efforts to satisfy endlessly recurring needs, to preserve themselves from a thousand forms of misery; and we know that they can dare to hope for nothing more than the preservation, for a short time, of the consciousness which makes this suffering possible. And behold! In the middle of the mess we see two lovers making sheeps-eyes at each other. Why do they clothe it in such mystery? Why so shy and shamefaced? Because lovers are traitors. They work in secret to perpetuate a state of affairs which, without their meddling, might come to an end. Now a girl, at least, marries for sensible, solid reasons—money, and position, and so forth."

John feebly kicked his heels against his chair, but Randolph had found a new text, and went on.

"Why, after all, should we blame a girl for being ambitious? Are men, then, totally free from that fault? Most men give their lives to it."

"Men," broke in Guy, "are usually ambitious because they love their wives and children, or wish to win a woman, or have a desire for fame. But they rarely mix ambition with love, and scarce one but would sacrifice ambition for love."

"Doubted. Besides, consider—a woman has only one way of exercising ambition; that is, to make a brilliant marriage. But men have a thousand ways. They have money, power, fame to seek for always; they can be all their lives bettering themselves. A woman can only do so once. After marriage she has no field except a limited social possibility; and even that depends upon the husband she has chosen. It is certainly very unfortunate that this one opportunity of worldly aggrandizement should be found in love, which we like to keep somewhat poetical. It is sad that what to a man is the highest period of his life, when he shows the noblest emotions, should be to a woman the lowest, when she displays the most sordid motives. Undoubtedly in a love affair the man usually appears better than the woman. He is particularly ideal, she uncommonly real. That is why he is the one that is ridiculed. Who ever laughed at the beggar maid for marrying King Cophetua? But how can we blame the dear creatures for using the one chance they have? Besides, it may be the affair of instinct, not of calculation. We learn from St. Herbert Spencer that those creatures survive which have tastes best fitted to their environment, so perhaps we have evolved a breed of girls with hearts only capable of loving eligible men."

Guy was impatiently tapping the window-pane. John smoked grimly. Randolph, though usually a tactful man, went on.

"A philosopher like you, Strang, should learn to take women as they are. I am willing to admit that every girl starts in life with an ideal romantic enough to suit Guy himself. But she soon learns that she cannot realize the ideal; and the next best thing is to idealize the real. And it is easier to get money and position, and idealize upon that foundation, than it is to realize true love and attempt by idealizing to supply money and position. Ah, if it were not for the plain, practical good sense of our American girls what would become of us! Bless the dear creatures—bless them!"

"Oh, stop him, somebody," groaned John, feebly. "Please pass the tobacco-jar, Guy, and ask that sour-minded Cassandra if he will *please* be so kind as to go to the devil—where he belongs."

"My boy, if I only had a devil to go to, I should be perfectly happy. A devil, or a wife, or something of the sort—something to believe in, at all events, whether to cherish or eschew. A dear old Bible verb, that last?"

"Randolph," said Guy earnestly, "do you seriously, at your age of twenty-seven, pretend to disbelieve in all women?"

"How grave we are, all of a sudden! But please don't accuse me of saying things for effect. I may say things half in earnest—but that is quite different. Really, if I could say anything wholly in earnest, I would. But I am more in earnest in my half-earnestness, than that amiable old blatherskite I heard preach last Sunday was in his whole earnestness. As for women, they

'Ever prefer the audacious, the wilful, the vehement hero,
  She has no heart for the timid, the sensitive soul; and for knowledge,—
  Knowledge, O ye Gods!—when did they appreciate knowledge?
  Wherefore should they, either? I am sure I do not desire it.' "

"Well, but answer my question—and stop that drivel of quotation," added Strang.

"Well, O Yankee, well—if I disbelieved in all women, I should be wholly in earnest in saying so; which, from the nature of my character, is impossible. Q. E. D. Seriously, then—Did you ever read, in the *Demi-Monde*, Dumas's allegory of the *pêches à quinze sous?* He says, you go to the market, you find a basket of peaches: they are large, ripe, fresh, fragrant, perfect—one franc apiece. Next to this basket you find another. It contains peaches of the same size, the same appearance, apparently the same freshness and perfection. But you examine each one closely, and you find in each one just something lacking. Here it is a speck; this is a bit hard; another a trifle over-ripe. They are peaches *à quinze sous.*"

"Well?"

"Well. I don't deny that genuine girls still exist. I suppose they still grow, like sound claret and pure Havana tobacco. But they are not found at every dinner party; they are not to be got at each market in Tattersall's. And this is how: the most fatal of gifts for a woman is fascination. If she once gets that, she loses the natural desire for the love of one; she must have the admiration of all; and becomes— not a *pêche à quinze sous*, but a *pêche a quinze francs.* Did you ever go to the exhibition of a horticultural society? There you will find baskets of peaches *à quinze francs.* They are far superior to ordinary peaches; larger, rounder, richer; not a fault in their fragrance, not a blemish in their bloom. There they lie, admired by all that come to the fair, with the steady, lasting blush of beauty, not of modesty. All praise them ; most of us desire them ; few dare touch them; none can afford to buy them. You may look on all sides of them; in their perfection you will find neither speck nor stain. But what is the end of them ? Who knows ? They are peaches *à quinze francs ;* they are *show* peaches, not grown to be eaten. Perhaps some poor fellow has been wretched because he could not get them ; they care little for that, they are there to be admired. So they stay till the end of the fair ; every one has seen and praised them : they are the beauties of the show. But then what becomes of them ? Perhaps some nabob buys them ; perhaps they are musty and have to be thrown away ; perhaps some poor fellow gets them when the fair is ended, esteeming himself very fortunate, and finds them rather flavorless, after all. They have exhaled their fragrance ; their inner sweetness has gone to preserve that velvet bloom you admired in the market last week ; they have been too long in the crowded, perfumed hall. Now the show is over, and perhaps the happy possessor would rather have the ordinary fruit of to-day, fresh from the orchard. See, there they come ; cool and sweet in the basket, and only thirty sous apiece ! For God's sake," Randolph ended, almost fiercely, " beware of peaches *à quinze francs !* "

" Humph ! " said John. " That all ? "

" That is all."

" Well ! "

" Well," said Randolph, languidly, as if ashamed

of his previous heat, " Dumas has warned you against the peaches *à quinze sous—du demi monde.* I warn you against those *à quinze francs—du grand monde.* Selah ! It is spoken."

Guy, all in thinking how different Annie was from the girls Randolph had been describing, saw his motive, and approved it.

" I wonder whether any of the girls we know are *pêches à quinze francs,"* said he.

" Damn it," cried John, "what are you two fellows driving at ? What's the moral of it all ?"

" The moral is, you shouldn't pay over twenty sous for a peach," laughed Guy.

CHAPTER XXVI.

" Je suis pêscheur ; je le sçais bien ; Pourtant Dieu ne veult pas ma mort, Mais convertisse et vive en bien."—VILLON.

GUY often regretted that he saw so little of Philip Symonds in these days. Norton Randolph was all very well, but he missed the genuine, healthy gayety and animal spirits of his dear old friend. And Philip was not living in a way he altogether approved of, Guy would sometimes fear. In some ways he even seemed a little weak. His business of stockbroking was rather a mystery to Guy. He believed it was all right ; many gentlemen he knew were in it, but even the terminology—the puts, calls, margins, bulls, bears, pools, corners—was repulsive to him. It seemed an unhealthy, hazardous sort of thing for a business, and, such as it was, he feared Phil did not stick to it very closely. Guy tried very hard not to have priggish prejudices ; perhaps he recognized wine and cards and fast horses and women as sources of pleasure necessary to some men, and not permanently degrading. Yet he never could joke about them quite so lightly as some of the men he met in New York and Newport used to do. Randolph himself, despite his cynicism, was singularly averse to dissipation.

11

Be not shocked, dear matrons who read these pages; we are beginning to reach the complexities of civilization in America; we are no longer in that curious little Arcadia formerly New England, which perhaps still exists in the imagination of New England women. We are in the world and of it; and if you send your son to Cambridge, New England, it will be like Cambridge, old England, and he will meet all kinds of men, no longer scholars in an academy, to think of vice as something that exists only "across the water." And if Phil Symonds fell easily into the easier path at twenty-five, with fifteen thousand a year, and little or nothing to do, and sought to realize a little Paris of his own in sober Boston, it was not for his companions of his own age to play the parent to him.

Still Guy did not like it. And as much as he could—for, after all, Phil was his old friend and hero, and Guy was a gentleman—he hinted to Phil his disapproval, and Symonds did not like it, and used to snub him, swear at him, or laugh at him, according as they were in a crowd, alone, or with one or two friends. Meantime Guy, being given, heart, soul and imagination, to the love of Annie Bonnymort, and working all he could, and only resting to think about her; and Philip so given to dissipation that, instead of dissipating his energies in various pursuits, he most conscientiously concentrated them all on his pleasures; the moods of the two friends did not harmonize, and they saw little of one another. While Guy was going like a school-boy to his lessons every day, and studying his profession that he might make a fortune for the lady he wished to marry, Philip was the hero and giver of suppers and dinners innumerable, and was spending his fortune, but not on the woman he wished to marry. And withal everybody liked Phil and spoke a good word for him, and half the town called him by his first name. He was a handsome, manly fellow then, with deep blue eyes, and a yellow, military mustache, and a fascinating dash of wild oats about him. Withal, he was the very top of the fashion; young ladies secretly admired him, and told romantic stories about him; mammas thought he had a fine fortune, and it was a pity he did not settle down; and all the masculine world swore he was a damned good fellow; an easy-going, good-hearted fellow, as Randolph would admit. Lord John Canaster had long since left town, with a deep respect for Philip's powers as a poker player; but the genial William Bixby had arrived in a Cunarder in a state of collapse, and, upon being revived at the club, was slowly getting over the effect of ozone, sea-air, and too much sleep, and building up his exhausted constitution on brandy and soda, early morning card parties, and tobacco smoke; and between Bixby and Symonds was a noble emulation. The following summer all Newport was astounded at the pace they made. Polo, anise-bag hunts, were not as yet; but the speed of yachts, and the bouquet of wines, and the points of horses were understood and appreciated even at that early date. And of all these things of mammon, it was a question whether Symonds or Bixby had had the most added unto him; though each would courteously have yielded the *pas* to the other in seeking the kingdom of God.

It is possible to spend a fortune, even in America, though a country properly designed only for making one. And Tom Brattle, who was impecunious, used to complain piteously of the way Phil wasted his. Perhaps it is true that Tom did his little share in the devouring thereof. But Tom's modest needs were so cheaply satisfied, that his frugal stewardship in other directions made his entertainment rather a saving to Phil than otherwise. Give him a berth on Phil's yacht, a handful of Upmann *exquisitos* a day, and a reasonable quantum of fizz (though he honestly preferred gin and ginger-ale), and he was quite content. But it grieved him to the soul to see Philip sling around liquors, and money, and cigars, among the general herd, or lose a thousand dollars a night to Pat Flush, of nobody knew where, when cruising with the New York yacht squadron. For Thomas Brattle was a prudent youth, with old Bay State conservatism, and never " raised" the " limit" under a "full house," aces up.

Thus it happened that Phil's foresail began to shake in the wind a little. For whereas his father had left him a cool three hundred thousand, his trustees wrote him that in future he could not safely spend over seven thousand a year. His mother had been left her bare legal share, under his father's will ; had promptly married again, and was now devoting herself to a second family of children and a High Church chapel. Moreover, Philip Symonds was not a man to take petticoat aid in money matters, as

he thought to himself. Yes, he reflected, as he wandered up Mill Street one evening from his yacht,
Bixby had proved too many for him. Bixby could
stand it.

For Bixby was the offspring of an Americo-Paris-
ian banker, of no particular extraction, who had
meant his sons to dazzle their way into home society.
With that end in view, he had given a long course
of extravagant and somewhat vulgar entertainments
to all Americans of position, who came to Paris, with
the usual result that the invited fellow-citizens
laughed at him, the uninvited yearned for his notice,
and his home compatriots gaped from afar. Norton
Randolph, who had, among other bits of curious
knowledge, some acquaintance with the ancient
Saxon law, applied the name of *snub-wites* to these
rich offerings upon the shrine of society. And Bixby,
père, was snubbed all the same. Now, however,
what the father's wealth failed to achieve, the son's
good fellowship was rapidly accomplishing ; Billy
was decidedly a *lion* in Newport. And poor Philip
could no longer emulate him in the splendor that
gilded his career.

Philip was certainly one of the most popular men
in society, except among his intimate friends ; and
as he walked into the little club that day, scene of
the defeat of John Canaster, *cum proeliis multis aliis*,
the cloud upon his brow drew many a sympathizing
inquiry from his friends gathered about him. Shak-
ing them off with a shower of repartee and chaff,
much as a Newfoundland dog does water, he went
into an anteroom and called for brandy. Philip had

superb physical health, and was proud of it, and had usually too much good sense to play with it, as foolish little Bixby did. So that when he called for brandy at five in the afternoon, I thought something was up; and Norton Randolph and I being there, though he did not like us, he was led to talk, and more or less to confide in us and condemn his lot.

"Yes, by Jove!" he concluded. "I don't see anything left but marriage. I always knew I should come to it some time—in fact it was quite cut and dried for me long ago, by my family. But I did not think it would be so soon."

"Not before you were cut and dry yourself, eh?" said Randolph, smiling.

"Well, we must all come to it some time. Eh, old fellow?" slapping Randolph's shoulder, "with some nice, rich girl, it might not be so bad. *Décidemment, mon cher, je me range.*"

"That is," said Randolph dryly, "having spent your own fortune, you want to spend some nice girl's?"

"Damn it, Norton," replied Phil angrily. "I wouldn't take that from any fellow but you! No—but you see it's the proper thing, I suppose, for a fellow to marry. For instance, I now have ten thousand a year—a married man can live very well on that. But a bachelor can't possibly manage with less than twice as much. Why, hang it all! I couldn't on thirty!"

"Really?" laughed Randolph. "I thought it was the other way."

"Why, no. You see, if a fellow is by himself, I

wants a yacht, and a T cart and pair, and a few saddlers; and then his travelling and dinners, and so forth—flowers he gives girls—poker, and so forth—and—and other things. But of course, if a man is married he does not want a yacht, or flowers, or many horses, or other things."

"True," said Randolph. "I did not think of that."

And then Phil went off elated; and I heard him sowing his new ideas broadcast among the other members of the club. This entire absence of reserve on his part was one of the things that made him so universally popular. Every one believed himself to be his bosom friend.

We sat there in silence, Randolph puffing his cigar. Among the carriages passing through the avenue came Mr. Bonnymort's staid old victoria, with Miss Bonnymort and her maid. She was passing the summer in Newport; but they lived more quietly than most of the people there. I thought she did not look quite happy as she drove by. She cast a hasty, unquiet glance into the club in passing, which was a strange thing for Miss Bonnymort to do. "There goes a very lovely young lady," said Randolph. "Would there were more like her!" The remark was so unlike him, that I looked to see if he were quite serious; but he smoked on, apparently unconscious of my observation. Shortly after this he seemed to become rather blue, and gave short answers to my remarks. Just then Philip Symonds came back, in his usual high spirits again. "By the way, Phil, what do you hear of Guy?" said Randolph.

"Guy? Oh, I haven't heard for——yes, I have, too, though; I had a letter this morning. Gad, I forgot to read it. Grundy's out in Arizona, mulling over mining or something or other." And Phil pulled out a letter, addressed in Guerndale's familiar cacography, and tossed it to Randolph. "Read it aloud, old man," said he, "while I light a pipe." Randolph hesitated for a moment. "Oh, go ahead. We haven't got any secrets."

"'My dear Phil,'" began Randolph. "'I am going to bore you with a line or two; though I fancy you have many things better to do than reading my letters, and probably won't, for a week. However, I am safe in Arizona, which, just now, is a fine country to make you value a whole skin. I have investigated several mines or claims already, but have not found much of anything except fine scenery and sunsets. Perhaps it is lucky I haven't, as a gang of Mexicans and half-breeds dodge about the hills in my vicinity, apparently with the intention of annihilating me when I do. Still, the air is wonderful, and the country lovely; and I enjoy the fresh, out-door life. Lane, who is out here with me, you know, has gone to the fort for reinforcements; meantime, camp is rather lonely, but I maintain a man ought to be able to get along with himself for company.

"'I hear great stories of your success in Newport, as well with men and women as with horses and yachts. Still, I can't say that I envy you. But one thing I do want to say, old fellow; and I want to write this time about you, not myself. I hear you are very free, not to say wildly extravagant, at Newport. Now, Phil, old boy, do brace up. If you knew ' "——

"Oh, damn it all, cut the sermon!" cried Phil. "I know what he's driving at."

Randolph turned the leaf, and went on impassively:

"'By the way, you remember very well what I told you long ago about a certain old friend of ours. Well, I have now a great favor to ask you. They are, as you know, in Newport this summer; and I wish you would write once in a while and tell me something about——' The rest seems to be private," said Randolph, and he handed the letter back to Phil.

Just then we were interrupted by Tom Brattle, who burst into the room, gasping inarticulately:

"Bixby—for God's sake! For God's sake—Billy Bixby!"

"What the"—various expletives—"is the row?" we cried as one man, rising from our seats. But Brattle was choking with excitement and quite speechless. All that we could make out was that we were to get into his carriage and come with him. So we crowded into a lumbering barouche and there gathered from Brattle the whole story. It was serious enough; but I cannot still think of it without laughing.

It seems that William Bixby, though a careless, happy-go-lucky youth, at all times prone to such enjoyment as the good things of this life afford, and only too ready to put his trust in whatever substitute he had for Providence, was yet subject, as was only known to his best friends, to dire attacks of the

11*

blues. No one knew the why or wherefore of this strange caprice of a system far from atrabilious, but his sudden reappearance in America, following on a somewhat erratic European itinerary, had aroused suspicions; and a habit he had of referring in Manfredian tones to "Woman," when in his cups, had led his friends to believe that his blues were engendered of human causes, and that said causes were of the gender feminine. And yesterday, I mean the day before that evening, while on his yacht, and bearing sixty nautical miles or thereabouts southeast-by-east from Block Island (though how the devil did he ever get there, suggested the mariner Brattle, unless he was steering for No-man's-land in the hope of finding no Woman there), in a blue flannel shirt, with the blue sky above him, and the blue sea beneath him, drinking blue ruin with a crew clad in blue, an attack of the blues came on him so far exceeding all other attacks of the blues that not only did he not recover from this attack of the blues on the following day, but, having drunk all the afternoon, and gone on drinking all the evening, over poker with Pat Flush, and continued drinking through the night when at the wheel with the skipper, and started fresh the next morning with his other guests, he sat down again that afternoon to poker with Pat Flush (whose winnings amounted, by that time, to considerably above two thousand dollars) and, growing gloomier, offered said Flush to bet him double or quits that he, William Bixby, would drink a laudanum cocktail then and there, said beverage consisting, as he kindly explained, of equal parts, one

ounce each, of brandy, absinthe, and tincture of
opium, making in all precisely three ounces of po-
table fluid which, however, even Pat Flush's limited
knowledge of materia medica declared to be not
wholesome. And said Flush, being unusually close-
hauled himself, and inclined instinctively to follow
the impulse which led him to see a good bet and
take it, having promptly closed the wager, Bixby,
to his horror, had produced a small tumbler containing the cocktail in question, and, having swallowed
it, became, shortly thereafter, unsociable and inclined
to sleep. And having at that moment Brenton's reef
lightship on the lee bow, with a stiff breeze from the
southeast, Pat Flush, sobered by his scare, went
about and crowded on all sail for Newport harbor,
first detailing two of the crew to walk the deck with
Billy, who, for their pains, regaled them with a
monologue of original profanity which, for ingenuity and variety, has seldom been surpassed, even on
blue water. And finding a head wind up the harbor,
Flush had landed below the steamboat-wharf and
taken Bixby in all haste to the city hospital, regard-
less of the fate of his bet (though he afterward declared that he believed the bet would have been off,
in any event). Here he left Billy in charge of the
resident physician and three guileless young internes
from a neighboring medical school; and going off
to seek Bixby's friends, found us at the club.

When we fairly got at the truth that Bixby had
probably poisoned himself, I do not know what
the other men felt, but I was never more cut up
in my life. Philip nervously asked a great many

questions which Flush, of course, could not answer. Randolph smoked silently all the way, tapping the window-pane. Flush was ghastly pale, and I verily believe would have paid double the bet to see Bixby himself again. It was late in the evening by this time ; Thames Street was almost deserted ; and, as we drove by the docks, we looked out and saw the tracery of Bixby's beautiful yacht against the sky. The master had brought her into the harbor since Flush landed.

"Whom are we to write to ? " said I, " if Billy ——"

"I only know of his father in Paris," answered Phil. " We can telegraph to him."

"Don't say that Bixby committed suicide, if you do," said Randolph.

I shuddered at hearing the name given to it. After this we were silent until the carriage pulled up at a low brick building, with a wide door, which, for some reason, suggested stretchers to my mind, and the carrying them out through it. Flush told us Bixby had been left in charge of the three students and a male attendant, who would do all for him that could be done. It was a long, narrow room, with a row of empty beds down either side ; quite dark, except for a single gas-burner which flared over a group of men in the further corner.

Implements of surgery, hot water, and black bottles were on a table at their side ; and the three medical students and the attendant were all grouped about poor Billy, who was wide awake, smoking a black cigar, and instructing the attendant and the three medical students in the mysteries of unlimited loo.

CHAPTER XXVII.

" As ships, becalmed at eve, that lay
  With canvas drooping, side by side,
Two towers of sail at dawn of day
  Are scarce long leagues apart descried."—CLOUGH.

WHEN the sun rose, one September morning,
and peered over a ridge of the Cordillera
de Rio Gila, in Pima County, Arizona, he was doubtless much surprised at finding Mr. Guyon Guerndale, of Dale, Massachusetts, awake and awaiting
him in the valley beyond. Not, perhaps, so much at
the early hour—for the sun, having summered and
wintered the earth on all sides, must have observed
that white men rise earlier in Arizona than they do
in Belgravia, where, indeed, it is frequently impossible for him to see them through the smoke,—but at
the unexpected presence of any white man at all.
And Guy himself welcomed the sun with a sigh of
relief; and, rolling over upon his side, filled and
lighted a short, clay. pipe. After this, he gave
himself up to the beauties of nature, the pleasures
of memory as personified in Miss Bonnymort, and
the pleasures of hope as embodied in his expectation of seeing her on his return to Boston.

As a miser takes his treasures from his chest, Guy took up in his memory the several hours or minutes he had passed in her company that last year, and turned them over in his mind. It was now two years since he left college; and for one year he had definitely sought to win her love. She seemed very fond of him—only a month before he had had a letter, saying how much she missed him that summer,—and he doubted whether he ought to wait any longer. Why not now tell her of a love which he had long sought to let her see? True, he was not rich; but he had lately had some flattering successes, and with a year or two at Freiberg he felt that he should soon stand high in his profession. . . . It was a curious thing, by the way, that he should have been led to adopt this profession. Mining had once proved the ruin of his family, as in the case of greedy old Guy; and he, this present Guy, hoped to work their restoration to what they had left and the recovery of what they had lost. . . . He took the old jewel, still uncut, out of his locket and looked at it curiously. It seemed dull and pale in the broad daylight. So, for this stone, old Guyon, his ancestor, had lost his life and their fair name. He wondered who it was that first gave credence to that strange old superstition about the ill-luck which would attend the family as long as they retained the diamond. And Guy looked at the locket, with its proud motto, *Seule la mort peut nous vaincre*, and put the stone back in its case, and fell to dreaming.

Dreaming: for his summer's work was done, and well done; and the sun grew warmer, and the morn *ing* was sleepy and hot, and the turbid little rill at his side had a tinkle like the clear brook he remembered in years gone by, falling from the woods behind the old brown house at Dale. . . . What a queer, gloomy child he must have been before he had known Annie! How she had changed him! But since he saw her he had never changed, except, he hoped, to grow more worthy of her. Yes; he had done well so far; the past was past and gone; he would live the old story down, and go out into the world. The fair, broad world was sweet, after all, and a worthy thing it was to succeed in it, though not in the way his poor father had wished. He could never have the faith of a priest; though, with Annie, he could find that faith in mankind and the world which his father had lacked. . . . And he would keep the diamond, and wear it in a ring if he chose. The old tale of ill-luck must have begun in the time of the witches who were hanged at Salem. Or, better still, he would put the stone in a ring and give it to Annie Bonnymort; and so he would lose the diamond when they two were happy together, that the old prophecy might be fulfilled. . . . Yes, he would go back and ask Annie to be his wife. She had now been two years in the world; she had seen enough of other men not to have him fear entrapping her with a childish attachment. But she had known him so long, and he had loved her so dearly; even if she had liked him in a different way, it was for him to say the magic word that might translate her affection into love like his, the love of man for woman. She had seemed to care for him more than ever this past year. Her sweet manner had almost embarrassed him at times; and it had been hard, so hard, for him to keep from throwing himself at her feet and telling her all. His constraint had even been evident, so that she had upbraided him with being cold and forgetting their old promise. Now, thank Heaven, it was all come to an end, and all might at least be frank and open between them—at last, and forever.

Two things yet gave him trouble—the lives of his mother and of his dearest friend. For poor, lonely, widowed Mrs. Guerndale was growing old before her time, and more and more retiring from the world and within herself. Only the past was alive to her; the present was dead, the future did not exist. She barely wrote to Guy now; and he sighed as he thought of her dreary life. Then there was Philip. The dear old fellow! How much, too, he owed to him; how near he was to being perfect! Yet Guy confessed to himself in his reverie what he never would have allowed any one else to say—Philip was weak in certain ways. His very weakness sprang from his virtues, his kindliness, his good-fellowship, his careless generosity. Still, he *ought* to be different. But then, after all, how could he help it? He was so popular with every one, and his friends were not all of the best sort. Guy wished he would write oftener. Still, Phil was never much of a correspondent, from the time he wrote home to Guy, ill at Dale with a fever, that he had "likked Arther Salsberry because he sed you was ded."

Here Guy's morning meditations were interrupted

by Mr. Lefauconeur Lyndhurst Lane, of Boston, who came out of camp in scanty attire for his morning tub, for which necessary ceremony it was his wont to construct an elaborate dam in the nearest little stream to camp.

Faucy Lane, of Guy's class in college, who was now, on account of his supreme amiability, known among the members of the expedition as Fawkes, had been chartered, as he expressed it, by a number of Eastern capitalists to go out and explore a number of mining claims they had purchased. He went in company with a Californian mining expert, and some of the capitalists who knew young Guerndale had engaged him to follow and serve by way of check on the notoriously brilliant imagination of the mining expert in question. Lane knew nothing of mines, but as it was the intention of his uncles to make him treasurer of this one, it was thought advisable that he should see it. This was the last claim they had to examine, and on the morrow they were off for El Paso and civilization.

Guy went on smoking, and did not notice the proceedings of Lane, who, after endeavoring to tub successfully in what he asserted was an extremely muddy stream, began to scrub himself with a highly civilized flesh-brush, much as he might have done in the paternal bath-room. The mining expert, too, whose ablutions were less elaborate, was mysteriously busied in his tent, so that Lane had shouted once or twice before either became aware that his presence was desired. Then Guy hurried to the brook, and found Lane on his hands and knees

quite unclothed, and gazing into a particularly turbid pool which, it was evident, his body had just left.

"Look here!" said he. "I think I've found a
gold mine."

Sure enough, floating in the clayey cloud in the
water were a number of little yellow specks, rapidly
settling; and among the more earthy motes, where
the sunlight shone through it, was the unmistakable
metallic glint of gold.

"You have done it, this time!" laughed Guy.
"Send a gentleman, after all! For no one but a
gentleman of precise habits would have found it necessary to take a tub in the nearest little pool to
camp!"

"All the same," Lane answered, beginning to
wriggle into a shirt, "the water was beastly dirty."

The next day they packed up traps and turned
their faces to the East. The first of October they
were in San Antonio; thence to Galveston, and by
steamer to New Orleans; with a dozen good claims
behind them, and packages of reports and surveys in
their pockets. And as the hills of Arizona and the
sand and cactus of New Mexico gave place to the
parching alkali plains of Texas, and that to the Llano
Estacado, and then pasture-land and prairie, Guy
turned his face to the northeast each morning and
counted how many miles nearer her the past day had
brought him.

CHAPTER XXVIII

* And on his guide suddenly Love's face turned
And in his blind eyes burned
Hard light and heat of laughter ; and like flame
That opens in a mountain's ravening mouth
To blear and sear the sunlight from the south
His mute mouth opened and his first word came :
' Knowest thou me now by name?'"—SWINBURNE.

NEW ORLEANS, with its low, broad streets, running *up* to the river ; its boulevards,. with the little green strips of park in the centre ; its foreign-looking stone houses ; its quaint French markets ; its "shell road," glory of jockeys and languid Creole women ; New Orleans and its delights, after the arid asperities of Arizona, proved too seductive for Lane. And this was the how of it.

Lane, wherever he went, carried the air of Boston about him like a nimbus of east wind. The only concession he was ever known to make to Trans-Carolian habits (it may here be necessary to remind less classical readers that the holy town of Boston a sacred river pours around, yclept the Charles), the only modification this pure Anglo-Saxon ever permitted in his ancient British habits, was the carrying a revolver. For Lane fancied that the average extra-Bostonian American usually began conversation with a pistol-bullet. Now he never would have used his own weapon ; moreover, he never loaded it, and had no cartridges. Upon severe provocation he would have dropped it, and struck from the shoulder in the good old Saxon way. Still, he carried a pistol for the moral effect ; and this, he used to say, was prodigious, especially upon himself.

It so happened, that among the men who most did frequent the rotunda of the St. Charles Hotel, Lane passed for an Englishman. And it was upon a tacit understanding to this effect that he was one day invited to join the company of Southern chivalry who pressed about the bar in the consummation of a standing drink. Lane did not drink ; but he was so considerate a fellow that he would not have made the sign of the cross in hell for fear of injuring the susceptibilities of the devil. So he complied, or was upon the point of complying, when a somewhat drunken fellow, pushing between him and his host, knocked the glass from his hand, with the remark that he, Lane, was a damned Boston Yank. At this point, Lane so far forgot the calm of good-breeding as to " punch " the interlocutor's head.

The other drew a long, curved knife.

Lane promptly covered him with his (moral) revolver, and at once became himself the focus of the revolvers of the rest of the company. Tableau.

It was from this scene that Lane was extricated by Colonel Huger Gayarre, late of the Confederate army, with whom he dined upon the same evening, and with both of whose two daughters, as far as his sense of propriety permitted, he incontinently and impartially fell in love. Thus it happened that Mr. Lefauconeur Lane remained behind in New Orleans, where, as rumor hath it, the course of true love ran pretty smooth.

Wherefore, our hero found himself alone, one evening, smoking his cigar on the stern of a steam-boat, in the broad expanse of Lake Ponchartrain. Far behind him was the faint line of the reedy, fever-haunted shore ; and the wake of the steamer, yellow and blue with phosphorescent flashes, sparkled into more creamy foam in the wave-way of the moon-light.

He was strangely happy that night; so happy that he could not bear to sleep and forget his happiness. And it was lovely, out in the moonlight, above the sound of the water. He had not seen her since June —of course he was thinking of Annie ; whom else should he think of ?—and should he sleep, he could not be sure that he should dream of her. And some-thing in this night reminded him of that night he remembered in Dale, long ago. No, he would not go in. So the silent shores went by ; and the wilder waters of Borgne ; and the moon rose and set, and the dawn came ; and when they came into Mobile, the sun rose, and found him still sitting on the deck, his eyes closed, and a pipe fallen from his lips. The foolish fellow should have taken a fever, but that there is a special providence for lovers.

Then he risked his life upon a decayed ferry-boat, with red-hot, rusty boilers, resting on bricks upon the flat deck, and open to the winds of heaven, save where piled up and walled in with bales of cotton.

Such of the steam from these boilers as did not escape, worked a reluctant stern-wheel, which urged the craft up the long bay to Tensas. Here Guy landed, and found a village—consisting of a wood-shed and a stump—at the end of a railway track. The stump formed the butt-end, being put there to prevent trains from sliding into the river, and, from its appearance, had frequently been "bunted" into.

Alabama. Endless dark forests of tangled growth, with low glades and swamps and underbrush and gloomy recesses, intertwined with long festoons of Spanish moss, now old and brown, clinging to the living trees, feeding on the fallen and dead ones; then uplands, with an occasional farm-house—a lazy, weary country, with the blight of poverty upon it. Mile after mile of peach-orchard, now barren of foliage, with trees stunted and small, though in spring they must have filled the land with fragrance and pink blossoms. At night, supper in a shed by the railway, served by a tall, dark, serious Southerner, who wore a broad hat of white felt, and went gloomily around with trays of fried bacon and corn-cakes. The only light came from a blazing fire of pitch-pine knots, kindled upon the side of a car-wheel, set high upon three posts. Then again, the weary rumble of the cars, while Guy slept restlessly and grew more impatient as they neared the East.

Georgia. Still the peach-orchards; then an occasional town, left desolate by the war; and huge sandy forests of pine. South Carolina—dank woods, swamps, with rice plantations, cotton fields; occasional openings, with old high mansions of palmetto-

wood, falling in decay. Charleston, the city of a
lost cause, half burned and not rebuilt, silent and
still, with the grass growing in the cobble-stones by
the wharves. And so to sea; and he grew more
eager, as they crossed the blue ocean of the Gulf
Stream; then the fury of an autumn gale off Hatteras; at last New York, and Guy found a letter
from Randolph:

"MY DEAR GUY: I am off again. I wish once more to study my
native land from the proper distance, that I may get the perspective
right. Moreover, I want to buy a silk hat in London; when I have
got one, I may return. But I do not think I shall. My mother is too
damned fashionable. She is now engaged in marrying off my sisters; and I cannot breathe in her elevated social atmosphere. Besides, I should be in the way, and should very likely punch the heads
of the pretenders. At present, only two of the latter have been found
who will pass muster. One is a wealthy New York *lion*, descended
on the one side from King Solomon or David, and on the other from
a banking-house in Flanders. The other is Sewell Norton, the little
fool who roomed under me at Cambridge. He has not so much
money, but his great-aunt married my paternal grandfather, and my
mother's second cousin was his grandmother. So, you see, it would
simplify the future ramifications of our family tree. He is not treed
yet, however; and my mother is riled that I did not snail Canaster for
one of the girls. A devil of a way of showing gratitude to him for his
kindness to me in England! Worse than all, Mamma wants to marry
me, and has got hold of some underbred creature in Newport, with a
mine in Nevada. So I escape.

"Guy, I shall expect to see you in Europe, and want you to let
me know when you come—will you? And one thing more—pardon
my ungracious hint; I know he is a friend of yours; but unless you
can improve Symonds, I would not be too thick with him. Good-by.
The usual address, Boulevard St. Germain.

"N. R.

"—— Club, December 2, 187-."

Guy read this letter somewhat impatiently; and
then, crumpling it angrily, he threw it aside. It was

not like Randolph to seek to come between him and
his oldest friend ; what could he mean by it ? For a
moment he was almost offended with him.   However, he had no time to think of Randolph now, or
Philip either, for the earth burned beneath his foot
until he got home. So Randolph was going wandering about the world again ? Poor, idle, unhappy fellow ; he was greatly to be pitied.   Guy hurried to
take the first train, and left the letter unanswered.
He must see Annie ; he could not bear another day's
delay. He must see her, before all else ; before even
he made his report to his employers. If he got
home by six, he might call the same evening. Then
perhaps old Mr. Bonnymort might leave them alone,
as he had done once or twice before ; and then—and
then Guy's heart beat so fast that he could not think
of what would follow.

So Annie, dear Annie, he thought, while the train
rolled rapidly through the clear winter's day, and
the bare, brown New England hills, with their rugged shoulders, came about him—after all, it was a
dear, rough old country, and he envied not Randolph
his life abroad. Now Dale was off in that direction ;
well, he would go there in a day or two. He wondered how she would greet him. How slow the
train was. Then the sun set, and the night gathered around, and he thought only of Annie—ah, if
the train should be too late—and of her only, when
at last they got there, and he drove rapidly through
the streets. He found his rooms empty. Strang was
away ; but he was rather glad of this, so he donned
his evening dress, the first time for nearly a year,

and dined hastily and alone. Seven o'clock—how
early could he call? He decided that a quarter to
eight was the earliest possible hour, and at half after
seven was in the street. He could not have told why
he allowed fifteen minutes, when the walk to her
house took only five. But there he was, and he
could not go in yet. The evening was terribly cold,
with little icy needles in the air, so he walked up and
down the street to keep warm. At last, the third or
fourth time he looked at his watch, it was time to go
in. He felt that his voice was husky, and his pulses
throbbed so that it made him almost giddy to go up
the steps ; but, with a trembling hand, he pulled the
bell.

"Not at home, to-night," said the man, indifferently.

It was like a plunge into ice-water. He thanked
the servant mechanically, and told him he would
leave no card. Then a rush of disappointment came
over him. He tried to laugh it off. How absurd !
What difference did it make whether it was that
night or the next ?

Still he did not quite know what to do. Phil was
away ; Strang was away ; Lane in Louisiana, Randolph in Europe. Where could he go ? There was
no one he thought of but Brattle. Well, he could
not bear to be alone that evening, and Brattle was
better than nobody. So he went to Brattle's house;
there was the same endless smoking and drinking
and gossip, Bixby and a few other men playing
whist. Bixby told a long story, to which Guy did
not pay much attention. However, they seemed glad

12

to see him, and he told them about his life in Arizona, and Lane's gold mine. Brattle seemed very much taken with all this, especially with the story of the discovery of gold. He wished he could strike something of the same sort. Gad, you couldn't do much in that line here, unless you get hold of a rich girl, like Symonds. Who was Symonds going to marry? asked another man.

"What Symonds—not Phil?" cried Guy.

"Why, yes, of course. He is engaged to Miss Bonnymort. Haven't you heard?"

"No," said Guy, calmly. "You see, I have been away almost a year." And, after staying a few moments more, he went out into the night.

CHAPTER XXIX.

"I am he that was thy lord before thy birth ;
I am he that is thy lord till thou turn earth :
I make the night more dark, and all the morrow
Dark as the night whose darkness was my breath :
O fool, my name is sorrow ;
Thou fool, my name is death."

OH, Phil, Phil ! That Philip Symonds could have betrayed him ; of all other men in the world but Philip !

For betrayal it seemed ; Guy did not stop to think whether Phil had remembered or attached much weight to his old confidence.

His oldest friend, the other member of the old trio in their childhood—Philip, who had been, as he thought, courage, and manliness, and frankness and kindness itself ; to whom he had been so loyal, and whom he had thought so true.

Years before he had told his own hopes to his old chum in college, his schoolmate and companion Philip had come between him and Annie, as he had felt, with a child's instinct, that first day when he saw them from the old churchyard in Dale ; and then he had thought only to be a good friend ; to lead him with his careless laugh from that moody loneliness in which he had been sinking as a child; to urge and cheer him through the rough companionship of school and college, to win his trust and love. And then—this.

It was not that he had lost Annie. He could bear that. Of course he had been wild and presumptuous and mad and conceited and a fool to hope to gain her love. He might have known that her kindness was only the warmth of friendship, flowing to him, unworthy, from her kind and gentle heart ; he might have known she was not for him ; the very fact of her always having known him so well made her see his weakness and unworthiness, and the distance there was between them. How could he ever have hoped, still less ventured to ask her to link her bright life with his poor career ?

But to have lost her so ; to have lost his dearest friend, all that remained to him ; with the loss of her, to have lost faith and friendship. Ah, poor, absurd, cynical Norton Randolph, with his whimsical grim moods. Had there been some method in his madness? Some sense in his sermons ?

He was not angry with Philip ; no, he could not be angry with him. It was not the wrong to himself that rankled ; it was that Philip, his last ideal, his first hero, should have been like this ; that Phil *could* have been like this. He felt that he would gladly forgive the wrong if he could have his faith in him restored.

Ah, why had he done it this way ? Why had he not told him—this or anything ? Anything, so that Guy might have saved his one friend and his faith in him. Now, all was gone ; all, all. There was nothing left

him in the world. Nothing, nothing, nothing. There
was nothing worthy in the world save Annie, and
she was lost to him forever.

"Annie !" he sobbed. "O God !" And the young
strong man, with his bronzed face and heavy beard,
walked reeling in the road, repeating the woman's
name over and over again.

He had been chiding for years the folly of invest-
ing our Deity with human attributes, and ascribing
to him pity and sorrow and revenge. He had indig-
nantly denied that the Existence, in and for itself,
could go out from itself, and stoop to change the
course of its own being, at the weak wailing prayer
of some suffering mortal. He had maintained that
birth and death and sorrow and old age were the
steps by which the soul purged itself of itself, and
rose up into the eternal ; and now what comfort in
this fine-spun philosophy ? This calm philosopher
cried to God for aid and sympathy like a child. As a
child he had never so done ; now first as a man his
cold theories gave way, and he cried out in his sorrow, nor once remembered that he had never so
cried before.

Where was he ? he came to himself with a start.
Unwittingly he had wandered over the long bridge.

Above him was a winter sky, blue-black, sown
thick with stars twinkling with coming wind. The
city lay behind him, across the pale still river, painted
with many lights ; in front of him a row of stone
houses, straight and high, cast black bars of shadow
far over the water. Here and there a brighter light
marked some scene of gayety ; in one house the

windows were ablaze, and the light came streaming through the white and red curtains, and a faint sound of music floated over the water. In the back of another house near by, that he well remembered, shone one lighted window. It was her room, he knew. His eyes were still dry, but he leaned his hot head upon his hands, and sobbed once upon the railing of the bridge.

CHAPTER XXX.

GUY was roused by a dash of cold wind upon his face. He looked up and saw the stars on the northern horizon fading in blackness ; a gust came sweeping over the river, with pricking darts of snow, He rose and faced it for a moment ; then looked at his watch. It was after midnight, and, with a firm step, he strode back to his rooms. They were dark, cold, and lonely ; the fire on the hearth was in ashes, and the clock had stopped. He drew out his trunks and began to pack—a gloomy occupation at best. At four in the morning all was done. Where was he going ? He did not know—he cared less. It did not seem to matter much how he used a broken life. What should he do ? What did he wish ? He did not know. Throwing himself on a sofa, he buried his face in his hands. They seemed icy cold as he pressed them to his head.

Yes, he would go to Dale. And so lying, he fell

into a dreamless sleep; and it was morning. A dull morning, with a steel-gray, working-day sky, shrouded in falling snow, which lay in muddy drifts about the street. Outside, muffled men tramped laboriously along, nerving themselves to work with thoughts of home and children. Their duties called them down-town. Guy had no duties, he reflected; and the town was weary. Loneliness he did not mind; for a moment he felt thankful that all his friends were away, and he could go off alone.

The servant entering, brought in his coffee and a telegram. It was from a doctor in Dale, saying that his mother was very ill. He sent for a carriage, and loading it with all his trunks, drove to the station. Stopping at a florist's, he got a basket of red roses and sent them to Annie without a card. She was probably sitting in her warm morning-room then — he wondered whom she was thinking of. Probably of Philip. Ah, how could Phil have deceived him? Had he really meant to do so? And Guy tried hard to imagine himself in his place, and to make excuses for him. Strangely enough, he thought more of him than of Annie, as the train trundled on over the muffled rails. It was storming heavily, and the jangle of the wheels was dulled in a cushion of snow.

The train was nearly empty. It had come into the city with its morning freight of men and school-children, and the cars were hot and close, and the air was sour. The smoking-car was worse: foul with tobacco smoke, like an echo of profanity. He went back and took a seat. In front of him were two

thin, sallow-necked women ; a tawdrily dressed girl
and a commercial traveller were the only other occupants. It was less cheerless to look outside, where
the snow fell thick through the dark green forests
and the empty wooden villages. Evidently the tawdrily dressed girl was seeking to win the attention
of the commercial traveller, and after the first stop
they came back and sat together, eating cream-
cakes.

His feet and hands were cold ; he had forgotten
his gloves, and his fingers were grimed with dust
and cinders. The atmosphere of the car became intolerable. He went out, and, unmolested by the
brakeman, sat upon the rear platform and watched
the storm. The feathery snow-flakes danced after
him in the wake of the train, and their cool touch on
his face gave him a faint sensation of relief. He
drew the old diamond out of his locket and looked
at it long and earnestly. Should he throw it away !
and see if better days would come ? It seemed paler
than ever in the dull light. Should he fling it in the
fast-gathering drifts ? He could not attach much
weight to the old story now. Life was dull and pur-
poseless enough. It was time for him to give up
romance—even the romance of sadness.

He went back into the car. The girl was talking
in a high, flat key, telling her companion that he was
"horrid." From this and other remarks, Guy in-
ferred that the man had kissed her.

Hours went by ; and the same great stretch of
barren country loomed through the windows ; and
Guy looked at the diamond which now could never

12*

be hers. Then he smiled a little contemptuously, and put the diamond back in its case.

No, he would not give it up. After all, there was some virtue in courage. Perhaps it was worth while being brave. Such as it was, he would live his life out, as he had laid it out for himself, fifteen years before. If there was no happiness, there should be no sorrow. Only a dull emptiness of both. There should be no more dreaming.

What was real? These people about him. He looked around and felt a positive hate for them all. What was real to the man? To sell such goods as he had, for such prices as he could get. He was better off, after all, than Guy himself; for Guy did not value the price, and had no goods to sell if he did. The reward he sought was not exchangeable for goods. Did high and pure and lovable things really exist? He supposed they did. Some people must have found them, they were written about so much. But La Rochefoucauld said people wrote much about ghosts, and for that very reason—that no one had ever seen them. He would take Randolph's advice, and not look for the birds of this year in the nests of the last. Bah! what a fool he was to think so much. There was that girl opposite—a ribbon and a cream-cake and the coarse admiration of a man satisfied her. And she would marry and propagate others of her kind.

Well, since gold was all, he could get gold. Doing good was a conventional phrase, and meant nothing. Or, at most, it meant giving to others the gold that one despised one's self, because others could be content with it and the sensual comfort it brought. True, one might relieve positive pain, vulgar want; but what a half-measure was this! At the best only a palliative. To be a clergyman, for instance—that was romanticism of a sort; but how could he do that? Romanticism was done with him. All men were either unhappy or contemptible. All he could do as a father-confessor would be to advise the unhappy people to kill themselves, and for people who pretended to be happy he had no sympathy—rather contempt. True, he himself meant to go through with it all, but it was not a course he could honestly recommend to others, especially such others as suffered from the positive wretchedness of want and squalor.

Yes, he meant to go through with it all. Dissipation was simply repulsive to him; vice was foul and unendurable. Besides it was wrong and cowardly to seek distraction from a noble sorrow, that he might not feel it quite so much. He would ride straight, whatever happened. And so, with still, empty eyes and compressed lips, he alighted at Dale.

He found his mother delirious, and the one old servant moping, drinking tea in a corner. For five weeks he was with her, watching her by night and sleeping in the morning. Only in the long afternoons did he get out and wander through the wet, brown woods. Most of the old nooks he had known were hidden in snow, or bare and unlovely with rotting leaves. The Bonnymort house was closed and boarded up, and he passed long hours wandering through the shrubbery about it. He never went to church, and rarely to the village, and heard through the servant of ill-natured comments of the neighbors, which mattered little to him.

One afternoon he heard the tinkle of the brook behind the house, like a faint voice of spring, and followed it up as he used to do years before, to the little basin where he had first met her. In the shade was a gray shelf of ice, but near the rock was a few feet of open water, and through its black surface he saw the soft, green mosses waving, as if beneath the brook it were still summer ; and, as any country school-boy might do, he took his penknife and cut with labor her initials and his. It seemed as if he must leave some record of his love before it was buried forever. "She will never see it," he muttered, as he went home.

That evening he found a letter from Annie—a sweet, kind letter, sympathizing with him in his mother's illness, and telling him how much she felt for him, even in her present happiness. Each kind word was a stab to him ; but he read it through, and putting it down, thanked Heaven that she at least was left to him, and prayed that Philip, false to him, might be true to her. In the night his mother opened her eyes and spoke "Guy."

"Yes, mother."

"Guy, dear—are you here ?"

'Yes, mother."

"Forgive me, dear."

Guy bent and kissed her.

"Have you got the stone I gave you ?"

"Yes, mother."

"Are you happy?"

"No, mother."

"Neither was your father."

There was a long silence, and when Guy looked at her again her face was no longer so ashy pale as it had been. It even seemed that a faint flush was upon her cheek; and looking at her face more close-ly, he saw that she was dead.

The funeral was quiet, but in deference to custom the house was thrown open, and the neighbors came in rusty black dresses, and talked in half whispers, sitting upright upon horse-hair chairs until the min-ister, in a halting, constrained way, made a long prayer. At the grave Guy wished a part of the ser-vice of the English church, but the minister objected to set prayers. Still, Guy took an old prayer-book with him; and, turning the leaves noticed the book-plate and coat-of-arms, "Godfrey Guerndale—1743," with the motto, "Seule la mort peut nous vaincre."

He left the old servant to live in the house, and went away from Dale.

Book Fourth.

CHAPTER XXXI.

Chiappino.—It seems you never loved me, then?
Eulalia.—   Chiappino!
Ch.—Never?
Eu.—   Never.
Ch.—   That's sad—say what I might
There was no helping being sure this while
You loved me—love like mine must have return,
I thought—no river starts but to some sea :
If I knew any heart, as mine loved you,
Loved me, tho' in the vilest breast 'twere lodged,
I should, I think, be forced to love again—
Else there's no right nor reason in the world !
                              —R. BROWNING.

GUY thought often of Norton Randolph these dark times. He had trusted Philip ; he had half distrusted Norton. But now he felt himself more akin to him than ever. Something about his calm reserve of belief, his flippancy, or what was superficially flippant, seemed natural to him. . . . After all, *nothing too much* was the motto. Serious things were always half ridiculous; there was nothing more foolish than to take the world *au grand serieux.* Everything was half good, half bad ; half true, half false ; half worthy. Life was a compromise ; the times of reality were olden and gone ; it was a world

of *if*, *but*, and *perhaps*. . . . Bah! What was the use
of thinking about it? He had lived too much in
wild country, among animals and plants. Nature
was frank, but mankind was not. . . . There was
only Annie in the world, and of her he might never
think; yet even then her memory seemed to make
things plainer for him. . . . He would live it
through; he would go on as he had planned. Courage—gayety and courage—was the manly part.
Norton was right in taking life with a smile.

And so Philip was lost to him, and Annie, too. If
she were only happy he could bear it. But if it
might have happened in any other way than this!

If only people were frank, it seemed that one
could pardon them everything else. He could not
bear to lose Philip. Philip had been all in all to
him; he had embodied the broad, real life, the
strong stir of blood and animal spirits, for which he
had left his shrinking childhood. Was his old idol
really shattered? Perhaps he had never really
known; perhaps he had forgotten.

These thoughts came to Guy while at breakfast in
a New York hotel. Then the door opened behind
him, and he heard a strong, well-remembered voice.

"Why, Guy, old man, I have found you at last.
Where the deuce have you been keeping yourself?
I heard of your mother's death——" And Philip
was in front of him, holding out his broad, brown
hand.

Guy started up for a moment; and then sank back
in his chair. Phil's face was redder than usual, and
there was a forced *bonhommie*, almost a swagger, in

his manner. His eyes met Guy's only once, and then but for an instant. Guy drew back his hand.

"Philip, have you forgotten what I told you two years ago?"

Phil hesitated a moment. "Why, what ——" he began. Then again his glance met Guy's, and he changed his mind. "Come, come, Guy, don't be a fool. I thought that old moonshine of yours was over, years ago."

"You knew it was not," said Guy, in a low voice. "You might, at least, have told me."

Again Phil hesitated; then, as if in a burst of irritation, "Good God, man, what are you mad about? I cannot imagine."

"It is just because you cannot imagine," said Guy gloomily.

Phil walked to the window, and there was a moment's silence. He came back and took a chair next Guy's. "Come, old fellow, give me your hand, and let bygones be bygones. Don't be so damned cranky. Even if I did know, all's fair in love and war, you know. Hang it, man, don't be a fool. There are plenty other girls in the world as good as Annie Bonnymort——"

"Please don't mention her name here," said Guy gloomily.

"Why, —— —— your cheek," cried Philip, with an oath. "I'll mention her name when and where I like. Who has a right to do so, if I have not?" Philip forced his voice to a cry of indignation as he ended; then rose, and strode angrily across the room. Guy was silent.

"Come, come, old fellow, don't let us go off in this way," Philip said, as he came back. "Where are you going to?"

"Freiberg."

"Well, brace up, and take something to drink with me. There's a good fellow, and don't be angry—— thank God you aren't hooked."

"You really must pardon me," Guy broke in. "I must go down-town—I have an engagement." And Guy rose and left the room, not once looking back.

It is pleasant for none of us to lose the approval of one who has always loved and admired us. Phil was careless in most things, but it sobered even him for a moment. He called for a glass of brandy and soda, and drank it savagely. "Good Lord, who would have thought the poor devil would have been so cut up?"

Philip was furious. Any one who could have seen his expression then, would have wondered at his popularity. His heavy features were not so pleasant to look at when his good-nature was gone. Gradually, however, the stimulant restored his self-esteem; and he rose, content with himself and his actions. "Anyhow, I tried to be friendly with him," he muttered, with a shrug. "It is not my fault."

Good-natured Phil never thought it was his fault, whatever happened; and the world was only too apt to encourage him in this opinion. He was such a good-hearted fellow.

So they parted—Philip pettishly, Guy sadly. He could not piece and patch his old friend together to make him whole again. That day he busied himself about his departure, and in twelve hours the hills of Neversink were fading in the western light.

The steamer rolling heavily, all the other passengers had gone below, and Guy was leaning on the bulwark, over the gray waves. He had always meant to write once to Annie, but had given it up. " So," he whispered, "she will never know. It is better so. She will never know—never know——"

He bent over the stern and looked at the yeasty wake and listened to the murmur of the troubled sea. His head sank, wearily, for a minute ; then he rose and paced the deck. In all his life he would never, voluntarily, think of her again. In that moment he had buried his love for her ; and perhaps, in all his life, he had never loved her so much.

And so, she would never know.

CHAPTER XXXII

"Through many a night toward many a wearier day
   His spirit bore his body down its way.
Through many a day to many a wearier night
   His soul sustained his sorrows in her sight.
And earth was bitter, and heaven, and even the sea
   Sorrowful even as he."—SWINBURNE.

TWO weeks at sea, and a stormy voyage. Scarce
one day of sunshine ; at most a passing gleam
between the billows of white cloud blurred upon a
watery sky. The ocean was angry ; now slate-color,
now olive-green. At night the clouds were blown
away, and left cold spaces in the zenith, where the
stars would come out and blink and tremble in the
storm. The wind kept always in the northwest, and
moved long, steady waves, with gray jowls, which
opened and showed white teeth of foam.

There were many passengers, mostly Jews and
Manchester salesmen ; one inexplicable lady ; some
rich Americans with their families, making the grand
tour ; a couple of young students. Guy walked rather
dreamily among them all. By day he usually lay in a
rug on the deck and read or dozed, while the young
feminine portion of the ship's company paced up and
down, arm-in-arm with the more presentable of the
male travellers, and scanned curiously his brown,

quiet face, as he lay asleep. The mass of the male
persuasion stayed in the smoking-room, betting, telling stories, drinking, and making the place foul.
The younger men vied with each other in talking of
their exploits and displaying their knowledge of life.
Most prominent among them was a man of forty or
thereabouts, with a fat neck and three days' growth
of black beard ; they all hung upon his words, and
were happy to pay for his drinks. On the second
day out he brought up a poker table, and was busy
with organizing pools on the ship's run. Guy fancied he was a professional gambler. Guy rather
avoided the smoking-room or "fiddler ;" but at
night he left the cabins, and the red eye of his cigar
would gleam in the darkness, as he walked the decks
from stern to forecastle.

At last, one evening, they sighted the rocky bones
of Cornwall. Guy kept out-of-doors, and at four in
the morning he saw the sunlight come over the green
Devonshire uplands. Then the coast receded, and was
nothing but a hazy, blue wall ; until evening, when
they passed the chalk points of the Needles, and cast
anchor in Southampton water. He remembered that
he was probably the first of his family to return to
England since old Guyon. But he did not go ashore,
contenting himself with looking at it. It had been a
favorite idea of his to return, when he should be married, and look for the old manor in Durham, or what
might be left of it. He might at least hope to find
some old brasses of the Guerndales in the chapel or
church. He wondered who guarded it now. Perhaps no one ; the Devil was probably not so keen

after good old St. Cuthbert's bones as in days of yore. He now knew that the Church had attached a false value to such antiquities.

That afternoon they went down the Solent; by Cowes and Ryde, with their pleasure fleets of yachts; into the Channel at night, and on the next day the petty ground-swell of the German Ocean, with a few spars or spires stuck endwise on the horizon line, to stand for Flanders. . . . He wished he had asked Annie to write to him. She would not have thought it strange. . . . Yet why?

Bremerhafen, and land, the next morning. A quaint little brick town, with brick houses and pavements, and tarpaulin-hatted children, red and rosy with frequent scrubbing. The children disposed of and safely off for school, the entire female population turned to and scrubbed the pavements. Domestic interiors, with the hausfrau in the court-yard scrubbing, and the herr in the doorway smoking. Visions of a life of comfort, going to the market, eider-down —*bürgerlich*, to a degree, Randolph would say. Did Randolph himself never yearn for a domestic interior?

A shrill whistle from the station round the corner. Only one first-class carriage in the train, which all the American tourists squabbled for. Himself in the second-class coupé, with the lady of the voyage, dressed in black and a veil. American-like, he refrained from speaking to her; Americans, contrary to the prevailing impression, being the most reserved people in the world. Out the window a comfortable, farm-yard sort of country; evidences of plenty of rain, and lack of water-courses. Easy, squatting farm-houses, with low, white-washed walls, and huge projecting straw roofs, looking like mushrooms. A clatter of ducks and geese, birds and bees, in the garden. As the train went by the little brick station, with its name grown in flowers beside it, a uniformed station-master popped out and presented arms—apparently with a broomstick—while his hastily dropped pipe lay, still smoking, on the pavement. A shriek, longer than usual ; a tunnel ; Bremen.

More country, still flat, and very green and yellow, like a colored lithograph. He took a book and tried to read, but, despite himself, his eye wandered to the window and the perspective of hedge-rows, widening and closing, as the train rushed by. Hanover ; then, late in the afternoon, an old city, fortified within high walls, Magdeburg ; a great Protestant stronghold in the days when men fought for their faiths. The railway-carriages and freight-cars, painted green, were all numbered—" 3 horses—36 men," " 12 horses —60 men," and so on. He wondered why ; then he saw that they were all requisitioned and apportioned for case of war. The thought struck him oddly, and caused him a vague wonder that there was anything left to fight about. But, he reflected, the rank and file did not care what they fought about.

Blobs of water came on the window, through which the landscape looked distorted and plum-puddingy. They still had the coupé to themselves—himself and the lady in black. He noticed once that she had large, dark eyes ; and late in the twilight, when

she thought he was asleep, he saw her put her handkerchief to them. Suddenly he felt the tears in his
own eyes ; and, with a start of surprise and impatience, sat upright. At the next station he got out
and walked up and down in the rain, stamping his
feet and swinging his arms as if to restore the cir-
culation. At last they got to Leipsic, and he fell
asleep.

He was roused at two or thereabouts, when they
came to the Elbe ; and he found that the bridge over
the river had been carried away, and it was necessary to be ferried over. The little steamer had to
make two trips ; half the passengers shivered and
swore on one side of the river, while the first load
went over ; then the first load swore and shivered
on that side of the river, while the second load went
over. The weather was a gloomy drizzle ; and the
great stone piers of the broken bridge looked gaunt
and high in the mist. Then another long ride, half
unconscious, and a bright flare of gas. Dresden.

Would der Herr have a bed ? It was then sunrise ;
and the first train for Freiberg left at seven. No ;
he would take coffee and a cigar in the terrace over
the river. The waiter was horrified ; it was impossible ; but Guy had his way. So he sat there, liking
to see the sunlight break into the city and up the
narrow streets, and to watch the market-place take
life, and the long bridge, and the swift, brown river.
Then back to the station and Freiberg ; and there,
in the high morning, Guy took a room at the hotel,
and fell asleep.

In the afternoon he got up and took a walk about

the town. It did not seem to be much of a place. He had come here because he had heard of the School of Mines ; and supposed, lazily, he ought to go and have a look at it. He remembered, with a smile, Norton Randolph's story of how he had gone to Heidelberg. He had arrived at Mayence with a general impression that there were universities in Germany ; and, ringing the bell, had asked the waiter the way to the nearest one. He wondered where Norton was now.

Freiberg. Well, he was here, and settled for two or three years. What should he do ? He had walked all over the town in a couple of hours. Should he go up and have his name entered on the books, if that was the proper thing to do ? He supposed there was a dean, or somebody who kept books. Meanwhile, he threw himself upon a bench in the promenade above the town, and smoked cigarettes. The town looked hot and stupid ; the streets were deserted ; below him was a sentry, walking to and fro monotonously. A sudden weariness came over him. He was tired—tired of seeing so many cities and towns, and resting in none of them ; but he could not rest. Now he had been here six hours, three and a half of which he had slept ; and he was tired of this place. He did not like it. The country was flatter than he had supposed. Ah well, he would go to Zurich and try that. The school might do as well, at first, as a more special school. And he could learn German, which was, of course, necessary, as well there as at Freiberg.

Back to Dresden, late in the evening, again to the

astonishment of the sleepy waiter, who regarded him as an uncanny guest, with ghoulish and unnatural habits, who slept not at night, but smoked and drank strong coffee. This time, however, he went to bed; and, in the consciousness of being off for Zurich the next day, slept long and peacefully. Toward the morning, he had a dream of the woman in black in the train.

13

CHAPTER XXXIII.

"Am Grabe der Liebe wächst Blümlein der Ruh'."—HEINE.

EARLY in the next day, Guy started for Zurich.
No sooner was he fairly off in the train than
he distinctly regretted that he had not stopped at
Freiberg. After all, what difference did it make to
him where he studied? That day he went through
Bavaria, presumably; but Guy never remembered
anything of his travels in that country. He was
quite certain that he came to a place on the Lake of
Constance; subsequent biographers have identified
it with Friedrichshafen; whether rightly or not, I do
not know. At all events, the lake was there, a very
faint and clear blue, with a bluer rim around the
shore, and high, dreamy forms of cream-color and
white on the southern horizon. This Guy noticed
and remembered; but he cared little in those days
for beauty of landscape. The greatest beauty brought
only the more sadness into his moods, as it seemed
to him.

At Zurich he found the semester was over, and the
next was not to begin until August. There was
nothing for him to do then, at all events. What was
he to do? He supposed that he might as well travel
for a few weeks more. So he went on to Lucerne.

As Guy's reminiscences of that charming little city began and ended with Thorwaldsen's lion, he is supposed to have spent most of his visit there in contemplation of this work of art. He did remember, however, that one evening found him lying on his oars in a boat upon the lake, and a great impatience of all things was upon him.

He had been trying never to allow himself to think; and he had driven himself on, over the earth, urging his mind away from all thoughts that to most men are dear. For, he had reasoned, what was there better for him? Why should he, now, be any more alone in a strange land than in his own? What was there left to him in his own land, that he had not here? He had but himself; he was seeking to make, for himself, what he could, of himself. That must content him.

Yet, he had left nothing behind him, and he had left everything; he had brought nothing with him, and he had brought everything. He was impatient of it all, and impatient with himself for being impatient. He seized the oars, and drove them vigorously through the water for a score of strokes; then they fell once more from his hands, and the boat drifted. The purple shadows crept out from the land and folded it from him; the white, gleaming waters deepened to color of lead. A trivial tinkle of music came from a pavilion on the shore, and from a boat near by the chorus of some song from an opéra-bouffe.

Again, he grasped the oars and pulled back to the town. He landed, and wandered about the streets,

which were crowded with summer excursionists,
vulgar Englishmen and unpleasant Americans; the
latter walking, with their wives and daughters, in
the gardens by the Kursaal, or sitting at tables and
taking ices or other refreshments. Two or three
young American girls were there, overdressed; near
them two French *cocottes*, also overdressed; one or
two men following, and ogling both groups equally.
Two fat men, with broad, cloth hats, low vests, and
diamond shirt-pins, sitting and discussing the Chicago pork-market; probably the fathers of the girls,
Guy thought. One gentleman, sitting alone and
smoking cynically. Guy started, as his eye fell
upon him; then he went behind some trees, and
walked rapidly away. It was Norton Randolph.
Why Guy avoided him, he could not have told; but
he felt an odd repugnance to meeting him, which he
afterward regretted.

After walking along the quay a moment, he turned
and went back for Norton; but he was gone. Well,
it did not matter. He knew his address and could
write to him, even if he did not find him in Lucerne.
His impatience came upon him once more. Oh, he
could not bear this. He must get away again—
alone, by himself, away from this common, comfortable crowd. Taken *en masse*, he seemed to hate his
fellow-creatures. He must leave cities, for a time;
it did not matter much where he went. So he
packed up hastily that night; and leaving his trunks,
started the next morning with a knapsack and a
stick to "have it out with himself."

He went up the lake in a small steamer, and

ashore at Altdorf. The higher snow mountains had a strange charm for him as he studied them from the deck of the steamer. They seemed to float so calmly in the upper sky; they were so cold, and pure, and far off, looking down upon this world as from a world of dreams. So he set out on foot, strongly, up into the opening of the valley; and when Norton Randolph was dawdling over his coffee, in Lucerne, Guy was far up in the gorge by the Devil's Bridge.

Though walking rapidly, and with a grim vigor of exercise, he looked about him little, and did not see much of what was around. His way was dusty and hot ; private carriages and lumbering diligences kept passing him, presumably on their way from Italy ; and the rock-walled road seemed little less *banale* than the quay at Lucerne. He found a quiet nook in the Reuss, below the Devil's Bridge, and took a plunge in the river, and then lay for an hour in the sun, smoking his briarwood pipe, with his hat pulled over his eyes. He had brought a few sandwiches with him, upon which he made his luncheon, intending to avoid hotels as far as possible. Late in the afternoon he came out in the wider valley around Andermatt, where, or at Hospenthal, he had expected to stop for the night. The inn was crowded ; upon the piazza he saw a pile of alpenstocks, encircled with inscriptions burned in the wood, commemorating visits to the Rigi, Staubbach, Pilatus, and other equally memorable exploits. They all bore the chamois-hook at the end, which marks the tyro in mountaineering ; and from the dining-room windows

came the loud, shrill monotone of his native accent.
In front of the inn lounged a few Englishmen,
goggle-eyed, knickerbockered, white-veiled.

Impatiently, Guy turned away and walked on
through the valley. He had had a vague idea of
going on, over the St. Gothard, into Italy; but was
weary of the heat and dust of the highroad, and now
wished to go still farther into the mountains. He
had brought with him a map of the country; and, on
consulting it, decided to leave the main road at
Hospenthal. So he turned aside into the smaller
road, and, leaving its upward windings, began to
climb up the steep incline of the Furka. But he
was fairly tired out; every moment he felt tempted
to throw himself upon the alpine roses growing at
his feet, and watch the sunset light flung far over
the green lowlands below him by the huge ice
mirror of the Galenstock. At last he reached a
little inn at the summit of the pass, where he found
quiet and a room for the night. He smoked a pipe
on the balcony overlooking the Rhone glacier, went
to bed at nine, and slept twelve hours.

Still he wanted to get away; the severe physical
labor was like rest to him, and he wished to plunge
farther yet into the heart of the highlands. He tried
Meyringen, and wandered a day or two in that valley, and upon the Grimsel. The quiet of the Alps
was grateful; he worked hard by day, and at night
slept peacefully; while the five giants of the Oberland
—the Eagle, the Monk, and the Maiden, the Horn
of Terror, and the Dark Horn of the Aar—kept watch
above.

Still, he was restless; the roads were thronged with travellers; the snows were still far off. He was under the spell of the mountains, and wished still further to explore their solitudes. He left the Oberland for the deeper shades of the Pennine range; taking the Rhone at its source, where it bubbles from a cavern in the broken glacier, he followed the little stream through the upper Valais; a thinly peopled gorge, where the sun does not shine an hour a day, and he saw the most repulsive forms of goître. Then a diligence brought him to Visp, where he spent the night, and early next morning bent his steps southward, up the valley. Here he found no carriage road, but a rough path that wound tortuously through a growth of firs, clinging to the side of the cliff, and chilly with the spray of the glacier-streams roaring at its base. High above him was a hamlet, hanging on the very brow of a precipice. It was cool, almost too cool in the early morning; no ray of sunlight was yet to be seen above the mountains on his left. Now and then he heard the tinkle of a cow-bell, but he met no one until, after three or four hours' rapid walk, he saw the quaint little village of St. Niklaus ahead, with its shining tin belfry. The path became the main street of the village; but there was scarcely room to walk between the huge manure-heaps which adorned the front of every house.

The valley of Zermatt has now become a commonplace of tourists; but they can never change the savage grandeur which gives it its charm. As Guy walked on beyond St. Niklaus, the valley widened; the scarred cliffs on his right seemed even higher than before ; their bleak faces were cleft and riven by the frost, and by the earthquakes which have more than once depopulated the place. But between the mountain walls was a wide level of soft green, and upon the other side the huge knees of the Mischabel. No human being was in sight. High up on the right, in a hollow scathed by falling rocks and land-slides, lingered the lowest skirt of a glacier, old and gray, shrinking now far up in its lair to escape the summer heat, and leaving the worn stones smooth behind it. As Guy walked on, the valley seemed to close before and behind him ; no tree or green thing was visible, nothing but the cliffs and the torrent between them. Then Guy turned an angle in the cliff, and looked up and saw the Matterhorn before him.

A long time he must have lain and looked at that view that many of us now know so well. In front, the wide, warm valley, dotted with chalets at its upper end, and just above them the great green wedge of forest that seems to force itself through the two living streams of ice that wind on either side. Then again the long sweep of the woods, and the barren slopes ; and far above these, resting on huge rock shoulders, a snowy sea ; and out of this, with one strong leap the eye scarce dares to measure, rises a single shaft of rock and ice, piercing the very zenith as it glitters in the sunlight with its coronal of snow. For the Matterhorn is a cathedral that no man has wrought ; nor can man lie down beneath its shadow and think of man alone. The very villagers at its base do not grow sated and indifferent, as is the wont of natives living in such scenes; they speak of it with awe and fear; long they would believe the mountain supernatural, and said no man should ever stand upon its crown. And Guy gazed at it from the earth, and felt that in all the world there was no form of things inanimate like this.

Great billows of gray cloud swept its snowy shoulders; but the sun shone full upon the highest peak, clear in the upper blue. Guy lay still, in the long, sweet grass of the valley, and forgot to think of himself and even of her; the peace of the mountains was upon him, and the passion in his heart lay stunned into silence.

13*

CHAPTER XXXIV.

" ——Or chirrups madrigals, with old, sweet words,
Such as men loved when people wooed like birds,
And spoke the true note first."—AUSTIN DOBSON.

STILL many minutes Guy lay drowsily, at peace
with the world. The summer day wore on, and
the full sunlight came down into the valley ; the
birds flew low over his head. A dense perfume came
from the crushed grass thick with wild flowers ; the
numberless Alpine insects filled the air with the
beating of their wings. A strange, sweet sound came
to his ears, a low and liquid melody. He listened
dreamily a long time before his curiosity was aroused ;
he was curious a long time before he got up to see
what it was. The melody was well known to him ;
it was an old German song that came to him cool
and sweet, from some wooden instrument, like water
from a wooden pipe.

Guy sat up and looked about him. The sound
seemed to come from a little chalet near by. On
coming nearer, the chalet proved but an empty cow-
house. It stood hard by a coppice overrun by thick
vines, and in the depth of this thicket there was a
rush of water, pouring in a cloud of mist from some
unknown height, and trickling in little slower

streamlets to rest in a pool in the green meadow below. The door of the hut was open, and Guy peered
in curiously. The place inside was empty and now
disused, but still sweet with an odor of old summers,
and there in the shade lay a yellow-haired youth.
He was lying on his back, playing on some wooden
instrument, and his blue eyes were half closed. The
boy did not see Guy for a minute, and went on
breathing his melody through the wood. Behind
him lay a knapsack, which served for a pillow ; and
beside him was an old German student cap and his
alpenstock. This was of oak, not turned in a lathe,
but hewn, and rounded smooth at the upper end.
Near it, wound in a coil of rope, was an ice-axe.
Guy, with his grave face, stood at the doorway looking in. His shadow fell upon the boy, and he looked
up and spoke before Guy could disappear.

"*Herein!*" said he pleasantly. "I see ; you heard
mein Schatz, and were by her called hither. Fine
morning ! Pardon, Herr, that I do not rise to receive you. It is not mine, the castle you behold ! "
and he smiled, opening wide his blue eyes. Guy felt
an inclination to laugh, observing which, the boy
laughed merrily. Then as Guy, with true Anglo-
Saxon diffidence, hesitated upon the doorstep, "Ach,
pardon, sir, that I do not receive you, but will you
not come in from out of the sun ? She is so warm,
efen for de beerts, out in de vallée." This in English.

"Please go on with your playing ;" said Guy, "I
like to hear you." The boy needed no invitation, and
had already begun some new melody. Guy clasped

his hands over his knees and leaned backward. They were sitting on the hay with which the earth floor of the hut was strewn, and little sunbeams came in through the chinks between the logs in the wall. "Do you like it?" said the boy, suddenly stopping. "Most often you English do not know music."

"How did you know I was English?" said Guy, amused, and rather abruptly.

"Ach! I know you are English; for you are trafilling for pleasure, and you are here in the Switzerland, and it is summer, and the world does not make you glad. But I do not think you are English. You come from America? Not so? You are American."

Guy laughed. "Ach, I knew you did come from America!" and he broke into a laugh of sympathy. "America! I, too, haf been in America, and I shall go there again!" And the boy laughed louder; and seizing his instrument began to pipe the shepherd's song in Tannhäuser. Guy was much delighted, and, turning over comfortably, proceeded to fill and light his pipe. The manners of his young friend were so frank and simple that one could not help being easy in his company, and Guy already felt as if he had known him for years.

"You haf a fine country," the boy went on. "Yes, it iss wonderful, your country. And you haf great railways, and machines, and fabrics. You are very ingenious in your country; and your climate, it is *wunderschön*. Ach, you are grand fellows in your country. But you do not know, none of you, to be happy." And he garnished his conversation with another oboe *obligato*.

"Do you think so?"

"Oh, yes, I am sure. You are all free in your country, and—what you say?—equal; and you try, each one of you, to be bigger than the other; and you work too hard, and you are unhappy if you are not so greater; and you grow tired. Oh, yes. That iss not the way to be happy. Now, in the Vaterland we are all so different, one from the other; but we do not think that makes nothing; and we do not envy one the other. One is happy if one sees what iss fine in the world, and what is beautiful in the country, and if one feels what iss great, and loves and iss loved. But no, you, most of you, do not care for that in America."

"Do you always take your—your flute with you?" said Guy, for the sake of something to say.

"It iss no flute, it iss oboë. Yes, I do take her always with me. She iss mein Schatz. Ach, you know what that iss? Yess? You know, I haf also another Schatz—my true Schatz. But she iss not here. No. She is far away.

> ' Schöne, helle, goldne sterne,
> Grüsst die Liebste in der Ferne,
> Sagt, dass ich noch immer sei,
> Herzekrank und bleich und treu.'

Yes," he went on, suddenly stopping his song, "she iss in America."

Guy lay by, little disposed to laugh, and more touched than amused by this childish confidence. He had been fifteen minutes with this fellow, and he was already giving him his heart history! If Shakespeare had been a German he never would have written that line about daws and wearing one's heart upon one's sleeve. The boy began a prelude upon his oboe.

"You do not climb ? You do not know the mountains ? "

" How do you know ? " said Guy.

" You haf no ice-nails on your shoes. But it is a fine thing, climbing; to be so high over the world. Ach, you, too, should climb. Then you would smile."

Guy smiled very decidedly at this.

" I should like to try, but I have no experience. I once thought of trying Mont Blanc," he laughed.

" Ach, de Mont-Blanc—he iss noding, nodings at all. He iss but one big—what you call him !—blateau. You should come vid me. Will you come with me ? " cried the boy, excitedly. "Ach, permit that I do give you my card ! " and, with a sudden effort for formality, he produced a pasteboard, on which was printed :

ERNST GUTEKIND,

Posen.

Guy took the card gravely, and handed him his own.

" Ach ! " said Gutekind, " your last name is strange. I do not know it. But your first is a goot name. You haf one Ritter Guyon in de ' Faery Queen.' "

" Have you read Spenser ? " said Guy, surprised.

" Oh, yes, I haf read Spenser ; he is one great poet ; he is fery sweet ; he is not like one Englishman. We all do study English in our schools. You haf also one other great poet, whose—whose *Vorfahr* wass one Guyon. He was Shelley. He wass better than all your others. But you—you study not German?"

"I have read some German," said Guy. "Goethe, Kant, Fichte, Schopenhauer——"

"Der war auch ein Narr!" cried Gutekind, savagely. "Ach, no! You should read Jean Paul, Schelling—Heine, he was too sad; and Schopenhauer, only what he wrote of æsthetik was goot; his head was turned round the wrong way. But you haf not told me—will you not come with me? Ach, say that you come, and I will show you what are the Alps."

Something about the boy pleased Guy; and, in a humor, he consented. Gutekind jumped up and seized his hand enthusiastically; and, sitting down by his new friend, proceeded to expand in new confidences.

"I haf left home that I might be among the mountains once more," said he. "We men who are always in the affairs, you know, the false things seem real to us; and we forget what is true; and our minds, they do not keep clean. So I wished once more for the Alps, that I might make high and pure my soul with them. Ach, your friend was sometimes right; it is only when we are one, united, with the pure idea, that we lose what is wrong and—and irdisch. I did wish again that I might go up into the *Luft;* that I might leave there what I did not wish to remember. And then I shall go home, and then to America!" laughed this imaginative young mystic.

"And what do you do when you are at home?"

"I am a fabrikant of cannon," said Gutekind.

CHAPTER XXXV.

"In Heaven a spirit doth dwell,
　Whose heartstrings are a lute. . . .
　Yes, Heaven is thine ; but this
　　Is a world of sweets and sours ;
　　Our flowers are merely—flowers—
　And the shadow of thy perfect bliss
　　Is the sunshine of ours."—Poe.

ALL about the little pine-wood village of Zermatt
are huge knees and buttresses of mountains
whose peaks, far distant in the sky, are unseen from
the valley. Only the Matterhorn, full in front, soars
into the blue, like a huge splinter of ice, cleaving
the heavens. But the morning sunlight comes dancing down over miles of falling glaciers ; vast ter-
minal moraines fill the valley and, to the east, the
wooded flanks of the Mischabel roll away, and the
great snow shoulders of Monte Rosa. And Guy felt
the mighty consolation of the hills ; he was happier
that night than he had been for many a long day, and
slept well and quietly, for the Matterhorn and the
Mischabel and the great Weisshorn range held him in
their arms, and shielded him from the world. True,
he had walked nearly thirty miles that day ; it was
late in the evening before they reached honest Mr.
Seiler's little inn, and the last few miles had been

enlivened by the cheery company of little Gutekind.
For Guy had taken a fancy to him ; he liked the
freshness and simplicity and the honest blue eyes of
this young artificer of engines of destruction.

And Gutekind had conceived a vast admiration
for Guy, and grew ten times more enthusiastic, himself, when he saw Guy's evident enjoyment of the
scenery and the walk.   He was up, bright and early,
burning with delight, and wild to get up into the
highness, as he expressed it.   Even Guy caught a bit
of his fever, and found himself earnestly endeavoring
to persuade a guide that the Cervin might be attempted through the flecks of cloud which were
clinging to its sides.   But Gutekind grew shy at
this ; it was too much.   "Perhaps to-morrow," he
said ; "one might always try.

> ' Je réfiendrai à la montagne—foilà tout !
>   Je réfiendrai à la montagne—foilà tout !
> Bour ébouser ma pien-aimée,
> Celle que mon gœur a tant aimée-e-e—
>   Foilà tout !   Foilà tout ! '

We might well, however, go to walk ?" he added.
"We haf all the day to rest."

So they followed the gorge up to the base of the
glacier, and there in a little green recess under the
rocks, hollowed into a roof by the torrent, Guy lay,
through the afternoon, and smoked his pipe; and little Gutekind sat beside him, and played on his oboe,
and sang snatches of song, and talked a curious mixture of common-sense and sentiment.   Above them
was piled the ugly moraine of the Boden glacier—
great rocks, and débris, and blocks of old ice, crusted

at the surface with dirt and gravel,—for the old age of a glacier is not beautiful, when the snow coverlet is gone, and the purity is lost, and the clear violet ice becomes gray and honeycombed, and it sinks to die in the hot valley, giving birth to the torrent that bears its name.

But anything, apparently, made Gutekind happy; and he sat laughing and singing, piping on his oboe, and running off occasionally to gather some Alpine rose or gentian, intensely blue. He had hopes, he said, of an Edelweiss; he wanted one to send to her; but they were too low for them yet. And Guy looked at him with amusement and perhaps a tinge of contempt, and wondered what Norton Randolph would have to say to him: for all Americans are intolerant of expressed sentiment, and Gutekind was after all a bourgeois and took the world quite *au serieux ;* while Randolph was familiar only with that world which society is pleased to call *the* world, *le monde où l'on rit, le monde où l'on s'ennuie.* But they were screened far from this world, that day; and the torrent falling beside them came too fresh from the skies to be quite earthy—just a touch of rock-grit to give it strength. So Guy lay watching it, dreamily, and thought to-morrow he would be up in the snows whence it came, and quite forgot to smile at little Gutekind. He remembered how in his childhood he had so lain and looked into a browner brook with softer motion, and he threw a scarlet leaf in the water and watched it eddy around, and wondered if the little rock-rimmed pool up by the edge of the wood were just as it used to be. Then he bent his

brow over the stream, and the water reflected his
face and ran on with a new shadow; while Gutekind
played idly on his pipe, then laid it down and sang in
French with his queer German accent:

> "Si fous croyez que che vais dire
> Qui j'ose ai-ai-mer—
> Je ne saurais bour une embire
> Fous la nommer."

Guy flung himself back, somewhat impatiently, on
the grass. "Herr Gutekind, do you remember the
war ?"

"Ach, Gott, yes !" said Gutekind with a start.
"Why do you so suddenly ask me, do I remember
the war ? I believe well—I was a soldier myself."

"You—you a soldier in the war? Why, you were
too young !"

"Ach, no. A man is nefer too young to be shot.
I haf been all through the war. It wass schreklich
—it was terrible. No, no. I do not like the wars.
I seek always to forget all that I haf seen of war.
Ach, do not let us think of him here !" And seizing
his oboe, he began the brook melody of the pastoral
symphony ; then his face grew serious, and he laid
the instrument down again.

"Ach, yes. I haf killed many, many men. You
should see our cannon. They were fery fine, our
cannon, and they did fery well ; and my father, he
did get the Iron Cross. I was—what you call him ?
artillerist. But nôh. The war was not a true war.
Then, I was a boy, and I thought it fery fine—all
fery fine indeed."

"I should like to go to a war," mused Guy.

"No, no—you would not. You think you would like him, because you are sad and trübselig, oh! I can see. But nôh. To see men killed as if they wass cattle, it is not nice. Poor fellows! and to many of them the world so sweet."

"I thought you Germans were all pessimists?"

"Himmel, nein! das sind die Narren. No, you come up with me to-morrow in die Luft, and I will show you how the world is wunderschön, and then you will nefer forget it. Ach, yes, this world is bad enough if you think the thoughts of him, and you look at him with the eyes of him, and you do not see the soul."

"Truly," quoted Guy, "he is a fool who abuses this world; for he has none other."

"Yes, yess; you haf one other, that is outside of, that is beyond this. And it is the licht that comes from the outside that makes bright this world. No; the men they are all Selbstsucht, egoist; and they seek the happiness of this world; and then they are not happy. But haf they right to complain? Haf they then ein Recht nach Glück? Nein, nein, not here; and this world is not the true. But yet there are lights in the world; there is musik, and beauty, and memory and the poetry, and the *erhaben*, the sublime, and lofe; and they are not of this, but of the true world; and they are true. Ach, do not gomblain to me of this world; it is only der Grobian, der Grobian who iss not happy."

And little Gutekind rose quite angrily; and Guy walked back with him as he stowed his oboe in a case, and strode along with his hat stuffed with wild flowers. Soon his face cleared up, and he began again with his snatches of song :

> " Ich bin die Prinzessin Ilse und wohne im Ilsenstein ;
> Komm mit nach meinem Schlosse, wir wollen selig sein."

"Do not you think that I am Christian," he said, suddenly turning to Guy, as if it were suggested by the song. "Oh, no ; the Bibel, it iss a goot and a beautiful book. But it iss not all of the truth." And the same evening he got into a quite furious discussion with an English divine who conducted the service in the inn on Sundays and risked his neck over ice-slopes on week days. Furious, that is, on one side ; for Gutekind uttered his most appalling pantheistical doctrines in the callow and childlike manner that was peculiarly his own. The curate, who had not read a dozen theological works in as many years, much less philosophy, and was chiefly conversant with J. C.'s work on whist, was shocked, and retreated terrified behind the thirty-nine articles and St. Paul. But, as Gutekind evidently considered the latter a far less trustworthy and unprejudiced authority than Strauss, he calmly masked these positions and proceeded to rout the Englishman with Spinoza and Schelling. "Either," he would say, "something—whether mind, man, or matter, we do not know—exists outside of God, or it does not. In the former case, der Herr is an atheist ; for his God is not infinite, that is, not God at all. In the latter case, der Herr, like myself, is a pantheist ; for every· thing, even der Herr himself, is a mode of God."

Pinned behind this dilemma, the clergyman stared helplessly at Guy ; but he was engaged in conversation with a charming Russian countess, who clapped her hands at Gutekind's worst speeches, pouted when he admitted the existence of any deity at all, and confessed, in soft, broken English and a musical voice, to being something of a nihilist ; she tried her best to fascinate Guy, retired to her bedroom somewhat disgusted that he did not make love to her, and was, as Gutekind expressed it, "so charmed to be so charming."

Gutekind had a horror of the *femmes du monde ;* but Guy heard him softly humming, as he came up-stairs—

> " Ich glaub' nicht an den Herrgott,
> Wovon das Pfäfflein spricht—
> Ich glaub' nur an dein Auge
> Das ist mein Himmelslicht."

Guy went to sleep in a moment ; but at two o'clock Ernst Gutekind came and knocked at his door. "The morning iss fine; it is time to depart," said he.

So Guy got up, feeling wretchedly uncomfortable. His room was very cold and dark, and it seemed almost impossible to dress by the light of the one tallow dip the inn allowed ; however, he struggled wearily into his clothes. His mountain boots had been wet the day before, and the huge nailed soles and leather sides were damp and stiff, and greasy with fresh tallow. Footsore as he was, it seemed an endless task to stamp them on, but at last he did so, and limped down-stairs. There, in the gloom of the general room, he found Gutekind and a trio of guides. It was a dismal start; even Gutekind seemed quiet and subdued, and the guides whispered together, morosely, in one corner, as if they were plotting a conspiracy. One of them had made some hot coffee, a bowl of which Guy drank, and felt a bit better. Finally, they sallied forth into the little village, Guy stumping along like a cripple.

Still, as they plodded up the steep path, silently and in single file, Guy gradually forgot his stiffness in the picturesqueness of the scene. The night was cold and damp; the nearest mountains, where they could be seen, gleamed a ghastly white in the moonlight. They were walking through a wet pasture: first a guide, then Gutekind, then another guide, then Guy, and after him the last guide. The men kept silence; they wore peaked hats, and cloaks slung gracefully upon one shoulder; the effect was of some midnight party of banditti. The long valley behind them was all in a shimmer of moonlight; but, as they wound up the alp, the moon sank behind the Weisshorn and left them to the faint light of the stars, and the valleys all in the darkness, with only the vague sky-line to mark the mountain.

There was something strangely beautiful in it all. In the exhilaration of the morning air, Guy's fatigue disappeared; he forgot all but the climb before them; slowly, imperceptibly, other thoughts and memories faded away. The darkness itself gave a solemn grandeur to the scene; the guides marched silently, with steady steps and bowed heads; Gutekind, looking up, was whispering a song. They had left the grass, and were on a long slope of shale;

beside them was a mound of worn and rounded rock, along the edge of which they took their way. From below came the hoarse roar of a torrent, as omnipresent in the Alps as the murmur of the waves by the sea. A wall of white became dimly visible above and ahead; they were come to the edge of the snow. Here the guides halted a moment, and Guy looked behind.

It was darker than ever. Hill and valley were alike undistinguishable; the very stars were paler; all was pitchy black. It seemed to Guy he could scarcely see the sheen of the snow around him. No ray of dawn appeared.

Suddenly the jagged ice-peak of the Weisshorn, twenty miles to the west, flamed—blood-red. He started, as at a blow. Nothing to be seen but this scarlet patch, hung mid-high in the darkness, against a black sky.

Then a minute, and a rosy flush fell upon the Matterhorn, and a tender glow like ashes-of-roses spread slowly down over the vast snow-fields in front, in infinite gradations of soft pink and white. And now, peak answering peak, each in turn flashed, like warm marble, into light; only the lower glaciers kept their chill, ashy white; and all above them was the day. But still the valleys were vast gulfs of darkness, like Dante's Malebolge, unpierceable by any power of star.

And so, group after group of snowy pinnacles turned scarlet, and red, and rosy, and glitter-white; and yet the huge chasms yawned below, and the night brooded in the valleys. At last a sunbeam, glancing full upon the icy surface of the Matterhorn, fell down and backward into the long valley like an arrow from the sun ; and they saw the birth of dawn below. At first, the deep valleys were shrouded in a sea of mist ; then, as the sunbeam cleft the cloud, the gray veil wavered and rose slowly upward. They felt its chill breath as it rolled by them ; the mists of the night ascended, like incense, at the rising of the sun ; and there came the sweet morning smell of the woods and meadows, and the tinkle of bells and little rills, far down below.

And Guy turned thankfully to the bread and meat before him, and forgot that he had forgotten the beings of the lower world.

14

CHAPTER XXXVI.

"Die Mutter faltet die Hände ;
Ihr war, sie wusste nicht wie ;
Andächtig sang sie leise
'Gelobt seist du, Marie.' "—HEINE.

HOW little tourists know of the true charm of
the Alps ! Ladies, who walk on the prome-
nades and terraces of the large towns, drive sleepily
in their comfortable private carriages over the military roads, buy wood-carvings and crystals at the
chalet-shops, or even, perhaps, venture in boats on
the lakes ; parties of "personally conducted," de-
lighting in casinos and bands, in railway ascents of
the Rigi, charmed at evening illuminations of the
Giessbach, eloquent over the adventures of the Mau-
vais Pas. And now even Zermatt is invaded by these
latter tourists, and the warm recesses of the Val Tour-
nanche—and next they will be for bedecking the Matterhorn himself with electric lights. But there is still
a world these do not know. They frequent only the
carriage passes ; the dusty roads, and the hot, broad
valleys, where only a glimpse of the distant snows is
vouchsafed them, like a dream never to be realized,
and the fag-ends of the glaciers hang down, dirty
and uninviting ; and then they go back to Birming-
ham and talk of Switzerland.

But no one knows the secret of the mountains unless he meets the high Alps face to face ; unless he sees all their moods, and grapples with all their dangers ; unless he spends days above the snow-line and only descends to sleep. Then he finds another world than ours, a world, like Nirwana, above the evils of birth, and death, and change; swept by keen, clear winds, or lulled in the stillness of the stars. It is a world eternal, and its colors are white and blue ; the red and green of the earth are far removed ; no plant lives, no green thing moves, no moss grows ; the valleys are lost and forgotten ; nothing is seen but the billowy sea of ice, shining white, save where the crags of rock break through the foam of the snow ; and the icy waves lie motionless, as if stilled at a word of God. Far below may be heard the falling of water, the rending of rock, the rush of the avalanche ; but the masses of the mountains are at rest, and the high peaks seem to say, in Dante's words :

> " Dinanzi a me non fur cose create
> Se non eterne, ed io eterno duro."

For at such times we forget that Helmholtz places the duration of the sun itself at seventeen millions of years.

Over the mountains is the calm of eternity, and the peace of the high places enters into the soul.

All that week Guy and Gutekind were above the line of change, and it was a week which Guy never forgot. He learned to know of the mountains : he won a love which he would never lose. Rarely, at

night, would they even descend so far as to seek
shelter in some chalet or hay-filled hut; oftener they
lay, wrapped in blankets, on the snow itself and fell
asleep watching the stars. For none of the pains
that come from the earth and the damps of night are
known in these upper airs; only the radiance of the
light there blinds the eyes of those who live in lower
places. So Guy would lie at night, vaguely remembering that below in the world there were many men
who went up and down, to and fro, troubling themselves; and then he thought how well the mountains
fitted Dante's description of the higher angels, for
they lifted their great white faces

> "All radiant, with the glory and the calm
> Of having looked upon the front of God."

Then Gutekind, who rarely sacrificed his oboe except in actual climbing, would bring it out and pipe
sweet melodies to the echoes of the Mischabel. And
Guy would watch the shifting curtain of the clouds
below them, while Gutekind twined edelweiss for
his "Schatz" in America; and only rarely, when
they caught a glimpse of some far valley through a
rift in the fleecy floor, would they wonder what
might be going on in the under world.

One day Guy has often described to me. It was a
day when all things seemed too lovely to leave;
each charming picture, as they wound up the ascent,
seemed to woo them to rest there and go no further.
They had spent the night in a little chalet in the
Saas valley, and purposed to ascend the Dom. So
they toiled vigorously over the pastures, and up the

precipitous Fee glacier, and by seven in the morning had reached the snow above the ice. Most of the higher peaks were in front; but, as they turned, they saw far to the east and south, where the mountains dwindled away, and fell, in brown, purple, green foot-hills, to the distant plains of Lombardy ; and far on the horizon, below the sun, a blue mist floated above the Lago Maggiore.

Guy had a moment of weakness ; let the rest of the day care for itself, he thought, and he threw him-self down upon the last soft bed of alpine roses. There he lit a pipe, pulled his cap over his eyes, and flatly refused to move. Gutekind, nothing loath, though making one or two feeble remonstrances about the length of the day's work, and the proba-bility of soft snow in the afternoon, threw himself down beside Guy ; and both became lost in the pure delight of the view.

"Ah," said Gutekind, "I wish that I had here my oboe." Then, after a long pause, "Oh, I do wish that I could bring her here. She is like you Ameri-cans ; they are not strong.

> ' Sie hat mir Treue versprochen—
> Und gab ein Ring dabei! '

But, ah, you do not know of whom I speak ? I do not speak of my oboe now ; I speak of my feins Liebchen."

"Oh, yes," said Guy with a smile, "I have heard you mention her."

Gutekind hummed a song or two ; then suddenly, he spoke impulsively :

"Yes, I haf told you a little; but I did not tell you all. I said that I was come here to the Alps because I did wish to rest from my business. But it iss not true—no, it iss not true. Let me tell you why I haf come here; it is because I shall see her; I shall now go to Amerika myself and I shall see her."

"And are you going to marry her?"

"Oh, yess. I shall marry her. I haf been betrothed to her now—ach, it is nearly five years. But now it iss all over, and I can go, and so I am so happy, weisst du. I haf been working for her, that I might get a home; and now I haf won it, and I can bring her to my own house, and she can haf all that she shall want. Yess; I can give her all."

"But why do you come to Switzerland?" queried Guy.

"I could not go to her from my work and my business and all that I haf seen. No, I did wish to come here first, that I make high my mind with the mountains and haf my rest before I do see her. Oh, I haf had a hard time—a fery hart time, do you know. And then I did wish to write to her that I come. It is since five years now that I do lofe her. And she said then that she did lofe me; but I—I was young, and I could not keep my wife as she did need. So, I came back to Germany, and I worked that I might get things of my own. For my father, he iss rich, but he has many sons and daughters; and he did not like me to marry her, for he thought that her health it was not good, and she would not make a good wife. And so, I did go to work; but then the war came, and I wass of the Landwehr, and ach! the war was terrible. And I did not hear from her only once in the war; and then I was wounded, and I could not return to my work for two years more, and the waiting, it did make me more ill."

"Where does she live?"

"She iss in New York, and her name is Fannie—Fannie Batts."

"And now you can marry?"

"Yess, I haf done very well—oh, fery well indeed, in my business. And I haf a house for her, and there is a garten, and a droschke that she may ride, for she is not always well——"

"And so you are going to New York to marry her there?"

"Yes, I am going. She has always written to me,—not so often as I—but then, you know, she was not strong, and it was hard to wait so long, and then it is not easy for a maiden to write, it is not—not *sittlich*. And her father he did object to our marriach, because I was a German and poor. But now he will let it be. Ach, Herr Guerndale, my dear friend, you must see her. She is so lofely!"

Guy lay silent.

"But ach, you too haf lofed?" broke in Gutekind.

"How do you know?" said Guy, forcing a laugh.

"Oh! I know. You forget to talk; and you do not care whether you stop on the *névé*. And you do not laugh at me."

Guy's laugh came naturally, this time.

"Ach, my friend, do not fear it. I tell you this world it iss vain and little worthy; and love and beauty, they are gifen us to keep us mindful that it iss not all." Then the boy went on with his song snatches, and Guy's mood grew quiet; and so they forgot the time, until Gutekind suddenly came to himself, and gave the word to advance. Then the ill-matched pair, roped together, went up the *arête*.

But this long delay made them late. It was three o'clock before they stood on the highest peak of the Mischabel. Guy was reluctant to leave the view; for the Dom is the highest of all the Swiss mountains and overlooks the northern Oberland. But Gutekind was more prudent; he spoke of long and tedious ice-cutting, and the young German was an admirable mountaineer. The slopes were far too steep for a *glissade;* still, fortunately, there was no new snow, and the crust was icy and firm. But cutting steps is a tedious process. They got into a long couloir; and at dusk, had only reached a little snow plateau at its base, somewhere above the glaciers over Randa. So, little loath, they postponed the final glacier-climb to the morning light, and had their supper, side by side, at the base of the cliff.

It was quite dark, that night, and they talked long and kindly together; Ernst Gutekind speaking of his love, Guy listening silently to the simple, sweet-minded fellow, and contrasting his friend's happiness with his own future life. Again and again the boy ran over his old story, until his earnest voice was hushed to silence and his fair head lay back upon the snow, and his tender blue eyes closed in sleep.

Guy lay awake for some time. The night was still and starless; now and then broken by a distant flash of cloud-lightning, or a fall of snow. He must have fallen asleep, an hour or two, for then he awoke, about midnight, and heard a thunder of falling rock. The sound came from above, louder and louder; finally, with a crash, the main crag rattled along the centre of the couloir, striking flashes of fire as it bounded from the jutting rocks back to the ice again. A shower of smaller stones fell about them; then the long after-thunder came up from below, a prolonged reverberation of echoes; and again the night was black and still.

Guy was nervous and frightened. He got up to ask Gutekind to change their resting-place. But a small stone had struck him, and the boy was dead, and his yellow hair dabbled with blood, and his brain beaten into the snow, and Guy could just see his pale face looking up into the darkness.

14*

CHAPTER XXXVII

"They said that love would die, when hope was gone.
And love mourned long, and sorrow'd after hope ;
At last she sought out memory, and they trod
The same old paths where love had walked with hope,
And memory fed the soul of love with tears."—TENNYSON.

ALL that night Guy lay, with open, weary eyes, and watched for dawn. The little plateau was of small extent ; he dared not move in the darkness. At first he was utterly unnerved ; he wished that he could weep, or faint like a woman ; then he waited and watched for another fall of stones. But none came after the one that had been fatal to his poor young friend. His eyes were dry and tearless ; and he stood up and swung his arms in an agony of self-reproach. Was his life so dark, then, that it cast a shadow on the paths of those he met ? Was there really a curse upon him ? If there was mercy in heaven, why had poor Gutekind been the one to be killed ? Bah—there was no heaven ! and he laughed aloud, with a voice that sounded strange to him ; then he put his head back upon the snow, and strained his open eyes to see the dawn.

It grew colder, as the night wore on, and more silent ; the looser stones, now frozen fast, ceased to thunder down the mountain ; the distant lightning stopped, the sky was clear, and the cool air restored his strength and calm. With the first twilight of the morning he got up again, and laid a handkerchief across the boy's face, and folded his arms upon his breast. In doing this, he found around his neck a ribbon, and with it a small gold locket. He opened it, and found inside a portrait of a pretty girl and a little wisp of yellow hair, and Guy thought of the poor girl, far away in America, who had loved this boy, and he left the locket with its owner, sleeping there in the eternal snow.

It was a dangerous climb, down over the glaciers to the little village ; almost impossible for him alone, with no rope, no one to hold him while he chopped the steps. But the concentration of mind and muscle did him good ; and he worked his way manfully ; *Seule la mort peut nous vaincre*, he thought, and bah ! there was no God ; his life was charmed. So thinking, when he had leisure to think at all ; risking his life a hundred times, sliding boldly down the steeper slopes, careless of crevasses, it took him all day to reach the plain, and it was already evening before he could bring the news to the inn.

A party of search was at once made up for the next morning, with a number of guides, and Guy as leader, for he was determined to go back with them, despite his exhaustion. Getting five hours' profound sleep, they were off at two in the morning. A party of six or seven men, with rope and axes, they accomplished easily in a few hours what had taken Guy all day ; but they found no trace of poor Gutekind. Guy was certain of the spot, but the fresh snow was now gone, and it was evident that the heat of the day before had caused an avalanche which had carried with it the body of the young German.

He wrote to Gutekind's parents, and told them that he would stay at Zermatt awaiting their instructions. He could not bear to write to the poor girl in America, telling her of the death of the young lover she was even then expecting. So he wrote to a friend in New York, asking him to make inquiries about her and to break to her the news, for Guy knew that Gutekind's father had had no acquaintance with her. And every day, for that and several weeks, he searched the Mischabel glaciers for a trace of the boy's body, but without success. It was probably buried far beneath the ice of the lower glacier.

At last, a letter came from the father "thanking him for his trouble" and begging him to abandon a useless search. Guy thought, somewhat bitterly, that the boy's death did not seem to affect them overmuch. Then, for the first time, the sense of blankness in his own life came over him again. But not for long. Guy felt that the mountains had taught him a lesson, after all ; his strong bodily health gave him a less morbid mind ; he would go on to the end. So he turned and set his steps for Freiberg ; but not before he had himself walked around into the Saas valley and got the old oboe that Gutekind had been so fond of, which Guy chose to keep without asking his father's permission. Then he left the terrible Oberland, and never again returned to Zermatt, but never lost the memory of a single day of the six weeks he had passed there that summer. Spite of all that had happened, he kept his love for the high mountains; and most of his vacations, in following years, were spent in other valleys of the Alps.

He went back to Lucerne, arriving there late in September, and found a letter from his friend in New York. "After getting your last," he wrote, "I tried to find a Fannie Betts. I have only succeeded in discovering a Fannie Bates; but she is engaged, and about to be married, to a young man from the West. She is a pretty girl, with yellow hair and blue eyes, but rather ordinary, I fancy. . . . She had allowed some attention from a young Prussian engineer, who came over here five years ago and was reported to be engaged to him; but her friends say that was only a flirtation. At all events, she is shortly to become Mrs. Thompson. I send you her address; under the circumstances, I did not think best to tell her of Gutekind's death" —— Guy threw the letter aside. He thought of the young German, buried in the snow, and wearing her picture at his heart, and decided to leave her in ignorance of her lover's fate. Perhaps it was better so, for both; and he remembered his mad outcry that night, and thought the course of nature was not always blind.

Then Guy went to Freiberg, and studied there and at other universities, four years. At first, he often used to sigh for courage. He had resolved to go on to the end, but it is hard to go through life for no better reason than the fancy of *noblesse oblige*. It is hard to have courage, lacking faith and hope; it is hard to have faith and hope without love. What hero would be brave, fighting for no cause   Still, he thought of poor Gutekind, and tried his best; once or twice, too, in the beginning, he thought of Annie; she had passed from his life, and yet he felt that he would not lose his memory of her for all the world.   Her memory was yet his own, and he did not count the sadness that it brought him.   The first day that he went to a lecture, he found himself, as of old, writing her name across the blank page; then he set himself again to forget her after that.

The month after he got to Freiberg, he had a letter from Lane, telling him of Annie's marriage to Philip.   Occasionally, too, he heard from Randolph and from Strang; but the former was away on some characteristic trip in Central Asia, and the latter hard at work, bridge-building in Dakota, for a Boston railway corporation.

It is hard, writing a brief history of a life, to convey to the reader's mind the idea of the lapse of so long a time as four years—four years passed in strong effort, but with few outside occurrences of importance.   For, after the first few weeks, Guy worked very steadily.   He was not all the time at Freiberg; a semester or two was passed in other schools.   There was, of course, no necessity for so long a stay abroad; but Guy could not bear the idea of going home; he felt no impulse, as yet, urging him to active employment in his profession.   Strang often wrote, asking him to come; and Guy as often answered with excuses.

In the summer of 1874 (I happen to remember this date, although not quite sure of many before this),

Guy had a characteristic letter from Lane. Lane was a very good letter-writer; for the world, to him, consisted in the havings and doings of people and society; and though his horizon was rather limited, his letters were full of personalities and amusing observations upon the men and things of which he commanded an extensive view from his social eminence in Boston. He rarely observed such parts of the United States as lay beyond a somewhat limited circle in the Eastern cities; when he did, it was with a mild surprise that the national character was so little influenced by his Boston Faubourg Saint-Germain. Lane's opinions were so assured, and his prejudices so very positive, that his character was completely negative. "My dear Guerndale," he wrote, "though you have owed me a letter, for a long time, I keep, as you see, my promise of writing to you. There is not much to write about, to you who have been away so long from Boston. I hope you are coming back soon; really, if you do not, you will be quite forgotten; except, of course, among your friends. Boston is very much changed, of course; the fire has even improved the city. There are several new churches; one quite the finest in America," etc. "You will be surprised to learn of Miss Kitty Cotton's engagement; still more so, when you hear that it is to John Strang. People here are very much surprised that she took him. He is not a Boston man; and she must have had plenty of chances. However, you know him quite well; so he has doubtless written you." . . . . "The new president of Harvard is becoming quite radical, and there is much talk about it. I suppose the papers over there have told you how Grant is misconducting himself. Mrs. Bill Willing has been left a lot of money, and has a brand new carriage and footmen in livery, with a coat-of-arms on the panel. Of course, people laugh a good deal when they think who her grandfather was." . . . . "I suppose you heard of old Mr. Bonnymort's death. He had grown quite feeble of late, and they say there had been disputes between him and Symonds. Symonds has been living rather extravagantly; they say he has been speculating largely, and has given up his business." . . . . "Tom Brattle is off in a yacht with Symonds this summer. He has been quite devoted to Miss Ruthven of New York; people say he would marry her, if he had money enough," etc. So John was going to marry Kitty Cotton after all, thought Guy, and Randolph had been wrong. He wondered that John had not written to him, and went to Dresden and bought a set of china to send to his old chum. Shortly after, he got a warm letter from Strang; it had been sent to Freiburg in the Black Forest by mistake.

Guy worked very hard the following winter. He wrote a scientific thesis which gained him much praise. He had one letter from Mrs. Symonds, written very cheerfully, but saying little about herself. Guy read it many times, very carefully; for he liked to think that her life was a happy one.

One summer, two years after he went to Freiberg, Guy met the Symonds, at Baden-Baden. Annie was sitting alone, in the garden by the Kursaal, when he

saw her ; she looked rather pale, he fancied, and
started when she first saw him, and then became
quite flushed with the pleasure of the meeting. She
talked to him confidentially and kindly, like an old
friend, but very quickly ; Guy was very grave, and
as he thought natural. Annie kept glancing behind
her nervously, as if to see whether Philip were coming ; he had gone into the play-room for a moment,
she said. Curiously enough, little was said of him
or of the last three years ; they both talked mostly of
earlier times, although Guy studiously avoided referring to the scenes and sayings which were brightest
in his memory. He spoke much of his studies and
of the interest he took in his profession ; he said
once how fond he had been of her father, and saw
the tears come into her eyes, and grew wild at the
thought of having given her pain. She was very
sweet, and her manner even more charming than
ever ; and she talked brightly of the future, and of
her life at home, and of seeing Guy back in America.
But her face was pale and worn, and it touched Guy
to the heart to see that she seemed used to being
alone.

It was an hour or more before her husband returned. He greeted Guy warmly, and wanted him
to join him over supper and a bottle of wine with a
lot of jolly men he knew ; but Guy made a pretext
of an early departure the next morning, in excuse.
Philip's face was red, and he was stouter than of old ;
his old jollity had not left him, but he was louder
than usual in his manner. He told Guy of Bixby's
marriage " to a silly, countrified, insipid little thing

—the last girl in the world you would have thought Billy would care for." Philip seemed to have quite forgotten their old difference ; and Guy, too, treated him very naturally ; and congratulated himself, when he went back to the hotel, that he had so well kept his secret from Annie, and had so little betrayed, that night. But as he did so, he angrily brushed away a tear that came upon his face ; and he lay awake long hours, haunted by the tired look in her sweet eyes, the look that had crept into them again when Philip came back. "Oh, God," he murmured, "is she unhappy, then ?"

But the same night, when Annie went alone to her room, she fell upon her knees, and wept. For all the long years he had tried to win her love she had never known ; and now he had tried to keep it from her, and the light of sorrow came to her, and she saw far down into his heart.

CHAPTER XXXVIII.

"O why, why did you love me all these years?
Why not grow cruel to me, as I to you?
Had both been false, neither had had to rue
One thing, nor shed, as I do, hard vain tears."
—W. H. MALLOCK.

I WONDER, after all, is there a higher courage than that we term *dogged*—the courage of despair? The word would seem to indicate a reproach; as we call a man a dog of a Mussulman, or Christian, as the case may be, allowing for all prejudices. But if a man can have higher virtues than courage and truth, I do not know them; and if any man has more of these two than many a dog, I do not know him. No; dogs were given to men as models of character; the common metaphor is unjust, and the superfluity of kicks over halfpence most deplorable.

So Guy lived and worked four years, doggedly; for his courage had outlived his hope. And if in that time he never once thought of Annie, he thought, most of the time, that he had resolved not to think of her. But he kept to the old motto and his own resolve.

We can control our actions, but not our moods. And despite himself, there would come days when illness or enforced idleness gave Guy leisure to think;

then his reveries were not as light as in old days, and the thought would recur that he had been called out of himself into life by Annie, and he could not help thinking that, although he had tried so hard, he had not yet learned how life could be without her. He could not reach back with his mind to a time when he had not loved her ; he could remember nothing before ; and it seemed to him that his present life was more like a dream than were those childish days, and would be less clearly remembered by him in days to come. Four years of his life—no, six, ten—were clear ; all the rest was vague. His love had been to his life like a river, and given him all that was in it of brightness and of good ; all that was in him worthy had come from her. And now that she was gone, his life was dry and barren, and the bloom was dying, and the weeds sprang up.

But no—*Seule la mort peut nous vaincre,*—and Guy would choke these thoughts aside, and bend his will back to work, and seek to comfort his heart with the thought that she, at least, was happy. Alas, it was harder to do this after the meeting at Baden, and so it was the more urgent that he should never think of her at all. No, he never would again. Besides, she had forgotten him ; and thank Heaven, she would never know what his life was. And thinking these things overmuch, he thought that he was not thinking of her, and found it hard.

I dare not say how many times, when Guy was thinking thus, Annie was alone in her great house and softly crying. Perhaps it was as well that Guy never saw the tears in the tender eyes he loved ; Guy

was far in exile, but there is compensation in all
things and perhaps it was as well.

Poor Annie. I cannot bear to tell this part of the
lives of Guy and Annie—I must hasten over it, saying briefly what I learned long afterward. For if
there was one thing right in Guyon Guerndale's
strange life, it was the love that made that life so
sad ; and Annie Bonnymort had a heart as warm as
the divine love, and a soul that came from high
Heaven, as any one might see who looked in her
eyes. It was her nature to love with a love that
might have saved many a worse man than Philip
Symonds ; yet could she never love again what once
she knew ignoble. Had there been one spark of
greatness in him, magnanimity of any kind, whether
for good or evil, he would have understood her,
possibly adored her. But Phil was a good fellow, a
jolly companion, tolerant of others and expecting
tolerance for himself ; contemptuous of things he
could not understand, he had that most worthless,
most hopeless form of conceit, which is self-content
without self-respect. An average man, he saw that
other men were like him, weak, easy-going, sensual
—in his life Annie was out of place.

Yet they might, as people say, have "got along"
together, while the sunshine lasted. But Annie was
now a woman, and hers was not a nature to be satisfied with "getting along together," which Phil could
not be expected to know. For what had she to complain of ? He was kind to her. Probably most of his
men friends would have sided with Phil ; for he was
a good-natured fellow enough ; the world had always

treated him well, and he was willing to treat the
world well, his wife included. Everybody always
liked him ; while he was living a fast life in Paris,
everybody liked him ; when he married Annie Bonnymort for the fortune he knew was hers, everybody
liked him ; even when he lost bets and could not
pay them, everybody liked him. While he lived
royally, and kept his horses and his yacht, and entertained his friends, and showed a gentlemanly
taste for breeding setters, and had the carelessness
in money matters of a good fellow who squanders
his own money as freely as his friend's, all spoke well
of him. Not many men stopped to notice that his
pleasures were such as his wife could rarely share,
or remembered that Phil had long since spent what
remained to him of his own fortune.

So Phil lived these few years, and kept his flow of
spirits and his fine physique and his jolly goodfellow-
ship, and grew more popular than ever as it seemed ;
and none of the ladies in his fashionable set but
envied Mrs. Symonds her carriage and her jewels
and her style of living, and perhaps the husband who
so freely gave them all to her—out of her money.
And when Mr. Bonnymort died, Phil built himself a
fine new house ; and not to know Phil Symonds
argued yourself unknown—if you were a man, be it
said ; for Phil was a man's man, exclusively, and
hated the society of ladies—ladies whom he could
not entertain in his own way with a few chosen
spirits among his friends. I fear some ladies were
willing to take him on his own terms ; for Phil was
an easy-going fellow, and took life easy, and liked

easy company and easy manners. And for one thing, I am glad that Phil kept no accounts, and his wife never saw or knew all the ways in which her money went ; Annie did not think much of the money. The best horses Phil bought did not drag his wife's carriage. Phil, indeed, was very well content to leave his wife alone, and had far too modest an opinion of himself to see why that proceeding should leave her unhappy. He had an uneasy feeling in her company : doubts, incipient questionings, a nervousness as unwonted as it was unwelcome.

No one ever heard Annie complain of her husband, no one ever even saw her look unhappy, except perhaps her maid ; but she tried her noble best to keep her love for him, and to give him love for her, which Philip never had. People whom she met in society thought her rather proud. As for Phil, he liked her well enough ; but what could she do with him? His world was not hers ; he did not understand her, he did not even care to try. Phil was contented enough with life. He did not want anything more ; why should she ? Though she tried her best not to show her sadder thoughts to him, Phil was conscious of a mute disapproval on her part, and it angered him when he thought of it. Did not all the world say he was a damned good fellow ?

I suppose Annie had loved Symonds ever since the two were children. But I do not believe she really loved him after they were married ; and it was the struggle she made to love him still which almost broke her heart. Hers was a nature which found it easier to love than to make compromises ; her insight was too clear to make a shrine where there was no divinity. Like Guy, she could deceive herself once, but only once; and she could have forgiven her husband any crime or fault, save those that made her despise him.

After that summer when she met him at Baden, she often thought of Guy; and she knew too well why he stayed in Europe, and did not come back, though he must have learned his profession long ere this; for Guy, by this time, was nearer thirty than twenty. But Guy was still a boy at heart—now young, just as, when he was young in years, he had seemed old. The picture of what the world ought to be was yet as fresh in his mind as when he was eighteen; in this best way of all ways, Guy never lost his youth. Alas for him, perhaps; and yet I think that was what made some of us so fond of him. As for Annie, I used to hear from my wife of her; she had known her very well as a girl; and she told me how lovely she was, and what a noble woman. I think even then my wife thought Annie and her husband were unhappy together; of course, I did not know all these things until long afterward.

Well, here were Annie and Philip and Guy; and it was perhaps hard to see how that somewhat insouciant divinity who holds the web of fate was to unravel their fortunes. As I said before, I suppose in smooth waters Philip would have steered well enough; he and Annie would have got along together, and I should not have been at the pains of writing this story. But a time came when Philip suddenly woke up to the fact that his second fortune was going, too. So, he gave up his yacht, and a horse or two, and in a flush of grateful self-approbation, went to work ; that is, he began again his old business of stock-broking.

Still, when the first flush of self-esteem was over, he felt that it was infernally hard that he should be cut down in his income ; the domestic expenses entailed by marriage were heavy, after all. Well, it was all the more necessary to make money quickly. So, with some money of his wife's and a nominal hundred thousand advanced by old Waterstock, he went into partnership with Jim Waterstock, son of Waterstock aforesaid, of the old (that is, twenty years established) firm of Waterstock, Proxy and Company. Old Waterstock was out of business, but was given out on change to be their sleeping-partner ; and Proxy put them into one or two good syndicates, and they did well. For all the world said Phil was a jolly fellow, and deserved to get along ; and get along he did, though I doubt if he knew much of business.

Guy knew very little of all this. He heard, from other men, of Phil, his popularity and success, but not much of Annie. She had written to him once or twice when he first came abroad ; but she never wrote after the meeting at Baden. This made Guy unhappy, not divining the reason ; but he strove to comfort himself with the thought that she was happy and had forgotten him.

So Guy worked hard in Germany, and his courage gave him strength ; and he said to himself that it was all over, and everything was right, and they were all very happy, and it was time for him to go home. Strang had been writing many letters to him, urging him to come. Strang was married and settled. It would be very pleasant to see all his friends again, Guy said to himself. And he would try to succeed, and realize his old dreams and ambitions. He did not quite see, in these days, why he had chosen mining engineering; it was a selfish profession, good only for making money; he would have wished for something more public, more generally useful, scientific or political. However he must do what he could with himself and it. He would see Annie again when he returned; he was thankful that the world spoke so well of Phil. He hoped at least that to her he had never shown what might be in him unworthy. And he tried hard to remember his old fondness for Philip, and to like him as much as ever, and to persuade himself that he had been wrong in condemning him. Guy was a fine fellow in those days, broad-shouldered and deep-voiced; for he had lived a straight, sober life, and his eyes were deep and tender, and his face firm-lipped and heavy-bearded.

And Guy himself was feeling the glow of success, that spring. He had done what he had proposed to himself; he held a high reputation in the scientific department of his universities, for he had been to more than one. And again he would say to himself that Annie was happy; and, as for him, why, he was successful, and no doubt he too would be happy some day; as the old Saxon bard said, the foundations of happiness were a suffering with contentment,

a hope that it might come, and a belief that it would
be. And after all, as Norton used to say, we have
no right to happiness, and it is childish to cry because
we have it not. He often thought of little Gutekind;
poor little Gutekind who had taught him so much.
He kept the old instrument upon which the boy
used to play ; and sometimes he would take it from
its case, and think, while looking at it, of that hot
afternoon in the deep valley when he had heard poor
Gutekind playing to the cows, and his shadow had
fallen on the threshold, and the boy had looked up
with those simple blue eyes of his.

Ah, well. He had done what he had proposed ;
now he would go back to America. Spite of all, the
prospect did not excite Guy overmuch ; and he made
his preparations for the journey quietly and quickly.
A few days before he meant to leave Freiberg,
he had a letter from Lane. It was like most of
Lane's letters ; containing much the same sort of
talk that one uses to make conversation at a "party-
call."

"I have been meaning to write for a long time ;
but one's social duties take up so much of one's
leisure, although really I cannot say what I have
been doing." . . . "There has not been much
to write about ; the weather has been beastly, this
spring." . . . "One or two engagements, none
of them particularly interesting, as they have been reported any time these fifteen years." . . . "Tom
Brattle is doing very well, and I see him often ; he
is treasurer of one of his uncle's mills, not far from
ours, and we often go down together. Have you

seen anything of little Bixby? They say he has married somebody abroad ; at all events, he has not been seen over here for a year or two. I believe Strang has taken his wife off to Arizona or Alaska or some such place, but I do not know." . . . " Some people have turned up here, calling themselves Darcy, with letters to my people. They say they lived a long time at Dresden ; did you ever hear of them there, and do you know anything about them? I suppose you were sorry to hear of Symonds' failure. It seems he has been speculating with his wife's money and a little of other people's, and has lost all her fortune besides his own. I am afraid he has behaved in a rather shady way ; there is a good deal of very dirty scandal about it. They talk about false pretences and that sort of thing. They say Mrs. Symonds is very ill. Symonds himself cannot be found. Meantime, another woman has turned up and is making a good deal of trouble. I do not believe he treated his wife very well. It has quite ruined his reputation in Boston, though I believe they are more used to that sort of thing in New York. It has made a great deal of talk, as Symonds was a well-known man, popular at the clubs. I never liked him. Waterstock, his partner, has been arrested. It is fortunate that Mrs. Symonds has no children, as she is left quite destitute. We are all very sorry for her, but of course there is nothing to be done." . . .

Nothing to be done? An hour after getting this letter, Guy was in the train and going westward. All his energy of action had come back to him ; and

when he took his seat in the railway carriage, it was
with bright eyes, and a flushed, firm face. The impulse of a new life was in him ; he had not done
anything with such a will for years. For four years
his life had been repression ; now it was action, and
he sat upright in his seat, and watched the country
fly by, almost with a smile upon his lips.

He took out Lane's letter again ; it was the first
time he had found to read the end of it. It contained nothing but gossip and commonplaces. He
crumpled it in his pocket, lit a cigar, and looked
out of the window again.

Then first he found time to think. Hitherto, his
action had been rather impulse than resolve. He
sat, watching the hedge-rows dash by in rapidly
changing perspective. He watched the trees on the
horizon, and remembered how he used to think,
as a child, that there were more trees beyond
them, and beyond these more trees again, and so
on till the mind grew weary. They were in the
plains of Bavaria, and the day changed into night
with the long, faint twilight of a country without
hills.

Suddenly, in all its plain hopelessness, the thought
stood out in his mind : What could he do ? Lane
was right, speaking for himself ; much more for
Guyon Guerndale. What was he to do ? What
right had he to help her ? Could he go back to her,
and thereby reveal to the evil world a love he had
so long kept secret ? And if he went to her, what
would the world say ?

His clenched hands relaxed, his head sank helplessly upon his breast. Then he had a moment of rage. God! who cared what the world would say? But then he knew that Annie would not think as he did; nor would he wish her so to think.

His mood left him, and he broke down. He had the compartment to himself, and thought aloud. So Annie—Annie whom he loved—was in grief, and he could do nothing. She might be crying, broken-hearted, at that very moment, and he could do nothing to help her. He might as well be dead. And there was no hope—none, none, none. It was an agony of impotence. "Oh, my darling!" he whispered; and then, over and over again, "oh, my darling; oh, my darling!" Then he rose to his full height, and, stretching out his arms, looked upward, and the place grew dark before his eyes, and he fell backward on the floor.

When he came to himself, it was Frankfort. His face was wet with tears, and he saw that he had been crying. It seemed to him that the night had been one long dream. But now it was over, and he had learned what he had to do. It was decided; and he saw his life lie wearily before him. He had learned that he could not go back. No; he could do nothing. God help her; he could not.

He stopped at Frankfort, and, taking a droschke, drove to a hotel in the rain. Then the thought of stopping seemed intolerable; he drove back again to the station; in a last revolt against his powerlessness, he wrote a hasty telegram proffering aid, which he sent to her in America; resolved, after that, to resign himself to all things. When he got to Mayence, the rain was breaking away in great bronzed clouds ; suddenly he bethought himself of his walk of four years before. He could do nothing better while waiting for an answer, if answer there should be. So he bought a knapsack ; and hastily putting a few things into it, he started on foot down the Rhine.

CHAPTER XXXIX.

"L'espérance est la plus grande de nos folies. Cela bien compris, tout ce qui arrive d'heureux surprend. Dans cette prison nommée la vie, d'où nous partons, les uns après les autres, pour aller à la mort, il ne faut compter sur aucune fleur. Dès lors la plus petite feuille réjouit la vue, et le cœur en sait gré à la puissance qui a permis qu'elle se rencontrât sous nos pas."—A. DE VIGNY.

AT about eleven the next morning Guy came to a little inn, standing in a vineyard, near the hill of Rheinstein ; and, entering the garden, un-slinging his knapsack and putting it on a table, he sat down, called for a schoppen of wine, and looked vacantly across the river. A man was sitting at the next table, smoking a cigar ; and Guy watched the smoke-rings curl from his lips, as he also looked vacantly across the river. His face was thus turned away, so that Guy watched him for some minutes before he rose with a start of surprise.

"Norton Randolph !"

"Hallo, Guy !" said the other quietly. "So you have come ? I told you that you would, you know."

Guy, overcome with amazement, was silent for a minute. Randolph went on, calmly smoking.

"What a wonderful chance ! How did you come here ?"

"If it comes to that, how did you come here ?"

laughed Randolph. "Do you suppose that I, too, was not surprised, when I saw you come in? But I knew you would come"——

"You saw me come in? Why did you not speak?"

"Why should I speak? I did not know that you wished to see me. You did not, four years ago, at Lucerne."

"You saw me there?"

"Certainly, my boy."

"And did not speak?"

"For the same reason. You evidently wished to avoid me."

Guy was silent again.

"But I am glad to see you, dear old fellow, all the same," cried Norton; and he gave his hand a strong grip. "Now you have come, as I told you, and we can travel together"——

Guy changed color a little, and began to speak, rather hastily. "What's the news, old fellow? Where have you been — in America? tell me." Guy's voice was a little uncertain; he was tired with a long walk; he did not quite know what to say and turned his eyes away, nervously.

"Where's the waiter? Damn that waiter!" broke in Randolph, with unnecessary vehemence. "Excuse me a moment, till I go and get that waiter, and a bottle of wine"—— And Randolph walked hurriedly off to the inn.

Guy looked across the river to the sunny bank opposite, and saw the rich, brown light, falling on the vineyards. The view grew blurred, and wavered

15*

a little in his eyes. Then he got up, and, forgetting Randolph, walked nervously about the garden. It must be time for her to have received his telegram ; he hoped she would answer. After all, what could she say? His offer was but an empty condolence. He wondered where Symonds was. If he only knew, he might persuade him—he might perhaps help in some way——

"Hallo, Guy!" shouted Randolph after him. "I found them, at last. The servants are pages to King Barbarossa, I fancy; but here is a bottle of wine, and I think it is good. It is Assmannshäuser."

"Oh, I can't drink in the middle of the afternoon," said Guy with a laugh.

"Nonsense, my dear boy. All times are alike for good wine. Pull up, and sit down, and look at the world through a wine glass. Claude Lorraine's is nothing to it, for putting on a gloss. Sit down, sit down, let us have rest from our labors."

"Lazy as ever?"

"Better to sit than to stand ; better to lie down than to sit ; better to be dead than either ; says the wise Hindoo."

"Gloomy as ever?"

"Well, I try not to cry at the world because I can't get what I want ; still, I am pretty sure that every man who shoots himself has good enough reasons for it. The only doubt is whether he does it for the right ones."

"Cynical as ever?"

"Hereditary trait, my boy. It is recorded of my

orthodox Calvinist grandfather, that the harder his
schoolmaster whipped him the louder he laughed—
thereby, perhaps, redoubling the anger of the peda-
gogue. The less I see that is agreeable, the broader
I grin. Perhaps the world treats a man all the
worse for it ; but I can't help that."

" I sometimes wonder why you don't make a
book, utterer of bad aphorisms."

" Because the aphorisms are bad. But tell me,
what have you been doing with yourself, these last
years ? "

" Oh, I've been at Freiberg, studying. And
you ? "

" Well ; I have been doing very little with myself.
I never do make very much of that article. As a
gentleman, I cannot but feel a little the falsity of
my position in this world. Still, I have escaped the
toils of matrimony, thereby doing my little best
toward diminishing the evils of this life. Just
now, I am walking down the Rhine on a tasting-
trip. Yes," he added, seeing Guy's puzzled look,
" a tasting-trip. I concluded that my taste in Rhine
wines was defective. So, I am walking down the
river ; and at every vineyard I stop and have a bottle."

Guy looked at Randolph to see if he was quizzing
him ; the old twinkle was in his eyes. " And where
do you go then ? "

" I don't know where the deuce we *shall* go," said
Randolph, meditatively. " I want variety ; and had
thought of going to Tiflis. Then a fellow I know is
getting up a North Pole expedition at his own ex-

pense ; and he gave me a bid to join him. But I
object to cold and darkness and bad grub. I like
excitement ; but I want to take it comfortably.
Now, there is Timbuctoo—the last European who
saw that city escaped with what remained to him of
his life in '47. Timbuctoo, certainly, has its charms.
—— Where shall we go ? You decide, most ingenious Don, and I will be your trusty Sancho."

"Where shall *we* go ? Why, I must go back to
America " ——

"Oh no, my dear fellow, not so fast ; don't do
that. The last thing I heard, there, was a salvo of
artillery announcing the election of our old friend
Hackett to Congress, and he had won the ballot by
proving that his chief opponent had maintained improper relations with his parlor-maid. Hackett is
quite the man ; he has come out as a blooming
infid is president of a society for erecting a
monu. .ent to Pontius Pilate, and goes to and fro
telling his constituents that there is no such place
as hell. By way of proving it, they send him to
Congress."

"Why don't you go to Switzerland ?" said Guy.
"I might almost like to do that with you ; I should
like to see the Matterhorn again."

"My dear fellow, don't speak of that infernal
mountain. Often as I have seen it, it always reminds me unpleasantly of the Lord, Hackett to the
contrary, notwithstanding. No, no ; I want some
place where life is easy, and the air is hot and lazy
and unsuitable for the propounding of ultramun-
dane conundrums, and people live and breed and

die with equal indifference, and there is nothing in the world or, at all events, out of it, to think of. Now Bulgaria is a fine country. I met a fellow the other day—Canaster, you knew him—who was going down to take a look at the seat of war. He had lots of letters and all that sort of thing, and was going to be a great swell in the Russian headquarters as the son of a Whig duke. He'd put us up to things, and we might take a look at the fighting. Do you know, I have sometimes thought I should like to see some fighting." And Randolph stopped for a moment to cut his cigar.

"I once saw a dog-fight in a barn," he added, meditatively. "I didn't like it very much. But the dogs only fought for a bone ; and down there they are fighting for the Christian religion. At least, so the Czar says. I tell you what, Guy, that's not half a bad idea! Let's turn crusaders! The modern paladin, if that's the proper name and all that sort of thing. We'll be the heroes of a new Chanson de Roland. Who says romance is out of date ?"

"What a whimsical old idiot you are !" said Guy, with a smile ; and he stretched out his hand, cordially. "No, no. I can't go. It is awfully kind of you to want me with you ; but really, I must go back to America."

"Ah well, my preux chevalier ; perhaps it is as well you should go back to the lists of fashion and the listlessness of society. You haven't been quite enough of a carpet-knight ; I have been too much of one, and I am tired of the *tapis*, and what is on it as well. Apropos of gossip, I hear your old friend Symonds has got into a devilish disagreeable row."

Guy was silent.

"Frankly, I used to wonder at your fondness for that man. If there was ever a man with the breeding of a gentleman and the nature of a cad, it was he."

Randolph spoke rather strongly; but Guy went on smoking. For once he did not answer to defend his friend.

"How Miss Bonnymort ever could have married him, I could never see. She seemed a very nice girl. Poor woman, I suppose she is wretched enough now "——

"She thought he was all that was fine and noble and brave—as we all did,"—— began Guy, almost angrily; but his voice grew a little husky and he finished with a glass of wine.

Then there was a long silence between them. Evidently, Guy would say nothing more; and Randolph watched him gravely, as they sat smoking in the dusk. Then he got up, resting his hand lightly on Guy's shoulders, "Come, old fellow, it is getting dark; we must find an inn." And they walked back in the evening to Bingen.

The next day, Randolph and Guy took a long walk among the hills above the river; and it seemed to Guy that his friend had never been so charming a companion. Every weed of a whim, conceit, or quaint opinion that had sprung up in his idle mind for the last year, he brought forth and served in a sort of salad for Guy's amusement. And with all

his raillery and cynicism, there was a delicate tact
of manner which made his hearer laugh unwound-
ed. It even seemed to him that there was a kinder
undertone in Randolph's mood than he had known
of yore. He spoke little of present or personal matters, far less did he mention Symonds again ; and
many a time Guy found himself laughing more
cheerily than he knew. After all, it is so easy to
laugh ; so pleasant a thing, even if it be with a
catching of breath now and then.

It was late in the afternoon when the two came
out on the brow of a hill, above the valley of the
Nahe. There is a little village, and a church, upon
the sunny bit of land between the rivers ; and
coming to a grassy bank, they sat down to rest ; or
rather, Randolph did ; and Guy joined him, laughing at his laziness. Yes, said Norton, he supposed
that he was lazy. American fashion, he intended to
assume a new coat of arms, to be borne by his descendants. He had adopted *argent, a Randolph* (to be
represented by an Indian brave ; " for you know,"
said he, " we claim descent from Pocahontas ") *azur,
regardant, smoking a pipe of peace. Supporters : dexter,
a Randolph recumbent ; sinister, a Randolph couchant ;
all of the second. Crest : a Randolph dormant, bearing
a mark of interrogation. Motto : Born tired.* " I
think," said Randolph, " with the expressions of the
various Randolphs properly ennuyé, that will about
suit." Then Guy smiled a little, and Randolph
went on, poking the moss off an old tombstone with
his cane. He was gradually bringing out an epitaph which seemed to be in Italian. Randolph

uttered an exclamation of surprise; and, after scrap-
ing away a little more of the moss, bent down and
read the line :

" + *Poco amato* + *molto amai* + *pace ho.* + "

"How strange!" muttered Randolph. "What an
odd little line to be mouldering away up here behind
the moss!" And pulling his hat over his eyes, he
lay back and looked at the sky. His mood had
changed, and he said nothing for a long time, but
murmured the line over to himself. "I want to
learn it by heart," said he. "It is a queer, soft bit
of Italian to find up here under the gray German
sky. I wonder who the old boy was (for he was a
boy) who wrote it and wanted it put on his tomb.
Poor fellow! he probably was in exile up here, and,
for some reason could not go home to die. How he
must have walked along by the river of an afternoon, and watched the sunlight over on the brown
vineyards, and the shadows come creeping up from
below; and then he would look to the south and
long for Italy—or for some one in Italy, more likely.
The poet (for he was a poet) must have gone pretty
deeply into the heart of the world to write like that.
There are more things one can love than a woman,
and vainly."

"Set not your heart on the things of this world "—

"And you *will* be a pessimist; for then you set
your heart on things you cannot find in this world.
And they say that you and I have no other. Bah!
no—I am not a pessimist. The world is jolly
enough as long as you like it. Pessimist? No,

my boy. Life is too sweet, the world is too charming a jumble for that. It is like the dream of a drunken god, who has slunk away from some stupid conversazione of the divine society, and has fallen asleep upon a single star; and he does not even know himself that he is creating all that he dreams. And the vision is so sweetly fantastic, so wildly gay, and often even, by some chance, so reasonable, so consistent—for instance, the Iliad, Moses, Napoleon, gunpowder, Potiphar's wife, the United States Congress, Cora Pearl, the battle of Marathon, Henry Ward Beecher, the game of whist, Shakespeare, liberty, are all separate happy thoughts in the dream of creation of this drunken god. But it will soon be over, and the god awakes, and rubs his heavy eyes, and grins. And all our world has gone into nothing. It has never existed at all."

"John Strang would say that you were a fool, and that your folly was not even original," delicately suggested Guy.

"What is so rare as true folly? Humbugs, asses, and idiots are common enough, but true folly is as rare as true wisdom; in fact, it is a kind of madness resembling wisdom—wisdom that has gone mad for knowing all things—wisdom that has found out too much, and gone mad as the best refuge possible under the circumstances. The ancients were wise; they honored madmen as prophets; we hold all prophets madmen. Do you remember that delightful fellow up in your old village at home—Solomon Bung? By Jove, I wish we had him with us! What a dear old chap he was! And how he would enjoy rambling idly with us over Europe, and looking at the carcasses of dead and gone pomps and vanities! He would be as picturesque a figure over here, in his mental attitude at least, as is Fortuny's shepherd, sitting and piping lazily upon the fallen column of an old Greek temple. Well, I remember talking with him, one summer's day, as he sat fishing by the old pond near your house. He was telling me the history of some old crony of his, and talking of the lot in life he had, and making criticisms of life and society by the way.

"'Wa'al, you see,' said he, 'old Sam Orcutt, he never had no kind o' luck. An' he was a nice man, too. Fust he travelled all roun' the world on a ship, an' meantime he went an' married Sue as was Sue Slater, daughter of old Slater as used to drive the stage. But his employers, they made all the money; for old Sam, he never had no luck at all ; and finally, he settled down an' kep' the store at South Chatham. An' he lived nigh onto thirty years at South Chatham, an' then he struck a streak of luck an' died.'"

"'You seem to take a dark view of life, Mr. Bung,' said I.

"'Wa'al,' said he, 'I dunno. P'raps life wouldn't be so bad, ef there warn't so many darned fools roun'. An' as for this world, I suppose the Lord might 'a' made a wuss one; but, thank God, He never tried.'"

CHAPTER XL.

" Elle aurait pleuré, si sa main,
Sur son cœur froidement posée,
Eût jamais, de l'argile humain,
Senti la celeste rosée.
Elle aurait aimé, si l'orgueil,
Pareil à la lampe inutile
Qu'on allume près d'un cercueil,
N'eût veillé sur son cœur stérile,
Elle est morte ; et n'a point véc
Elle faisait semblant de vivre ;
De sa main est tombé le livre
Dans lequel elle n'a rien lu."—A. DE MUSSET.

THERE is a little castle on the river below Bingen. It lies on the bosky brow of a hill,
high up above the Rhine ; and below you may see,
from its weed-grown terrace, the dusky forms of the
Seven Mountains ; and above, the straight blue
river. For it is blue, from that height. And year
by year, the vines twine closer about the old, worn
stones ; and the moss gains strength and greenness
as the rust grows redder on the gates. The people
who lived there are forgotten ; their own descendants do not know of the old Stammschloss ; they are
obsolete and gone. Perhaps their grandchildren
drive droschkes, or travel for German woollen mills,
or shoulder needle-guns in the ranks of the Prussian

army. Only one daughter, being a poor girl, made
a *mésalliance,* and was duly cursed for it, in the last
century, with a Frankfort Jew; and her descendants
are well known in places where the pulse of the
modern world beats thickest. But even they have
lost sight of the old tower; they no longer spin their
cables across the river to net the ships that go by, or
descend the precipitous slopes of the Rhine valley
to plunder the passing traveller. No; they are
scattered far away from the ruined castle; but they
are great on loans and discounts; count their noses,
and you would find a syndicate to fund a national
debt; generous noses, generous only as to their
noses, they ply their traffic at board and bourse, and
would turn up their noses, if it were possible, in
scorn, at the franker modes of plunder of the forefathers of that maiden, their ancestress, who de-
meaned herself, and now lies dead and buried in a
silver casket—God rest her soul, if there be a God,
and she have one.

Well! Here, at the base of this old ruin, for it was
a ruin, sat Norton Randolph. This ingenious citizen of a great republic looked well by a ruin; his
blue cigarette-smoke did not shake the old stones,
and he lay idly by them, looking appreciatively at
the world, or such part of it as was spread at his
feet. Guy was with him; but Randolph was distinctly thoughtful, almost abstracted—a rare thing
for him whose mind was always open for the
thoughts and doings of his friends, little as he
seemed to care for his own. "'*Molto amai—poco
amato—pace ho,*'" he muttered, after a long silence.

"That epitaph seems to run in your mind," said Guy.

"I sometimes wonder, Guy, how our modern ethics are really going to wear. I am curious to see a fellow, born and bred on Spencer and science, *aux prises* with them, under a strong emotion. Every strong will must have some check or motive, just as a steam-engine has a governor, or fly-wheel. Now our neat utilitarian, society canons, our tangible, every-day aims may work beautifully for ninety-nine; but what is to become of number one hundred? Take a fellow of strong will and imagination, ardently in love, for instance. He is quite out of place, you know, in our play at life."

"It seems to me," said Guy, "that you talk a good deal about the things you jeer at."

"I don't jeer at things; the world does. Cervantes wrote the Don Quixote of chivalry; who is to write the Don Quixote of love? Zola, perhaps. Heigho; love was the last good motive left us. Guy, my boy," Randolph went on, changing the crossing of his legs, "don't go back to America."

"I must."

"Nonsense. You won't find what you want, if you do. Immortality is the dream of an egoist fool; love is a fancy, now growing obsolete; power is impossible in a free country, except the power of corruption; money is contemptible. None of them will satisfy you just now. Be sensible. The past is gone; the future does not exist; the present—— well, the best thing you can do about the present is to sit over here and think about it. Come along

with me, old fellow, down the Danube, and we'll
talk it over. We'll go and fight the paynims, my
boy! Think of that! We'll serve under the banner
of the cross, and polish off the infidels!"

"I ought to go America."

"Ought!"

"Norton, if I did not know you never said what
you meant—if you were not—ah!" said Guy, impatiently. "I am tired of hearing this groaning,
this complaining, this weakness made a mode by
Musset and Heine. Suppose their worst; and that we
do believe in nothing, and there is no God to tell
us 'Be a good boy and you shall have so and so,'—
have we not all that half the great men of the world's
history have had? Did those poor, so-called benight-
ed atheists of Rome or Greece sit down and whine
about the world? Is there no merit in bravery?
And are we worse off than they? Suppose we do
not know what is coming? If a clock knew that it
was to be destroyed the next moment, would it not
go on striking the hours until that instant arrived?
Whatever happens, cannot we go on striking our
hour? I am weary of this complaining that the
gods have not thrown light enough on our path. Is
there one moment in life when a noble soul does
not clearly know which action lies before it to be
done? And even if the impulses of a noble soul
can err, even if they are not inspired, then all of it
will come to an end at death; and thank God that it
will. You men who cry because you cannot believe
what a priest tells you of Christ: was poor Greek
Sophocles a Christian when he prayed that his lot

might lead him 'in the path of holy innocence of word and deed, the path which august laws ordain, laws that in the highest empyrean have their birth, of which Heaven is the father alone; neither did the race of men beget them, nor shall oblivion ever put them to sleep; for the power of GOD is mighty in them, and groweth not old.' Grant that we know not that those laws are true—what merit in our courage if we did? Let us act as if they *were* true. And if we do think falsely, we shall die nobly and die forever."

Randolph was silent.

"Heaven knows," added Guy, with a sigh, "the doubts of all these men are too much like our own for us to blame them. I do not mean that I am always free from them."

For once, Randolph made no answer; but an hour afterward, as they were walking home, he spoke.

"Guy," he said gravely, "we have talked, in our time, badinage and nonsense enough. I am not sure that you will remember, among other things, my once giving you my views on peaches *à quinze francs?* Well, I was thinking of that when I spoke, this afternoon, and of a fellow that I met once, in the far East, and knew quite well. In fact, it was he that made the text for my sermon. Poor little fool, he fell in love, madly, passionately, wildly in love, at nineteen, with a girl, beautiful, gay, fashionable, and a year older. He was just the romantic, enthusiastic youth, and withal wilful and clear-headed, whose head could once be led away by his heart. How she laughed at him! By Jove, how she

did laugh at him! Well, the poor boy was sensitive
and proud, but older than he seemed, and a strong
enough character in some respects; and he caught
her unlucky trick of laughing; and the damned
habit stuck to him. As Heine says, a man can go
laughing away, stuck deep in the heart, and go on
laughing and trallera—trallera-la-la—and not even
know that he is stuck deep in the heart—and tral-
lera-la, la-la, la-la—— Well, this one was a man of
the world, not a passionate shepherd, nor a heavy
villain; so he never did anything very remarkable,
but went on laughing. And the worst of it is, he
got over caring for her. I suppose she would take
him now, if he came back. I doubt not, she has
grown tired of her throne of fashion, at one-or-two-
and-thirty. But she was a *pêche à quinze francs.*
Everybody in general was so taken up with admiring
her, that nobody in particular thought of loving her.
She was too perfect a peach for eating; and now
the show is nearly over, and the doors of the fair are
closed to her, and fresher, more fragrant peaches
have taken her place in the stalls; and perhaps the
beautiful girl is not a happy woman.

> " ' Elle est morte ; et n'a point vécu.
> De sa main est tombé le livre
> Dans lequel elle n'a rien lu.'

"Perhaps the little boy who hankered after her
might carry her off now, if he chose to try. But he
does not care for her now; and yet he cannot forget
her, and he remembers her as she was once, and the
picture will not leave his mind; and he could not

seriously make love to her, for he has caught her old trick of laughing ; and yet he does not particularly see the use of caring for anything else. So he roams about the world ; for he has money enough, poor devil, to go to the devil with, only he still keeps an old Puritan prejudice against the gentleman in question. And she is pointed out as Miss So-and-So, who used to be the great belle ; and her temper is a little dubious, and she uses rouge." Randolph delivered all this rapidly, like a lesson, learned by heart ; then he went on, more naturally " Oh, well, it's no use, as old Sol Bung used to say. Let's go down and have a smoke—*cras ingens*—and —and damn the rest of it."

Guy shook his head, and Randolph went on, talking carelessly, urging him to spend the summer with him in Europe. Randolph, having touched Guy once, had seen that he did not wish to talk with him of certain things ; so he never again referred to Symonds. But he told me, long after, that his meeting Guy was not such a curious coincidence as it seemed, as he had tracked him all the way from Freiberg, where he had arrived a day too late.

"Old fellow," Randolph went on, "you aren't fit to go back to work now. You haven't had fun enough this four years. Take pity on a lonely friend, and wait till the autumn. We'll have a jolly old roving summer together." So he talked hastily, all the way back, while Guy was silent. Coming down through the wood path, Randolph spoke again of the verse he had found, which he said was worth a bushel of Swinburne: *Molto amai—poco amato—pace ho.*

A steamer was passing below them on the river : few people were on the deck, but Randolph swore he could smell the Bass's ale as the bottles were uncorked in the cabin. Below them, down the river, they saw the smoke of some new foundries.

Guy, too, thought much of the little Italian verse as he walked along to his banker's. He remembered with wonder his long speech to Norton in the afternoon ; the spirit which prompted it seemed to have left him, and his doubts were crowding back. What a kind, pleasant fellow Randolph was ! Still, he was glad he had kept his secret. It was better that he should always do so. He began to wonder a little about Randolph himself ; but this thought was driven from his mind by a telegram he found at the banker's.

" Thank you very much for your message ; but please do not come back. A. B. SYMONDS."

Book Fifth.

CHAPTER XLI.

" Le monde, une sottise ! Ah ! la belle sottise pourtant ! C'est, selon quelques habitants de Malabar, une des soixante-quatorze comédies dont l'Éternel s'amuse."
—DIDEROT.

IT is less than a month after their walk on the Rhine, and Guy and Norton are sitting at a littl: round table on the Chaussée in Bucharest. The year is the eighteen hundred and seventy-seventh of our Lord ; and, although only the last week in May, the fierce Roumanian summer has already begun. The day has been intensely hot, and the world only awakes with the approach of night. Randolph's fair face is already of a bright bronze, against which his long moustaches gleam golden ; attired in a light lounging suit, he sits drinking the lime-juice and water, cooled with snow, while Guy, whose face is a darker brown, is beside him. Around them, under the rather ineffectual shade of the lime-trees, is a gay procession of Roumanian beauty and Russian valor ; these gallant officers doubtless deserved the fair, for they were confidently discounting future bravery, and getting their deserts in advance.

The avenue of the Chaussée is filled with carriages, bearing ladies on their evening drive, their white muslin dresses and bare necks and shoulders shining pleasantly in the twilight. The broad brows, full lips, and handsome faces of this old Roman race contrast curiously and favorably with the long, white moustaches, the small eyes, and high check-bones of the Cossacks, or the heavier, darker features of the Russian moujik. The gay little city is gayer than ever to-night; illuminations gleam in the gardens, strains of dance-music ring out into the narrow streets; the empty day is over, and the pleasures of the night have begun. Old and young, poor and rich, moral and immoral, all seem equally to be enjoying life—a general and delightful indifference to everything between pitch-and-toss and manslaughter pervades the populace. Guy is amused, and Randolph, who is always mildly entertained by the world in general, finds the world more than ever entertaining to-night.

Very few people now remember that over across the river, to the south, are Turks. The pink blossoms in the garden are very sweet, the winds are stilled, the dust lies quiet in the roads. Overhead the stars, large and serious, look down upon the red and green lights of the garden. But people do not look at them; for every woman in Bucharest is visible to-night, and their dark, round eyes are rounder than ever with admiration of the splendor of the foreign soldiery. If any woman can resist a uniform, it is not the Roumanian. Here it is a Circassian officer, lounging by, gorgeous in light blue with silver lacings and accoutrements; now a group of Montenegrins, ablaze with scarlet silk and gold ; then a party of sober-clad Russians, looking more serious than the brisk young Roumanians : for are they not fighting for their father Czar and the Holy Church ? A Russian officer comes up to address Randolph, leaving his carriage at the curb, with his pretty, somewhat faded, young countess. Randolph goes up to speak to her, and Guy hears her soft musical voice, and pretty broken English, but makes no move to join them. So the count, all complaisance, takes Randolph's seat, and tells Guy of the great review of the Russian army at Kischeneff, when the declaration of war was read to the army by the bishop of the church ; and how the soldiers cheered, in a long hoarse roar of delight ; while Alexander II., the Peace Emperor, sitting upon the earth, his elbows on his knees, burst into tears. It will not be a promenade, this war, he says ; for the Turks believe in what they fight for, as the French did not when the Germans marched on Paris crying Fatherland, and the peasant soldiers threw their arms down before the enemy, and cried that they had left their wives and children, that the harvest was still ungathered, that they did not wish to fight, and the Comte de Paris, fighting also for an Emperor he did not own, had to beat them into battle with his sword.

Guy and Randolph have come up the Rhine, and walked through the Black Forest, and traced the Danube, from the little stream at Donauwörth to Ratisbon. There they found a boat ; and so came down, below the white Valhalla, with its marble foolery of a foolish king, below the endless green hills of the Bohemian Forest, where Schiller's Robbers lived and Consuelo, to Passau ; and on through river scenery which dwarfs the petty Rhine, by the great marble convents and monasteries, and the old city of Linz, perched above the Danube, with the Austrian Alps gleaming in the background ; down through the whirlpool and the rapids, by quaint little churches and villages and old, forgotten castles ; by St. Michael, where the six little clay hares upon the roof of the church still remain, to remind the simple villagers of some old winter, when the hares ran over the ridgepole on the snow ; by Durrenstein, where the castle yet is seen below whose windows Blondel sang to his caged master, Cœur-de-Lion ; by the huge walls of Klosterneuburg ; by Vienna ; down through the broad Hungarian plains, where the peasant and his six great oxen still scratch the earth with the forked stick of antiquity ; into the Iron Gate, which breasts the brown Danube waters with its walls of browner rock ; out of European civilization into Belgrade and Asia, even on to Bucharest. And Randolph has been a very charming companion to his friend, and Guy would say that he enjoyed the journey very much.

So it happened that the two sat here, under the dusty lime-trees in the park of Bucharest ; in this careless little city which laughed and drank and made love between two warring empires. On the morrow, they were to leave Bucharest for the front, if Lord John Canaster had gained permission. The campaign had now fairly begun ; the Russians were about to sow torpedoes in the Danube, and there were rumors that they intended to throw a pontoon-bridge across the river at some point below. The two armies were about to close ; and a Yankee skipper, pacing the deck of his ship at anchor in the stream, was even then profanely cursing because he had been compelled to leave his moorings before he got his cargo on board.

In front of them, in a canvas theatre, a third-rate French company were performing opéra-bouffe ; and the under-officers eagerly spent their hard-earned rubles in hearing a last laugh before they left for the war. Randolph was quite at home in all this scene ; as he said laughingly, he was the vic-tim of democracy, and was out of place at home, where the country was getting along very well, under the administration of Mr. Hayes, and he had been as good as told that his services were not wanted, in the meanest capacity. But for Guy it was otherwise ; Guy was rather off his beat, Ran-dolph said ; which Guy, also laughing, denied, and said he was as well there as anywhere else.

Guy had been to the banker's that day, to see if there were no letter for him from Lane ; for he had written to Lane, and asked him to write what he heard of Annie. But there was none, and so he sat, playing idly with his locket, and listening vaguely to Randolph, who was using all his powers to entertain him and win him over to his own gayety. So sitting, Lord John, returning from Ploiesti, met them, as he had promised to do when he left them the day before.

With him was a handsome young fellow, in the

uniform of a cavalry private. Canaster had obtained
the required permission for Guy and Randolph, and
now desired to present to them his friend, through
whose influence it had been granted—the Prince
T——. He was serving as a private from preference,
as he said, and because, being himself a diplomat, it
was not thought best for him to be put over men
who had spent their lives in the army. He made
this explanation, seeing Randolph look curiously
at his coarse blue uniform, gray overcoat, and black
leather helmet. It seemed to Guy that Canaster, too,
was a very different fellow from the heavy, coarse
man of pleasure he had known years before in America ; his eye was brighter and more clear, some of
his flesh was gone, and there was an air of frankness
and determination about him which became him
well.

The four sat a long time, smoking and talking, under the lime-trees ; the prince burning with enthusiasm for the war, Canaster alert at the prospect of a
fight, Randolph suave and companionable as usual.
Here there was no talk of horses, wine, and women ;
few stories were told and no scandal. Randolph
talked of the social condition of Turkey, of the political reasons for the war ; Canaster of what he had
seen of the front and of the state of the soldiers ;
Prince T—— of the purpose of the Czar and the
hopes and loyalty of the army. The country was
united, he said, for the people all loved the Czar ;
even the nihilists, he said, were silent in the common danger ; there were many of them in the ranks.
When they got up, Randolph hoped that he might

see his Highness often, now that they also were going to the front.

"Oh, no," laughed the prince, "you are swells and
go with the councillors and the household, to look at
the war. I, you see, am nothing but a private under
orders, and go to fight." They walked back with
the prince to his quarters, outside the city, and saw
his sheepskin blanket, and his horse, hung all over
with tin cups and kettles for the rough bivouac, and
tasted the sour brandy and dry, hard bread. Guy and
Randolph had two rooms in the best hotel of the
town, where they had a table d'hôte of seven courses
and a French cuisine. This was to be the last night
of it, said Randolph, as they entered the quaint
Eastern inn, with its central court-yard and brick-
floored, windowless bedrooms opening on glass gal-
leries ; the last night they were to pass in a bedroom,
with a bed in it and sheets.

So they both slept long and soundly ; and in the
morning were up betimes to search for horses.
Canaster's jockey knowledge helped them in this.
Then Guy found a little time yet to go to the
banker's again, in search of a letter from Lane. · But
there was none ; and early in the afternoon they
started for Ploiesti.

16*

CHAPTER XLII.

"There was, in the temple of Memphis, a high pyramid of globes, piled one upon the other; a preacher, questioned about these globes by a tourist, told him that they represented all the possible worlds, and that the best world of all was upon the top; the tourist, curious to see this best of all possible worlds, clambered up the pyramid; and when his eyes were fixed upon the top globe, the first thing he saw was Tarquin violating Lucrece."—LEIBNITZ.

THE slow weeks of preparation passed by; the Russians kept up an incessant but quite ineffectual cannonade across the river; and finally the vanguard of their army crossed the Danube. All this time, the Turks lay idly behind their earthworks, and watched the hostile pageant as if it were a militia parade. They were evidently hoping that something would turn up to prevent it; but, for the nonce, their confidence in Allah was misplaced, and nothing of the kind occurred. However, this attitude of the enemy had the effect of exciting the boundless admiration of Norton Randolph, who praised their consistent and philosophic fatalism, and regretted deeply that the stern etiquette of war forbade his crossing the river to make them a friendly call. But Sistova was occupied; and this place in Bulgaria had so lately been Turkish that he thought it worth while to obtain from the authorities permission for himself and Guy to visit it. So, one June morning, buried in a cloud of dust, they were riding along the military road—Randolph in high spirits, Guy rather quiet, as was his wont in those days.

Already the blight of war had scarred the country, on both sides of the river. Many of the villages were in ruins ; the broad stream, filled with torpedoes and patrolled by gunboats, deserted of all shipping, ran beside them. The road was a foot deep in dust, and crowded, not with soldiers, but with stragglers, pedlers, peasants ; the throngs of camp-followers who seek to fish in waters troubled by war. Many of the peasants, seeing their civilian's dress, would stop and beg of them ; they knew it was of no use begging from soldiers. A huge cloud of dust rose ahead of them, dense, like yellow steam ; when close upon it, they saw that it was caused by a regiment of mounted Cossacks, squatting high on the shoulders of their horses, with their long lances, and chanting a barbaric war-song, to the marching music of whistles. Guy and Randolph caught up with them, and rode slowly past them to one side, noticing their tangled hair, motley dresses, and small, fierce eyes. Before each sotnia was borne the banner of the holy war ; and long after they were left behind and lost in the dust, came the shrill scream of the whistles. Randolph asked Guy, somewhat grimly, if he felt like a crusader.

Somewhat grimly, for they had seen much of the dirt and misery and horror of war, these past few weeks, and had grown more sceptical about the accepted reasons, diplomatic, social, or religious. It was difficult to believe that the Turks were worse than the Kalmucks, and all the optimism of Candide would be needed to prove that either race would do much good by killing the other. One thing was certain; they had seen a great many men very miserable. They had seen the hundreds and thousands of the Russian army, marching in misery to probable death, with dogged, brute valor, for which they were rewarded with the sum of one ruble a month per man. They had seen these men, starving on one pound of bread a day, and only hoping for the ration of coarse beef twice a week that had been promised them by the government, and stolen by some contractor. They had seen a great review of the army of invasion, held before the Grand Duke in person, where the wretched rank and file, ill-fed and ill-clad, walked by him in silence, and only the flat swords of the officers and their own fear of Siberia could call out a cheer. They had seen the wretched invalids, seeking admittance to the army hospitals, scourged like hounds upon their naked flesh lest they should be shamming ill. What wonder, thought Randolph, that these men do not fear Turkish bullets? They had talked with the officers, too; many, of the lower grades, were nihilists; and these would boldly condemn the war and the government and all things that make Russia Russia—less fearful of Siberia, now that the Czar needed their lives to fling away upon Turkish trenches, and talking more freely in consequence. And they had seen the miserable, degraded people, for whom this army came, looking stolidly on while their own deliverance was wrought, fearing their Russian captors little less than their old Turkish masters, and quite as willing to work them evil where they safely could ; lying always, stealing when they found a chance, and robbing and murdering in their own turn such Turks as had not fled.

Now and then they passed a wretched Bulgarian village, with filthy houses, half buried in the earth, windowless, with low doors, and openings in the reed-thatched roofs, through which, while the smoke struggled to get out, the light might struggle to get in. These hovels were so deep sunken in the ground that the eaves were level with the soil, and pigs might be seen rooting upon the roof ; when they caught a glimpse of the interior, they saw that the floors were of damp earth, mouldy with fungus and alive with vermin ; upon them rolled and wallowed indiscriminately the domestic animals of the household, dogs, pigs, and poultry, and the naked children.

All around the villages lay broad, rich lowlands, scarcely cultivated, gay with yellow colza and pink dog-roses, and dotted with ponds, their margins fringed with broad bands of purple iris. They had never seen a country with such a wealth of wild flowers. The sky was blue without a cloud, and in the clear air they saw incessantly white puffs of smoke, across the plain, at the base of the Turkish position, and heard the dull thudding of the cannonade. So riding, they crossed the long bridge of boats, between two caisson wagons, and came into Sistova.

In this little city, the first important place that had been occupied by the Russians, it was a day of rejoicing. True, the Turkish quarter, the best part of the town, was deserted. The walls were riddled with shot and shell, the windows broken and the sashes gone, the houses pillaged and bare. But about the market-place the houses were gay with bunting, the windows full of faces; and in the square, rimmed by a double cordon of Russian infantry, stood the Christian bishop, holding the pale blue banner of the Church to welcome the Grand Duke and the army of liberation. Two little girls, one on either side of him, chosen from among the cleanest of the Bulgarian village maidens, stood with trays of bread and salt. And all around, in the background, crowded the Bulgarian populace, peering with their vicious faces and small, eager eyes to see the Grand Duke. There seemed to be no women between fifty and fifteen; the Bulgarian maidens, on being married, become hags without any intervening state of matronhood.

Close guarded in a hollow square of lancers, the Grand Duke rode slowly up and dismounted. As he did so, the bishop bowed, bending forward his banner; the children kneeled, holding up their trays. The Grand Duke, clumsily crossing himself, broke off a bit of the bread and ate it, and pretended to partake of the salt, while he was sprinkled with holy water at the hands of the bishop. A salvo of artillery completed the ceremony. The Bulgarians looked on in silence, lacking either the will or the intelligence to cheer.

Guy and Randolph sought through the wretched town for such accommodations as the place afforded.

Already the streets were thronged with drunken soldiery, robbing and rioting where they could, bearing their plunder through the streets or hurling it into large fires at the street-corners for sheer wantonness when they could turn it to no use. The Bulgarian population shrank silently into the narrower lanes, waiting, like vultures, their turn for plunder when the soldiers were sated. Not a Turk was to be seen ; all seemed to have fled the place.

The Americans would have fared hardly for quarters, had they not met Canaster and young Prince T——, who offered them a share in their own. The prince, in a moment when few subalterns were sober and trustworthy, was acting as aid ; but Canaster rode a little out of his way to show them the house. In outward appearance it was the best they had yet seen, and belonged to the Cadi, the only Turkish resident who had dared to remain in the town after its capture. He had relied for his safety on a long life of benevolence to the Christian population ; and something in his pluck or manners had impressed the soldiery, so that his house had escaped pillage. All the servants had run away, Canaster told them, but his daughters remained with him, closely confined.

Canaster knocked at the door, and receiving an answer in very good French, they entered. The house, as usual, was of stone and plaster ; but the entry-way was large and scrupulously clean. Randolph stopped to wipe his shoes carefully upon a mat, and the others followed his example ; then they passed under a superb curtain and entered a spa-

cious room with a beautiful mosaic floor, the walls
ornamented like those in the Alhambra, with texts
from the Koran intertwined. In the centre of the
floor, on a rug, was sitting the Cadi, a venerable
gentleman with a long white beard, to whom Canaster
presented them both in turn. The Turk rose gravely,
bowed in courteous fashion, told them that his house
and all it contained was at their service, and that
he regretted sincerely that the terror inspired by
the army and companions of his honored guests had
caused his servants to flee the houschold, so that it
was quite impossible for him to offer them suitable
entertainment; he invited them, however, to a seat.
So saying, he resumed his own with dignity and continued to smoke. Canaster took his leave, the Cadi
rising and bowing to him as he went out. Norton
Randolph, who was greatly pleased with the manners and address of his host, sat down and sought to
draw him into conversation.

Guy walked back to look after the horses; and
when he returned, the two seemed to be getting on
so well together that he did not wish to disturb
them. The windows of the room opened upon a
true oriental patio, walled so high that there was
but a small square of blue sky visible above. The
sides of the house were thick with vines and broad-
leaved plants that threw a green shimmer into the
water of the fountain, plashing in the court-yard.
Here was a basin of clear, cool water, grateful to
one who came from the heat of the open and the
parched roads. In the grass-plots at the corners
grew all manner of fragrant flowers, roses in rich

abundance ; and here Guy threw himself down, listening to the distant cries of pillage and the tread of troops, that came scarcely to him through the massive stone walls which barred him from the street. Louder sounded the tinkle of the fountain near him ; and so, thinking of moss-grown pools, and of cool waters ebbing from lips of stone, or from forest margins as the little brook used to do in Dale, he fell asleep.

Randolph awoke him.

"The old fellow has promised to have his daughters get us some dinner," he said. "I am anxious to see what they will be like."

Surely enough, Randolph had so insinuated himself into the likings of the Cadi, that this was the substantial result of his amenities ; and going into an adjoining room, they found a dinner that Randolph declared to be the best he had eaten since they crossed the Rhine. Everything was clean and well served ; and the curtains, portières, and marbles would have caused envy on Fifth Avenue. But in one thing Randolph was disappointed ; the daughters did not make their appearance. "Ah, well," sighed Randolph, "the old fellow is quite right ; we certainly have not had a fitting introduction." And after dinner they smoked their host's pipes in the greenery of the cool patio, and had some excellent coffee, prepared by the fair invisible hands.

"Guy, my boy, I feel ashamed of myself. I'm a Goth—a Vandal—a Hun—anything else that is vulgar and barbarous and intrusive !" growled Norton. "Don't you ? Why, compare this side of the river—

the cleanness of this house, the beauty of this place,
with the dirt and squalor and degradation of those
wretched Servians! And our dignified, patient host,
with his cultivation and his courtly manners—I
don't know when I have seen a Christian to compare with him! And we claim to be for liberty and
enlightenment, and come bursting in here with a
horde of ignorant, thieving Kalmucks, and a Czar
who wants to make these people like unto them!
As if one creed was not as good as another, as long
as it. turns out a gentleman! And a better gentleman than that respectable old Double Bézique, or
whatever his title is, I never saw."

Guy smiled, as he usually did when he saw that
his friend's freaks were meant for his own amusement, and the latter went on :

"Just think of that old boy's hospitality—con-
joined with a delicate social instinct for his daughters' acquaintance, because we are Christians. I feel
tempted to renounce. As if there were such a thundering amount of difference between a cultivated
Turk, who believes in God, and that Mahomet was
His prophet, and a nineteenth-century Unitarian,
who believes in the same God, and Christ, or
William Shakespeare, as I heard that intelligent
minister of yours say one day, up in Dale! Bah,
Guy! I'm disgusted. Let's change sides."

"Norton, old fellow, don't you think we are rather
too fond of changing sides—you and I ?"

"Yes, Guy. . . . But, after all, it doesn't
make much difference. . . . And that's the
trouble."

After this, the two men went on smoking, idle and silent, until they were startled by hearing a heavy crash at the front door, and a turmoil of soldiers in the house, and a clatter of Cossack dialects. Guy started up to go in ; but they were met by the Turk, who came calmly out of the room, carrying with him his heavy pipe, as the crowd of soldiers rushed by.

"Qu'est-ce——" began Randolph ; but the Cadi waved him to a seat.

"Ce n'est rien, messieurs. Ne vous gênez pas, je vous en prie." And after he sat down, and Randolph had resumed his seat, he told him that the soldiers had discovered that there was a loft in his house filled with tobacco ; and the noise was caused by their efforts in plundering it and fighting over the spoils. "But the ladies——" cried Randolph, starting up. "Are in a place of safety," said he. Norton offered the Cadi his sympathy ; but the latter assured him there was no need, and thanked him gravely.

"Ça ne fait rien," said he. "D'ailleurs, que faire ?"

Surely enough, a procession of half-drunken Cossacks came back through the room opposite, bearing in their arms huge bundles of tobacco, like over-dry hay. And at the same time a pungent snuffiness came out through the window, and set them all to sneezing.

When Guy and Canaster went to bed they found in their rooms a bath, towels, beds neatly made up, and all the appliances of a comfortable night.

Whether the dread of the advancing army had caused the fleas also to leave, is uncertain ; possibly they feared the vast and voracious host of fleas which the invaders brought with them ; certainly there were none in the chamber. The best couch had evidently been reserved for Randolph, who was not ready to join them, but still sat below, smoking with the Cadi—the two, as Lord John remarked, thicker than thieves.

Guy was awaked once in the night, by Randolph, about midnight. "Come down and help, old fellow ; there is a gang of drunken Russians at the door, and the Cadi is down, trying to pacify them ; and they want his daughters."

The two waked Canaster, who swore viciously on being roused, and swore yet more viciously on hearing the purpose of their waking him. They crept softly down, in their stockings, and found a dozen drunken soldiers rioting in the room where they had lately dined ; and two of the drunkest ones had seized a silken curtain-cord, and passed it with a single knot around the Cadi's neck, and so were pulling the cord in opposite directions, one at either end, and asking the old man where his daughters were. His long white beard was knotted in the cord, and his face was purple ; but he showed no other evidence of emotion, still less any intention of yielding ; and it gave Randolph acute pleasure to see Canaster knock these two down, while he and Guy, with their revolvers, induced the others to move into the street.

There, however, they clamored about the door,

and, others coming, the dispute became serious. Guy was meditating emptying his revolver among them; Lord John stood against the door-post, and growled like a bull-dog; while Randolph exhausted the French, German, and a portion of the Russian languages in endeavoring to persuade a lieutenant to keep his men in order. This the latter professed his utter inability to do. Usually, he said, they were very good fellows; but he was quite without control over them when not in the ranks. Luckily, at this juncture, the Prince T—— appeared. He told the men his real rank, and ordered them away. Only one of them made any resistance; cursing the Czar, and all the—whatever term in Russian corresponds to damned aristocrats—he sprang at the Prince, who shot him twice, in rapid succession, and he fell, seriously wounded, upon the cobble-stones. The rest, leaving their comrade, slunk away like whipped hounds; and the Prince and his three companions went back to their beds, first examining the man, whom they found to be dead. The Cadi went to attend them, thanking them gravely, but with tears in his eyes.

"Well, Guy," said Randolph, after blowing out the candle, "what do you think of war, now?"

CHAPTER XLIII.

" So go forth to the world, to the good report and the evil !
    Go, little book ! thy tale, is it not evil and good ?
    Go, and if strangers revile. pass quietly by without answer.
    Go, and if curious friends ask of thy rearing and age,
    Say, ' I am flitting about many years from brain unto brain of
    Feeble and restless youths, born to inglorious days :
    But,' so finish the word, ' I was writ in a Roman chamber,
    When from Janiculan heights thundered the cannon of France.' "
                                                                    —CLOUGH.

GUY and Randolph stopped some weeks at Sistova ; but Guy remembered very little of this part of the summer, when he and Randolph afterwards talked it over. Despite all the change and noise and fatigue and fighting, it seemed dull to him, and his time hung heavily on his hands. He rarely thought much ; he had given up thinking ; but the war seemed to act upon his mind like an anæsthetic, and his sensibilities were deadened. Then, he was never alone. For some reason of his own, Randolph kept always with him, seeking to amuse him by an infinite variety of moods and fancies, to excite him by stories he heard of the fighting that was going on about them ; now trying to provoke him to argument by his old half-earnest indifference, now raising a laugh by some grotesque absurdity, now soothing him to smoke with him in idle companionship.

Norton was distinctly out of conceit with the Russians ; this much was evident. " I say, old boy, we can't desert our colors when under fire, can we, now ? " he would say. " Come, young Godefroi de Bouillon, how much personal interest do you suppose these besotted Bulgarians take in the true Cross ? " Or, again, he would lament his fate in being always mixed up in things he could not believe in. " Why," he complained, " even under fire, I believe I should be only half in earnest. Heigho ! I wish the old Cadi were here ; then there would be somebody to talk to." For this aged gentleman had been shipped, with his daughters, to a place of more safety, leaving, when he went, his house and all it contained at the disposal of his " American preserver ; " and its most secret apartments were now in their undisputed possession ; but alas ! the charming inmates had flown.

Up to this time, the invasion had been war only in form—an armed excursion. The Turks had been steadily repulsed through the whole line of the Danube. General Gourko had flung an advanced guard through the Shipka Pass, beyond the Balkans ; and the complete success of the campaign seemed assured. Perhaps, for this reason, Randolph had begun to sympathize with the weaker side.

But now there came a change. Gourko had got too far from the main army, and had much ado to maintain his position. While he was still staggering in his foothold at Fort St. Nicholas, Osman Pacha had been winding himself up, like a spider, in Plevna. The Russians around him were throwing up earthworks, in rather a desultory way ; and one morning they found that Osman had suddenly occupied the heights of Loftcha, near by, and commanding Plevna ; and that their own trenches were quite too low for comfort. So the news reached Sistova that a general attack had been ordered ; and this attack, it was whispered, had resulted in a serious repulse. Thus it came to pass that division after division was called before Plevna ; and the two armies lay there, facing one another ; and around a camp-fire in the northern one were our friends, the non-combatants.

Already the rough, warlike life had left its mark upon them, though they had not actually been in battle. It is hard, in the field, to retain a vestige of the refinements of civilized life. Canaster was there, in a garb unknown to St. James Street ; Norton Randolph was there, quite as indifferent as ever, now that he was under the guns of the enemy, but undeniably dirty (dirt, he said, after all, was only matter in the wrong place, and war was the right place for it) ; and young Prince T—— was there, disgusted with his cavalry regiment, which lay useless in the background, and fighting on his own hook, like a Tartar as he was—a very cream of Tartars, as Randolph affectionately called him ; and Guy was there, too, feeling a certain grim enjoyment in the excitement of the thing, forgetful of most things, though wondering now and then why he heard no further news from Lane.

All that night there had been a scream of shells and a roar of rifled cannon ; and the mist and the cold, and the barrenness of the place of bivouac, had made it a *nuit blanche* for most of them. It was a dull day; there was little doing, though the cannon, out of courtesy, kept up a harmless interchange of compliments; Canaster rode to headquarters for the mail, while the others of the party gave themselves to sleep, to make amends for the discomfort of the past night. In the afternoon, after Lord John's return, Guy disappeared for a long time, and Randolph lay lazily watching the men at work strengthening the entrenchments. In the evening an orderly was sent to warn Canaster and his friends that their position was one of some danger, and to advise them to go further to the rear; but their tent was just put up and comfortably arranged, and they decided to stay and see it out. That night was quieter; the ineffectual cannonade still continued, but by that time they had got used to it, and all slept well.

Guy slept unusually late; for when he went out, the sun had risen and the mists were clearing away. The cannonade was less active, for the Turks were all at morning prayers; and our four Christians, including a newspaper correspondent, were seated by the fire, smoking clay pipes, and playing whist at a ruble the point. It was really almost still; the long, wailing cry of the Muezzin could be heard from Plevna, and Randolph was just telling Guy that he felt all the old delight of cutting chapel at college, when the Prince threw down his cards and pointed to a long, dark line, winding among the wheat-fields in the valley. It was of a dun color, the uniforms of Islam being none of the brightest, and might well

17

have been taken for a religious procession, but for the flash of the steel points against the corn.

"You are right!" said Randolph. "They certainly intend to pitch into something. The hypocritical beggars! just when we thought them safe at prayers!"

That it was an attack, was evident. All along the Russian lines began the clatter of preparation; and the place where our friends were might not be safe many minutes more. The correspondent of the London paper, only stopping to remind Randolph that their score was a treble and three, hurried back to his companions. Guy and Randolph looked at one another; and each saw what the other wished to do. Canaster and Prince T—— had already transformed themselves into irregular infantry. For alas! by this time there was no lack of spare pieces and equipments. The two Americans followed their example. "We don't want to run away," laughed Randolph, apologetically. "And if we stay here, we might as well do some rifle practice, in self-defence. Besides, they have given us a fair *casus belli*—they interrupted our quiet game of whist."

So the four stood there, in the fresh summer morning, grasping their rifles. Guy's piece was an old weapon that had belonged to some Roumanian, and the cartridges would not fit; he did not care, for he had the bayonet, and only wished it for purposes of defence. Besides, it was not likely that the Turks would come so near, for bayonets were rarely crossed in this war; and if they did, he reflected that he should probably run away.

Near them was the group of newspaper correspondents, brave fellows, to whom the dangers and
hardships of war came as incidents in a profession
of peace and civilization. Most of these were hastily
jotting minutes in their note-books, their horses
tethered close behind ; but as the enemy came nearer,
many of them grasped pieces and thrust their note-
books in their pockets. Even after this, and in
every lull of the engagement, they would lay down
their smoking muskets to pull out a note-book and
make a hasty memorandum of some point of ar-
rangement in the attack, or of some sight or scene
to be recorded. The bivouac of our friends was between a regiment of the Eighth Army Corps and a
company of Roumanian infantry. For the Prince
T——, though nominally a private in a company of
cavalry, was very much of a free lance, and usually
got leave, when it was certain that his own detach-
ment would not be wanted in the front, to fight where
he listed, and as often as he liked ; which latter was
most of the time.

Three long, sinuous streams of soldiery were now
seen to be winding down from the entrenchments of
Plevna. The cannonading had totally ceased. The
two great armies lay silent, face to face ; but between
them was the broad valley, filled with yellow cornfields, and adown its centre shone the sun. As Guy
watched, he saw a Turkish officer come out of the
entrenchment. He was mounted on a red horse,
and Guy could see him point with his sword, although more than a mile in distance lay between
them. He pointed with his sword directly toward

the Prince's little group, turning his horse a little as he did so. Suddenly there came in Guy's mind a memory of that morning, years ago in Dale, when he rode with Annie to call on the widow Sprowl, and looked across the valley and saw the old horse with the stumpy red tail, standing beside the cider-mill. Strange things are these sudden rushes of the memory to slight occurrences, long forgotten ; and as Guy looked across the valley to the Turkish officer on his red horse, he seemed again to see the New England valley in the smoky autumn air ; and the quiet meadows, and to hear Annie's sweet voice coming out through the blinds of the house where the widow Sprowl lay ill.

Then there came a roar of cannon, rending the silence, making the clear air tremulous. The foremost column of the attack was now half-way through the wheat ; and the wind of the burning powder swept down through the yellow cornfields, bending the grain, and a great flash of scarlet came over the valley, where the red of the poppies came up through the yellow. Then the smoke of the cannon lowered down in front of them, and the sun turned red, and all was hid from view.

An hour or more they stood there, not firing, but watching for the enemy ; while all around them the crackle of the musketry drowned the dull thudding of the cannon. But all this time nothing was to be seen of the attack. The soldiers about them, particularly the young Roumanians, were wild with excitement, firing in the air, firing it mattered not where, so long as they got their bullets off in the direction of the Turkish approach. The balls which had been dropping about them spent, now flew straighter over their heads ; and even, once in a while, a man would be wounded, to show that the attack was in earnest. None of our friends would fire, but stood there waiting ; though the suspense was well-nigh intolerable.

Finally, Randolph touched Guy's elbow softly, and pointed below. Far down the slope of the line of defence, perhaps a quarter of a mile, they saw a figure through the smoke. It was that of a man, tall and splendidly built, running upward. He bore a red battle-flag on his shoulder ; and some few paces behind him swept a long line of soldiers, dim in the smoky dust, coming up with their bayonets fixed. A great shout rose from the Russian lines, and all their fire converged upon this point. The smoke, doubled in density, fell between them again like a curtain. "Are they still coming?" cried Canaster. His voice was hoarse with excitement ; and dashing his cap to the ground, he began firing repeatedly into the mist. But no ; that attack was repulsed. The Turkish column had fallen rapidly down the hill, and was re-forming behind the bodies of the slain.

A moment's breathing-spell was given them. The Prince, hearing a rumor that a charge of cavalry was to be attempted, rushed hastily back to his quarters. Canaster stood, panting with excitement, opening and shutting the lock of his gun. Randolph borrowed the old oiled-rag, with which he began to clean his own piece ; his clothes were full of dust and his hands and face smeared with oil and burnt powder. He looked at Guy ; there was an unwonted gleam in his eyes, and neither thought of going back. Just below, on the glacis, was a wounded horse, winding around like a kitten, in his death-agony. " By heaven ! There he is again !" cried Randolph ; and sure enough, from another direction, they saw the same tall figure rushing up, stopping now and then to cheer forward the dark line that pressed upon his heels. In one hand he now had a musket, and in the other he still bore his banner ; thus armed, he came along upon the run, stopping every few minutes to reload, and sticking his flag in the earth, when the main body would catch up, then picking up the banner and rushing on far ahead of them, he would calmly discharge his piece, and with the utmost *sang froid* stop to reload as before. " That is a splendid fellow, Guy," cried Randolph. They could see his long black hair, so long that it whipped his face in the wind, and even his white teeth and his strained eyeballs and his dark features working with excitement. A red silk scarf was bound about the top of his head, and his dress and arms shone, yellow with gold.

"Fair play, at all events," muttered Randolph ; and before Guy could stop him he had sprung out upon the narrow edge of the earthwork. Calmly he levelled his gun, like a fowling-piece ; the man with the red silk scarf seemed to see him, and a little spurt of flame leapt from his gun almost before Randolph's. Both reports were lost in the noise of the battle, quite unheard. Randolph sprang back into the trench ; the Turk turned slowly round. poised himself a moment, threw his banner, spear-fashion, far down the hill into the ranks of his friends ; then fell to the earth like a tree. At the same moment, the Russians gave a great shout, as four long lanes were opened through the Turkish ranks ; a second after came the thunder of a new battery, just placed behind them. There was a moment's check ; then the entire body of the enemy fell back in wild confusion into the valley.

The order for a charge of cavalry was soon given ; and Canaster threw down his gun and ran for his horse, determined, as he swore, to ride with them a bit. Many of the Englishmen joined him, Guy too ; only Randolph refused, saying he had had enough of fighting, that the attack was repulsed and that was enough. As he spoke, the way was cleared for the cavalry ; Prince T—— rode among them, waving his hat, as he passed, at Canaster and Guy, who threw themselves on their horses and followed close behind.

Randolph, left alone, stayed gloomily by their quarters, out of humor with everything, himself most of all. He felt as if he had committed a murder. Poor fellow ! how brave he had been, and how devoted to his cause ! How he had striven that his country might win ! How pluckily he had led the charge, returning to it again and again, cheering on his followers, never losing the flag he bore, saving it even with his last heart-throb ! And who was he, Norton Randolph, a careless cosmopolitan, an idle rover, a weak, good-for-nothing dreamer, that he should

take this man's life ; that he should still the strong
pulses of a man who used his life ; that he should
meet him, whoever he might be, and shoot him like a
widgeon ? Because he was on the wrong side ?
Bah ! Who could tell what was the wrong side in this
world ! He had not even the excuse of believing in
the cause he fought for, like those poor devils of
soldiers down in the valley. What enemy had this
man been, or all Islam, for matter of that, to Norton
Randolph ? This was a fair exploit, truly, for his
philosophy. And where was Guy ? A pretty fellow was he, Norton, to butcher a Turk in cold blood
and let his friend go off alone on a charge of cavalry.

Such was the tenor of Norton's thoughts, as he
looked impatiently round the scene of their bivouac.
The little plat of grass was burnt and trodden, and
cut with heavy wheels and the hoofs of horses. In
the centre were the ashes of the camp-fire, still
smouldering, and among them the pack of cards
which had been hastily thrown down when the game
was broken up. The overcoats and blankets lay
carelessly around the fire-place ; Guy's was there,
among the others. As Randolph looked at it, he
uttered an exclamation of surprise. A letter, in a
lady's handwriting, had apparently fallen from one
of the pockets of Guy's overcoat ; there it lay in the
ashes ; and as Randolph picked it up, he thought
he had seen the handwriting. The letter must have
been contained in a bundle that Canaster had
brought them the day before. Randolph thought of
Guy's long absence that afternoon ; although Guy
had never told him anything, he knew much of which

his friend thought him ignorant. For a moment he hesitated ; he wished very much to know who had sent that letter. For Guy's sake he wished it. But no ; he could not open it. And as he turned it over to put it back, he read the letters on the seal.

Randolph hurriedly crumpled the letter, and thrust it in his own pocket ; then he grasped his revolver and ran back to the place where their horses were picketed. Mounting his own he rode rapidly down the hill in the direction of the cavalry pursuit. It was still an hour before sunset, but the smoke was hanging low over the battle-field and he could see nothing ahead. One or two soldiers cried to him to come back ; but most of them were lying down to rest, or busied with carrying away the wounded, and none the less did Norton ride straight in the track of the cavalry.

17*

CHAPTER XLIV

At last . . . forever.

"FORGIVE me, dear Guy, that I write to you. I am now quite alone in the world; and, though I have seen you so little of late years, I feel that there is no one else to whom I can say what I have to say now. You were Philip's dear old friend, were you not? He is now in Europe—where, I do not know. But you will see him, and tell him to come back to me, for I am very ill. You know his nature, and can do this good, both for him and for your other old friend,

"ANNIE B. SYMONDS."

This letter was left behind in Guy's overcoat as he rode down into the valley that day, with the words of the letter burning in his brain. For twenty hours he had thought upon them; first stricken with all the anguish of his love, then by his old dull despair. What did she wish him to do? Whither was he to go? He could not tell. Her letter was so strange; he could not understand it. He had not even known that Philip was in Europe; then how could he hope to find him? And what was he to say to him, if he did? Why should she have written to him? How could things be so bad that she should have turned to him for aid? A month before, she had begged him not to return.

And yet, through all this, there ran a strange thrill of happiness; almost a flush of some new hope, for he saw that he had never been so near to her as now—now, when she turned to him, though it were but to reach the lover through the friend. At last, she had gauged his friendship aright. And he thought of this again as he rode, and spurred his horse as he did so, and went on with the foremost.

What was he to do? Whither was he to go? Now, at least, for these few moments, there was no choice. For this half hour, whatever lay beyond, his life was clear; some strange impulse had led him to this charge, and now he could not falter back, for all around him rode his friends. His friends; new friends indeed, made the day before yesterday, but already welded to him in the heat of war. In front was riding a young officer who had shared his dinner with him, one day of fainting and fatigue; here beside him rode another, who had told him of his home and hopes, in the strange, close confidence of the day before the fight. And there, before him, lay Plevna and the enemy; rightly or wrongly, the enemy; and the bullets that whistled by his ears angered him, and the booming of the cannon, and the flutter of the crescent flag.

Again he spurred his horse, as he came down the hill into the open, with the rush of many riders on either side; and he felt the savage joy that all the horsemen shared, as he leaned forward, and heard the hasty message that the army was behind them. Faster still, they cried; and he leaned well forward on the horse's neck, and pressed his shoulders, and felt the quick breath of the gallop and the strain and play of. the mighty muscles beneath. Now they were riding through the bending grain; and the scarlet flash of the poppies came up through the wheat, and other red gleams where the corn was trampled and the roots were steeped in blood. Here and there, in the full speed of the charge, his horse would suddenly swerve aside, and he saw these places, where the grain was beaten down, and a careless heap of man and horse lay still amid the straw.

No time was there to stop and look; as yet, no one of them had fallen, and they rode straight ahead and with no sign to guide them but the roaring of the Turkish cannonade. No enemy was to be seen; they were riding into a brown cloud of smoke, cleft here and there by the pink glint of the cannon; but the sound of the guns was fused in one vast murmur like the sea, and louder came to Guy the quick beat of his horse's hoofs and the humming of the wind about his face.

Then, as he rode, there came a new surge of life in his heart. Three great pulses; and the stirred blood tingled in his temples and his loins; his brain grew clear and high, his heart was full, and once, once at least, he knew that he was living, and he felt the human passion and the strong delight that make swift motion and the life and air so sweet. O the brave, gay world! he was glad to be alive, glad to be on the right side of the broad, rich earth, beneath the high and open sky! He lived anew, and he loved his new life, and the hoarse cry of the men behind him sang in his ears like the sound of a trumpet; the sweep of the charge and the noise of battle were like sweet music; he was drunk with awakened life, and he thanked God for it, and prayed for victory, and drove the rowels in his horse's loins. "Huzza!" the men cried, and he cheered in answer, and standing in his stirrups waved his hat high before him, and as he did so, the brown cloud that was ahead quivered and opened, and his very soul leapt from him far from the earth —then he seemed to be falling, falling in a rush of air, with the thunder of the cannon in his ears.

CHAPTER XLV.

" Les animaux lâches vont en troupes ;
Le lion marche seul dans le désert."—A. DE VIGNY.

SO the second assault of Plevna was tried, and
failed; and the long evening shadows drew
across the field where twenty thousand men were
slain and Guyon Guerndale lay dead or dying. A
large, still star came out over the hill, as the sun
sank down behind it; the smoke of the battle rolled
away, and the mists of the night rose up; the cica-
das were chirping, and the evening noises of the
fields began, as if the blood were drops of dew
and no darker red than poppies stained the corn.
Though men may war as much as ever, the fields of
battle are no longer haunted, even in the first dark
night; we have disenchanted them as well; we have
driven away their spirits, good as well as evil. No
need now of Valkyries to bear the souls of men in
battle slain. No grimmer figures than the ravens
circled in the air this night; and the low murmur-
ing that there was came only from such poor hu-
mans as had not had the good fortune to die, or
from those who moaned that they were long in dying. These little spots of conscious matter went

out like taper-flames; and left (we know) as much behind them.

Guy, however, was not dead; though, for a long time, he lay unconscious. Now, in the twilight, his eyes were open; and it seemed to him that he never in his life had had a calmer mood. But for the numbness in his side, he might have been lying there to watch the sunset light upon the hills. His horse had fallen dead beside him; but Guy was not bruised, for the brute had been fond of him; and when a fragment of the same shell had wounded both, he had stepped (as horses will do) between his master's limbs and fallen just beyond.

Here, for an hour or more, Guy lay; happy either in his restoration to life, or in the relief of many things that death would bring. The day before seemed now to be removed from him by many years; now, when perhaps there was to be no day after. He thought of Annie's letter as of something that had happened in his childhood. "I would have tried," he murmured; and then lay dreamily looking at the faint light. All the cannonade had ceased; the camps were lost in the dark slope of the hills; around him waved the wheat, pale-amber in the gloaming. It was as still as an old summer evening in Dale, by the meadows or by Weedy Pond. He wondered, would some strange chance ever show to Annie the letters he had carved there, by the little brook? He did not care very much. The brooks ran blood, here, to-night. So thinking, he fell asleep.

Suddenly, almost immediately, he became wide

awake again. A furlong from him he saw a group of dark figures bending down amid the corn.

"My God!" he muttered. He grew faint and sick, and a wave of ice came about his heart.

"Oh, my God," he thought, "not this!" And his tongue grew dry, and he trembled in his limbs like a coward.

He was thinking of the week before, when they had seen the Russian killed and wounded, who were left on the field after the attack. They had gone there in the morning, and in the night the Turks had done their work. Even the bulls in the arena will show some mercy, and do not gore a dead horse; but these mad fighting fanatics knew no emotion but rage. He had seen limb torn from limb, great red crescents gashed upon the breast— O God, not this!

But all around the field of battle, as the night grew dark, swarmed the Turkish irregulars—Circassians, Bashi-Bazouks, mad Asian savages—prowling among the slain like ghouls; robbing and rifling the pockets of the dead, stripping them naked; tearing out the entrails of the wounded before their faces; hacking and mutilating the bodies of both, in a lust of horror and of gain.

The place where Guy lay was so near the Turkish batteries that they dared to come on foot; and he could hear their low chatter as they passed behind him. Sooner or later, they were sure to find him. Beads of cold sweat stood out upon his forehead; ah, had he but a knife, that he might kill himself— that he might at least kill himself first.

Perhaps he might yet die before they found him. Annie, dear Annie—he thought of her again at this moment, and wished that something might bring him to her mind. He even stopped to imagine her sorrow when she heard; and the thought of her sweet pity made it easier to bear. He was thankful that he had not her portrait with him for those fiends to find.

He heard a low shout, not far off; and his heart stood still, and the wave of ice poured down his spine, as he saw a figure, pointing in his direction. Every conceivable pang of fear was crowded into that one moment. There was no one to save him— no one. He so prayed that he might die. Now he saw another figure, coming swiftly toward him on horseback. Apparently, the first Turk had not seen him; but there was no hope now. Courage, courage—that was all. The horse would discover him, if the man did not. As the horseman dashed up, the horse was checked back, thrown nearly on his haunches; and Guy uttered a cry, half-suppressed, and then bit his tongue and set his teeth for doing it.

"Guy?"

"Norton!"

"Thank God!" echoed Randolph; and, dismounting hurriedly, he lifted Guy tenderly upon the horse's shoulders. Then he mounted again, and so sat in the saddle, with his left arm tight on the reins, and his right supporting Guy, waiting for a favorable opportunity; just as the nearest group were bent upon their plunder he turned the brave

horse with his spur and gave him his head across
the fields.

So far, Norton had ridden out unobserved; but
this change of direction revealed him to the enemy.
They had hardly ridden a hundred yards before they
heard the shout of discovery; a moment afterwards
a dozen bullets hurtled over their heads. After the
first shock of surprise, Guy had recovered his presence of mind, and with it a sense of the peril his
friend was braving for his sake.

"Norton, Norton," he whispered faintly, "please
leave me—dear—old fellow—please—leave me! You
—cannot save—both! And I—am wounded—mortally—" The words came in syllables, uttered with
difficulty, broken by the gallop of the horse.

"What, Guy? Don't talk so much, my boy.
You're wounded, you know," Randolph's calm,
pleasant voice came back to Guy. "Steady, old
fellow—we'll do it yet!"

The cheery tones revived Guy like a cordial; and
there was a soothing, satisfying ring in the well-
known voice. Guy could not see Randolph's face,
and he was too weak to make reply; so he shut his
eyes again, and gave himself over to his friend.

But was this Norton Randolph?—idle, luxurious
Randolph, of the old lazy indifference and cynical
carelessness?—could he be this man with the face
pale, but lips firm set, and a hard glitter as of steel
in the dark gray eyes? Where had he got the close
seat in the saddle, the nervous strength that wound
his arm around Guy's shoulders, the quick eye that
guided him among the groups of the enemy, now

hastily mounting and dashing in pursuit? Only the old calm was still upon his face, and his set lips and flashing eyes belied it; and the veins stood out upon his small hand with its steady grip upon the bridle. Guy had a delicious sense of security as he let his head sink back upon the strong arm about his neck, and felt the long, swinging gallop of the noble horse; and here he must have lost consciousness. The last he remembered was the cool rush of the wind by his temples; and he saw Norton's yellow moustache just above his eyes, and heard the distant rattle of the musketry.

It was the very boldness of Norton's sally that saved him. A defeated army are none too apt to linger about the scene of the repulse; and here, under the batteries of Plevna, with the Russian pickets a mile away, who was to recognize an enemy in the horseman that rode out so calmly toward the Turks? The plunderers thought him one of their own number, no doubt, and bent upon a similar errand. It was only when he turned and spurred his horse away again, with Guy across the saddle, that the Turkish skirmishers discovered him. Then the bullets fell around him, and with shrill cries of rage they mounted and gave chase. But the bullets scattered harmlessly; in that late dusk a horseman was not visible above a hundred yards. They spurred on their horses, screaming for very anger that their booty should be taken from them. Randolph's horse had double weight, and he was already partly winded with the ride out. Could he hope to escape? After all, they were wretchedly mounted; and his own was a noble animal, and knew what was wanted of him. They would not dare to follow him very far.

And in a few moments many of them stopped, and began firing again; but their aim was even more uncertain than before. Now Randolph heard only the gallop of a single horseman behind him. He thought of the man he had killed that afternoon; but no, loaded as he was with Guy, he could not stop to draw his own revolver though he heard the man firing at him as he rode. "Ah, hit a man in the back, will you?" he growled between his set teeth. But he could not drop the bridle to return his fire; and he only drove the rowels deeper in his horse's flank, and lifted Guy farther up upon the pommel in front of him.

And riding so, Norton Randolph brought his friend into camp.

CHAPTER XLVI.

" Mähnt mich nicht dass ich alleine
Bin vom Frühling eingesperrt."

AFTER this there were many dreamy days, and
Guy lay in his bed, half-conscious, half-re-
membering, much like an infant, whom we may
fancy, sleeping or awake, mingling the memory of
the last world with the first vague consciousness of
this. But if Guy was dreaming, Norton Randolph
was always in his dream. The past and present were
mingled in his mind ; but Norton was ever with him,
about him, controlling his movements, determining
his surroundings. Guy knew in his first fever that
he was being moved ; then, later, that he was moving
again ; that he was no longer in camp, nor near the
scenes of war, but in some far-off place which was
high and quiet and cool. Here the days went by
more softly, and the noon light was like twilight ;
but most he dreaded to awake in the night ; only
even then Norton seemed always to be there, in the
black loneliness. At last a time came when he
awoke ; but the effort of being awake was exhaust-
ing to him, and he could do little more than lie still,
as if he were sleeping. So lying, he heard a low
hum of voices by his side ; they seemed to take him

back to college, and to old college days, as if all that had happened since were a dream, and he had but fallen asleep in the deep window-seat, some June day, under the swaying elm-branches, and awaked to hear the men around him talking. He was still too weak to feel surprise; he could only lie and ponder vaguely; then he opened his eyes wider, and saw first an open window with white curtains, and a stir of summer air, and through this a line of hills, with white walls and squares of sloping vineyards. This was not college; so he lay still and wondered.

For Randolph, unwilling to trust Guy to the army hospitals, had managed to get an ambulance, and moved Guy to Bucharest, with some army nurse or wearer of the Geneva Cross as attendant. And then, under her advice, he had taken his friend still farther north, to Pesth. Here, in a cool, high room, with the brown Danube beneath him, and the cliffs and villages of Ofen beyond, Guy had been placed; and the nurse, a member of a Catholic sisterhood, had stayed with him.

So it happened that when Guy awoke this day he found beside him his old friend; and with him was another figure, short, familiar, dressed in a light check suit; and both were conversing in low tones lest they should disturb him. Then, after another moment, Guy looked down, and saw a white press of bandages; and suddenly the memory of the cavalry charge rushed back upon him, and he knew that he had been wounded, and remembered those terrible minutes when he had lain bleeding in the long grain, and how Randolph had come and lifted him upon his horse, and they had started on the ride for life ; and then he must have fainted, for the rest he had forgotten. Here he grew weak again, for so much reasoning had tired him ; then, after a quarter of an hour's rest, he spoke, but very faintly, and in a queer voice :

"Norton, old fellow—have I been very ill ?"

The two voices stopped suddenly, and Randolph came quickly to him.

"Guy !" Guy made a weak effort to stretch out his hand. "Hush ! don't move, old boy—it's all right ?" And he stood by the bedside, and looked tenderly down upon him. "Don't move, my dear old boy; you're all bandaged up, you know. Quiet's the word ; take it easy for a day or two ; and you'll be on the right side of the soil next week."

"All right ? Well, I should say so. He's good for a dozen dead men yet ; and if any man says he won't be up next week, I'll knock him into the middle of it." And no less a person than Mr. William Bixby came smiling up. "Thanks to Randolph here, you know."

"Billy !" whispered Guy, "you here, too ?"

"Aye, I should think so," answered Randolph, "and Billy's been here many a day and night when you were farther off than the doctors cared to follow you. Now quiet, old fellow—you never would keep quiet, you know—and in a day or two we'll tell you all about it ?"

"I *have* been ill ?"

"Well," grinned Billy, "even old Dr. Wayland would have given you a certificate for prayers. Now brace up, old man, and go to sleep, or else you'll wake the baby. Keep your pecker up, and you'll be on deck in no time!" And Guy tried to respond to Bixby's smile of delight, and these two amiable nurses walked on tip-toes out of the room. Guy was tired with so much conversation, and his head fell back upon the pillow and he must have fallen asleep again; for when he next woke it seemed to be some other day, and he was conscious only of some silent, watchful presence, a woman with a white bonnet, and still, dark eyes; eyes that reminded him so strangely of some one whom he had seen before, but he could not remember where.

Then there came long days when it seemed that all he could do was to lie and drink in the light, and feel the cool air upon his forehead; days when he barely knew that he was alive, before he thought much of life, or of the world, or what he should do when he came back to it. Perhaps these were the happiest. It was the dreamy, half-life of convalescence; he was just conscious of the color of the hills, of the fragrance in the air, but was still too weak to think, too weak even for memory. The white-hooded woman was always there; but when she spoke it was in French, though with some foreign accent, it seemed; besides, he never saw her face, but only her eyes. And Norton and Bixby, too, were with him by turns, nearly all the time; though he rarely cared to talk much, even with them, and only felt grateful for their kindness. He would speak when he was stronger.

Then came the next stage, when all his thoughts made one long reverie, and only his imagination was at work, weaving scattered memories into day-dreams, before self-consciousness and care. In these days he would lie propped up on pillows (for his wounds were bandaged still, and made it dangerous for him to move) and look out through the open window, and see the white walls change from gray to white, and then to yellow, and then again to blue, as the sunlight and the shadows went by, and the noon was past and the evening came. It was a pleasure to him to watch even so small a thing as this ; and the deep blue vault of heaven and the crowded grapes, fast ripening on the hot, white walls. He used to look at them and follow with his fancy the process of the vintage ; the merry labor of the gathering, and then the red days of the press, and the laying away in deep, cool cellars, perhaps to be uncorked again in some distant year, and drunk by some gay student-party, such as he remembered years ago at college. How vivid in his mind were those old days! And now he was lying here, middle-aged and wounded, watching the grapes ripen that would be wine for other men, now boys ; wine which they, perhaps, would drink as quickly and as carelessly as he had used to do, years before. He could hear their drinking-song, now.

Opposite was a huge monastery, white-walled, with windows few and narrow ; how gloomy it must be inside, this great, stone prison, with narrow apertures for light, shutting out the summer with the cold, dead rock. It reminded him of the great fortress of the monks at Klosternenburg, which he remembered to have seen that summer.

18

It seemed years ago, now, that week when they came down the Danube ; and they had gone into the cobwebbed cellar with an old monk, and there, from the midst of the fungus and the dampness, in a vault like a grave, he had lifted up a jar of wine, and un-sealed the stone lips, and the wine came pouring out, cool and bright, like yellow sunlight. Then he had not thought so much of it, but now he remembered how the monk had seemed to taste it ! And he could fancy himself a monk, immured, forgotten, with all the little that there was of his life behind him ; and how the wine would bring sweet memories of long-gone summers, and the fragrance of the vin-tage time, and the sparkle and the merriment of life and light, as it gurgled from the cold stone.

Then Randolph, coming in, would talk with him long and pleasantly ; but his manner would be dif-ferent from the Randolph we have known, and I shall not try to set down here what he said. Perhaps he would speak of little Bixby, and say how patient and devoted he had been through all the weary days of Guy's delirium, though now and then he had asked Randolph to take his place. Or he would seek to tempt Guy with many schemes of what they would do together when he was well ; and in all his talk would be no taint of bitterness, but only earnest purpose and resolve. Guy would listen, smiling faintly ; but though he was gaining strength, there was a weariness upon him and he did not care to talk much of his future life. Sometimes Randolph would blame himself for having led Guy into this danger ; but then his friend would check him with a smile which said enough. From now henceforward there was no shadow in the trust between these two.

Now that Guy was well enough to be left alone, Norton felt that he ought to return for a day to their quarters with the army ; as well to get the things that they had left behind as to thank Canaster and others for their kindness. Bixby was expected back the next day, so that Guy would not be alone ; and the night before Randolph's departure he sat late into the evening, talking quietly with Guy. Guy made him tell the story of the ride back into camp ; and sought to thank him in words, for the first time, which Randolph nervously avoided. It was the least he could do, he said, after bringing a better man out on one of his own fool's errands. Then he began talking about home and life and work. Hitherto they had never spoken to each other of the past ; nor had either told the other of himself ; although, perhaps, for lack of confidences, their confidence in one another was no less. But that night they talked a little more of their own lives ; and then made many plans for the future, and for going home, and even for co-operation in some work. Then Randolph told Guy that it was no mere chance, his having met him on the Rhine, but that he had followed him thither from Freiberg.

Then began another conversation on such themes as men will use, who, speaking of the world to come, are thinking chiefly of the world that is. So, gradually, they came to deeper things ; and Randolph re-quoted back to Guy his favorite lines from Sophocles. Here in the darkness, in the seriousness of Guy's illness, the veil of shyness could be drawn aside, and one could speak the thoughts that usually remain thoughts only. But strangely, the accustomed manner of each was changed; perhaps Guy was too tired to take his usual side. However, Guy listened approvingly for a long time; he sighed a little, with fatigue, when Norton came to an end, and asked him to change his position on the pillows. Then Guy insisted on Randolph's lighting his cigar, which hitherto he had foregone in the sick room; and Norton did so, and Guy looked through the darkness for his friend's face.

"Guy," said Randolph finally, "I want to tell you something—you remember the long story that I told you near Bingen, that afternoon, about the man that I met in the East?"

"Yes," said Guy.

Randolph stopped a moment to trim his cigar. "Well," he said, slowly, "it was not all quite true. I never met such a man. The man I was thinking of was myself."

Then Randolph sat silent for a long time, the red spark of his cigar fading and glowing through the darkness. Guy must have fallen asleep; for when he woke up, his friend was gone.

CHAPTER XLVII.

"Il n'y a pas un homme qui ait le droit de mépriser les hommes."
—A. DE VIGNY.

NOW that Guy's fever was conquered, he was considered out of danger. It was simply a question of healing the wound, which was a slow process, though it was well encased in a complication of bandages. It was a serious wound ; and undoubtedly, had not Norton turned up when he did on the night of the assault, Guy would have slowly bled to death. As it was, it seemed to Guy like being born into life again ; and even now he was too feeble to have that life seem quite real to him. At first, his perceptions were hardly more vivid than an infant's ; but as he grew stronger, he began to think, and the thinking only brought weariness and trouble. It is so happy, sometimes, to be too ill to think ! It is so much easier to bear troubles than to grow weary with foreseeing them ! So Guy would lazily abandon himself to his sensations, or listen distantly to little Bixby's kind chatter, who every day came to his bedside with a new lot of gossip or the latest paper or the last Parisian comedy, telling him of what the world was doing—that world which had been such a vague conception to Guy. But little

Bixby's talk was less dubious than of old, and his stories of a more reputable character ; and he rarely took anything to drink, and if he did, it was after dinner. Guy once spoke to Bixby of this reform, and Bixby blushed up to his ears, as if being rallied for an effeminate weakness.

"The fact is," said he, apologetically, "that before I was married, I said—that is, Emily likes—in short," he concluded desperately, "I conducted my court-ship on such a high moral plane, that I'm damned if I've been quite able to get down off it ever since !"

"My dear Billy, do you know that I never once thought of your being married ? Excuse me ; I'm not more than half awake yet, you know. But where is Mrs. Bixby ?"

"Emily ? Oh, she's up at Vienna. I get a letter from her every day—— "

"At Vienna ? And you've been staying down here on my account—— "

"Sh ! Shut up, my dear boy—she approves of it. It's all right. Which is more than she does of the B. and S., I can tell you !" added Billy, with a com-ical *moue*. "Besides, I went up to see her nearly every day while Norton was here, you know."

Guy stretched out the hand that was on the sound side of his body, which Billy received, and laid back, like a bird's egg, under the coverlet. "Where is Norton ?"

"Now that you are beginning to look like some-thing," answered Bixby, "he has gone back to the army for the traps, I believe. He hasn't been able to get there before, you know ; but he has had lots

of letters from Canaster and a fellow that he calls
the Cream of Tartars. He said he'd be back again
by to-morrow or day after; so I told him I would
stick by you till then, and keep you out of mischief.
So go to sleep, old man, and don't make an ass of
yourself; and when you're better, I want you to
come to Vienna and see Emily."

Guy smiled; and then he turned aside and pretended to doze, not wishing to keep Billy from his
morning walk; and he, after watching Guy for a
few moments, pulled a large cigar out of his waist-
coat pocket, and looked at it admiringly, and then
back at Guy, and then at the cigar again; after
several minutes of these alternate glances, he pulled
out a penknife and carefully cut the mouth-end.
At this point Guy judged it proper to simulate the
gentle breathing of a person who is asleep; and
Bixby, after looking at him again, went out softly,
speaking a word to the nurse in the anteroom as he
closed the door. Guy lay there, thinking of the
kindness of this man, who had been a mere acquaintance of his in college, whom he had not thought of
four times in as many years. With Norton, of
course, it was different. He cared more for Norton
than for any man in the world. But little Bixby!
Two men more unlike than Bixby and himself could
not be imagined. Ah, if, years ago, any one had
prophesied to him that these men would be first in
his mind at this moment! And irresistibly his
thoughts reverted to Philip; and, for the first time,
he remembered Annie's letter.

Annie's letter! Where was it? He put his hand

to his pocket as if to feel for it; then he remembered that he was lying in bed, and that, of course, it must be in his overcoat, where he had left it the morning of the fight. His overcoat was hanging up at the end of the room; and he knew he could not move, much less walk, without loosening his bandages. Could the letter have been lost? He could not bear to have it lost. He had taken a long walk when he read it, and he did not remember very well. The nurse heard his sigh of impatience, and, seeing his motion, brought the coat to him.

"Monsieur desires to find something? The coat is as he left it."

Truly enough, so it was; and in the pocket Guy found the letter, which he had almost hoped to be part of his fever dream. The coat was blood-stained in places, having been used as a wrapper when he was taken from the camp; but Norton had carefully restored the letter to its place, and there it was, slightly crumpled. Guy took it out, and managed to open it with one hand, the nurse tactfully turning away as he read it.

Philip. That was it; he was to find Philip. But where was he? Ah, he could not think now; he was too tired. It was all weary and far off; he had even hoped it was all a dream. For so many days he had forgotten it; from the moment of the charge of cavalry all seemed so different to him. Now, and in the future, all should be changed; a new life had begun for him; all the old failure should be forgotten and gone. Again he put it from his mind, and tried to spin a day-dream of the future as he

had used to do in the old days. But despite all the
efforts of his imagination, all that Norton had said
to him the evening before, it seemed cold and indifferent; more like the project of an old man than
the vision of a youth. Thinking this, his weariness
overcame him, and he fell into a doze; and the
hours slipped over his closed eyelids into eternity, and
the day went by as many another had gone before it.

Late in the afternoon he woke again. He was
more feverish than before, and did not feel so strong.
Bixby had come in, and was telling him that he had
brought a friend to see him. Guy turned nervously; it seemed to him that all this had happened
once before, and he knew, before the door was
opened, who was coming in : Philip Symonds.

Bixby had met him at the Victoria Hotel, seeking
their whereabouts; and had brought him hither,
thinking of course that Guy could see his old chum
at any time. Besides, Philip had said that he wanted
to see him ; hearing at Vienna of his wound, he had
come down expressly for that purpose. He only
made a visit of half an hour, talking loudly in a sort
of rude imitation of his old manner. He was glad
to have found Guy, he said ; but Pesth was a damned
dull hole, and now that he had seen him, he thought
he should have to go back to Vienna on the morrow.
Guy could say very little ; throughout the interview his face was very pale, and he kept his eyes
fixed on Philip's. The latter seemed rather to avoid
his glance. Perhaps both felt that there was so
much that might be said, and so little of which either
cared to speak, that the conversation suffered from

constraint. Bixby, usually unobservant, noticed
this; but he ascribed Guy's silence to his weakness,
and kept up most of the talk with Philip himself.
Philip spoke critically of the relative attractions of
Paris and Vienna, and dwelt much upon his damned
hard luck at Monaco; he was no longer as fine-
looking as he used to be; he had grown stout and
coarse-featured; his neck was very thick, and the
small blood-vessels in his face were swollen. There
was a curious nervous twitching under his eyes. He
was disgusted with Buda-Pesth, he said; the cook-
ing at his hotel was very bad, and the wines vile. Besides, he was deuced lonely; there wasn't a white man
in the place to keep him company. He had tried to
get Bixby to go with him to a dance of Hungarian
women that his guide was to get up for that night;
but Bixby wouldn't go. Well! he said awkwardly,
he supposed he must be going. He was glad to have
seen Guy; he would be right as a trivet in a day or two.

Despite the nurse's caution, Philip spoke in a loud
tone; Bixby went out a moment and left Philip with
Guy. There was a flush in Guy's face; but he said
nothing. This embarrassed Philip; he had hoped,
when he came, that Guy would behave like a good
fellow, with no more damned nonsense; so he had
assured himself, for Phil's was an easy nature, forgetting injuries as well as favors, and he always
judged others by himself; but despite his mental
assurance, he felt a little embarrassed at this moment. Bosh! he said to himself, the fool couldn't
have kept cranky about nothing for five years. Besides, he had ulterior motives for wishing to be on

good terms with Guy ; so he confidently held out his hand to say good-by. Guy could not, in truth, give him that hand on account of his wound ; but Philip did not know this. The color deepened in his face ; he thought the act was intentional, and remembering his old patronizing, half-contemptuous friendship for his friend, found it the harder to bear. However, it would not do to break with Guy just then, when he alone could be of service to him ; so he crushed the oath between his teeth. It was hard to have to control his temper—with Guy, above all men.

"I wish you would come again to see me," said Guy, in a low, constrained voice. "I want to see you once alone."

Philip growled an ungracious consent ; he was angry enough, but then he, too, wished this interview.

"You are very kind to come at all," added Guy, seeing that Philip was offended. "How is Mrs. Symonds?"

This was too much. Philip turned angrily upon his heel, and came back to the bed. "I don't know," he said, rudely. "I haven't heard for some weeks. Why do you ask me that?"

"Because I wished to know," said Guy, feebly. "I heard she was ill. Have you not heard from her lately?"

"I heard last in Paris. She was well enough then. I have had to travel too rapidly to get many letters. If she had known I was going to see you, very likely she would have sent a message, but she didn't," he added, with a sneer.

"She isn't with you in Europe? How long ago did you hear in Paris?"

Philip could stand it no longer, but broke all self-restraint in a furious oath. "I am too poor now to drag a family around Europe with me. I had to fail in business. Didn't you hear that? I have lost all my money." Philip walked rapidly up and down the room. Guy closed his eyes wearily.

"God knows, I have worked hard enough," said Philip, after some minutes, changing his tone. "I tell you what, Guy, poverty is all very easy to bear when you are alone; but when a man has a family to support—— I have been all over Europe, trying to get some chance. And all I can say is, I have had damned hard luck."

Phil looked at Guy; his eyes were still shut, and his face was now very pale. He drew his chair up to the bed, and sat down.

"That reminds me, Guy, that I wanted to see you about something. I know you've been in a sort of a huff of late years; but you aren't the sort of fellow that bears malice, and I know you will lend a fellow a hand. Now your friend Norton Randolph——"

Just then Bixby came back, and Philip stopped directly. The nurse was with him; and seeing Guy's face, she said he must have rest immediately. Philip got up to go, taking his leave rather clumsily. Even his good-nature seemed to be gone; and Guy heard him angrily disputing with Bixby about some refusal of the latter, as they left the room.

Guy had a relapse that evening, and all the night was in a high fever. Poor Bixby, who had hoped to be in Vienna, stayed faithfully by his side; and the next evening Randolph returned from Bucharest.

CHAPTER XLVIII.

" . . . How he that loves life overmuch shall die
The dog's death, utterly. . . . "—SWINBURNE.

FATE had certainly treated Phil Symonds rather unkindly. Blest with health, wealth, and many friends ; handsome, good-natured, well-born, popular ; he had lost his own fortune, that of his wife, all his friends, and most of his popularity ; and now, at barely thirty, he was drifting around Europe like a vagrant, and would probably be forced to borrow money of the last man in the world to whom he wished to be under an obligation. So he thought ; and, as he expressed it to himself, it was hard luck. So firmly conscious was he of his own deserts, that the approach of any evil seemed an injustice ; it was not his fault, and he had not deserved it. He had never done a wrong to any one, he reflected. All his friends had always liked him, and now they all went back upon him. Besides, he had never been used to adversity, and it was harder for him than it would be for another man. He had done his best. Now, to-day, he had been to see Guy, and had all his trouble for nothing ; and, in return, Guy had had the impudence to meddle in his own affairs.

As he thought of Guy that night, he came as near hating him as he was capable of hating any man. Phil was not a good hater. He was always indulgent enough to his friends' faults; what did he care, so long as they did not affect him personally? They usually gave him rather a sensation of pleasure, than otherwise. Had he been Guy, Phil reflected, he never would have cared a damn what his friend did, or how he fulfilled his domestic relations; and that day he had more than ever been conscious of a critical attitude on Guy's part, and something made him feel what it was that had most excited Guy's disapproval. And it seemed as if, in some way, all his misfortunes could be traced to Guy's disapproval. Now he thought of it, when he looked back to any step in his life which had proved unfortunate, he remembered Guy's sour face, or some cursed sermon of his. And how much he had done for the man! How he had helped him, and pushed him, and stood up for him, and would have lent him money if he had asked it! What a friend he had always been to him; at least, until he turned cranky about nothing and made a damned fool of himself. All these reflections came to Philip as he was sitting in a sort of dance-house in Buda, much frequented by male tourists, where, for a florin or two, may be seen dancing of a piece with the famous flea-dance in Egypt.

Then there was his wife. Somehow or other, there seemed to be a sort of connection between Guy's disapproval and hers. In their disagreeable side, there was a certain resemblance between them.

He now remembered to have seen the same expression in her face which he had seen in Guy's, that afternoon. She too was turning from him, and was false just when he most needed her. She did not even take the trouble to write to him, now; it was two months since he had last heard from her. To be sure, he had left England unexpectedly, and had been travelling too rapidly to get many letters. When he left her, in a fit of passion, he had sworn he did not care whether she wrote to him or not; but now that Guy cared to hear from her, he cared too.

Why had Guy spoken of her that afternoon? Had he had news from her? Of course, he, Philip, had not lately got her letters. He had made up his mind very suddenly to run up to Vienna, before returning home. As long as he was abroad, he might do something for his own pleasure. Besides, it was important for him to see Randolph. As for the letters, he would telegraph to have them forwarded from Nice or London. It was like Guerndale's infernal meddlesome check, blaming him, though. Did he really remember that old flame he had had for her, as a boy? The little ass! As if any girl was worth remembering five years. Phil's language, when communing with himself, was rather intemperate; and he sat with his hat over his eyes, and did not see much of the dancing. But indeed this was not very good—that is, bad. He had seen better—that is, worse—in Paris.

If he had not been a devilish good-natured fellow, he would not have stood this from Guy. Now he thought of it, and any man but himself would have

thought of it long before, Guy had never behaved
like a friend to him. He was always throwing a
damper on everything, when they roomed together
in college ; and he had only stood it out of kindness.
Besides, he had not forgotten that time at Worcester, in the race, when Guy had been mean enough
to refuse him the commonest favor and prevent his
making a cool thousand or two for his trouble. Then
he believed he had set Norton Randolph against
him ; and Randolph's influence would be very valuable to him now, in certain quarters ; for his brother-
in-law was one of his chief creditors.

Damn it, what did Guy mean by saying that his
wife was ill ? When he left home, she had been well
enough to be infernally disagreeable. The thought
recurred again—could she have written to Guy ?
She had acted like a fool when he came abroad ; and
perhaps, woman-like, she was just fool enough to do
this. And Phil, who perhaps cared little enough for
his wife himself, suddenly felt a rage of jealousy
against poor Guy.

Phil thought he was more sinned against than
sinning ; he did not know much about business.
Certain it is, that when they had to suspend, he
was as much horrified as any one. He had always
been used to the indulgence of his friends ; he
had supposed most of them to be good fellows ; and
when they came swarming down upon him for their
money, just at the most inconvenient moment, like a
pack of tradesmen, it seemed to poor Phil as if the
world were all changed, and he stood aghast. His
partner was much less surprised ; he was busy about

town that day, and left Phil in the office to bear the brunt of it alone.

Then, he remembered, there was some infernal nasty talk about false pretences ; and, Lord knew, he was guiltless of that. He had, of course, had some of his wife's money in the business, just as his partner had had a hundred thousand of his father's ; but as for talk about ostensible capital, or guaranty, that was all nonsense. Waterstock had taken out the money and paid it back some weeks before ; and, of course, he had done the same with his wife's, that is, he had not formally given it back to her, because she could not understand about business. In fact, he complained very bitterly of Waterstock's conduct. He did not understand it ; if there had been anything shady it was in Waterstock's part of the business ; Waterstock had all the experience ; he did not believe Waterstock had lost a cent by their failure. There was no doubt of it, Jim had treated him very shabbily. He, Phil, had had nothing left of his own money ; only a beggarly twenty thousand dollars, and that belonged to his wife. The creditors, many of whom pretended to be his personal friends, had behaved like a parcel of vultures, prowling round and grabbing anything they could get. They had even got scent of the twenty thousand of his wife's ; which, however, he did manage to keep, and went to Europe with it, for it was fairly hers, to see the English bondholders of a railway that he and Waterstock had controlled. And even there his enemies had followed him, and made such an infernal stink that all his own offers were refused, and that chance was lost. When the election took place, half the English proxies were sent against him. God knew, he had done all he could; the fact is, the world treated him unkindly; and so Phil concluded his bitter reflections with the usual comment that it was hard luck, damned hard luck, particularly for a fellow like himself.

Then there was Annie, too. By God, she had treated him like a pick-pocket. She had made a regular scene when he left home, opposing his coming abroad, throwing obstacles in the way of the last chance he had to restore their fortunes. As if he was not doing it all for her sake ! The Lord deliver him from a woman, when she mixed herself up in business. However, reflected Phil, the real reason probably was that she was angry about his mistress. It was natural enough, he supposed; and it *was* unfortunate the woman made such a row, and at just the worst time, too; his usual luck.

And here Philip mentally paid his wife the compliment of supposing that she had grudged him the twenty thousand dollars of her money that he brought with him. Perhaps in this inference our old friend was a little hasty. It was excusable, no doubt; Phil was in an unusually bad temper that night, and he certainly had been very unfortunate. Besides, the true reason never occurred to him; which I fancy the reader will have little difficulty in divining—namely, that Annie had read what the papers said about her husband's failure, and was only too willing to spend the last of her own money in getting a little kinder judgment for the man she had loved. Even if their right was doubtful, she preferred the creditors should have it ; Annie was so old-fashioned as to be proud in such matters. Phil did not have such weak sensibilities, and would not hear of it.

All Phil's thinking did not seem to lead to much good. His cud of fancy was bitter, rather than sweet, that evening. After a time he grew tired of it, and gave himself up to the dancing ; but the sight rather bored him than otherwise. He had had still worse luck since he left London ; most of the twenty thousand had been left at Monaco. Phil was not the metal for a desperate gambler ; when he saw only three or four thousand remaining, he grew frightened. He had never known what it was to be absolutely without money, and he trembled at the prospect. Then, one night, an acquaintance of his was found with a bullet in his head, and Philip had no mind to follow his example. Three or four thousand were not much ; but they were enough to finish his European trip, and take him home ; and, once there, his creditors would begin to show some decency ; or, hang it all, his mother would do something for him, even if she did have a beggarly brood of children. So thinking, Philip had come to Vienna before all his money was quite gone at Monaco. However, certain other expenses had intervened ; and not many thousand francs were left by the time he got to Pesth. The one definite result of his reflections, that evening, was a determination to see Guy again in the morning, and Randolph, too, if possible. Meantime, his troubles were too great to bear sober ; Phil was utterly unused to anything like serious care, and he could not stand it. He was a sociable fellow, moreover, and could not bear to drink alone ; so, for want of a better man (and Phil never had any false pride or snobbishness about him), he invited the commissionaire to a bottle of wine ; and the two made a night of it together. It happened that this night prolonged itself into two nights and a day ; the acquaintance in Pesth possessed by Phil's new companion was extensive and curious, though unhappily rather expensive to his friends ; and it was late in the morning of the third day when Phil returned to his hotel. If his francs were counted in thousands before, hundreds could manage it now ; and Phil swore, as he stumped wearily up the grand staircase, that he would see Guy as soon as possible in the afternoon, have it over, and get away from the infernal hole by night.

Guy had had a serious relapse on the evening of Philip's visit ; so much so, that Bixby was frightened, and telegraphed at once for Randolph. All that night the fever never left him ; and the next day he seemed to be worse. His delirium was a bad symptom ; he talked rapidly ; most of the time he fancied himself back in the war ; now he was riding in the cavalry attack ; now he was lying wounded, and the murderers were coming ; then he would cry that it was Norton, and thank God for it. Then he thought himself back in Arizona, and was possessed with the idea that he was making a long journey, and must travel very rapidly, that there was some one in Boston whom he wished to see; he frequently tried to get out of bed, crying that he could not wait for the next train; and it required all Bixby's force to hold him down. In the afternoon he grew a little quieter, and Randolph got back. He heard from Bixby of Philip Symonds' visit; and as Guy was now better, he persuaded Billy to go to Vienna, as he had intended, now that he was there to take his place.

For several hours, Randolph sat there, with the nurse; the woman touched Guy as tenderly as if he had been her son; and as Randolph watched her careful movements, he thanked her with a look, silently. Through all his delirium, Guy kept his secret; he had never once spoken of Annie, but mentioned Philip's name repeatedly. Norton asked the nurse if he ever spoke of any one else; but she said not, except that the day before his mind had run much upon woods and brooks and walks in the country with children. Randolph showed some surprise that she understood so much English, so the nurse told him, still speaking in French, that she knew that language; then it occurred to Norton that her French had an English accent, but he forebore to question her further.

Late in the afternoon, Guy was silent for some hours; then he turned, and, opening his eyes, muttered something in a low tone, not like the tone of one who is delirious. It seemed to be some sentence which he repeated again and again. The nurse bent down and listened.

"What does he say?" whispered Randolph; and

bending forward himself, he took Guy's wrist in his hand. As he did so, he looked up, and noticed the nurse's eyes, which were very soft and deep.

"*Seule l'amour peut nous vaincre?*" said she.

Remembering that it was probably Guy's old family motto, he corrected her:

"*Seule la mort peut nous vaincre.*"

"*C'est la même chose,*" she answered, abstractedly. Randolph, at any other time, would have felt an inclination to smile, the speech sounded so incongruous from the lips of a nun. But he kept silence, and, listening himself, heard Guy once or twice repeat the phrase. Then he sighed, and fell into a natural sleep. Randolph dropped his pulse. The access of the fever was past.

"Thank heaven," said Randolph, "he's all right again." And he got up with a long breath of relief, and walked up and down the room. The nurse had resumed her knitting, and sat demurely in the corner.

CHAPTER XLIX.

" Once he had loved, but failed to wed
A red-cheeked lass, who long was dead ;
His ways were far too slow, he said,
To quite forget her."—AUSTIN DOBSON.

NOW that I am so near the end, I wish to say
why I, John Strang, of Dale, write this book.
It is because I loved Guy.

For I knew Guy very well, much better than he
ever supposed. I knew him as a boy in Dale, at
school, at college, and for two years we lived together. Many of these things I learned from Norton Randolph, long afterward, and from others ;
and some things, which I could not know, I have
put in out of my own head, using a biographer's
privilege. And even besides the facts and incidents, there are many places where Norton's hints
have helped me ; but still, so far as I could, I have
written this from what I know ; and put down Guy's
own thoughts as I knew them to be, not my own.
For, as I said before, I knew Guy much better than
he thought ; and, though I fear he did not know it,
I loved him. He is the only man I have ever met
to whom I should think of applying this word. And
so I have tried to write the history of his life. It
was a strange life ; and it was a strange story—that

of the old diamond, which Guy's ancestor found, and Phil's ancestor quarrelled with him for. Strange things happen occasionally, even now. It was only a coincidence, of course ; at all events, it is now off my mind, and I leave it with the reader.

I sometimes feel that I should like to have my old friend know of this ; and that I, at least, did not misunderstand him. And yet it was so difficult to understand him, that I fear I have failed to bring him out before the reader as he stands in my memory. Yes, yes ; I know very well that his life was morbid—wasted, if you like ; very likely, he acted foolishly ; perhaps even his character was weak ; you and I would not have done so, I know. I doubt not, Guy himself would have been the first to acknowledge this ; for he had a poorer opinion of himself than any one else could possibly have. All the same, I loved him.

Yes, Guy was a curious fellow ; and we all know what that phrase means when applied to a man by his acquaintances in a club-room. Both his distrust of himself and his admiration for his friends put him at a disadvantage. I doubt if they always gave him credit for either ; just as I think that Don Quixote must, in his day, have been thought rather arrogant and egotistical by the good people about him ; yet heaven knows there was never a more unselfish creature than the dear old Don. And, as Norton says, Guy was a little like him. He was forever looking for this year's birds in the nests of the last. And it was the very old-time simplicity of his character that made it hard to understand. He took life too seriously; and never could accept a compromise. By the way, speaking of that most merry, most sad conceit of Cervantes, Norton Randolph called my attention once to a point in the book which I had never noticed --that among all the Don's adventures, the only one where he succeeded, where his knight-errantry was of use, where he did not make a fool of himself, was when he dissuaded Marcella's followers from the extravagances of love. Even in Don Quixote's day, says Norton, that was the only one of the real old follies left—and that was why he succeeded. Pity the Don had not met Guy. And even of Norton himself, I sometimes shrewdly suspect—however, so, no doubt, does the reader.

To return to Guy. He was a dreamer, of course; the world he had in his mind was not this second planet from the sun; the men he had in his mind were not those we see about us; and yet something made him always act as if they were; and I feel convinced he always would have acted so. Guy was no fool; he could easily have seen human weaknesses, meanness, evil motives; but he would not stoop to recognize them. He was an impracticable fellow. Even if he found his ideal false, he preferred to act as if it were true. When his friends changed, he refused to let himself be altered. He would rather be deceived than mistrust. He never would have got on in the world. Perhaps he is well out of it. I do not know that he ever believed very much; but he started by believing in three things—truth, love, and friendship—and, to my knowledge, he never recanted. I do not believe he was wrong; but, even if he

19

was mistaken, I know that he would have preferred to have been so. And he never would have acknowledged the mistake ; he was too proud.

Somehow or other, despite his being a curious fellow, it is astonishing how many men remember to speak kindly of him now. Take Bixby, for instance —never were two men more different—and yet when he told me what he knew about that unfortunate summer of Guy's on the Danube, the whiskey and water was not strong enough by half to account for the moisture in the eyes of so old a toper, even though he has reformed. Well, well! Let me say what I know about the other men, before I tell how Guy and Annie were made happy.

William Bixby, as the reader knows, is married, and now the father of several children, and has already shown signs of becoming a very strict parent, who will look carefully behind the items "books" and "charity," in his sons' college accounts. Billy lives in New York, has his favorite seat in the Union Club, in one of the windows on Fifth Avenue, plays more whist than poker, rarely drinks before dinner, and never goes to Paris without his wife. He must have inherited a good half million from his father ; and although the old man was the first possessor of this fortune, the descent cast has tolled the entry, as a lawyer would say, and Billy's social position is now safe beyond attack. Bixby has begun to dabble a little in politics, and he was a delegate to the Democratic National Convention which nominated Hancock.

Seth Hackett, on the other hand, is an ardent

Republican, and a prominent member of the party "machine" in Pennsylvania. He is adroit in management and very popular with the masses ; and, if he does not go too far, will go very far indeed.

Vansittart, I believe, has gone to the dogs ; and I am very sorry for them.

Tom Brattle is quite rich, and is coming out as a prominent man in society. Although four or five and thirty, he is a great amateur of girls ; he has his happy hunting grounds at Mount Desert and Newport, and is doubtless a brave who deserves the fair, though hitherto he has led no one to his wigwam. His heart resembles nothing so much as a tennis-ball, flying from one racket to the other ; but thus far he has kept it safely over the net.

Lane is cutting his waistcoats to become one of the solid men of Boston, and will very likely die a member of the corporation of Harvard College; he chose one of his cousins to become his wife, and is fond of entertaining titled Englishmen. He must be worth considerably over a million ; but he rarely leaves Boston now, as it is so difficult to get to London without passing through New York. Although he does not wholly approve of me, he treats me with much consideration when we meet, and we talk about Guy.

Where Philip Symonds is, I do not know ; all I can say is, that he has not been seen in America, by his creditors, at least. He had some dispute with his mother, and will have nothing to do with her ; and, of course, his half-brothers and sisters rarely speak of him. I know that he stayed some time with Lord John Canaster, in England; and then he left there, with some awkward debts, as I have heard, at a club where his host had introduced him. I believe that Canaster paid the debts, and since then there has been a breach between him and Symonds. Since his failure, Phil has never been engaged in any steady business; they say that he complains bitterly of the enmity of his creditors. He is continually making new friends, and as frequently discarding them. There were rumors that he won largely on Foxhall's victory at the Grand Prix, and afterward that he was ill of the delirium tremens at Paris. That is the last I have heard of him; but I suppose he will come in for something when his mother dies, and is lying low until that event shall occur.

As for me, I suppose the reader guessed who I was, long before he came to this chapter. I have done very well in business, and am now one of the richest men in Denver, where I have been settled for a couple of years with my wife and family, on account of some large engineering interests in Leadville. But Mrs. Strang wishes to return to Boston, so I am trying to arrange matters to live in the East. The people were so kind as to elect me member of Congress from Colorado; and this will enable us to live in Washington.

I have not been in Dale these five years. I believe the place is much changed; but the old brown house still stands. There bids fair to be an interesting lawsuit about it. It was left, with all Guy's property, to Mrs. Symonds, in a will made shortly after Phil's failure; and now, as Guy left no heirs, near or remote, he being the last of his family, there is a question whether the property escheats to the national Government or whether the State can claim it by right of sovereignty. There never has been a deed of the property since the original grant of the Crown "to be held as of the manor of East Greenwich in Kent."

Ned Dench never married Mandy Shed; she became a hospital nurse and did very good work in the East; finally, embracing the Romish faith, she joined some foreign sisterhood. Perhaps it is as well; for Dench himself pledged some of his employer's funds to procure money with which to invest in copper stocks. Although his books were ingeniously kept, a certain fondness for fast horses and "style" made his employers suspicious; the panic of 1873 made it impossible for him to square his accounts, and the discrepancy was discovered. Dench was terribly frightened and made a clean breast of it, at the same time restoring what he could of the money. Even then, I think Miss Shed would have married him, had he been true to her; but in the high tide of his prosperity he had formally broken the engagement, and she had gone to Europe the summer before—the same year in which Guy went abroad—meaning to study her profession of nurse in foreign hospitals. Dench himself got off with five years in the State prison.

As for old Sol Bung, he grew very blue one autumn, being kept indoors by the rheumatism. He used to sit and sun himself in the garden; but steadily refused to be visited by the Rev. Hanna, professing little anxiety about his soul. "He never believed in no devil, anyhow," he said, one afternoon, "and as for his eternal welfare, he guessed he'd chance it on the Lord;" and the next day he was found dead, with his chair still tilted back against the sunny wall, and his pipe broken in his lap. He was a kind old fellow, and a philosopher; and Guy always liked him.

Norton Randolph comes to see me, now and then. He is travelling about the world, much as ever.

CHAPTER L.

Rückkehr auf den Grundton.

" In la sua voluntade é nostra pace."—DANTE.

G UY woke up the next morning with the words
of the old motto still in his mind, as they had
been there when the fever left him. He had come to
himself again ; it seemed to him that he remembered
all that he had so far done in his life ; yet his head
was clear, and in his thinking was a grateful sense
of calm. Only the days of fever were lost ; he took
up the thread of his life where it had broken, that
day of the charge and his wound. His first thought
was of Philip's visit, and of Annie's letter, which he
had read again, as he fancied, the day before. *Seule
la mort nous vaincquera,* he was saying to himself ;
then he turned and asked the nurse if any letters had
come for him. It happened that a mail had arrived
the day before ; and as he was now safe from further
fever, she gave him the packet. Something made
him wish to read his letters alone ; so, after smooth-
ing his pillow and propping him up in the bed, she
left him to himself and went about some out-door
errands of her own.

It was now high noon ; the room was darkened,
but through the window Guy could see the blinding

whiteness of the walls, the ripening vineyards, and, in the air, the trembling waves of heat. His face looked wasted and pale in the strong light. On the coverlet lay two or three letters, only one of which was opened ; that was from Lane, and told him of Annie's death.

Guy sat, propped up among the pillows, as the nurse had left him. Randolph had not yet been there that day ; and the nurse had not come back, though she had now been gone an hour or more. But Guy was out of danger ; and both were tired with two nights' watching.

As Guy thought to himself, it was fortunate that he was alone. And yet he was strangely calm. No need now to trouble with his speech to Philip, when he came that day. Nothing further lay between them ; it was all over between him and Philip and Annie, at last. As he had said, years ago, in another way, at last ; at last, forever.

So Annie was dead. It was kind of Norton not to come back. He could not talk with him now. To-morrow he would ; yes, to-morrow. But to-day he must be all alone with himself. He hoped Philip had not heard of it. Could he have heard of it the day before ? Ah well ; it did not matter ; nothing mattered now.

He had loved Annie—he had loved Annie even yesterday—but now it was all lost. He had loved Annie ; and she was dead. That was all he could think of now. And yet, he could bear it so calmly ! So calmly now ; it was all so simple and clear ; no more confusion or doubt. And she had written to him ; it was only the month before that she had written to him. Yes, he would see Norton to-morrow, and they would make arrangements for the future then ; to-day it did not seem as if there was to be any future. Life seemed so old a story, and so long, so very long, ago.

Seule la mort—had he not tried ? There had been those five years, and then—and then this letter. He had loved Annie, and she had died of a broken heart.

Perhaps the old story was right, about the locket. He had meant to give it to Annie, but he had not done so. And now she was dead and he kept it still. There it was on the table, and the diamond still inside it.

Curious, he found himself almost believing in the foolish old tale. It seemed like yesterday, that boyish trouble, that evening in the marsh, when Sol sat fishing, and told him the old story in the twilight. Poor little Guy ! how he had cried. It did not seem so hard to bear now. And then he had gone home in despair, and told it all to Annie ; and she had cried for sympathy, and he remembered her soft hands upon his face.

His eyes were dry, but there began to be a faint flush upon his cheeks, and his forehead burned. Ah, there were many strange things in this world, after all ; perhaps it was well not to laugh too much at old superstitions, at old crimes that left a stain behind them. He remembered his old boast of boyish pride, his resolve to keep the stone and regain all that they had lost ; after all, had he done better than his father ? It is easy to laugh in the daylight.

19*

He thought of his old dreams, dreams of youth—were they realized now in riper age? What had he done with his life? He had loved Annie and she was dead.

Yes, he might still go on. So he would try; but first fling the cursed stone away. Even if he did not care so much now. Where was it?

His thoughts began to wander again. The fever had come back; but he did not know it, and to his sick imagination it seemed as if all the evil came from the stone. The old story was the one idea in his mind. Anything to hurl the diamond from him. There it was, still near him, in the locket. Well! he would try the fates. So they never should be happy while they kept it. He would hurl it away, anywhere, so that it were lost to him. Annie!

Guy lifted himself upon one elbow, and looked about the room. He was very weak! truly, he had not known that he was so weak. There were strange blazing lights upon the wall. The bandages troubled him; he could only move one arm, and the nurse was not there. Perhaps she was in the next room? No matter; he would get it himself; he alone must throw it away.

With difficulty he got upon his feet; then his head throbbed terribly, and in a moment of weakness he sank back. Courage! It was only a few steps. His thoughts were all confused now. Annie stood before him beckoning; the floor seemed to shake and quiver before his eyes; but there was the table, and upon it the fatal locket. In three steps he reached it; grasping the locket, he wrenched it open, using both hands, and took out the stone ; then his strength gave way, and reeling back, he fell heavily upon the bed. The effort loosened his bandages, and probably opened the wound, for the blood came through, staining the sheets ; but in his delirium Guy saw nothing. Soon the loss of blood relieved the fever, and his consciousness revived ; but he lay looking at the stone. Should he then abandon it all ? Should he lose it forever ? For a long time his eyes were fixed upon it ; then he looked down and saw that he was bleeding. He looked at the blood indifferently, upon the white linen, as if it belonged to another person. Perhaps he ought to ring. He might bleed to death if left alone.

He tried to think, but again his thoughts became confused. How pale the stone looked ! Where was the bell ?

Suddenly his arm grew weak. His hand fell back upon the coverlet, and the diamond rolled upon the floor, away from him.

When Philip got back to his room that morning, he found a telegram. It had been sent to London, and from there to Nice, and then to Vienna ; the date was nearly a month before. It was a great shock to Philip. He had never fancied that his wife was seriously ill. It was an hour or more before he could collect his thoughts. What was he to do ? Could Guy have heard of it ?

After all, it was more than ever important for him to see Guy. He must get back to America immediately. If Guy had heard of it he would not refuse him a loan under the circumstances. Good God! how suddenly it must have happened. And just at the worst time, too, when he was so far away.

With a trembling hand, Philip made his toilet. His head was not quite clear, and he dashed his face in a bowl of cold water. Early in the afternoon, he was at Guy's door; the nurse was not in the ante-room, so he went in softly. It was best for him to see Guy alone.

The room was darkened, but he saw that no one was there. He went up to the bed to speak to Guy. An open letter was lying on the coverlet, which was stained with blood; and Guy was dead.

Philip stood for a moment, horror-struck; then turned to give the alarm. As he stepped back, he saw something glitter on the floor. He suddenly re-membered Guy's diamond; stooping, he picked it up and thrust it in his pocket, then walked hurriedly out of the room. When he got into the light, he took it out and examined it carefully.

The diamond was only a crystal, after all.

THE END.

Standard Works of Fiction,

PUBLISHED BY

CHARLES SCRIBNER'S SONS.

———•◆•———

MRS. FRANCES HODGSON BURNETT'S NOVELS.

———————

THAT LASS O' LOWRIE'S. One vol., 12mo, cloth, $1.50; paper, 90 cents.

"We know of no more powerful work from a woman's hand in the English language."—*Boston Transcript.*

HAWORTH'S. One vol., 12mo, cloth, $1.50.

"Haworth's is a product of genius of a very high order.—*N. Y. Evening Post.*

LOUISIANA. One vol., 12mo, $1.00.

"We commend this book as the product of a skillful, talented, well-trained pen. Mrs. Burnett's admirers are already numbered by the thousand, and every new work like this one can only add to their number."—*Chicago Tribune.*

SURLY TIM, and other Stories. One vol., 16mo, cloth, $1.25.

"The stories collected in the present volume are uncommonly vigorous and truthful stories of human nature."—*Chicago Tribune.*

EARLIER STORIES. Each, one vol., 16mo, paper.

Pretty Polly Pemberton. Kathleen. Each, 40 cents.

Lindsay's Luck. Theo. Miss Crespigny. Each, 30 cents.

"Each of these narratives has a distinct spirit, and can be profitably read by all classes of people. They are told not only with true art, but deep pathos."—*Boston Post.*

———————

*** *For sale by all booksellers, or sent, post-paid, upon receipt of price,* **by**

CHARLES SCRIBNER'S SONS, Publishers,

743 AND 745 BROADWAY, NEW YORK.

THE CIRCUIT RIDER. A Tale of the Heroic Age. One vol., 12mo, extra cloth, illustrated with over thirty characteristic drawings by G. G. WHITE and SOL. EYTINGE. Price $1.50.

"The best American story, and the most thoroughly American one that has appeared for years."—*Philadelphia Evening Bulletin.*

H. H. BOYESEN'S NOVELS.

FALCONBERG. A Novel. Illustrated. One vol., $1.50.

"It is a good story, out of the ordinary rut, and wholly enjoyable."—*Chicago Inter-Ocean.*

GUNNAR. A Tale of Norse Life. One vol., square 12mo, $1.25.

"This little book is a perfect gem of poetic prose; every page is full of expressive and vigorous pictures of Norwegian life and scenery. *Gunnar* is simply beautiful as a delicate, clear, and powerful picture of peasant life in Norway."—*Boston Post.*

ILKA ON THE HILL-TOP, and Other Stories. One vol., square 12mo, $1.00.

"Mr. Boyesen's stories possess a sweetness, a tenderness, and a drollery that are fascinating, and yet they are no more attractive than they are strong."—*Home Journal.*

TALES FROM TWO HEMISPHERES. A New Edition. One vol., square 12mo, $1.00.

"The charm of Mr. Boyesen's stories lies in their strength and purity: they offer, too, a refreshing escape from the subtlety and introspection of the present form of fiction. They are robust and strong without caricature or sentimentality."—*Chicago Interior.*

QUEEN TITANIA. One vol., square 12mo, $1.00.

"One of the most pure and lovable creations of modern fiction."— *Boston Sunday Herald.*

"The story is a thoroughly charming one, and there is much ingenuity in the plot."—*The Critic.*

*** *For sale by all booksellers, or sent, post-paid, upon receipt of price, by*

CHARLES SCRIBNER'S SONS, Publishers,

743 AND 745 BROADWAY, NEW YORK.

KNIGHTS OF TO-DAY; or, Love and Science. By CHARLES BARNARD. One vol., 12mo, $1.00.

"A volume of dashing, lively stories, in which the romance of love is mingled with the romance of science in perfectly artistic proportions. The stories are really fascinating."—*Cincinnati Commercial.*

THE ADVENTURES OF CAPTAIN MAGO; or, A Phœnician Expedition. B.C. 1000. By LEON CAHUN. With 73 illustrations by P. Philippoteaux. Translated from the French by Ellen E. Frewer. One vol., 8vo, $2.50.

THEOPHILUS AND OTHERS. By MARY MAPES DODGE. A book for older readers. One vol., 12mo. $1.50.

"The whole series is very clever, and makes a volume of most amusing reading."—*British Quarterly Review.*

SAXE HOLM'S STORIES. Two Series. Each one vol., 12mo, $1.50.

"Of these stories, we have simply to say they are charming, written in a most chaste, quiet, and yet somehow intense style, and thoroughly beautiful in their spirit and their lessons."—*The Christian Register.*

HANDICAPPED. By MARION HARLAND. One vol., 12mo, $1.50.

DR. JOHNS. Being a Narrative of Certain Events in the Life of an Orthodox Minister in Connecticut. By DONALD G. MITCHELL. Two vols., 12mo, $3.50.

THE COSSACKS. A Story of Russian Life. Translated by Eugene Schuyler, from the Russian of Count Leo Tolstoy. One vol., 12mo, $1.25.

RUDDER GRANGE. By FRANK R STOCKTON. A New and Enlarged Edition. One vol., 16mo, paper, 60 cents; cloth, $1.25.

THE SCHOOLMASTER'S TRIAL; or, Old School and New. By A. PERRY. One vol., 12mo, Second Edition, $1.00.

⁎⁎ *For sale by all booksellers, or sent, post-paid, upon receipt of price, by*

CHARLES SCRIBNER'S SONS, Publishers,
743 AND 745 BROADWAY, NEW YORK.

www.ingramcontent.com/pod-product-compliance
Lightning Source LLC
Chambersburg PA
CBHW022023110726
47901CB00006B/1641